freeing
VERA

freeing
VERA

Elissa Raffa

THE PERMANENT PRESS
Sag Harbor, New York 11963

Copyright © 2005 by Elissa Raffa

Library of Congress Cataloging-in-Publication Data

Raffa, Elissa A.
    Freeing Vera / Elissa Raffa.
        p.   cm.
    ISBN 1-57962-120-1 (alk. paper)
        1. Young women--Fictiion. 2. Teenage girls--Fiction. 3. New York
(N.Y.)--Fiction. 4. Children of physicians--Fiction. 5. Parents with dis-
abilities--Fiction. 6. Children of parents with disabilities--Fiction. I. Title.

PS3618.A37F74 2005
813'.6--dc22   2005048871

Printed in the United States of America.

Thanks to my grandmother, Rose Olleia, for getting me started; to the many family members, friends, and teachers who took an interest in my work; and to Hedgebrook, the Minnesota State Arts Board, the Astraea Foundation, the Puffin Foundation, and the Edelstein-Keller Program at the University of Minnesota for gifts of time along the way.

For MKS, with all my heart

This book is a work of fiction.

PART ONE

She's Gone • (1975-1976)

~ One ~

I wanted to get my mother a gun. I wanted to make her into another Janine Kennedy from Tallmadge, Michigan who I read about on the front page of the *New York Times*. Mrs. Kennedy had multiple sclerosis—suffered from it, the article said—and a husband who tortured her. He slapped her occasionally, it said in her sworn affidavit. But that was the least of it. It was all the times he refused to bring her a drink of water, refused to help her to bed, that pushed her over the edge. One night she waited up for him in her wheelchair, cradling a rifle in her arms. When he stepped from the dark of the night into the dark of their house, she blew him away. He had no reason to expect it.

What I wanted to know was how she got the gun—Janine, a woman who needed help with a glass of water. Someone must have brought her that rifle. Someone must have loaded it, propped it up. But she fired it herself. How long did she hold it, in the silence, in the night? How did she keep it steady, quiet her heart? Her arms must have been breaking. Someone had to have helped her, I just knew it. A teenager like me. Her son or daughter. I could have been her daughter.

Every morning, unless rain poured from the sky, I left the house at six-thirty to walk to school.

"Goodbye, Ma," I yelled on my way out the back door.

"Oh," she called out from her downstairs bedroom, "you're leaving already?"

The answer I gave was to slam the door, hoping it would wake my father up. Then for her sake, I'd cancel that wish and vow to be more quiet the next time.

The walk to the high school was less than a mile, but I avoided roads the entire way until the last stretch of Route 172 where there really was no alternative, unless you wanted to wade through a swamp. I hiked across

Mrs. West's back yard and into the swatch of woods that divided my parents' housing development from the next. At the gully behind the horse farm, I'd squat down to dip my hands into the shallow creek, and think of the water finding its way to the Hudson River and then the ocean. Then I'd walk again, and smoke a joint. The sky would brighten from gray to blue, and I'd arrive on the doorstep of my school at seven o'clock.

The only people there an hour early were the custodians, the cafeteria ladies, and the librarian. The linoleum floors always gleamed from the buffing they received the night before. Every day, I bought a cup of coffee, sweet and light—with two packets of sugar and a lot of milk.

"How you doing, honey?" Mrs. Esposito, who ran the cash register, asked. "How's your mother?"

I'd just shrug and smile, and push a strand of hair behind my ear, and she'd smile back. She wore a gray hair net, and kept a radio playing all day on the counter next to her. Darryl Hall and John Oates sang "She's Gone." Like every song about lost or unrequited love, it made me miss my sister Donna who'd run off to Ecuador with the Peace Corps and was living in the mountains outside of Quito.

The library was always empty, and although the sign on the door read, "No food or beverages allowed," the librarian never turned me away. Even when the school buses drove down the hill and the hallways filled with footsteps and voices and lockers slamming, no one came in. This quiet room belonged to me. Flat green carpeting, smooth formica tables, waist-high bookcases crisscrossing the floor. Early morning sun coming in at a slant. My cup of coffee, sweet and light—the way my father taught me to drink it.

Supper was over, the dishes done, my sisters and brother scattered to the shadowy corners of the house. My father still sat at the table—unusual that he was not napping. My brother and sisters were occupied with something called homework, but I wasn't even old enough for school. I drifted through the house, wandered in and out of dim rooms, hoping that something would capture me.

"Come here, Frannie." His voice was coaxing, ripe. We'd had no fighting at dinner this evening. He was inscribed in a circle of yellow light.

I balanced in the doorway, unsure that this was what I wanted. My mother entered from the kitchen and placed his coffee before him. She took two steps back. Her waist was tiny, her belted dress a lustrous purple-brown. She showed no signs of impending illness, but I hardly watched her. She and I, we balanced separately on the perimeter, watching him.

He said, "Come here, Frannie," and, "Vera, bring another cup."

Her shoes tap-tapped from wood to linoleum and back again. She brought the cup and saucer, another placemat, a spoon. Once more she went to the kitchen, this time returning with the pot of coffee and a tile to put under it. Then she left. The sound of her shoes traced an arc through the kitchen and living room, through the hallway behind me and up the stairs. I heard her muffled steps above us, the shutting of their bedroom door.

I entered the light, climbed into my chair at the table. Jimmy's place was to my father's right, mine to his left. Gloria and Donna sat with my mother at the end near the kitchen. But this night it was just Anthony and me.

He poured a splash of coffee out of his cup and into mine. Then he fixed both the same, with two spoons of sugar, and milk almost to the brim. He stirred—first his, and then mine. "Drink," he said. He lifted his cup and paused so we could drink together.

The cup warmed my hand. The milky liquid tasted soft in my mouth. It slid down my throat and traced a thrill along the edges of my tongue. I tried another sip. He looked at me, smiling, and waiting. I looked back, then drank again.

"You like it?" he asked.

I nodded, and drank a third time to show him. But I knew he wanted more—and what was the harm in returning a little smile? I took one more swallow of coffee, and let the sweet smooth tickling sensations grow outward into a grin. I saw the pleasure in his gray eyes. Then I slipped out of my chair and ran upstairs in the dark. I pushed open the door to the room Donna shared with me. She was ten. She studied at the desk, inside a small halo of blue-white light. I walked up close to her chair, and laid my head in her lap.

I didn't read books in my high school library; getting stoned ruined my attention span. Instead I skimmed the headlines of the *Times*, stoking my brain with news of hurricanes and earthquakes, civil war in Lebanon, Jimmy Carter's bid for the presidency—and keeping an eye out for some mention of Ecuador, although there never was any. The fragmented facts I pocketed served as social currency, bits I could swap with my friends in the art room later in the day.

We were the freaks, the artsy-intellectual clique—different from the greasers because we smoked dope instead of cigarettes, drank wine and tequila instead of beer, and talked about Nietzsche rather than cars. The groups were divided along what my friend Raymond Rothstein first pointed out were class lines, although every year a few crossed over, especially doctors' daughters like Donna who dated boys like Billy Paletta whose father was a plumber.

Our families could afford to send us to college but my friends and I claimed we wouldn't go. High school was hell; why throw away money on more of the same? There was a whole world out there to explore, and no more draft for the boys to avoid. Just to prove it about not going to college, we dropped out of Chemistry and Physics and signed up for two study halls a day.

Mr. Lombardi, the art teacher, had a double-size classroom—one side for pottery and sculpture, the other for printmaking and painting. He had a curly black beard and hip-hugger jeans, and let us hang out in the part of the room he wasn't using as long as we kept the noise down and didn't get him in trouble by skipping other teachers' classes.

We talked ardently about distant political realities, congratulating ourselves and each other for knowing more about the world than they'd ever teach in our boring classes. Our conversation ran wide and shallow, splashed here and there, did not spring from any experience, nor from having actually read the books. I chatted it up with the best of them, glad to discuss anything besides the true freakishness of my life. What was the truth of my classmates' lives? Fathers who kept late hours, disappointed mothers, sisters who shot heroin in the bathroom at the Holiday Inn. People dropped hints, but they never said. Just like I didn't say, Hey everybody look at me. I live in a remake of *What Ever Happened to Baby Jane?*, the movie where Bette Davis serves her crippled sister a rat for dinner. I found it by accident while flipping channels late one night. It scared me so much, I threw my body across the room to shut the TV off. At the time, I didn't know it was a horror flick.

The daily *Times*, my cup of coffee—these were my escape rituals which followed my walk-to-school cleansing ritual, all of which made it possible for me to fake like a normal person eight hours a day until September 16, 1975, when Janine Kennedy showed up in the bottom left-hand corner of page A1 and reflected my gothic home life right back in my face.

I spread the paper out on the table, kneeled on the library chair, lay my body nearly down on the newsprint to read more about her. She was a remarkable woman, continued on page A19, column 1. I drank down her story. But the thing I thirsted for I didn't find. No mention of a child or other suspect implicated in the death of her husband. Any cop with half a brain should have known she had help.

They booked her on first degree murder, but her attorney planned on using a new strategy called the battered women's defense. Although she declined to discuss the shooting in interviews, I knew why she did it. I knew what she must have been thinking. No penitentiary they could put her in would be worse than the one she was already in. At least they'd feed her in prison.

I'd fly to Michigan to sit in on her trial. I'd ask for a moment alone with her and hand over an envelope. A thousand dollars I raised for her defense fund. No—only forty, which I could easily have saved had I given up smoking dope for two weeks. She'd introduce me to her attorney and there I would be, testifying for her defense, the brilliant and hauntingly beautiful expert teenage witness. I'd become her friend, her confidante. I'd win her trust and together we'd win her freedom. Only then would I ask, Tell me where you got the gun.

I looked up to find the school librarian watching me. She wore a sticky smile, like it did her heart good to see someone actually reading the newspaper in depth.

"Can I have this section?" I asked. I rubbed the sweat and ink from my hands onto my blue jeans and prayed she wouldn't offer to help me out by photocopying the article that interested me.

"I'll save it for you," she said. "Come pick it up at the end of the day."

~ Two ~

Mr. Lombardi was into the Zen of art, which meant he'd go around for a week at a time taking pictures with no film in his Nikon. He said it wasn't necessary to entrap every vision in a photograph; sometimes it's enough to experience an image in passing. But the act of lifting the camera to one's face, of framing the composition in the viewfinder, of turning and clicking the rings and dials to set f-stop and shutter speed, would lead us to focus on details our brains would normally screen out. We'd see things through a Zen camera that otherwise went unnoticed.

Mostly I saw how people start posing the minute you walk into a room. They track your circuit through the room, shifting as you do, like you are the star and they are the orbiting telescope. Only it's the other way around, so when you decide to capture their reflection they're already positioned to throw you their best profile. It's a natural response, and I'm as bad as the next one—having grown up with a mother for whom the Hollywood motion picture cameras were always rolling, even when she slept or showered. Even when she sat up in the dark waiting for me to come home from my dishwashing job at the Steak and Brew and help her to bed. She'd wait like that on nights when my father didn't feel like helping her. On nights when he went to his own bed angry, and left her stranded.

"What are you doing up, Ma?" I switched on the living room light.

She was sitting in her wheelchair—hands crossed, ankles crossed, chin tucked daintily against her chest.

"Oh." She startled, then raised one hand to smooth the auburn and gray hair away from her brow. "I must have been sleeping. What time is it?"

"Three in the morning."

"You're getting home awfully late."

"What difference does it make?"

"You have to be at school in a few hours."

"I'll be fine," I told her. "What was he mad about this time?"

"No, nothing. He just took a nap. You know your father." She smiled winningly. "Hardly ever misses a meal. I thought his hunger would rouse him eventually."

"I can't fucking believe you haven't had any supper."

"Frannie, please," she warned. "You'll wake him." But I didn't give a damn about his sleep.

She wheeled herself to follow me into the kitchen where I found a left-over lamb chop and some escarole to heat up. "Frannie," she said when I banged the frying pan down on the burner. "Cottage cheese is good enough. Please, don't make things worse."

I slid the chop onto a plate and carried it to the table. Her hand shook erratically when she tried to cut it. I thought about laying my own hand on top of hers, about lending her my weight and warmth until her muscles became steady. But the air between us was cluttered with some invisible force, like trying to bring the north poles of two magnets together.

I reached for the fork and knife when she set them down, and cut the meat away from its bone. "It's not humane," I told her, "keeping you from eating and sleeping. How could I make it worse? What could be worse than this?"

"A lot of things. Trust me."

"You don't know how bad it already is."

11

"Maybe I don't," she said.

"You could have a better life."

"I have this life."

"You know, they build people kitchens where they can reach things and cook their own dinners." It wasn't what I meant by a better life, but it was something.

"I don't want a kitchen," she said.

The refrigerator kicked in and hummed loudly.

"Give me a push to my room?" she asked. "I feel tired now that I'm awake."

She turned her back to me so I could unhook her bra, but wouldn't let the bra drop until she'd slipped a nightgown modestly over her head.

"Do we need the Hoyer lift?" I asked.

"No," she said, "just help me with my balance."

Undress. Dress. Transfer to toilet. Transfer to bed. There was touching required when I helped with each of these steps, but we were efficient and impersonal in our transactions. I parked the chair right next to the bed, and set the brake.

"Okay?" I asked.

"Yes," she said. "Mattie will help me in the morning."

Mattie was paid to look after her while I was at school.

"Thank you," my mother told me.

"Goodnight," I answered from her doorway.

I had a recurring nightmare as a teenager. It started when I was around twelve.

I was on a train. It was the middle of the night, or afternoon, or morning, with stars overhead, or a harsh blue sky, or a warm mist of rain falling. A woman was hit by the train. Sometimes only I knew it. Sometimes other people, the conductor or the passengers knew, but they didn't seem to care. I was the only one upset that a woman was hit by the train. She was walking along the tracks, or walking across them, or she was a passenger—who jumped, fell, was pushed. Her body was thrown into the high weeds, or crushed on the track. I'd yell out loud that the train must stop, that someone must help me do something. Occasionally I pulled the cord. Usually the train kept going. Sometimes it stopped and the conductor and a few passengers climbed down, to humor me, to prove there was no body on the tracks. They pushed aside the tall milkweed and Queen Anne's lace—nothing there either. One time we found something fist-sized, something pink and pulsing, squashed on the rail, but it was just a chipmunk, they told me, small and insignificant. I tried to convince them that the woman was further back, that the train traveled quite a distance before it halted. They weren't concerned. The train lurched and started up again, slowly. The conductor and the other passengers walked alongside it, ready to pull themselves in before it picked up steam. Are you coming? they asked me. Sometimes I got back on the train. Often I stayed behind on the tracks. Either way, I'd wake up defeated.

All day I dreamed about Janine Kennedy, and for weeks after. Through lectures about sine curves and the law of supply and demand, I considered what she might look like. She was angular and blond, with a prominent jaw. She was dark-haired and round-bodied, with a prominent nose. She was ordinary in every way, except for the fire in her eyes. She had the look of someone who could pull the trigger. I inked her name in block letters on the pages of my notebook. I called on her, took her home with me, to work at the restaurant, everywhere I went. I introduced her to my mother, Vera, who thanked her profusely for providing such inspiration. Both suffered the same torment, and Janine acted with finality. And there she was, living with Vera—in a dormitory-like prison, in a cottage by the sea, in our house in Mount Kisco. There were Janine and my beautiful mother, both in their wheelchairs—at the A&P, the library, the rifle range, laughing together. But where would we ever get a gun?

Guns belonged to men, to TV westerns, to boys like my brother who went to Vietnam, to the streets of New York City. To my first cousin Al, twenty-five years older than me, and to Raymond Rothstein's father. Probably to the guys who sold coke and crystal meth on the bar at the Steak and Brew, but except for a taste every now and then I minded my own business, my bus pans of greasy dishes and racks of hot clean dishes, back in the kitchen. I had a hard time picturing any of the women in my family handling a gun—my aunts, my sister Gloria, already married with a baby and in medical school, my grown-up cousins in the Bronx, already married and on their second and third babies. Not even Donna—alone, I imagined, in a little stone house on the equator.

I knew that Al owned a gun because one time we went to his place instead of Aunt Julia's for Christmas Eve dinner. I must have been seven or eight. Jimmy lived in exile at Al and Marie's—he hadn't graduated from high school yet, or gotten drafted—and my cousins hoped to orchestrate a reconciliation between him and my father. Besides, my mother was not walking well, and it took only three steps to get in the cousins' back door instead of the long flight of marble stairs up to Aunt Julia's apartment.

I remember Anthony grumpy in the car, Vera wondering out loud if the flat box of Perugina chocolates she held on her lap was enough, and him saying it was more than adequate, we were the guests, they would feed us. Which wasn't fair since he never allowed her to invite her own relatives or his to dinner, and when Al and Marie, who were pushier than most, showed up uninvited they always brought pastries and a pan of eggplant Parmesan. My mother was saying maybe there was an A&P still open, maybe we could stop for an Entenmann's cake and he told her it wasn't necessary to bring an Entenmann's cake, they lived back to back with Lanzetta's, they could smell the cannolli baking in their sleep. So she changed the subject. She said how fun that we'd get to see the houses in the city all decorated with Christmas lights; people didn't go overboard with the lights up in Mount Kisco like they did down in the Bronx. Gloria, who was home from college for two weeks and couldn't squirm out of this dinner, said, "That's because everyone in the Bronx is a wop." He took a swing at her and Donna in the back seat. I was sitting in the best seat, behind him, out of his reach. Donna yelled, "I didn't do anything," and Vera yelled, "Tony, you're driving!" He pulled the car off the Bronx River Parkway and shouted at Gloria that she'd better apologize or get out and walk. She apologized.

The fighting was already well under way, and when we arrived at Al and Marie's it got worse. My brother was nowhere in sight. Anthony pretended he didn't care, but I saw him looking around.

"He's gone to a friend's," Marie tried to explain.

"How much longer for the eel?" my father asked.

The eel was roasting in the oven, and everyone was acting quite proud that we stuck to tradition and cooked one on Christmas Eve, although only Uncle Frank actually liked the taste. The tradition was you bake an eel and then you fill up on bread, antipasto, and linguini with clam sauce. But this eel took forever to cook. It looked like a stubby piece of black electrical cable and Uncle Frank kept poking it in its roasting pan and saying, "A little more. A little more." Cousin Marie put my sisters to work pouring water and wine and sent me off to play with her boys. They were ten and eleven. I followed them to the back of the apartment where the air felt cooler than in the kitchen and they showed me the gun their father kept behind the shoe boxes in the bedroom closet—a revolver, it must have been, with a fat round part by the handle. It was brown and black, wood and metal. I had just reached out to pet it like some rodent in my cousin Ricky's hand when my father filled the doorway, screaming like Godzilla at the top of his lungs.

"It isn't loaded, Uncle Tony," Al kept saying. He even tried to show him, but Anthony just yelled at him to stop handling that weapon in front of these youngsters. Did Al want to know about all the bullets he had fished out of people in the emergency room, all the knife wounds he had stitched up? He wanted to leave right away, and it's one of the few times my mother put her foot down. No, she would not drive back up to a cold house in the suburbs on Christmas Eve when all the grocery stores were closed and the kids hadn't eaten. So we ate, and my father sulked in the living room. Marie went back and forth, trying to coax Anthony with little plates of food, but he would not relent. In the early days, he settled a fight by depriving himself.

In the car before we got back on the parkway, my mother pointed out all the brick houses wrapped in multicolored lights with bright Santa's sleighs and reindeer in windows and on rooftops, and my father badgered her to confirm his outrage about the gun. "That's why we moved away from the city," he said. "We relocated to escape the threat of violence."

Anthony never socialized with other men, watched sports on TV, got drunk in bars, or settled differences with his fists, like Mr. Clark down the street, a corporate lawyer who got punched out in a tavern and died of a brain hemorrhage.

"What could they have been fighting about?" my mother asked.

"Who knows?" my father told her. "A business deal, a pool game, a woman." The last one, the woman, spat out like a bite of rotten fruit.

He didn't bluster or swagger in public, having found more refined ways to wield power—at work the scalpel, at home the bankbook. And what a miracle of medicine, that the cruelty he displayed at home could not tarnish the image he held of himself: a healer who worked all his life to aid the sick. That words did not count as weapons, and neither did hands, walls, doors; refusing to pay for college even to protect his only son's life—and as my mother's illness progressed, withholding of food and a bedpan and sleep.

The men Anthony saw most often were his patients—in need, in pain, under anesthesia. Under the hot white lights of the operating room he opened them wide, removed gall bladders, appendices, whatever ailed them, and stitched up the wounds. What more did he need to prove to them?

15

He didn't hunt, or associate with Mafiosi—in fact, he wouldn't admit the Mafia was real. This was his party line: that my friends who stopped by to pick me up—I never invited anyone to stay—should call him Doctor, not Mister, D'Amato. That I should always correct a person who asked if we were Italian—we were Italian-American. And that no matter who said the word "Mafia" in what context, I should interrupt immediately, leap to the defense of my people, and insist there was no such thing.

My cousin Angela, a couple of years older than Donna, told us of course the Mafia existed. If not for them, Angela could have been Nancy Sinatra—scratchy voice, white go-go boots, and all. Her father, my mother's brother Robert, showed great potential as a singer. For seven or eight months in 1951, long before I was born, he was a local celebrity with his own TV variety show, *The Robert Vittone Show*, which aired on a Newark station Sunday nights before Ed Sullivan. Uncle Robert would sing an opening number, introduce a couple of acts, and sing again before signing off. His voice was as good as the young Sinatra's, Angela claimed. And the Mafia offered him the same sixty-forty split they offered Frank. They'd set up as many gigs as he wanted—the Catskills, Vegas, maybe even Europe. No thanks, Robert told them, he'd see what he could do by himself. No son-of-a-bitch owns me, he told his family. Well then, the mobsters said, they'd see to it that he'd never work. And he didn't, because no matter how talented he was he couldn't get any clubs to book him.

My father always said his brother-in-law was lackadaisical, a ne'er-do-well who never became good at anything because he drifted from one job to the next. At least he could have done like Anthony's own brothers and entered the trades. This Mafia business was a load of bunk. There was always someone to blame for your own lack of ambition.

~ Three ~

Jimmy, the only son, was supposed to be the doctor. A doctor minimally, a surgeon ideally, to further the tradition Anthony started when he broke away from the building trades—the bricklaying, blasting, and stonework of his own father and uncles, brothers, neighbors, and cousins—and discovered a different kind of work that could be done with the hands. Work he could feel proud of—more risky, more technical. Work that could save lives. But Jimmy would have none of it. His refusal brought on their nightly battles, Jimmy's long stubborn exile, his drifting within easy reach of the draft board. Better to take his chances in Vietnam than consent to being remade in Anthony's image.

He resembled my mother physically, and Donna—more sinuous than sturdy. Gloria and I, both stout, took after our father. I'd think of Jimmy when I looked at Raymond Rothstein—skinny, and with a face as soft as a girl's. Only Ray wasn't Italian—he was half Jewish and half Puerto Rican, and he wore his black hair tied in a ponytail straight down his back. My brother kept his hair short, but even at an inch you could see the curl starting to form.

My memories of him roll like a grainy super-eight movie: Jimmy sneaking cigarettes down at the creek, building a flagstone patio out behind the house with Al, playing one-on-one in the driveway with Carl Delassandro. He slammed the basketball against the smooth black asphalt; I sat on the tin milkbox to watch. Bob Dylan played harmonica on the radio in the kitchen. My sisters complained about getting stuck with the dishes. Why did the boys get to play outside? Donna was only ten, Jimmy fourteen. I was still too young for dishes.

Jimmy going in for a lay-up, swinging huge flat pieces of slate off the back of Al's truck—with a twist in his hips, a shimmy in his spine. More than anything he looked like a dancer. He could have grown up to make disco movies, to land a part in the touring company of *A Chorus Line*. Even fighting with my father, he was in fluid motion. His head ducked, his shoulder turned, he only yelled back when he had to.

"A good-for-nothing." Anthony pointed a fork at him. "You'll never amount to anything."

It was 1964, and Jimmy had just started high school. They had this same fight every night at supper. Why did my brother sign up for shop, not chemistry? Why technical drawing instead of Latin? I didn't understand most of the details; all I knew was the pushing and prodding. I toyed with the fried smelts on my plate, and watched to see what Jimmy would do. He let two accusations fly by unanswered. He snatched the third one out of the air and slung it back.

"It's my life. Leave me alone."

My brother never said "Fuck you," like I would in later years. He was such a good boy, for a bad boy. Their arguments were so mild-mannered, so lethal.

"You're proud of your little job at the garden center," Anthony told him. "That's sufficient for a child, but where will you be at twenty-five?

You'll be answering to a boss. You'll be coming home from work every day with dirt on your hands."

When my mother said, "Please, Tony, we're having supper," Anthony turned on her.

"What use are you? You could have given me another son. Or you could explain to this one the value of an education. But you're too stupid. You didn't even go to college."

Vera said nothing.

"I pay substantial taxes," Anthony told her. "That school should be preparing my son for pre-med."

"I doubt they can force him," she said.

"You're worthless. What do you know about anything?"

Her face clouded over, and she rose unsteadily from her chair. "Donna," she said, "help me clear this table."

Anthony had no secretary in those days; he made the calls himself to reschedule his Monday morning patients. He dressed in a blue suit and striped tie to meet with the high school guidance counselor. When that conference proved, in his words, "unfruitful," he canceled another round of appointments and put on a dark grey suit to visit the principal. For the district superintendent, he switched back to blue.

The school authorities confirmed what my mother already knew: they'd leave it to the parent to negotiate about expectations with the child. But perhaps Doctor D'Amato would consider a compromise. He might encourage Jimmy to pursue a career in landscape architecture. That way, if Jimmy were to soften his stance towards medicine, he would already have taken the basic sciences. He wouldn't have wasted any time.

"Please think about it, Tony," my mother said. "Maybe Jimmy will come around on his own."

"Forget it," he told her. "Landscaping is for laborers. He can go for pre-med, or he can find someone else to pay the tuition."

Gloria went off to college to major in French and art history—good enough to attract a well-educated man. Footage from Vietnam started to air on the evening news: helicopters landing and taking off. Soldiers loading and unloading supplies. Guns pop-pop-popping in the distance. Vietnamese boys, their shirts untucked, running down city streets. I didn't think any of this had anything to do with my brother. My father's harassment of Jimmy ebbed and flowed, and the times he didn't push frightened me more than when he did, because he regarded my brother with such blank hatred.

And then one Holy Saturday, Al and Marie showed up on our doorstep. Anthony answered the bell in his sleeveless undershirt. Guinea shirts, Gloria used to call them—quietly, so she wouldn't get smacked. Al had an anchor tattooed on his forearm, and he carried a big *pizza piena*. Marie carried an Entenmann's coffee cake in a blue and white box.

Al said, "Happy Easter, Uncle Tony. Special delivery from my mom." Aunt Alida was my father's older sister.

"You shouldn't have." Anthony let them in and went upstairs for a shirt. "Frannie," he yelled, "tell your mother we have company. Donna, put on some coffee for your cousins."

"I'll do it," Marie said. "Don't put yourself out. Isn't Aunt Vera feeling well today? Our kids are playing at their grandma's, so we thought we'd take a ride in the country."

Al said, "Let's see the lay of the land," and he brought my father out back to plan the patio he had offered to build.

Jimmy ended up helping Al with the patio on a few sunny Saturdays in May. They dug up the lumpy clearing between our house and the woods, and then leveled it, and laid the stones and cement.

My cousin said, "If it wasn't for all these trees you could keep a horse on the place."

Whenever he and my brother worked, my father left for the hospital. "I'll be rounding on my patients this afternoon," he'd make a point of explaining.

Before we knew it, Jimmy was living with Al and Marie—working as Al's apprentice, and attending his senior year of high school in the Bronx. I couldn't tell whether my brother was rescued from Anthony, or thrown away by him, or given in trade for the patio.

My father took possession of Jimmy's bedroom immediately, stripped the pro baseball team pennants off the wall, and turned it into his at-home office. He moved the stacks of medical journals and his desk piled high with bills out of the downstairs family room to turn that space into what he called a more convenient bedroom for my mother. "It's much more sensible," Anthony said. Vera didn't use a wheelchair yet, but the stairs were starting to wear on her. The new bedroom was to be hers, not theirs.

My mother went along with the plan, her only complaint being moving the TV set. The whole reason to have a family room, in addition to a formal living room, was to keep the antisocial habit of watching television out of the view of polite company. But once Al and Marie absconded with my brother, we never saw any company at all.

19

Donna, who had griped chronically about Jimmy never doing any housework, now grumbled about how easily he was dismissed. "What if he doesn't like that school in the Bronx? He won't have a bedroom to come home to."

But Anthony was unstoppable, muscling furniture through doorways and up the stairs by himself, calling on Donna for a hand only when he absolutely needed it. And Jimmy must have liked his life in the Bronx well enough. He came home once in two years, and that was after his draft notice arrived. By then it was 1968, and I knew exactly what the newsreels from Vietnam might mean for him.

My mother sat in the living room weeping. Jimmy stood next to her chair. A blue and white taxi waited for him in the driveway.

"Why don't you enlist?" my mother asked him. "Maybe they'll send you to Germany."

He had grown muscular and brown from working outside all summer, and his hair was cut so short it had no wave. He said, "It's too late for that, Ma. I'll just put in my time and come home."

She said, "I'll pray for you, Jimmy. Now, please. Your father's at the office. Have the driver take you there to say goodbye."

"All right," he told her, but I was not convinced.

His shirt stretched tight between his shoulder blades when he bent down to kiss her. And then—even though I was nine—he lifted me up, and kissed me and set me on my feet again. After he left, I found his coin collection and a bag of M & M's on my pillow. That was it. My only brother gone. The sergeant who delivered the news about the land mine rang the doorbell at Al and Marie's house, not ours.

Half the time I wasn't sure if we lost Jimmy to the Bronx or the Viet Cong—except when people said simplistic things like only poor kids died in the war. I knew they were talking proportionally, trying to make a point about inequality, but they didn't help their point by saying "only." And there were the blurry days in middle school—in 1971, during the bombing of Cambodia—when people wore black armbands and refused to go to classes. They sat out on the front lawn of our school and chanted, "Hell, no, we won't go"—only a handful, three or four percent of the student body. They joked about all the ways to stay out of the draft—about saying you're gay when you're not, or pissing your pants. I didn't want to listen to their bragging but I didn't want to go to classes either. That's when I started going down to the creek.

~ Four ~

The ocean was my religion. In the beginning, the ocean was far away and practically unreachable, except by long stifling rides in the family Buick. My mother looked pretty in a blousy white smock and pale pink straw hat. She unpacked our sandwiches and complained that the heat made her dizzy. Jimmy and Gloria, thirteen and sixteen, wandered off in different directions, intent on being seen without parents or little sisters. Donna worked hard at digging a wet sandy hole big enough to bury herself in. My father, up to his waist in the surf, lifted me by the elbows and dunked me. In his hands I flew up into the hot hazy sky, plunged down into cold breathtaking water, up and down over and over, and we laughed together.

But soon I grew older, and wanted to run into the surf by myself. Anthony ran behind me, yelling about riptides and undertow. I shook his warnings out of my ears and raced to touch the magnificent water. He'd catch me and haul me screaming under one arm all the way back to our brown plaid blanket. Soon Gloria and Jimmy refused to come at all and when Vera complained about the extra laundry, all the sandy clothes, my father said, "Forget it then. We won't go." So the trips to the seashore ended. My mother grew weaker and my father meaner, Gloria went off to college, Jimmy first to the Bronx and then to war. The wailing inside me grew louder, and the ocean became a remote god—at least until Donna, who took me everywhere she went, got a boyfriend with a car.

Donna went to the beach to work on a tan. Billy went to be with Donna. She lay for hours flat on her stomach, or propped up in an adjustable lawn chair, holding a three-way reflector made of cardboard wrapped in aluminum foil under her chin. I sat all day watching the waves rushing in and draining out. I worshipped the ocean. Not the bay or the sound with their muted tides, fishy smells, nearly-whole empty shells littering the beach, but the ocean, unbounded and ineffable, whose waves bleached and pounded every scrap of life and all my disappointments into sparkling grains of sand.

Then Donna left town, first for college and then South America, and the ocean receded again. Close to home, I offered my prayers to the lesser deities of creek and swamp. But every day I'd pause to think about the distant powerful sea pulling all the water in the world back to itself.

~ Five ~

Mary Nathan was my mother's physical therapist. I thought she was a goddess. She wore sweat pants, drove a blue Ford station wagon, and carried a gym bag full of lotions and oils. She called on my mother every week, and touched her when nobody else would. Not me. Certainly not my father.

It wasn't the MS I felt squeamish about, not the incontinence or muscle spasms. The thing that stopped me from touching my mother was older than those symptoms, lodged deeper in my body. It mirrored the look I believe I saw on her face—reluctance? repulsion?—when she leaned over to pick me up from my crib. I always imagined her holding me at arm's length, more like a smelly dishrag than a live baby.

But Mary Nathan had never needed anything from Vera. She climbed right up next to her on the bed, to coax her muscles through their range of motion. "Push. Good. Push again. That's great. Now, can you pull?"

I'd hurry home from school on Thursdays just to stand in my mother's doorway and watch. Could Mary have scheduled those late afternoon appointments to see me? I thought so. I hoped so, at the time.

She had opinions, I could tell, about what was happening in our home. Mostly she kept them to herself. It was less what she said than what she didn't say. She never chattered like the neighbor ladies who came bearing prayers and pity, or library books and news of their children's accomplishments. She never insinuated that a cure was the highest prize. The experimental treatments performed on Vera would improve matters or not—in either case, she and Mary had work to do. Mary was sturdy and generous, so unlike the occupational therapist—a bland, frightened woman with insipid ideas about restoring my mother to her housewifely duties.

Week one: grasping a knife to chop an onion. Week two: opening cans of plum tomatoes. Week three: keeping a chair in the kitchen to take breaks while you stir the sauce. You'll be pushing a vacuum cleaner any day now, Mrs. D'Amato. But my mother had Mattie around to vacuum, and me to make the sauce. "Mrs. D'Amato," she warned, "I'll have to write in your chart that you are resistant to trying." Soon enough, the insurance company canceled her visits.

But Mary Nathan kept coming. Under her hands, Vera's muscles and joints became fluid. With Mary coaching, Vera stood, walked a few steps, sat back down again. "Protect what you still have." Mary massaged my mother's legs while she talked. "Then you can decide how to use it."

A wheelchair was a tool, Mary said, a means of conserving energy. By maintaining the ability to transfer from chair to toilet, Vera would expand infinitely the things she could do on her own. She could get out, talk to people, go to Mass, volunteer her time somewhere, maybe even enroll in a class at the community college.

But to Vera the wheelchair only signified failure, the end of the line, the end of a long slide down—from one hand on the wall, to a slim pearly-topped cane, then a thick graceless cane, then two hands on a collapsible aluminum walker. "How can I go out like this?" she'd ask Mary. "No one wants to talk with me."

"That's not true, Ma," I'd yell. "People still like you. Mrs. West talks to you." Anthony called her worthless, but why did she have to believe him? I knew better than to argue in front of a stranger, but this stranger was the only adult who made sense.

"Frannie's a troublemaker," my mother said to Mary.

Mary smiled at me and shook her head, but her hands on Vera's shoulder never missed a beat. I fled from the bedroom doorway to sit scowling in the living room. I hated my mother. I hated the whole world. I didn't hate Mary. I listened to her working in the other room—her bigger movements, my mother's smaller ones. I listened for the zipper on her gym bag, the signal that their hour was up. I sulked on the couch, the TV tuned to *Hollywood Squares*, the volume turned all the way down.

Mary would linger for just a minute on her way out to the car. She stood so close I could see the nap on her pant leg. She spoke confidentially, but never in a whisper. "I can see what you're up against, Frannie. I'm sorry. Saying so isn't much help."

But it was a huge help, and Mary always delivered. Always slipped me something in passing, some pebble of strength to add to the pile I hoarded. Best of all, she wasn't afraid of me. She didn't tell me I'd be prettier if I'd smile.

If a wheelchair was a tool at all, it was a tool of my father's intolerance. For although he hardly spoke to my mother over meals, rarely sat down with her to watch TV, never treated her to the opera or the movies, still Anthony insisted on taking Vera with him when he traveled abroad. They spent more time together in the Class A hotels of Moscow, Paris, and Vienna than they ever did in Mount Kisco—with no one there to protect her from his pace. How could she preserve her flexibility, maintain her independence, while they hurried from one historic site to the next? No time for her faltering gait, her hand on his arm; they had the three o'clock guided tour to catch. He'd unfold the wheelchair, command that she sit, demand that she allow him to push. She'd get out of the chair only to climb up or down stairs, then back in for the long piazzas and hallways. I didn't witness all this, but I did see the results. Vera came home from every vacation exhausted.

Even the most event-filled trip provided a break from Anthony's grueling hospital schedule. In the relative quiet, did he actually enjoy her companionship, or was he afraid to let her out of his sight for a few weeks at a time? I had heard her whispering with my grandmother on occasion about divorce, when I used to press my ear against the bedroom door. What about the Church, what about the children? they took turns asking. She'd lose the house, we'd have to scrape just to afford an apartment.

I myself relished the thought of a small apartment—empty, with bare white walls, our tartan plaid soft-sided suitcases unzipped in the middle of the floor. I imagined true peace, a clear space where my mother's long-lost exuberance could resurface. I didn't consider what we would sit or sleep on.

"You had spirit as a young woman," I overheard my grandmother telling my mother, "until you let your fiancé start calling the shots."

From the very first, Anthony had mandated that Vera was to socialize with no one—not even the women from her church or office. Rival suitors lurked around every corner. He attended medical school in Boston and came home to the Bronx every other weekend. He arranged to see his betrothed on alternate Sunday afternoons. Against her own mother's better judgment, Vera sat home the rest of the time. She proved herself worthy of marrying a busy doctor.

My mother kept her wedding picture in a frame on top of her dresser—she and Anthony striding arm-in-arm down the steps of the church. Her broad smile seemed genuine, not put on for the benefit of the camera. Her sacrifices had indeed paid off. The evidence of those sacrifices, of her life before Anthony, she kept at the back of her bottom dresser drawer—tucked under her pink, white and ecru satin slips. I felt the edge of the flat cigar box one day when I was putting away laundry. I lifted it out and pawed through the cache of snapshots.

They were small square glossies, black and white with crinkled edges: Vera stretched out on a blanket at the beach with her friend Antoinette, smiling at her cousin Gene who held a guitar, strolling on the boardwalk with her brother Robert. I glanced at the names and dates written on the back. I read fast, in case she insisted that I stop.

"Oh, those," she said when she came into the room and noticed me holding the box. "I keep thinking I'll make an album someday."

After that first time, I'd sneak a look every now and again. I'd open the box and try to put myself in the company of that happy young woman, to figure out how she became the woman I knew. Maybe my grandmother was right and Anthony was to blame, or maybe any marriage would have drained the life out of Vera. Either way, divorce sounded promising. I started praying for her to leave him, but she never solicited my opinion, never got further than an occasional threat.

"I don't have to take this anymore," she'd yell. "The kids are in school. I could make it on my own."

"You'll never find a job," he said.

And he was right. Before the whispering or threatening could develop into a plan, the bouts of dizziness had overtaken Vera. Except for Gloria's wedding, and Jimmy's and my grandmother's funerals, she rarely left the house unless Anthony dragged her with him.

Mary Nathan was talking on the phone in our kitchen. I stood in the dining room and watched.

"Doctor D'Amato," she said. "It's a matter of three or four days. As one professional to another, I urge you. No, I'm not a doctor. But I do think you're making the wrong choice."

Then without so much as "goodbye" she set the receiver in its cradle, and I knew Anthony had slammed his end down.

"You work with what you've got," Mary told me.

I followed her back to my mother's room.

"Okay, Mrs. D'Amato. A bit of a warm-up. Then I'll teach you a few things you can do on your own."

My father was taking my mother to Portugal and Spain. I had already hauled her suitcase up from the basement. The insurance company would drop Vera if she interrupted physical therapy for more than a month. Even so, Anthony planned a five-week trip. He could have shaved Cordoba or Mallorca from his itinerary, but he refused.

I begged my mother to speak up for herself, scolded my father to do right by my mother. Finally Mary Nathan got on his case, and failed. She wouldn't be coming to our home any more. So she worked with the last hour we had.

25

Vera reached her arm to the right, then crossed to tap herself on the opposite shoulder. "Five times, each side," Mary told her. "You can do it whenever you're sitting up."

She didn't suggest that Vera continue with my help. I felt both relieved to be left out of it and exposed as a bad daughter in my unwillingness to touch my own mother. I urged myself to try, to push my way in, to overcome that magnetic reluctance. Teach me, I imagined asking Mary. Show me—how to touch someone like it's the most natural thing in the world. An arm, a leg, casually, matter-of-factly. I bet Mary Nathan held and kissed her own children.

Teach me. Let me. But before these words could break the surface, I heard the tires skidding on asphalt, the car door slamming, the front door opening, the floor shaking under Anthony's stride. My mother held her breath and so did I. Mary's hands stayed true to their rhythm.

Run! I wanted to tell her. But it looked like she was in command. She was holding something back, so I did too.

Anthony stormed past me and into the room. Only then did Mary break her connection to my mother. She faced him. She glanced in my direction, but I could tell she was checking her exit, confirming Anthony did not have her cornered. His own momentum had carried him to the far side of Vera's room.

I felt a flash of glee: doing nothing could be a strategic choice.

Now Mary Nathan and my father stood on opposite sides of the bed. Soon they would be shouting across my mother's body.

But there was no shouting, no voices were raised at all. "Get out of my house." He spoke so calmly, it chilled me. "We have no further need. Isn't that right, Vera?"

"Please," my mother told Mary. "It will be better if you go."

I hung in the doorway, studying Mary. I needed to know what she would do.

"Dr. D'Amato. This is my last session. We have forty minutes left. I was just teaching Mrs. D'Amato a few stretches she can do on her own. Surely you'd agree—"

He said, "No. You've done enough. In one more minute, you'll be trespassing."

"Please," Vera told Mary. "Just go."

Mary picked up her towels and bag. "Goodbye," she said to all of us. She gave me no special notice when I stepped aside to let her pass. Anthony tailed her all the way out to the driveway and stood with his arms crossed while she backed her wagon into the street.

After she left, the fighting started. "You killed my brother," I screamed at him, "and now you're killing my mother."

The instant he looked at me, I ran. Upstairs, I slammed my bedroom door and leaned against it to keep him out, but he was bigger and pushed harder. I was caught crouching between the door and wall. In the scuffle, my hip bones proved strongest. One of them dented the plaster wall; the other splintered the wood of the hollow core door.

Inside the room, he unbuckled his belt and yanked it from its loops. I fell on my back, threw my legs into the air, kicking and kicking, but best of all, I laughed. Even if I was about to get pummeled, I would keep the upper hand.

Confronted with mirth instead of fear, he lost his motivation. Like a wind-up toy running down, he delivered a few feeble blows and quit. Much more effective to laugh than to cry out, "Please, Daddy. No, Daddy. Don't."

I thought Mary Nathan was gone forever, but then I saw her while my parents were in Portugal. I was walking home from school against traffic on the shoulder of the road. The blue Ford drove past, going in my direction. The brake lights flashed red as they disappeared around a curve.

When I rounded the bend, she was there, pulled over on the straightaway where she wouldn't get rear-ended. I crossed the two-lane highway and opened her passenger door. She drove me to the turn-off for our housing development, pulled the car onto the shoulder again and shifted into park. I sat in her front seat, my hands resting on top of my book bag, a tasseled wool bag from Greece that Donna had bought on the street in the city. Everyone else I knew carried khaki knapsacks from the Army-Navy surplus store in town, but they didn't have brothers who died.

Mary Nathan reached over and picked up my left hand, like she was going to start working the knuckles. But she just held it. Her own hand was drier than mine, lightly callused and warm.

"When do you graduate from high school, Frannie?"

"In two or three years," I told her. "Class of '77. '76, if I'm perfect."

"Two years would be good," she said. "Because honestly, Frannie, the best you can do is grow up and move away."

She set my hand down and gave it a couple of pats. That was my cue to get out of the car. Go into the world. Seek out the next person who would help me know I wasn't crazy.

~ Six ~

I took the *Times* home from school every day, and walked to town on Saturday and Sunday to fill in the gaps. I gnawed through newsprint, searched for an update on Janine Kennedy's case, but I couldn't keep up. Unread papers piled in drifts around my bed. I never even learned if she was brought to trial. I reread the original article every night before sleep, squeezing the words for just a few more drops. And one time I was reminded of something I should have known all along: Every person with MS is different. Janine might very well have acted alone.

Chances were she had her good days and bad, a fatigue that ebbed and flowed. There she was at the supermarket, walking and pushing a grocery cart. At home, walking from room to room, her hands seeking balance on walls, door frames, the back of a chair. No one needed to bring her that rifle. Chances were, it belonged to her husband, and he left it lying around. She picked it up and loaded it when she had the strength. And then she fired it herself.

If I had put a gun in Vera's hand, Anthony would have come home to find us arguing about whether or not she should pull the trigger. She barely protested the way he treated her.

"You'll lose your mind if you don't," I often said. I was in danger of losing my own mind. But she insisted we had to keep the peace.

"What peace?" I'd ask. "Show me where peace is."

When I was only three, I stopped climbing into my father's lap. I closed myself off from the songs Anthony sang me, from the channel of pleasure between us. A river ran in that channel, a high, rollicking stream, and beneath it a current of danger. Before I had words for it, I knew: I didn't want to be the only person he liked. I didn't want to compensate for his growing disappointment in my brother, for all the feeling gone to waste between him and my mother. I wanted justice, connection, a family, to break down the banks of that channel and let the energy spill through all the rooms of the house. When I was only three, I started fighting with him—sometimes throwing my body into tantrums, sometimes speaking out in defense of Vera and Jimmy, and always rejecting the kindness he offered. If he couldn't be nice to everyone, then he shouldn't be nice to me. I went on strike, and thought he would settle. Thirteen years later, he still hadn't. The only significant breaks in more than a decade of struggle came at the expense of my older siblings—of teenage Jimmy who threw away a lot more than an education, and teenage Donna, in Anthony's estimation a slut.

Even before I read about Janine, I had daydreamed about killing my father, about suffocating him with the pillow he shielded his eyes with when he slept. I savored the delicious martyrdom of going to jail on my mother's behalf, on my brother and sisters' behalf. Janine's story made clear to me how silly a pillow was, how mushy and ineffective. But it didn't teach me anything about what it would take to cross the distance— to make an actual homicidal decision, instead of merely wishing someone you once loved dead.

Nancy Levy brought armloads of vegetables, flowers, and herbs into the art room—including dazzling sunflowers on six-foot stalks uprooted from her mother's garden—for a day-long demonstration on how to make natural dyes from plant sources. Nancy was Raymond Rothstein's more-or-less steady girlfriend and, in my opinion, the most kissable woman on the planet. I never conjured up the nerve to tell her. Nancy and Raymond were both well known for messing around with lots of people, and rumor had it that all through tenth grade Nancy was getting it on with Kate O'Donnell, who was never seen in public without a boyfriend.

Rumor had nothing about me. I was pretty sure I'd be a lesbian someday, although I was possibly the only girl in my high school crowd who hadn't even made out with another girl. I needed to get safely out of my father's reach and behind a locked door before I could relax enough to indulge that interest. In the meantime, there were guys on every corner, and I loved the looks on their faces when I'd say "yes" just when they were getting all worked up to talk me into a little sex. Women who fell in love with men were stupid. I was intelligent, indifferent, and in control. I could telegraph "Why not?" preemptively, before the come-on had even started, could play with any guy's penis for a few minutes, all the better if I never saw him again. Half the time, I didn't ask their names. These were men, not boys—not hundreds, maybe a dozen scattered through my last year in high school. I let them pick me up hitchhiking, or walking down the street in New York, or sometimes at the Steak and Brew, although that felt dangerously close to home. At school, I let people assume I was inexperienced—and possibly a little daffy, the way I passed the hour in World Studies grinning at Nancy Levy.

Nancy had a running argument with Mr. Lombardi about the difference between true art and mere crafts. She said it was a feminist issue—

that although Mr. Lombardi challenged us to think beyond oil painting, he was too quick to dismiss traditional women's forms like quilting and weaving. He would never dismiss Christo, who built huge curtains and fences across different landscapes, as a mere engineer. In response to Nancy's challenge, he arranged to excuse her from morning classes so she could chop, soak, and simmer her plant dyes.

I found Nancy in the art room at lunch time, her red hair frizzing in every direction, her fingers stained crimson from peeling Bermuda onions. Kettles boiling on hot plates steamed up the windows all around her.

"Hey, Frannie," she said. "How was *The Battle of Algiers*?"

"Decent," I told her. "Except the white shirts made the subtitles impossible."

"Speaking of shirts, did you bring something to tie-dye?"

I had forgotten.

"Bummer," she said. I loved to watch her upper lip when she talked.

"I'll work something out," I told her, doing my best not to stare too hard.

I tried an experiment with some 18-by-24 sheets of drawing paper, folding the paper in half, then fourths, eighths, and sixteenths, and dipping the innermost corner into a vat of dye. Then I undid one fold and tried a different corner in a new color. The dyes were all very muted—brownish yellow, brownish red. Nothing green or blue through which I could express my fondness for water.

My favorite combination turned out to be purple and yellow. The colors ran together like a mostly-healed black-and-blue, and as soon as I saw this I had my plan. I made another sheet that matched, and hung both up with clothespins to dry. At the end of the day I rolled them up and took them home.

There was still a hole in my bedroom wall and a corresponding dent in the door, about eighteen inches from the bottom, punched through on the day of the fight about Mary Nathan. Unlike the bruises on my hips, the damage to the wall didn't fade or heal on its own. For more than a year, it had stayed as ugly as ever.

I taped my sheets of dyed paper over the smashed-up door and wall. Then I lay on my bed to admire my bruise-colored art work. I felt immensely satisfied, maybe even proud.

~ Seven ~

Raymond Rothstein's father owned guns, a room-sized collection of them, stored in one of the four bedrooms of their split-level house right down the street from us. The door to that room was not your average hollow core interior door that could shatter with a kick, but a heavily reinforced one, secured with at least three dead bolt locks, all requiring separate keys. Although you couldn't tell from the outside, the windows were wired with an alarm.

Raymond and I passed a joint under the beech tree in his backyard on a chilly September afternoon. It was too cold, really, to be sitting on the ground, but too soon to get cooped up indoors. The leaves had lost their fresh, summery wetness, and had faded to a tired leathery green.

"What does your father do with all those guns?" I glanced up at the window.

"He strokes them. It's like having a hundred cocks."

A hundred guns. Maybe Ray exaggerated. I envisioned smashing the window, grabbing a loaded gun, tearing up the hill to my parents' house with the alarm ringing behind me.

"But really," I said to Raymond, "what's the point of having them? He just buys them and puts them away, right?"

"He's not supporting any revolutions, if that's what you mean."

"Does he ever shoot them or anything?"

One at a time, Raymond told me, his father took the guns to the pistol range. That's how Mr. Rothstein spent his Saturdays. He would have welcomed his son's company, but Ray always declined. The guns gave him the creeps.

"I can swing an invitation for you next week," Ray offered.

"I think I'll skip it," I said. Still, I couldn't let up. "Inside that room, are the guns just lying around?"

Of course not. The guns were stored in locked cases, the ammunition in separate cases with different locks. "What's with you?" Raymond asked.

"Nothing. Just curious."

He stood up abruptly. "Let's go for a walk; I want to show you something."

We picked our way through the woods behind his house and out to the main road. Raymond held forth as we walked—about the effect of THC on the body's cells, the impact of overgrazing on the African grasslands. He was learning to be a potter, and planned to travel to Italy, Japan, Mexico, Kenya, to watch traditional potters at work. Nancy Levy, in addition to fiber arts, studied modern dance. I always felt bad in high school, hanging out with people who had talents and goals. My only goal was to get out of my father's house.

I saw two futures for myself, flipping back and forth like a Felix the Cat ring I once got at the dentist. Here's Felix laughing, here's Felix running. Either I'd play my cards right and take off like my sisters did—to Boston or some more distant city—or I'd end up living in the Bedford Hills Women's Correctional Facility right up the road from my widowed mother. As much as I wanted to get Anthony out of Vera's life, my interest in martyrdom was not consistent.

I worked five nights a week at the Steak and Brew—washing dishes and bussing tables, so I collected a share of the waitresses' tips. My dinners were free, and all the Michelob on tap I could drink. Every two weeks I deposited a paycheck, and watched my bank balance climb up and up.

That bank balance was my ticket to freedom, but I doubted whether I could leave my mother behind. Over and over, I saw myself taking off—walking to the train station with a suitcase in my hand. Every time, I'd get only so far and look back. My mother was sitting there, waiting. If I didn't take care of her, who would? So I'd set my suitcase down on the side of the road, and walk back up the hill to cook just one more supper. Only there never seemed to be a good time to go. I didn't want to leave her alone with Anthony, and she wasn't going anywhere on her own.

Raymond led me across the road to a wide, swampy field. A sign proclaimed that this was the future site of a professional office building. For now, the field was full of touch-me-not bushes—jewelweed—their flowers like small orange-yellow trumpets, with leopard's spots at the throat. I had seen them before, had noticed their beauty, but I'd never experienced the miracle of the seed pods.

"Touch one," Raymond said. It was green and about an inch long.

I did, and in one smooth motion the pod exploded, coiled itself into a spring, and threw its seed in every direction. I laughed, and touched another, and then another, marveling at how a simple plant could respond so quickly.

~ Eight ~

When Jimmy moved in with Al and Marie, Anthony stopped speaking about him, a cancellation made all the more complete because he didn't require that we do the same. The mention of my brother caused no ripple in my father's demeanor, as if we talked about someone Anthony had never met.

We didn't have much to say—only to comment that lamb chops were his favorite, or to speculate about how he liked his new school. The two or three times my mother drove Donna and me to the Bronx, and the details of Jimmy's life we gleaned from our brief visits—these we kept secret from my father:

My mother stood outside the door to my second grade classroom, dressed in a gray linen skirt and jacket and carrying a pocketbook, waiting for Mrs. Campbell to help me gather my things. She looked too dignified to be sneaking around on her husband, but sneaking around she was. I found it thrilling.

"It's a good day for a ride," she said when we got to the car. She meant stamina-wise more than weather-wise, although the day was sunny and cool.

We stopped at the junior high to pick up Donna, then got on the road. We were driving down to Greenwich Village first, to see my grandmother.

"I worry about her," Vera told Donna. "The neighborhood is getting rougher." My sister sat in the front seat, my mother's confidante. I eavesdropped from the back.

Just that month, Grandma's neighbor Mrs. Eiler's coin purse was stolen by a boy and a girl claiming to have a gun. It was probably a comb jammed into the corner of the girl's pocket. They often did that, Vera explained, they only pretended to have a gun. My grandmother insisted the neighborhood was safe enough.

Vera said, "Young people are becoming more violent. First the beatniks, and now the hippies."

"It's not the hippies," Donna told her, "it's the heroin addicts." My sister sounded so grown up, so worldly.

We found a parking space on my grandmother's block. I got out and looked around on the street. "Where are the beatniks?" I asked out loud.

"Shush up!" Donna hissed at me. I had forgotten the distinction between public and private.

I marched ahead to my grandmother's stoop, but waited for my mother to catch up before ringing the bell. Even on a weekday at noon, we held the security door open as little as possible. When the buzzer sounded and the hall light snapped on, Donna and I let Vera enter ahead of us. She climbed the stairs methodically, like she had to think about every step. We tried not to follow too closely. My grandmother watched from the top.

"Okay?" she asked when we'd made it about halfway. My mother didn't take the time to answer, so I nodded to show Grandma I'd heard.

Inside her apartment, she gave us each a kiss on the cheek. She said, "I'm so glad you came," which sounded oddly polite. But then the creases around her eyes deepened and she bestowed an extra smile on me.

"Take a rest," she told my mother. "I'll bake a little something with the girls."

My mother sat napping by the window with *The Ladies' Home Journal* open on her lap. I sat on the step stool in the kitchen while Grandma and Donna made brownies from scratch. Every ingredient, our grandmother instructed us, went back into the cupboard as soon as it was used. Long before she took the pan from the oven, the bowls, measuring cups, and spoons had been washed, dried, and put away, the thick smell of baking chocolate the only trace of our project.

Donna and I ate warm brownies, dusted with white powdered sugar, and drank milk so cold it gave me a headache while our mother and her mother whispered in the bedroom. My sister and I eyed the door, but neither of us made a move to go listen.

Then the bedroom door opened and the extra brownies were cut and stacked on a paper plate, and we were hurrying, it seemed—back down to the car, onto and then off the highway, and pulling up in front of a brick house I'd never seen before. We followed a narrow sidewalk between the house and the one next door and through a chain link gate, with Donna in the lead carrying the brownies. We rounded the corner into a strange back yard, and there were Jimmy and Al, with trowels in their hands, building a terrace.

One moment we were all standing there grinning, not knowing what to say besides, "Here, these are for you," and, "Thanks," and, "Better early for your birthday than late," while the paper plate passed from hand to hand. The next moment my mother grabbed a brick from the tall stack next to her. At least it looked like she was grabbing a brick, but really she was reaching for the whole stack, and if it hadn't been there she would have fallen over.

"Jimmy," she said, still trying to steady herself, "bring me that empty bucket for a minute." Her voice was as smooth as the skin on a drum, but underneath I could hear the panic.

Jimmy brought the bucket and turned it over, and she sat down. "Are you all right, Ma?" and, "Are you all right, Aunt Vera?" everyone asked at once.

"It's nothing," she said, "just the heat. Summer came on so fast."

But it was a mild day really, a day for baking, and I was wearing my red cotton sweater with buttons along the shoulders like epaulets. Al went into the house and came out with a tall glass of ice water.

"Won't the people mind?" my mother asked, but she drank. "Much better," she said and stood up again tentatively, testing her balance, brushing the white plaster dust off the seat of her skirt. "Okay," she said and we got back in the car. She held her hands at 10:00 and 2:00 on the steering wheel, which I would later learn in driver's ed is the way to maximize control. No one spoke. Donna and I watched our mother as she watched the road. It was if all three of us were driving.

"I need to lie down," she said when we got home.

Donna helped to start supper by lifting the big spaghetti pot onto the stove. I took the plastic wrapping off a quartered chicken and laid the greasy pieces in a glass baking dish. Donna sprinkled black pepper and oregano on top. Vera had roused herself before Anthony's car turned in the driveway, but this was the last time she ventured so far on her own. After this, we only saw Jimmy once. After this, my grandmother came to us.

~ Nine ~

Mr. Lombardi got us out of school for a day at a time and took us on marathon class trips to the city where he'd shepherd forty-five students through a dozen places: a SoHo loft with a real working painter, a West Village art theater that showed old Bergman films on a big screen, the Museum of Modern Art, two or three uptown galleries, and all the required bus and subway connections in between. Going to the city with him was definitely more interesting than the days Raymond, Nancy, and I skipped school to hang out on St. Mark's Place—smoking loose joints we bought on the street, thumbing through dense books about Eastern mysticism, and squandering our money on the inaccurate but accessible guidance we got from the Gypsy palm reader who hung a red neon outline of a giant hand in her window.

To demonstrate that art is everywhere, he also took us on a couple of day-long trips to the country. We'd pile into a school bus and journey into the hills of western Connecticut or upstate New York to visit artist friends of his—sculptors, printmakers, potters, and one time a guy who made gravestone rubbings. All had left behind their Manhattan lofts for big drafty barns with views of pasture turning back to woods.

Nancy had it right: Mr. Lombardi did nothing to dispel the impression that artists were always men—white men, in fact, but Nancy was not so precise. He brought us to look at as many kinds of art as possible, but not artists. Of all the works, the three-dimensional stuff impressed me most: Red Grooms's soft sculptures because we wanted to climb on them, a museum of hand-wrought iron tools because Patrick DePaulo challenged the teacher on the idea that tools could be art, and the sculpture we viewed in the front yard of a rickety wood frame house in Kent, because it was the kind of thing you don't easily forget.

Kent is a village on Connecticut's Housatonic River, a real-life prototype of the New England postcard scene. Our big yellow school bus bounced into town on a bright blue October day. Red maples flared on the hillside, offset by the purplish brown of the neighboring oaks. Mr. Lombardi was keeping our destination a surprise. We had just left the tool museum, but he wanted us to see something in town. Soon he was telling the driver to pull over in front of a weather-beaten grey house on a street of otherwise trimly painted white houses, so we could get out and look.

Someone had fashioned a crucifix from two rough boards, nailed a baby doll to it, and pounded it upright in the packed dirt of the front yard. The doll was female and naked, splashed with red paint. Beads and charms and other trinkets hung in strands from her plastic body and from the arms of the cross. A flat board, with at least a paragraph of lettering hand-painted in black and red, leaned against the foot of the sculpture. The words were clear but their meaning was not: thieves of children, damnation, crime. The whole thing read like a lot of ranting, and I got a headache trying to understand it. Mr. Lombardi ushered us back on the bus and, standing at the front, delivered a brief interpretive lecture.

The guy who made the crucifix lived alone with his daughter for a long time. When she was thirteen, Child Protection came and took her away. Mr. Lombardi told us this was how people make art out of the pain in their lives, by protesting the powers that are bigger than they are, that the father created his sculpture to express the anguish of losing his daughter.

I had never heard of Child Protection, but right away I liked the sound of it, the fact of those two words side by side. How many times had I lain face down between the roots of the fir tree and asked, Why won't Mommy, why won't Aunt Julia, why won't Aunt Alida, why won't the teachers at school? Why wouldn't someone challenge my father? I couldn't tell for sure how Child Protection worked. Just hearing those words together made the whole day shimmer before me, even if they did seem like the villain in the story.

"Mr. Lombardi," I called out from my seat on the bus, "what was the daughter's name? Where did she go?"

"How should I know?" he said, as if it were the most irrelevant question he'd ever heard.

~ Ten ~

I could have gotten a gun. I could have stolen one from Mr. Rothstein's locked room, or taken the train into the city to buy a Saturday Night Special, or waited until I turned eighteen and waltzed right into the hunting and sporting goods shop in Mount Kisco. I could have gotten my hands on a weapon, killed my father, claimed to have liberated my mother. I could've had my name in the news for five minutes. A few people might have noticed the continuation of a pattern, might have realized Janine Kennedy wasn't alone.

Although sympathy for my father most likely stopped me, at the time I refused to think about it. So what if Anthony loved me as a baby, sang me lullabies, held me close against his chest? That little bit of love could only stretch so far. It was my mother who should have been angry enough to kill him. It never really was my job. But she didn't want him dead; she wanted him to wake up and start loving her.

I could have gotten a gun, overcome my resistance to firing it, could have forced a change in my parents' thirty-year marriage. But that would have ruined my own chances of getting away.

I thought about painting in blood, but I was going for an end result, the brilliant effect of fresh gore, not the reality of stiffened brown blood. I surveyed my options: watercolor—too thin, but available at home. A tube of acrylic stolen from the art room—good texture and easy to get. A tube of oil paint stolen from Raymond's mother Anita, who was an artist—perfect

37

texture but smelly and hard to clean up, plus I'd have felt too bad about taking it. Lipstick.

I never wore lipstick, had never even owned any, but the minute I said it, I was hooked. Not the icy shades of pink and peach other girls my age wore, but deep red like Marilyn Monroe. Women in the movies were always writing on mirrors in lipstick, a luscious slide of dyed wax and fish scales on glass. That's what makes lip color glisten, fish scales.

Carla Gianetti, Donna's old best friend from high school, worked full-time behind the cosmetics counter at the Rexall drugstore. "I need to see some lipstick," I told her, and before she could reach for the rack of frosted peach I added, "Something really red."

"For your mother?"

"Yeah." I offered up what I hoped was my most darling kid sister smile. "How'd you guess?"

"I didn't think it was for you, unless maybe Halloween." She eyed me up and down: my unpainted face, my hair parted straight down the middle, my Mexican shirt with embroidered flowers, bought at the new head shop in town. Carla's own hair looked shorter and more teased-up than usual, almost like a hair-do. She wore her blue uniform smock-coat with the top three buttons unbuttoned, to show off the ribbed sweater and thin gold necklace underneath.

"How is your mother anyway?" About once a day somebody asked me this question. Vera was still alive, still putting on a happy face, resigned to her life of captivity.

"About the same." When I bothered to answer, that's the answer I gave.

"Oh, that's good. Tell her I say 'hi.'"

I looked at the testers—Rumba Red, Romance Red, Raving Red—but I knew zilch about what to do. Buying lipstick was as foreign as buying a gun.

"Here, give me your hand," Carla said. "Make a fist." She drew three strokes of red on the fleshy part at the base of my thumb. "What do you hear from Donna?"

"Letter about a month ago." I bristled at these questions even more than the ones about my mother.

"Same here. We must be due for a new batch. So you think your mom will like Raving Red?"

"Sure," I said, "I hope so." I liked the name, raving lunatic red, better than romance or dancing.

38

Carla reached into the case for an unopened tube and laid it on the counter. Then she raised her voice just a fraction of an inch, for the benefit of the other employees in the store. "Well, if it's not a surprise, you could wear those samples home and let her pick." She winked at me. "I've got to go unpack some boxes. Why don't you come back when you've made up your mind?"

"Yeah, thanks. I'll see you later." Some things would never change. As I watched her saunter to the back of the store, I slid the free lipstick into my pocket. Of course I knew how to shoplift, I was Donna D'Amato's little sister. Raised on robbery, just like Joni Mitchell said. All at once I damned Carla for making me miss Donna, and I loved Carla for knowing me, knowing Donna, knowing me and Donna together.

As a teenager, my sister was quite the thief. I was her admiring sidekick. Every Saturday morning for two years—after she got her driver's license and before she left for college—Donna and I went to the A&P bearing a fifty dollar check and a shopping list drawn up by Anthony. Our first stop, the manager's window where we presented the check for cash. Jerry, the manager, wore a red suit jacket and a diamond pinky ring. The very first time, when he asked for ID, Donna pulled out the temporary slip of paper that proved she'd just passed her road test. After that, he always greeted her by name. "How you doing, Donna?" he'd address himself to her practically non-existent chest.

My sister was as skinny as a birch tree, and wore baggy clothes with strong deep pockets. I was chubby and my clothes were snug, but I added normalcy to the picture. The more Donna padded her body with stolen groceries, the more we resembled each other. With me at her side, Donna could project herself as the good daughter—she who helps with the family chores. She could shake off the aura of suspicious teenager—she who requires surveillance.

Every week we came home with exactly fifty dollars worth of groceries, having paid for as few as possible. Anything we managed to steal turned to cash in our pockets. And these were the rules of Donna's game:

1) Every item goes in the basket first.
2) Only put something in your pocket if you're certain it's going to fit.
3) Experiment at home, not in the store.
4) Carry a purse, but never put anything you've ripped off into it.

5) Pay attention to price density—how much something costs compared to its size.
6) Turn your back to the one-way mirrors.
7) Use all available space on your body, but don't do anything that'll make you walk funny.

I watched her for weeks before I could push through my paralysis and slip a flat can of anchovies into my pocket. Eight ounces of cream cheese followed. I learned to mask my guilty look when the stock boys turned up our aisle. But no one could rival my sister.

The pockets of her jeans and jacket swallowed tins of tuna, cans of evaporated milk, tall bottles of ketchup, narrow jars of green olives, wheels of sticky figs. Most brazen of all were the pounds of hard salami and sharp provolone—sliced thin and wrapped in white paper by the woman in a hair net behind the deli counter. In one swift motion, Donna turned her back and slipped the parcels down the front of her shirt.

"Won't they know at the check-out?" I whispered.

"What?" Donna glanced back at the woman, who was busy cleaning the slicer. "You think she radios ahead?"

Just before we got on line, Donna would tuck a package of lamb chops or a London broil into her pants. "I look pregnant, don't I?" she'd murmur. "Pretty soon the rumors will fly: 'It must be that Paletta boy.'" She'd drive her cart up to the conveyor belt and unload only the bulkiest of items—a whole quartered chicken, four twenty-eight ounce cans of plum tomatoes, a net bag of ruby red grapefruit.

"How you girls holding up?" the check-out lady always asked. "That'll be twenty-five seventy." She never leaned over the counter to check the bottom of our cart for the laundry detergent and ten-pound bags of potatoes we'd have hidden there in plain view.

I felt as if the tin of allspice or ground cloves in my pocket might burst into flames under the cashier's stare.

While I stood there sweating, my sister wove her protective spell. "We're doing okay." She'd put the slightest tremor in her voice. But it was the cant of her body, the way she grasped the twisted yarn cord of her Greek shoulder bag, the way her hair fell in front of her eyes when she dug through the bag for money that broadcast what she intended the rest of the world to see: we were more acquainted with tragedy than other kids in town. Our brother died in the war, and now our mother was an invalid. We had to help her all the time. Weren't we managing nobly?

Outside the drug store, the day was windy and bright. I wrapped my fingers around the rounded-off edges of the Revlon tube in my pocket. After a stop at the stationer's and the post office, I walked home and got right to work.

The whole project took five minutes to complete. First I glued Janine's article, smudged but still legible, to an eight-and-a-half-by-eleven piece of plain paper: "Woman Arrested in Shooting Death of Husband." I circled the word "husband" in lipstick and drew an arrow over to the right-hand margin where I scrawled, in handwriting I did my best to disguise, "This could be you. Dead." Not as slippery as fish scales on a mirror, but pretty smooth, pretty satisfying. In the body of the article I drew Raving Red brackets around the description of the abuses committed by Mr. Kennedy, and another arrow to the bottom of the page: "This is you." Down in the lower right hand corner I started to write, "You can't escape your karma," and then paused to consider substituting "justice." It seemed like an inaccurate use of the word "karma," especially in conjunction with sending terrorist threats through the mail. In the end I kept it because I knew it would slow Anthony down, would give him something to think about before throwing my beautiful creation in the garbage.

Around the article I painted a raging lipstick fire, and cut out some triangles of paper from between the flames so the whole thing had a ragged edge. I laid my artwork down on one clean piece of paper and placed another on top as a blotter. Then I slid the sandwich into a large manila envelope, already addressed to his office. There was no point in sending it to the house. I didn't want to be nearby when he opened it.

~ Eleven ~

My parents didn't come to my high school graduation. I honestly preferred it that way. But when I came home late that night from a party at Kate O'Donnell's, I found my mother asleep in her wheelchair again.

"I thought things were better," I said.

"What is it?" she asked, startling awake.

"I thought things were better." And for the first time in my memory, I began to cry instead of shout. Tears welled up and slid down my face.

"Please, Frannie, don't," she said.

Her disability itself had worsened. Her leg muscles spasmed most of the time now, and she rarely got up from her chair without the Hoyer lift. But for several months Anthony's attitude had markedly improved, even though he never said a word about the art I sent to his office. We had been taking turns cooking and helping Vera. I had come to believe I could back away gradually.

"Things were better," I repeated, sniffling, as I helped her out of her clothes. I wheeled the lift from the corner over to her bed and untangled the chains and canvas sling.

"I wish I knew how to help you," she said.

"You can't," I told her. There was no helping me.

I got her settled and went upstairs to my own bed. The tears kept coming. I fell asleep, weeping and ashamed. In the morning, I woke up ready for a fight.

"Please, Frannie, don't," she said again when I started in on him in the kitchen.

"You're not a real doctor," I yelled. "You're a sadist, you're a quack."

On "quack" he lunged.

The next thing I knew, I was brandishing a knife—not a sharp or dangerous one, a flexible serrated knife for cutting bread. If I'd held a serious weapon, I wouldn't have known what to do with it. But just the fact of grabbing it off the counter, the flash of power I felt when I said, "I'll use it, too," made me recognize it was time to go.

The knife shocked him, stopped him in his tracks. We faced off for a few seconds, then I set it down with a clatter and pushed past him.

Upstairs in my room, I filled a backpack. Jeans and t-shirts. Summery peasant blouses. My hairbrush and savings account passbook tucked into an outside pocket. I stuffed an old soft-sided suitcase with long underwear shirts and heavy sweaters, my below-the-knee wool coat, a watercolor sketchbook and set of paints on top.

The door to my father's room slammed shut, and the bed springs creaked under his weight. One at a time, I carried my bags downstairs. I went to my mother who sat by an open window. Anthony didn't believe in air conditioning; he said the house was naturally shaded. But Vera's weariness always worsened on summer days like this one when the temperature kept climbing, the shade gave no relief, and she sat waiting to lap up the slightest breeze.

"Ma," I said. "I'm leaving. For a long time."

"Where will you go?"

"To Gloria's first, probably farther."

She said, "I wish I could do like a real mother and drive you to the station."

42

"Don't worry about it."

"Don't worry about me either."

At first, I stood above her, but then I squatted down and laid a sweaty hand on the vinyl arm of her wheelchair. "Listen," I said, "if you ever want to leave—"

"Don't be silly. This is my life. You'll have yours."

I should have kissed her goodbye, but she didn't move toward me either. She didn't split the distance.

"Be safe," she said, to which I could summon no answer. "How soon will you get to Gloria's?"

"Tomorrow, if I make the right connections."

"Call me," she said, and I promised I would.

I shoved my belongings out the front door into the blistering midday heat, and dragged them as far as the Rothstein's house. A sharp two-note high-low whistle made me look up just in time to see Raymond shinnying down from the middle branches of their beech tree.

His face shone with the exertion. "Let me help." He took my valise by the handle.

"Actually," I told him, "I was hoping you'd store that for me under your bed. I'll send you the money to ship it, once I get where I'm going." Better to look like a college student on vacation than a runaway.

Raymond walked with me down the hill—to the bank where I emptied my savings account, and then to the station where he sat with me while I waited for the next train into the city. I put a dime in the pay phone and called to quit my job at the Steak and Brew. Unlike all the times I had rehearsed leaving, I didn't once turn back.

~ Twelve ~

After Jimmy's funeral, a framed eight-by-ten glossy of him in his dress uniform appeared on my father's desk. My brother—dead, but no longer estranged—became the hero and I became the object of Anthony's desire, the next most likely candidate for a medical education. Donna was screwing up in high school already—not applying herself, my father said—skipping classes on balmy spring days to ride out to the beach with Billy. Gloria had finished her bachelor's degree and found her man. She had a husband in dental school, and motherhood right around the corner. I was eleven, in sixth grade, still a good student, and not interested in boys. I was his last best hope.

43

Instead of bullying me as he had Jimmy, instead of prodding and shoving and making incessant demands, Anthony became charming, coaxing. He meant to tease out my interest in the biological sciences, to drop hints of the pleasure he took in his work. Women, he frequently reminded me, could make competent physicians. There was one at the hospital—a Czech woman, a defector from Communism. He took great care pronouncing her name, holding each syllable, letting it roll around on his tongue. Some day, I too could qualify for this kind of respect. I could have a better deal in life than my mother.

We had a bookcase in those days—a tall modern built-in unit lining the west wall of the living room—but virtually no books. Anthony's education had been a technical one. Vera, who had never attended college, reminisced about the literature she read in high school. Our next-door neighbor, Mrs. West, brought over novels from the library—John Steinbeck, Pearl S. Buck. These my mother kept in a discreet stack by her bed. But no one spent much money on books.

One shelf of the wall unit held magazines—Anthony's *JAMAs* with their close-up color photos of ulcerated skin, a row of squat pale *Reader's Digest*, a taller row of yellow-spined *National Geographic*, and a pile of *Life* magazines too unwieldy to stand upright. For years we had only two books: a huge dictionary with fragile onion-skin pages, and a single-volume childishly illustrated encyclopedia. Baskets and bowls—inexpensive art objects—dotted the otherwise empty shelves. At some point, *The Godfather* appeared, my father's pride in Mario Puzo for making it to the bestseller list momentarily overriding his rejection of the whole Mafia business. "It didn't impress me," he reported after reading it. But there it stood—thick and black when you held it in your hand, but small in comparison to the two reference volumes. That year all the kids at school knew exactly what pages in *The Godfather* to turn to if you wanted to read about people fucking.

A couple of years after Jimmy died, Anthony bought a subscription to the *Time/Life* series on physical anthropology. Once a month, like a magazine, a book came in the mail: *Cro Magnon Man, Neanderthal Man, The Search for the Missing Link*. He lined them up on one shelf of the book case, perfectly uniform, the same brown cloth spines with bronze-colored lettering, even the same thickness.

"You can open them when they arrive," he told me.

I might have enjoyed slipping each one out of its cardboard box, being first to crack open the stiff cover, to turn the shiny pages heavy with clay.

But I owed it to Jimmy to accept no privileges, and left the books for Anthony to unwrap.

I couldn't resist pulling them down once they'd been shelved. I'd thumb past the charts of human evolution, the diagrams of skulls and bones. What captured me every time were the photos of archaeological digs, of modern-day men and women working painstakingly in far-off places, poring over dirt put through a strainer under a dry sun.

Once or twice that year, Anthony came across me reading his books. Passing by the archway that divided the living room from the front hall and stairs, he bestowed a warm smile of approval, and I did my best to ignore him. But in the long run, I lost my opportunity to let him down. He wanted one successor—any one would do. When Gloria presented herself, he dropped me flat:

I was thirteen, Gloria twenty-six. She and Michael and Baby Tina were back from Ann Arbor, visiting Michael's parents in Connecticut, acting— as usual—like Connecticut was the other end of the earth. Too far, Gloria said, to shlep what she called her entire family back and forth for Christmas with both sets of grandparents, but not too far to buzz over by herself for a meeting. She had important business to talk about, she'd told Anthony on the phone. He had taken to drinking espresso, brewed in a fluted aluminum pot on the top of the stove, muddy and black, with a splash of clear Anisette. He and Vera sat waiting for my sister at the table. I was the one who served the coffee.

Gloria let herself in and strode into the dining room past her old place at the table and without invitation took the chair that once belonged to Jimmy. I watched from the kitchen doorway. The whole room seemed to tip when she sat down, as if all the table's contents—the tiny upright cups and matching saucers, little stainless steel spoons, pot of coffee, plate of anise cookies with white icing and colored sprinkles that Billy's mother Audrey sent over to Vera—could have gone sliding and clattering into my sister's lap, but they didn't. When no one told her to change her seat, I hurried over to push a place setting in her direction.

"Daddy," she said, although my mother was sitting right there. She stirred her coffee while she talked. "I want to go to medical school. I've already been accepted at Michigan, but I need your help with the tuition."

"You—" he said, and I could hear him straining to keep the question out of his voice. I looked at him, daring him to look back, but he refused. He leaned forward, pressing his hands against the edge of the table, as if to right the balance. "What about your daughter?" he asked.

45

"My husband and I will work that out. There's no reason for you to say no."

"I guess you're right," he told her.

"I'm proud of you, Gloria," my mother said as I cleared the cups from the table.

~ Thirteen ~

I had run away to Gloria and Mike's once before. When I was fifteen, Donna left for Ecuador, and I was at my wit's end. My sister and brother-in-law proved useless. They oohed and aahed, made me a cup of hot chocolate, and put me back on the Greyhound to Port Authority. First they called my father to make sure, they said, that everything was all right at home.

Everything was not all right, I insisted, so loudly that they stole protective glances at three-year-old Tina who was playing with blocks in the living room.

They did offer to let me move in with them and finish high school in Ann Arbor, but I wanted them to intercede on my mother's behalf, not mine. Anthony had hired Mattie to help out a few hours a day. She worked at the hospital overnight, and treated her day job as an opportunity to sleep, napping on the couch with her cigarettes burning. She grumbled and sighed about fixing my mother lunch.

I understood resentment, and impatience. A few months before I ran away, Vera went into the hospital for an experimental treatment. She carried a box the size of a transistor radio in her pocket, with wire leads that attached directly to and were supposed to stimulate her spine. Implanting the wires was no big deal, but afterwards she had to live at the hospital for ten weeks so the neurologists and medical students could measure her neural responses each day while she sat, stood, and walked with a walker.

Maybe they'd see an improvement before sending her home, but I didn't bank on it. When she first went into a hospital—for a week of testing to diagnose the MS—I was only eight. I wrote "Get Well, Mommy" with colored pencils on handmade cards. But the older I got the more I could see that her physical disability would likely persist, and perhaps was the least of our problems.

Donna took a leave of absence from SUNY Binghamton that fall to be close at hand for her. The leave was temporary, she said, but in fact she never went back. She picked me up every day after school and drove to the hospital—down the Saw Mill and Major Deegan, past New York City, over the Triborough Bridge, and onto the Brooklyn Queens Expressway. There the traffic ground to a halt, the afternoon sun beat in through the windshield, and my stomach felt queasy from the smell of truck exhaust. Donna inched the car along and spun the radio dial to catch Crosby, Stills, Nash and Young and Marvin Gaye, and to avoid the Top 40, except for Stevie Wonder.

After the BQE came local streets—small ethnic restaurants down a half-flight of stairs from the sidewalk, and India Imports shops where patterned shirts and drawstring pants hung in the windows. "This is a nice neighborhood," Donna said the first time we passed through. "Maybe some night we can stop for supper."

But we never did. Donna knew how to hit every traffic light going both directions as it changed to green. I imagined her and me in a Greek or Cuban restaurant, at a candle-lit table for two, and the motion sickness I felt mixed with hunger and loneliness in my throat. We'd steal candy bars from the hospital gift shop to tide us over.

Vera always looked pretty sitting up in her yellow floral bed jacket, but she never had much to say.

"How's the food?" Donna asked every night.

"It's fine. You know me, I'm not picky."

"Should we bring you anything?"

"Oh, no, Donna. Don't trouble yourself. You already do so much driving."

Donna insisted it was no trouble at all, but it was a delicious, righteous kind of trouble, one that made us superior to Anthony. He showed his concern by phoning the doctors every few days to see how the experiment was progressing.

Donna clearly loved my mother. I thought I probably didn't. It was a lack I had lived with all my life, but not the kind of thing I admitted out loud. Even as a small girl, I never felt the impulse to climb up in her lap. Donna's, yes. Anthony's, maybe. Vera's, no. How do you love someone who perpetually says, "Oh, no, don't bother with me"? There was nothing to grab hold of.

"These are my daughters," Vera would introduce us whenever a nurse walked into her room. "My youngest two. Gloria, my eldest, is in medical school."

"All girls!" the nurses exclaimed, and my mother always agreed. We let her talk as if there had never been a Jimmy.

The hospital staff smiled and clucked over Donna and me. What good kids to visit so often. Vera seemed happy and proud, and I tried to be satisfied with that.

She was courteous to the nurses, not the least bit demanding. They'd come in at night and ask, "Do you want orange or grape juice?" and she'd say, "Whatever's easiest for you."

"I'll bet you'll enjoy orange tonight," they'd say, and I would thank God on the spot I didn't have their job. I would have said, "I'm here to get your juice, not make up your mind for you." I would have stood there, trying to force her to have an opinion, no matter who was down the hall ringing for a bedpan.

So I understood frustration, and annoyance. I had never particularly enjoyed my mother's company, and wouldn't have wanted the work of caring for a stranger. I wouldn't have wanted to be Mattie either—with three kids and two jobs. But I figured if you're going to charge money to take care of somebody in their own home, you should keep your grudges to yourself. You should not take a person who is habitually self-effacing and treat her like a pain in your ass.

I nagged at Anthony about paying a better salary to someone who could afford to give Vera her undivided attention.

He said, "Shut up, little girl. You don't know anything."

But I did know, and I expected Gloria and Mike to be moved by my arguments.

"You can't change things," they told me. "The best you can do is graduate from high school and get out of that house." Then they put me on a Greyhound heading back there.

Two years had passed since they first blew me off. This second time, I didn't expect much. I could have kept my seat on the bus, bought an extension on my ticket, bypassed their town altogether. It was just that—with Donna out of the country and unreachable by phone, with Jimmy and my grandmother long dead—I wanted somebody to know where I was going. Or *that* I was going, since I still didn't know where. West, I had decided. Maybe all the way to Seattle and the Pacific Ocean, where you could watch the sun setting into the water. Or maybe not that far.

From the bus depot in Ann Arbor, I traced the route I had taken before—up a shady hill, then across into glaring sunlight and around the back of a big gym to married student housing. Gloria opened the door. She eyed me and my backpack. I'd been in and out of train and bus stations for twenty-seven hours. My feet felt grimy inside my clogs, my breasts stuck to my ribs, my cotton shirt stuck to my skin.

"You've run away again?"

"I have six hundred dollars and a high school diploma. I'm moving away."

"Where are you going next?"

"Chicago," I surprised myself by saying. It was a compromise, less alarming than the West Coast. Downright plausible. There was a big lake there, if not an ocean. And once I said it, it sounded true.

She let me in.

Their apartment was just as I recalled it—flimsy 1960s construction, Danish teak furniture. Mike, who had dropped out of dental school to work at home as a writer, had just sold his manuscript, *First Impressions*, a detective novel about the science of forensic dentistry. He had splurged on a complicated new stereo which took up half the shelf space in their living room.

"Had to get a special license to drive that thing," he chuckled. His clothes looked new too, casual but plush.

Gloria and Mike left Tina, now five, at the next door neighbor's, and took me to a smoke-filled German restaurant on the far side of campus. They ordered rabbit stew, which tasted pretty good except for all the tiny bones. They poured stein after stein of beer and told me all about Mike's book deal and Gloria's surgery rotation. How lucky I was to have found her awake and at home. So I wasn't going to college; I had finally flown the coop.

"Your mother." Mike shook his head. "It's a pity."

Neither uttered a single word against my father.

"Your mother," Gloria said, "when she was pregnant with you, I walked in on her by accident and saw her big, naked belly. She went absolutely apeshit, screaming at me to get out of the room. She was that modest."

This was the story my sister gave me before sending me out into the world. In the morning, she wrote down the name of an old college friend in Chicago, and left a message with the friend's secretary that I might be calling.

"Say goodbye to your aunt," she told Tina.

I caught the nine a.m. bus, going west.

49

~ Fourteen ~

Southern Michigan looked exactly like Ohio, with cornfields on both sides of the freeway spreading to all horizons. No one lived on the huge tracts of land we sailed past—no farmers, no farm families, no barnyard animals. Every so often an abandoned house caught my eye, the paint gone from its boards, the morning light flashing through the cracks.

A pack of passed-out white boys had draped themselves over the last few rows in the bus. They'd been drinking and carrying on all night, it was plain, and were quiet now, except when one or another opened an eye and bellowed "Shut the hell up" at the woman sitting directly in front of them. She was black, and very small, not as old as I thought on first glance. She sat in an aisle seat, wearing a skirt, jacket, and pillbox hat even in the summer heat, her posture perfectly upright, and she sang spirituals—a slow and steady progression of songs which, as far as I could tell, never repeated.

"You've been singing all goddamn night," one of the boys said, but any profanity they hurled her way only fueled her commitment to keep on. She could have taken an empty place up front with the mothers and restless children, or the one I found halfway down the aisle next to a window, but she seemed to have singled the party boys out. "No one can keep me from praising my Jesus!" she'd call out every so often between songs.

As soon as I shoved my bag onto the overhead rack and settled down, an old man took the seat between me and the aisle. He wore a baggy brown suit and smelled of cigar smoke. "I'm changing my life," he leaned in to tell me, although I hadn't asked. "I'm going home to Wisconsin where there aren't so many Jews."

I thought about switching seats, but the only ones open were smack in the middle of a family of five or at the rear with one of the party boys. He was passed out for the moment, but was bound to wake up, look me over and say, "What have we here?" And I had pretty much decided I was finished with men. My life wasn't going the way I wanted. What better time than this bus trip to change it?

So I left the drunk boys to the Jesus woman, and I stuck with the anti-Semite. I turned my back to him and my face to the window, pressed my forehead against the smooth glass, and closed my eyes to the cornfields. I shut my ears against the singing and tried to imagine what I might be journeying toward.

PART TWO

Swimming Back • (1976-1977)

~ One~

I should have been afraid, showing up in a new city alone. Everyone always talked about the mean streets. Inside the Chicago bus station, the floor was gritty. Outside, the doorways stank of piss. All kinds of people walked by, including pimps. I was pretty sure I spotted one, a tall guy leaning against a post, pretending to read the paper while he trolled for new arrivals.

He would have loved to catch me looking uncertain. Are you lost? he would have said. Let me help you. So I kept my eyes bright, my step determined, and shook him and his associates off my trail. I carried my cash in a front pocket and stayed on guard against thieves. I needed to find a home, but I wasn't choosy. Any place would be better than the one I left behind, because in this entire city there was no one who had it in for me—me, Francesca D'Amato. No one cared one way or the other.

Eyes bright, shoulders back, I marched the six or eight blocks through downtown, under the rusty el, across the lanes of Michigan Avenue traffic and the broad plaza, as far east from the Greyhound station as I could walk. And there I was, confronting the lake—stunning and vastly turquoise on a breezy summer day. I stood on a cement wall, too high above the water to lean down and touch it.

It was deceptive, Lake Michigan. Waves lifted up and broke against the wall, but not wild ones. I watched the white-sailed yachts zipping in and out of the harbor, a wedge-shaped freighter crawling along the horizon, and tried to reconcile the great blue distances with the bland, salt-less smell. Maybe we could make a deal, Lake Michigan and I. Maybe life in Chicago would be simpler, and the lake would be big enough to hold me.

Two notices called out from the bulletin board at the Women's Center:
CO-ED CO-OP HOUSEHOLD SEEKS NEW MEMBER
and
LESBIAN FEMINIST HOUSEHOLD LOOKING FOR FIFTH.

51

Figuring there was no time like the present—Wasn't I a lesbian if I said so, and who was around to refute it anyway?—I copied down the number from the second flyer. I called from a phone booth on the street.

The woman who answered offered me an appointment for the following week.

"I was hoping for tonight," I told her.

A long pause, and then she gave me directions.

The house was red brick on the bottom, shingled on top, and unlike my cousins' houses in Queens and the Bronx—the ones with wide brick-and-cement stoops made for sitting on—this was a Chicago Northside two-flat, with a steep flight of wooden steps up to the door. Apartment buildings pressed in on the north and south.

"Look," I said as soon as the door opened, "if you want me to come next week, that's fine. I just need a suggestion about where to stay in the meantime. I've got money."

The door swung wider.

"I'm Frannie," I told her, and then correcting myself, "Fran."

"Arlene." She was square in her body like me, but taller and more fair. I had to tip my head back to look her in the eye. She motioned me to follow her upstairs. Two ten-speed bikes hung on the wall of the narrow stairwell. I had to take off my backpack and walk sideways to get past them.

"Is it just you, or you and a bike?" she asked.

"Just me," I hastened to tell her. "I figure I'll keep taking the el."

She nodded without turning around. "Wait here," she said, pointing to a sagging couch covered by a blue India-print bedspread. The afternoon light filtered through aqua paper shades.

Arlene disappeared to the back of the house, to what I guessed was the kitchen, where I heard women bickering in stage whispers about me, about whether to put me up temporarily while they considered if they actually wanted to live with me. "This is my home, not a drop-in center." "She's so young." "You're asking me to short-circuit the process."

"I'm asking you to be flexible." Only Arlene's voice was distinct. I strained to sort out the others, unsure of whether there were two or three.

Arlene said, "This is another class issue." I hadn't the foggiest idea what that meant, if she was talking about me, herself, or the other women.

"Who'll tell her no, if we finally decide no?" A clipped, crabby voice, the same one, it seemed, that spoke of process.

"I will," Arlene said. I could have kissed her.

They asked me a few questions about where I was from and how I had gotten here, and then they dragged a spare mattress out of the attic and into the unrented room. I tried not to look askance at the lumps and stains. We settled on fifty dollars for the week—one quarter of the monthly rent which covered utilities, shared food, Spic-n-Span, toilet paper, even the local phone service. I agreed to do my share of the housecleaning, and to pick up a dinner shift.

"Don't get too attached to being here." The crabby voice belonged to Jane, who happened to be beautiful in that great Jewish redheaded way I once thought peculiar to Nancy Levy. Beautiful, but awfully stern. I found myself wishing I had copied down the other number.

The phone cord wouldn't stretch from the living room to my new room, so I carried it out to the landing. I closed the door and dialed the number for Gloria's friend, to tell her I was safe.

"I've found a place to live," I said.

"Already?" she asked. "That was quick."

"I have friends here," I told her, softly, so they wouldn't hear me.

~ Two ~

These weren't just any lesbian feminists, these were socialist lesbian feminists. Justice was their religion. They talked all the time about power. They kept all kinds of books and newspapers stacked up around the house, and whenever I so much as glanced at one I learned something I hadn't thought about before. Like this article about using drugs I read in the bathtub one night, which said that getting high, far from being subversive, played into the hands of the system. It dulled one's interest in revolution, sapped one's stamina for effective action. The U.S. government condoned the sale of drugs in the inner city, I read, and had made them widely available to kids like my brother in Vietnam.

On the third night of my probationary week, Jane looked up from her gazpacho and told me, "Some of us are socialists," as if I hadn't gathered that already.

She and Mimi had spent the whole meal arguing about who had misplaced priorities—Mimi, who was trying to organize the Campbell's mushroom soup factory on behalf of the Socialist Workers Party, or Jane, who was running around drumming up interest in Cuba. Ultimately, it had to do with what kind of revolution we should be aiming for, and who would be in the vanguard.

I listened, said nothing, and to my great relief no one asked me to take sides. I was weak, unopinionated, always ready to agree with whoever had spoken last.

"How do you feel about socialism, Fran?" Arlene did ask me.

"I believe in it," I said. It felt silly, like saying I believed in Santa Claus. "But I've never—you know—joined a party or anything," all the while hoping this was the right answer.

"Join the crowd," Mimi told me. Party stalwarts like her were few and far between.

Willow, who had lived there only briefly, frightened me the most. At first I thought she and Mimi were lovers because they had the same wiry build and shared the attic expansion, but they were just willing to forego the privacy for fifty dollars each off their rents. Willow played the same Judy Collins album over and over, and sat at the kitchen table, even in summer, warming her thin hands around a mug of hot tea. More often than not, tears streaked her face. She let them flow, didn't wipe them away. She had no job. I never figured out how she paid her bills.

Arlene told me that Willow had been married once, for exactly twenty-four hours.

"Is that why she cries?" I asked.

"I doubt it," Arlene said. "She left him."

I didn't want to seem like her—a person with nowhere to be—and I didn't want to stay home with her either. So all that week I was under consideration and hadn't yet landed a job, I went out the front door every day and wandered the city to avoid moping around the house with Willow.

I wore a groove in the only route I knew—back downtown on the el, then east on foot to the Art Institute, which was air-conditioned. I took in Chinese platters and vases carved from glistening jade, Roman statues with ugly blank eyes, dazzling Impressionist paintings. But what drew me back time and again were the seventeenth-century Dutch and Flemish landscapes—all turbulent sea and sky, and hardly any land at all. I stood before them, rocking on the balls of my feet, fancying I could dive into their grey-green and yellow depths.

People painted at the museum, art students with easels set up in front of the Rembrandts and Cezannes. I cursed myself for leaving my paints with Raymond, but they were watercolors anyway, and I would have been too shy to use them in public. I did buy a new sketch book, a couple of pencils, and a ball-point pen. An artist, Mr. Lombardi used to say, must keep his materials close at hand. I made fast, sparse sketches—the square windows of the buildings across Michigan Avenue, the horizontals of the lake, the arcs of water in Buckingham Fountain.

I spent all day Saturday and Sunday at a Truffaut retrospective. The cinema was quiet and cool. At suppertime, I'd ride the el north again, turn

54

the key I had been trusted with in the lock of a place I couldn't call home, and join the socialist lesbian feminists for a meal of rice and veggies or cucumber soup in their sunny, aromatic kitchen.

Willow, Jane, Mimi, and Arlene needed to conduct a formal interview and deliberate over the results in two separate meetings before they could reach a consensus about me. How long had I been a lesbian? they asked. What was my ideal housemate? Did I know they were financially responsible to each other, that if one woman skipped out on the rent everyone's home would be jeopardized? Their decision got hung up on my age, which they believed was nineteen. I didn't tell them I graduated a whole year early and I meant a day, not a year, when I said I lived with my parents for a while beyond high school.

To prove I was not the sheltered, spoiled little girl they imagined, I put my very best into cooking and cleaning. I made a tomato, potato, and onion salad, and another of marinated string beans—cool but substantial food for a sweltering day. I scrubbed the bathroom on a rainy morning when I found myself miraculously alone. "Gone to my mother's. Be back tomorrow," read the note Willow left on the kitchen table. So I cranked up Bach's *Brandenburg Concertos* on the stereo and scoured the grout between the ceramic tiles.

I already thought of it as our mildewed grout, not theirs. Contrary to Jane's advice, I had indeed grown attached—to the place at first more than the people. I had come to love the deep porcelain tub, the chipped octagonal tiles that felt cool against my bare feet, the two tall windows facing east from my bedroom, the way the maple cabinets in the kitchen glowed like honey when the setting sun reached through a gap between the houses across the alley.

Surely, I fumbled the interview question about how long I'd been a lesbian. Saying my whole life, or since the day in first grade I looked across the aisle at Debbie Esposito sounded too flippant, but I couldn't tell them just one week. I told them two or three years, figuring that's how long I'd been falling asleep with my hand between my legs and Nancy Levy on my mind. Or Laura Nyro, who was so pretty in those photos on her album cover. But Jane, who let nothing slip, wrinkled her brow.

Arlene defended my inexactness. "Why not? Two or three years. Coming out is a process."

"Does your family know?" Jane asked.

"No," I said, without explaining how little family I stood to lose.

I was taking up space and they needed to decide if I should stay or go. So one night after supper they pushed back their plates, stood up in unison and moved to the living room. I went to my own room where I would be less tempted to eavesdrop, sat on my lumpy hand-me-down mattress, and pressed my back against the bare wall. I had nothing to do. I might have taken my dirty clothes to the laundromat on the corner, but didn't want to be absent so long. I sat. I worried. I made plans to go back to the women's center and call the other ad. I drew a picture of the gabled roofs outside my windows, and tried not to feel like an exile. These women had already eaten dinner with me six times; how could they not let me stay?

Jane knocked at my door, finally, and I scrambled up from my seat. "You're in," she said, and her mask broke apart into an unbelievably generous smile. I followed her out to the living room, where I was greeted with cheers and applause.

~ Three ~

First, there was the scratched-up, spindle-legged table I found at the Salvation Army and Jane carted home in her pickup truck. Next, I salvaged two wooden chairs from the neighbors' trash, and glued the rungs back into place. Motivation and desire took hold of me. I scrounged in the basement for brushes and sandpaper. At the hardware store, I bought pint-sized cans of enamel in every bright hue. In no time, I had covered my table and chairs—with lush climbing vines, fanciful birds, blazing orange suns, shadowy mountains, tropical oceans. Landscapes both inviting and unfamiliar, like nothing I had ever seen.

I bought a new double bed—mattress, box spring and metal frame—at a furniture liquidator's warehouse, twenty dollars extra for delivery. I bought pillows and sheets at Sears, and a thin forest green blanket which I hoped would beckon good dreams. First, I needed to beckon some money. My six hundred dollars was dwindling. It was time to start making a living in Chicago.

No restaurants, that was clear. At first I had loved my dishwashing job in Mount Kisco, had thrilled to the power of the water coming through the hose, the miracle of washing all kinds of messes down the drain. I chased bits of meat and cigarette butts off greasy plates with a vigorous jet of scalding water, but after a while the smells got to me. I'd needed to hold my breath against the huge clouds of garbagy steam that rose up around my head. By the time I quit, I had started to think of water and food as nasty.

So no restaurants. No taking care of babies, sick people, or old people. Sometimes I hated people with needs, sometimes murderously. I always begged my mother to want things, but I couldn't handle anyone wanting from me on a regular basis. I might have made it through a day, a month, even a year of behaving pleasantly, but the resentment I'd swallow would have shredded me from the inside. Better to accept this about myself than to pretend it wasn't so. Better to keep out of situations where I would likely become cruel.

So no nursing homes or day care centers. No offices, which would have required shaving my legs and squeezing my triple-E feet into pointy shoes. No cleaning mushrooms on the factory line with Mimi, or pushing lunch carts at the hospital with Arlene. Their jobs simply had no appeal.

As I lay in my new double bed, my imagination lit on this: I'd get a job pumping gas. Washing windshields, filling tires, checking oil. I'd take care of cars, not the people who drove them, and only for a few minutes at a time. I didn't mind the smell of gasoline; in fact, I craved its unwholesome sweetness—at least until I started breathing it eight hours a day.

~ Four ~

Sometimes in speech I find myself mixing up the words 'wedding' and 'funeral'—the crowd-gathering events in most families, and in mine virtually the only occasions my mother left the house through most of the 1960s and 70s, the only times my parents were ever seen together in public in New York. Until I was ten, I never went to either, and then in one overcrowded year I went to three—for Gloria, Jimmy, and my grandmother, in that order.

At Gloria and Mike's wedding, I wore something A-line and pale blue, trimmed with lace and a blue satin ribbon, but I wasn't petite enough or cute enough to be the flower girl. Mike's youngest sister won that contest. I swallowed my jealousy and pressed my throat against my spine, my spine against the back of the pew, to keep from belching it out. I brought home candy-coated almonds tied up in a little net bag.

At the funerals I sat tall, pressing together feet, ankles, knees, thighs, palms, fingers. Pressing elbows against my black velvet dress, my back against the wooden church pew, to keep my body from flying apart, my heart from beating on the floor. I clutched the holy picture with first Jimmy's, and then Grandma's, name and dates embossed on the back, and figured my losses in fractional numbers. Two of the six people I knew well—one third—gone forever, not coming back. Two of the three people—two thirds—I had even the vaguest inclination to rely on. Which left only Donna, until she went away. Until I could get out in the world on my own and start rebuilding.

After their wedding, Gloria and Mike went back to Ann Arbor. After my cousins' weddings, the married couple typically found an apartment in New York—too small, and not sunny enough, but their own. A baby always came, often two or three, and eventually a bigger apartment or a house. Every once in a while, there was whispering about divorce.

As to what comes next for the person who has died, I never knew what to believe. Not harps and clouds. Not worms and nothingness. As a teenager, I liked to imagine Jimmy and Grandma in some sort of overlapping individualized paradise—a hybrid of old lady and teenage boy heaven. In old lady heaven you get to swing all day on the porch glider, to look through a veil of morning glory vines at the view of an ocean beach. You sip lemonade with a sprig of mint and your breasts never sweat or stick to your belly. In teenage boy heaven you get to ride your Honda 350 back and forth on the stretch of road in front of the beach. You have no need for a helmet because you're already dead, and the wind massages your hair at the roots. Although you do the same thing over and over, it never feels like a trap.

And then once each evening, when the sky deepened to purple, my grandma would stand up from the glider, cross the road, pull her dress off over her head and walk into the bracing surf. Jimmy would put his bike on its kickstand, strip off his jeans and t-shirt, and run in to join her.

I wanted to join them myself some day, splashing and screaming at the cold. Not anytime soon because things were looking up, my luck seemed to be holding. And even when life with Anthony and Vera was at its worst, I absolutely did not believe in suicide.

Around the corner from my new home in Chicago I found a Catholic church, built of the same rough red-brown brick as the house, but with steps of smooth poured cement that unfolded toward the sidewalk to scoop me up. I pulled open the heavy wood door, and waited for my eyes to adjust.

I knew I was supposed to genuflect before the statue of Our Lady, but the gesture seemed false. Instead, I marched toward the statue slowly, matching her straight-backed posture with my own. She held no child; she stood with a snake coiled at her feet and plaster arms open, palms forward, delivering the power of healing love into the world.

At the end of my walk, I lit a candle for Jimmy and one for my grand-mother, flames that stretched and recoiled inside of cobalt blue glasses. I'm safe, I told them, and I miss you. I put fifty cents in the padlocked box—hoping it was enough for two. Between being the youngest and my mother's poor health, my Catholic upbringing had been spotty, but I didn't want to approach either of the old women muttering into their folded hands at the back of the sanctuary to ask.

So much for the dead part of my family. Back in my new room, I sat down at my gorgeous table and composed three letters. The first to my father, and an identical one to my mother: this is my new address and phone. You can write or call if you want.

I didn't have parents any more, not collectively. I had a mother, and a father. In order to begin my new life, I would deal with them separately. I would abandon my concern about how they treated each other. How he treated her, more accurately, although occasionally I'd swing around to believing she chose it. Either way, no more tying myself in knots trying to fix or explain her life. I was through with all that.

A family is just a bunch of individuals, I resolved. I mailed one letter to my mother, another to my father, a third to Donna in Ecuador. Mike and Gloria I ignored altogether. I didn't feel I owed them anything.

"I live with five other women now," I wrote Donna—leaving it to her to fill in the word 'dykes'—"and I work at the Standard station up the street. I'll last there while the weather's good. After that, who knows? I doubt I'll see New York for a while, but you can call—or better yet, come to Chicago. You are coming back, aren't you? Come and see me."

~ Five ~

I wanted my sister to visit me in my new life, to appreciate that I had, in fact, been rebuilding. Using Donna as the template, I had gone out into the world and found a half-dozen women who would offer me friendship and protection. True, they were lesbians, but Donna had known lesbians in college—even one of her roommates. And these women weren't my lovers; they were a whole tribe of older sisters. Women who had my best interests at heart, like Donna.

I wanted to show her off, to show her around, to integrate the two most gratifying parts of my life so far. True, I had never traveled to Ecuador, but that was in the southern half of the world, too far away and costly to get to, especially for a teenager who needed to save her own neck. Chicago was an easy drive from New York, especially for a person who'd made it to South America and back, who had finished two years of college.

I wanted Donna to see that I was making a home, the one she and I might have made if we'd been the parents. Finally free to excel at something other than fighting, I worked up domestic magic—with garage sale furniture, thrift store linens, bushels of fruit Jane brought home from Wisconsin. Every project was a song of gratitude—to Donna for teaching me what was possible, to my housemates for confirming my faith, to whatever unseen hand had helped me to get myself to Chicago and start to live. Through every creation I stitched together past and future, carried my longing forward into action, asserted my own definition of home. I wanted my sister to come speak Spanish with Mimi, roam the city with our girl gang, dance in our circle at the lesbian bar. But Donna never answered my letter, and she didn't return to the States for another whole year.

"I don't get it," I said to Jane. "Isn't the Peace Corps a two-year stint, give or take a couple of months for training?" Jane, who knew all about Latin America and the Sandinistas, was bound to know something about the Peace Corps.

"Tell you the truth," she said, "I don't think they take volunteers who haven't finished college. Plus the training is really rigorous. They use it to screen a lot of people out. Only the best can become instruments of U.S. foreign policy. You think your sister would have made it through?"

"I don't know," I told her. I felt like she had kicked me in the chest, but I recovered quickly enough. Donna was teaching English in Ecuador, I had the letters postmarked "Quito" to prove it. If she wasn't in the Peace Corps, she must've had a good reason for saying so. I'd get her to tell me all about it when she came back.

Jane said, "She's probably a missionary. It's a booming business."

"No way," I told her, "Donna's not religious. She spent Sunday mornings smoking cigarettes down at the reservoir when my mother thought she was driving me to Mass."

Jane just arched an eyebrow.

"I don't want to think about it," I said.

My father must have called the minute he opened my letter. It was evening. The sky was my favorite color—that heartbreaking, luminous color somewhere between blue and green and black. Heat escaped into the night from the sidewalks and the bricks of our house. I had filled the bathtub twice, as

I did whenever I came home from work. First to scrub away the smell of gasoline. And the second time to rest, up to my neck in cool water, to ease my burning skin. I was leaning forward in the tub, looking at my reflection in the chrome faucet and playing with the way my face changed when I tipped my head up and down. Up, and my chin came forward, my brow receded, my image was dominated by cheekbones and lips. I looked like I could be related to Ray Rothstein—even more to his mother Anita, who was Puerto Rican. When I tipped my head down, my forehead and eyes grew large, my chin weakened, and I looked like the little boy I used to see at the Ukrainian bakery.

So I was playing with my face, and thinking about how everyone on earth is related, thinking about all the different kinds of people—Greek, Arab, and Mexican, and some whose backgrounds I couldn't even pinpoint—who'd stop me on the street occasionally to talk to me in their own language, ready to claim me as one of their own. I was thinking about trying to capture this photographically, and about how you take a picture of a reflection without taking a picture of the camera, when the phone rang. It wasn't for me, certainly. I hadn't made any friends yet in Chicago.

But Willow hollered my name from the living room.

Well, then, it had to be him. He didn't allow my mother to make long distance calls. When I was a kid he was always yelling at her about the phone bill—about too many calls to my grandmother in Greenwich Village, and to Vera's cousins in Queens. I took my time climbing out of the bath and tucking a towel around me.

Willow held the phone against her stomach. "A man," she whispered, and then imitating him, "Is this the residence of Francesca D'Amato?"

"Hello?" I said.

"You're safe?"

"Safer than I've ever been."

Quiet.

"Everyone here gets to eat and sleep," I told him. "Nobody yells."

"Don't act smart."

I enjoyed our long-distance sparring. He couldn't hurt me except to write me out of his will, a fate I had already embraced. Water dripped out of my hair and pooled at my feet.

Did I have a job yet?

Yes, at a Standard station. I dared him, silently, to criticize it.

Didn't I want to attend college? Were any of my roommates students?

All but Arlene had graduated from college, but I couldn't afford the tuition. Another dare: just let him offer to pay. You didn't pay for Jimmy; I had already prepared my answer.

But he was cautious that night, skirting the bait, courting the future. Our conversation bumped and jostled along a rutted track. Then something new, nostalgia.

"Is there anything else you want to say to your dad?" Your old dad. Your old dad who loves you, but only if you say it first.

"Yeah," I told him. "Call any time." I didn't ask after my mother.

I felt potent when we hung up, energized. I was the one with a life ahead of me. I even liked him a bit; he seemed so pathetic.

My mother answered my letter with a letter. She was permitted a thirteen cent stamp:

Dear Frannie,

Sorry I was asleep when you called the other night. New York is an hour later than Chicago. I'm glad to hear you found a good living situation right away. It's important to me that my daughters are happy.

Nothing much to report, of course, except that it has rained here for a week. We missed your cousin Laurie's confirmation, but at least I sent a card in time.

How's the weather there?

Love, Mom

When *I* called? What a liar he was!

She'd typed the letter on a rickety old Smith Corona manual, using stationery I bought her every year for her birthday—dove grey Eaton, monogrammed with an elaborate V up in one corner. "Mom" was the only hand-written word—not in her once-perfect Catholic schoolgirl script, but halting and thick, like it took a lot of ink to ride out the muscle spasms, like it was her gift to me.

I sent back a short note: "The weather is pretty nice, especially near the lake. You could call sometime if you want."

The bit about calling just to goad her, but she ignored it. She did write back and every letter contained a question, one of the characteristics of polite correspondence I learned in fourth grade. The questions worked as they were designed to, they prompted me to answer. I racked my brain to reciprocate, but what do you ask a person who goes nowhere, who claims to want nothing? She did think. About what, she didn't tell me anymore. Except that, like me, she looked forward to Donna coming home.

~ Six ~

I used to know everything about my father's will. I learned it from listening to his meetings with Mr. Klein, the man who managed his money. Not eavesdropping, exactly. I was the one who poured the coffee. When company came—Mr. Klein, or Radke, the lawyer—I'd brew American coffee in the electric Westinghouse percolator, a stainless steel rocket ship with plastic feet. One scoop per cup and one for the pot. I'd bring out a plate of Stella D'Oro anise-flavored biscotti and curl my lip at Mr. Klein, who reeked of too much aftershave and eyed me up and down.

Mr. Klein advised my father on protecting his small fortune, on keeping it intact for his heirs. He never said "your children," always, "your heirs." It was, after all, Anthony's decision. He could leave every cent to Mother Teresa, or Saint Ann's Orphanage, if he wanted. If Vera would sign on the line. She sat in only when the lawyer came, when the decisions were all laid out and waiting for her shaky signature at the bottom of the page.

The men didn't whisper, they bellowed. This is how they talked: if Frannie has three children and Donna one— If Gloria dies before Donna but after Frannie— If baby Tina dies before her mother but after both her aunts; even with one heir really and truly dead, they acted like it was purely hypothetical. A game of Risk or Monopoly. Jimmy's name never came up.

My father worshipped genealogy. The object of his game was to keep the money flowing to his biological descendants, with no diversions to people related by marriage, love, adoption, or convenience. Anthony never named out loud for Mr. Klein the crimes that would snip the ancestral bond, that would leave Gloria, Donna or me as good as dead. But I saw how he brandished his last will and testament at my sisters, and how Gloria in particular hastened to do his bidding.

I was nine, Gloria twenty-two. She rang the doorbell and waited as if it had never been her home, as if she didn't still carry a key. Although she lived nearby in Connecticut, she visited only when commanded to do so. Jimmy was in Vietnam, Donna at the library. My father and mother held their places at the dining room table. I was the one who answered the door.

Even in 1968, Gloria didn't dress like a hippie. She wore a navy blue cardigan sweater, buttoned only at the neck. Although it was warm, even stuffy in the house, she didn't take it off. She turned her demitasse upside down on its saucer. This was a meeting, not a social hour; she wanted to know what this summons was all about.

"It's about sin," Vera said, and I was surprised by the confidence in her voice. "It's about you living with that man."

My mother didn't want coffee either, so I carried the entire little pot, and the tall bottle of liqueur, over to my father. I stepped in and out of the kitchen lightly, trying not to interrupt.

"It's only temporary." Gloria said, "until Michael leaves for dental school in the fall."

"I think you should marry him." This from Anthony. "So I won't need to rewrite my will. Do you hear me?"

"I hear you." Gloria stood up from the table and let herself out the front door.

Anthony and Vera sat in dreary silence while I cleared away the cups and saucers, the tiny stainless steel spoons.

"She's haughty, that girl," my father finally said.

Gloria and Michael waited about a month to announce their engagement. She moved with him to Ann Arbor but in my father's book, although cohabiting, they were no longer sinning. "Forget the Pope," he told my mother. They had made public their intention to comply with Anthony's wishes.

~ Seven ~

The first woman I went to bed with was Bobbie. Hers was the only offer to come my way those first six-and-a-half months in Chicago. I had bodyguards, of course, four or five friends at a time, and an air about me that said: I am complete, I have everything I've ever wanted. I felt only a twinge of jealousy about the bedsprings creaking at night in the other rooms of the house, only slightly embarrassed by having had sex with men but never with a woman. No one threw it in my face because they didn't know, not even Jane or Arlene.

It was the beginning of January, the night bitterly cold, the kind of cold that tastes like iron nails, that makes your lungs seize up. The inside of Moxie's was smoky and hot, the walls decorated with red and silver tinsel garlands and snowflake cutouts. My housemates, their lovers, and I danced in a circle. One at a time someone stepped into the center and gave it her all, encouraged by whoops and cheers.

I liked the center best. I could have danced all night to ridiculous songs like "Shake Your Booty," flushed, grinning, and sweating, using the slow dances as an opportunity to look around, to take a breather. Or I could have returned the gaze of the woman sitting, studying the dance floor, her long legs easily reaching the bottom rung of her stool, her back slouched ever-so-slightly against the rail of the bar.

Just by looking, she compelled me to look back. It was as if she pointed a camera at me, a camera that would capture my soul, would suck the juices right out of me. I met her stare and a path opened up.

"Do you want to dance? With me?"

"Sure," I said, almost indifferently. But I felt like I had agreed to jump out of a plane.

Her hair was the color and texture of dried grass, cut short once and now growing out. She was a whole head taller than me, but not as thick in her body. Her hips were nearly nonexistent.

Maxine Nightingale sang, "We're gonna get it right back to where we started from." We carved out a little rectangle of space amidst the other dancers, shuffled back and forth in place, our movements constrained by the press of bodies around us, but also by the way she locked her fingers around my wrist. Although she touched me, she didn't look at me; she danced with her eyes closed, and I felt a prickle of irritation. When the end of one song mixed into the beginning of the next, she dropped her hold on my arm and opened her eyes.

"Shall we?" she asked. It was a slow dance.

It seemed less complicated to say yes than no. While I stood there considering, she took one step in and placed her hand on the small of my back.

"I'm Bobbie," she said into my ear.

"Fran."

"I know that."

She'd been asking around. The same prickle of annoyance ran along my scalp, but I shook it away. I took another step closer, laced my hands behind her waist, laid my cheek against her soft cotton shirt. She smelled like clean laundry, like the clouds of steam that escape from apartment house basements into the chilly night air. Not an easy feat in a smoky bar.

Bobbie sang along with Diana Ross, "I've got the sweetest hangover I don't want to get over," right in my ear. "Stay and dance," she said, when my housemates started checking their watches. "I'll drive you home."

And I fell—for simple flattery, the knowledge that someone wanted me. The erroneous belief that I should act now, because this offer would not be repeated.

I took Bobbie home to my double bed, and I never said out loud: This is my first time. So this is what it's like to kiss a woman's collarbone. To lift her breast to my mouth. To burrow into the damp places between her legs, to taste another woman's cunt. This is what it's like to fall asleep with her arm draped over my waist. To wake up kissing, and right back into it, in the middle of the night. To have an orgasm with someone else there, someone who is paying attention. All the discovery passed by unmarked, uncelebrated. I acted so cool about this experience I had waited for my whole life.

The sunlight woke me up, great rivers of yellow pouring in through my unshaded windows. Bobbie was up already, standing across the room, wearing only her blue cotton shirt. She smoothed a hand across the top of my painted table, traced a vine along the back of the chair.

"Very beautiful," she said.

She seemed shy, almost taciturn, and I became chatty in response, telling her altogether too much about finding the chairs and painting them—details that added nothing to her appreciation, it was plain.

In the unwieldy silence that followed I said, "Come out to the kitchen. I'll make you some breakfast."

The kitchen was dark in the morning, shaded, a totally different climate from my room at the front of the apartment. I cooked scrambled eggs with Kalamata olives and fried potatoes with onions. All the while I kept chatting, telling Bobbie the most innocuous stories of my childhood.

Like the time my fourth grade teacher, Mrs. James, got into this huge power struggle with me about the number of kinds of olives in the world. Two, she said—black and green. This was our lesson for the day: black olives come in cans and green in jars. She had obviously never shopped anywhere besides the A&P, had never set foot in a Greek or Italian deli.

But I didn't know that then, I only knew she was wrong. "There are purple ones," I said. I didn't know the name 'Kalamata.' "There are purple ones and black wrinkly ones that taste really salty; I've had them at my Aunt's house."

Two kinds. Black and green.

Purple. And wrinkled. I couldn't let go, and neither could the teacher. We went back and forth for what seemed like an hour. What were the other nine-year-olds thinking?

"There are two kinds, black and green. Class, take out your math books."

I wasn't bold enough to keep arguing, but I did slam the lid of my desk, hard. I hated her. My face stayed hot all day.

Bobbie sat at the kitchen table, smiling and nodding as I told my story, and Willow scooted in and out a half-dozen times—to put water on to boil, set up a tea bag in a cup, change her mind about the flavor, pour the water, retrieve the tea after it had steeped. She ducked her head, as if to make herself invisible by avoiding eye contact.

"Willow," I said, "This is Bobbie. You want some breakfast?"

"Oh, no thanks," Willow said, "I'll get out of your way."

It was only nine o'clock. Everyone else was still in bed.

I was flying from refrigerator to table to cupboard to stove, laying the table with plates and glasses, stirring the potatoes, shaking the pan of eggs. Bobbie came up behind me and laid a hand on my arm. I jumped at her touch; it jangled the nerve endings all over my body. I shut off the flame under the eggs and turned to face her, my back pressed up against the stove.

"Why do you talk so much?" she asked.

I was at a total loss.

And then she asked, "Why did you pick me?" She smiled and kissed me, but I could tell it was a serious question. I would gain nothing by pointing out that she had picked me.

I told her about the smell of clean laundry, what a miracle that had seemed in a smoky bar. A B-minus answer, I could sense it. A-plus would have been something like, I knew right away you were the one for me. Less specific, more romantic.

The tension eased just enough. I squirmed away from her scrutiny and put our food on the table. We sat down and before I knew it I was telling her all about how I hated perfume and cologne. About how Donna and I would wrestle for the chairs furthest from Aunt Alida and Uncle Frank at Sunday dinners in the Bronx because otherwise you couldn't taste your food. We suspected my aunt and uncle were engaged in an escalating scent race, like the arms race. Alida believed I liked Aunt Julia better when really I recoiled from Alida's hugs and kisses because I didn't want her perfume clogging my taste buds all day.

Bobbie said, "You're lucky you got me after I quit wearing Old Spice."

"I sure am," I told her. Disappointment scrolled across her face.

I was supposed to say something on the order of, I'd love you with Old Spice. But I didn't love her. I wasn't particularly attracted to her, compared, for instance, to how I'd felt in the presence of Nancy Levy. Mostly I had responded to Bobbie's attraction for me, but she wanted more than a one-night stand.

I hadn't been planning one, I just didn't comprehend the pressure—to call her every day, to decide on Sunday morning what I'd be doing next Saturday night. We didn't sign a contract before we got into bed. Apparently, we signed it on each other's bodies.

After Bobbie came Wendy, and after Wendy, Nicole—each one wanting more than I did. And soon I was in trouble with my housemates.

Thursday night house meetings were pretty routine. We divvied up chores, and discussed whether or not Jane and Mimi could have meetings in our living room, and could men come, and wasn't it racist to tell Latino men they weren't allowed. We debated about whether Häagen Dazs was a grocery (to be bought with group funds) or a luxury, and about entirely banning illegal drugs in accordance with Socialist Workers Party policy.

"Why give the FBI an excuse to mess with any of our projects?" Mimi argued.

Willow knit during meetings, mittens and socks with tiny complicated snowflake patterns. Arlene brought big bowls of popcorn for everyone, with tamari and nutritional yeast instead of butter and salt. Nothing very personal or serious ever happened.

Which is why it caught me completely off guard when Willow said, "I'm tired of running into strangers at the breakfast table."

"Everyone has had somebody sleep over." Mimi jumped immediately to my defense.

"Not three people in four weeks."

"Three weeks," I corrected Willow. It was snotty, but all I could think of to do.

"It's nobody's business," Mimi continued. "We're not setting household policy to promote monogamy."

Jane, the one with the steady girlfriend, said, "Of course it's our business. We're not talking morality; we're talking too much traffic through our home."

"No problem," I said, cheating everyone out of further discussion. "I'll start sleeping at their houses."

But I didn't like sleeping at other women's houses, didn't like waking up in dim, unkempt rooms, the floors littered with clothes and books, pizza boxes and empty Mateus bottles. I hated drinking stale herb tea that tasted of dusty cabinets, offered up by women who didn't cook, who expected me to grab a candy bar when I got to work because that's what they did for breakfast.

I liked Nicole the best. She had sidled up to me at a Divest Now! speakout at People's Church. Her hair was black, her complexion light and freckled. She had dark rings around her eyes which gave them a certain hardness, and made her pretty in a tough-girl way. I thought I'd stick with her, not sleep around, yet try to keep it casual, not plan our lives much more than one date in advance.

But she was twenty-five, and kept talking about commitment.

"I'm committed," I said. "I'm not seeing anyone else."

She wanted a guarantee of every Saturday night, and calls from the Standard station on my lunch break. A definite plan for Valentine's Day, in my opinion not a holiday at all. She wanted to schedule a time to talk about living together.

I was bailing out a sinking rowboat, throwing out the demands I found unreasonable, but nevertheless struggling to keep the vessel afloat. She was the one who had the sense to call it off.

I missed her. In fact, I went out and found Alexis, who was just like her. She too lasted a few months instead of a few days—less taxing on the housemates, but even trickier to admit when things were simply not working.

"I'm not looking for anything serious," I'd make a point of warning before I kissed someone new.

"Oh, me either."

But in my opinion, they often were.

* * * * *

Between girlfriends was my favorite time of all. Between girlfriends, I could revel in being the best-loved little-dyke-sister in the house. I could drink up a wealth of affection, given freely, with no demands attached, or no unreasonable demands. I found it much easier to say "we" about a slightly amorphous group of four or five—Willow moved out and a student named Kelly replaced her—than about myself and any one woman. Between girlfriends, I missed the sex, but I didn't miss the price tag, and on moving day Willow gave me her copy of *Liberating Masturbation*.

Between girlfriends I spent Saturday nights painting if I wanted or watching old Barbara Stanwyck movies on TV, and I didn't have to explain to anyone why I'd rather be doing that than going to the bar with her. I painted self-portraits and landscapes, bright ones in layered translucent watercolors, and dark ones with only two tubes of oil paint—purple and yellow and the shades of black they made when I mixed them. Between girlfriends I never had to think up an answer to, "When are you gonna paint my picture?"

69

Between girlfriends my resolve sometimes slipped. I'd start to worry that I would never get another offer. So I'd take up with the next woman who looked at me, and soon find myself right back where I left off—making concessions while quoting from Emma Goldman on the evils of marriage. Between girlfriends I could quit resisting. I could relax.

~ Eight ~

All through my first summer in Chicago and into the fall my mother wrote me letters on dove grey stationery, each with a question embedded in it, and without fail I wrote back. My father neither wrote nor called, which I could have predicted. He was busy and stubborn like me. He was known to keep careful count, to see what he'd get before deciding how much to give. My mother was the champion of keeping up appearances.

But one day a letter arrived with no question, no invitation to reply. Instead, she had typed this closing line: "From now on, please address your letters to both your father and me."

So I was to make myself into a good daughter, like Donna, who always began her letters from Ecuador, "Dear Family," and had not once written to me in Chicago. Instead, I stopped writing and started calling Vera—on Monday mornings when I knew Anthony was seeing patients.

"Oh," she said the first time. "How expensive! In the middle of the day."

"Don't worry about it." Besides my blessedly cheap rent, all I ever spent money on was books and art supplies. Movies once in a while. An occasional bag of pot which, being frowned upon at home, could last me months. My transportation to and from the bar and one beer on the nights I went out dancing. Most days, I walked to work.

"I dreamt about Donna carrying a sack of flour," Vera said, "as real as if she was in the room. I think she'll be home from Ecuador soon."

"Tell her to come see me," I said.

"I wish I could come see you."

"You can. There are too many steps into the house, but I'll rent you a hotel room. A view of the skyline, the lake shore, you name it. You can get on a plane and come when the weather's good."

"Right," she said. "Wouldn't that be something?"

"I can't talk," she told me the second time I called.

"Why not? I'm paying."

She lowered her voice, as if the walls were bugged, "It makes things harder on me."

"So don't tell him."

"I've never been able to lie."

What about those visits we paid to Jimmy? I wanted to ask, but didn't.

"Let's go back to letters," I told her. "He has no business demanding I write to both of you. He hasn't written to me."

"No," she said, "don't trouble yourself."

The sort of trouble I must have been causing her dropped into focus, like one of those stereoscopic photos clicking into place in an old viewfinder: Vera sitting and Anthony standing about ten paces away, waving something square and white, a birthday card from Jimmy, away at boot camp. Anthony was screaming at Vera. Why had Jimmy acknowledged her birthday, not his? Vera's hands stayed folded in her lap. She didn't reach for the card. Small as she was, and shaky on her feet, she was no match for such an angry husband.

"He's keeping my letters from you," I said. "Just like Jimmy's."

"Let's talk about something else."

"He is, isn't he? He is." I hated myself for browbeating her, but I was a runaway cart. "It's a federal offense," I told her.

She said, "Yeah, well. Go tell that to a judge."

How had an energetic, happy young woman—the one smiling so magnificently in her wedding photo—grown so cynical, so hopeless, without even the briefest stopover at life-giving outrage? Or had the outrage all dissipated before I was born? I, in any case, had enough for both of us, enough for an entire family. I also had optimism.

She could get the mail while he was at work. The sliding door to her downstairs bedroom opened onto the patio, connected by a sidewalk to the driveway. The driveway was too steep, given the condition of her arms, but it was something Connie—Consuela, who had replaced Mattie and who lived in my old room now—could help her with. They could take a wheelchair outing every day to look for the mail. In bad weather, Consuela could go alone.

"Frannie," my mother said, "it isn't worth it."

I could send my letters with a return receipt requested, so the mailman would bring them to the door.

"I'm going to hang up now," she said. "Look how much this call is costing you."

My mother was always a fan of modern art, or at least the modernist influence on household design. The dishes we ate off of every night, for instance—a pattern of large grey and brown leaves strewn asymmetrically across a matte beige background, their unconventionality for her a source of middle-class housewifely pride.

For years, the A&P in town gave away free pieces of ordinary china—translucent white with prim blue flowers marching around the edge. I'd stand with my mother at the check-out lane, my head no higher than the conveyor belt, and run my hand over the smooth, cool dishes in the display. "We don't need that," Vera said every time. "We have much more interesting china at home."

She decorated our Christmas tree with all-white strands of lights—long before all-white became popular—and with hand-blown ornaments of turquoise and silver, amber and pink. So much more intriguing than red, green and yellow, she noted every year.

She had a deep, square wicker basket at Christmas time, spray painted metallic gold with silver pine cones and a bronze bow wired on. Not a trace of corny red ribbon. The basket held dozens of cards she received in December, maybe more than a hundred, from people who knew her before she was married. With my help, she would mail out just as many. In some cards, I'd write the questions she dictated: "How is your new baby girl?" In others, only statements: "I hope you and your daughter are well." I always knew which ten or twenty people she felt like extending herself towards, and the dozens more she kept at arm's length.

My first winter in Chicago brought rain that never turned to snow. It fell sideways when the wind blew, soaking through the rain pants I wore at work, soaking the trunks of trees and turning them black. After weeks of hearing nothing from Vera, I came home from the gas station one day to find a Christmas card, olive green with an embossed silver angel. Not a cute angel, but a tall angular one. And this note inside:

The tree is up. It looks beautiful.
Hope you are well.
Love,
*   Mom & Dad*

All, even the "Mom & Dad," spelled out in some unknown hand, probably Consuela's. My card contained no question—how impolite, how mean.

Fury overtook me. I turned it toward scrubbing the kitchen—not joyfully, creatively, whistling along with Bach as I liked to do, but bitterly, in silence, muttering to myself. I attacked the stove, the oven, the counter top, the refrigerator, the floor, throwing myself feverishly against one surface after another.

Arlene discovered me slouched at the kitchen table, still flushed and shaking. Everything shone, even the burners on the stove and the saucers underneath that catch the drips. "Letter from your mother?" she asked. "I hate to see you so upset, but the kitchen looks fantastic."

I dreamed I was on a train, reading a book, alone in an old-fashioned compartment for six with glass and wood doors. My left hand held a small paperback. Outside, the world was pitch black. Inside, yellow light warmed my compartment. I savored my book, my privacy, the rocking of the rails. Then I realized I was no longer alone, although the door had neither opened nor shut.

My grandmother sat in the seat opposite me, her hands folded in her lap. She peered out past her reflection into the world, then offered me the diffuse little smile she once would have given a stranger.

But I wasn't having it. "You made too many excuses for not helping my mother," I told her.

Her mouth stayed pursed in that pleasant smile, but her gaze sharpened to a point. "Then help her," she said. "Go and help her."

Everything dissolved into the black night—my grandmother, the train, the unseen landscape, and me. I woke alone in my double bed in a darkness muddied by the orange haze of the street lamp outside my window. I regretted not greeting my grandmother more kindly, this being her first visit since she died. But she didn't greet me either, didn't touch me or smile the smile she always saved for Frannie.

What is the proper etiquette for conversing with the dead? Only one encounter in eight years, so I said what was on my mind: She was your own daughter, why did you let her fade away?

~ Nine ~

I never said I wouldn't go back to New York. I waved a knife at my father, I set it down. I packed my bags and walked away. I caught a train and two buses, hurtled fast, fast through empty space, away from everything I had known and hated and railed against. Toward something I would need to imagine into existence. Like a skater who has fallen through the ice, I pressed up and up through cold water, heavy against my lungs, loud with the echo of my heart. Just in the split second before drowning, I found a place to burst through to air. I hauled myself out, I breathed. I invented a righteous life—a home, a job, daily contact with six or seven people, occasional sex, occasional bouts of painting in my room late at night. A routine that damaged no one. First, do no harm.

I never said I wouldn't dive in again, wouldn't swim back for my mother, for the sake of my conscience. Don't fight me, I'd tell her. I'll swim you to safety. I don't want to be an orphan.

I began by saving money, just as I had saved to run away, just as my grandmother taught me. "It's debt that kills the working man," she always said.

She used to take the train up from the city, and a taxi to our house, every couple of months at first, more often after my mother quit driving. She talked with me while my mother napped, when I came home from school. She liked Lipton's tea dark, with a wedge of lemon squeezed in, and left the tea bag in the cup while she drank it.

I'd sit by her side and draw pictures with crayons. The same picture over and over: a girl with black braids fishing off the end of a dock. I had never held a fishing pole. That girl at a lake was my best-loved peaceful fantasy. She had nothing and no one to oppose her.

Sometimes Grandma and I worked together to produce crafts for the church bazaar—sickeningly sweet soaps decorated with ribbons, beads, and sequins (to hang in your closet, she said, to make your clothes smell good), or felt covers in the shape of a top hat for the extra roll of toilet paper that sits on top of the tank.

"I've voted Democrat every single time," she'd tell me. "Republicans, banks, big business, they all trap the working man in debt. There's no freedom like a savings account, even if you do end up loaning it to the bank. The real old timers, you know, they kept theirs under the mattress."

Even then, at age seven or eight, I used to wonder, Why the working man? What about me, my mother, my grandmother?

"Never ask a woman to choose between you and the man she wants to marry," Grandma warned. "You'll be an unwelcome guest in their house. And don't ever be flattered by jealousy. Your mother should have given him the gate the minute he started acting like that."

She stored her craft supplies in a box on the top shelf of Vera's closet. At four o'clock, she'd pack everything away, wash her tea cup, and dry it.

The taxi called for her at four-thirty to take her down the hill to the station, well before Anthony came home at five-fifteen. "Just to be on the safe side," she always said.

I saved for a year and had a modest pile of money on hand when Jane decided to make the leap, take out student loans, and work on the prerequisites she needed for med school. Why anyone would even go near a medical school was beyond me, but Jane intended to practice a different kind of healing, more holistic and humanistic, to bring non-pharmaceutical solutions to the people by way of the community clinics. She'd model herself after China's barefoot doctors, who weren't actually doctors at all. In the U.S., she said, you needed those letters after your name just to get through the door of a clinic.

She sold me her pick-up—a 1969 Datsun, maroon, with pretty round headlight eyes and the best-cared-for engine in the world. I still walked to work, but the Datsun carried me safely home from the bar, and let me explore parts of the lake shore public transportation didn't trifle with. With a truck I could criss-cross North America some day; I could finally reach the Pacific Ocean.

Jane's girlfriend Kim had built a topper—a glorious wood one, polyurethaned, with a corrugated fiberglass roof. It was my own little room on wheels, with curtains in the windows and a bolted-in bookcase and storage cabinet. I laid down a foam mattress, an old quilt, and made a bedroom to take on the road.

"Go south," Kim told me. "You'll find the line where the soil changes from black to red."

Jane said, "Go west. And take Alexis. The Rockies will blow your mind."

But the romantic vacations and unexplored landscapes would have to wait. The invitation to Donna and Billy's wedding was sitting on top of my dresser.

Donna had turned up in New York in April, sneaking back under cover of night, it seemed to me. In the three months since her return she had sent one measly postcard, a picture of the wooden Indian that stood outside the tobacco store in Mount Kisco. She wrote, "I'm living at the Palettas'. I don't have any money," apparently her excuse for not calling. I myself had no excuse, except stubbornness. Then the impersonal news arrived in an envelope-within-envelope: Donna and Billy, the high school sweethearts, were to be married. Dr. and Mrs. D'Amato requested my presence.

I talked to Eddie, my boss at the Standard station, about giving me the whole month of August off. Eddie was Italian-American—five-five, but brawny, only forty, but almost bald, and he cultivated the same good-natured demeanor as my cousin Al. He loved me because I lasted through a winter.

"You can quit in the spring or summer," he told me when I had started, "just don't fuck me up by quitting in cold weather." And I didn't. In fact, I picked up extra shifts whenever he asked me, and paid close attention when he divulged small secrets: how to replace a frayed clutch cable, or coax more life out of a spark plug, or loosen the valve stem in somebody's tire so that no matter how many times they filled it, it would keep going flat.

Eddie never said my job was too dangerous for a woman, although he did arrange to put me on the day shift. He said, "You see a gun, or someone even claiming to have a gun, you give them what they want right away."

"So," he said now—reverentially, almost—"you're going to be in your sister's wedding." At, not in, but I didn't correct him. I could see from his point of view that someone's wedding was a serious obligation, one you didn't turn down even for your boss.

Do I look like a bridesmaid? I wanted to ask. But bridesmaids are made, not born. Even I could have unclipped my hair from its scraggly ponytail, wrapped it around electric rollers, swept it up in a mass of curls dotted with baby's breath, left a few tendrils to stray coyly down my neck. Even I could have squeezed myself into girdle and push-up bra, shaved my legs, swathed myself from bust to ankle in sea-foam green satin with mutton chop sleeves like Gloria's bridesmaids—if Donna had wanted me to. But all Donna asked was that I find the capacity in my heart to come celebrate this transition in her life.

No problem, Donna. I even borrowed an extra-fancy hippie-girl outfit—Jane's white cotton dress made in Mexico, with turquoise, green, and orange flowers and birds embroidered all over. I blew the balance of my savings on a gift, a hand-painted porcelain fruit bowl.

"I like this job, Eddie," I said. "I'd like it to be here when I get back."

"Go. God bless," Eddie told me. "Family is important. We'll cover for you, Fran. We'll put my nephew Danny on the schedule."

Even Arlene thought I would be in Donna's wedding.

"Not in," I told her, "at."

"Then why so many weeks?"

"I have other business to take care of." What business, if pressed, I couldn't explain. I saw my mother's face. I saw myself turning up my

76

parents' driveway in a maroon truck. Beyond that, I couldn't predict what might happen.

The morning I left, I tiptoed out of my room at five-thirty, sleepily oblivious to noise and smells. I carried a small box of art supplies, my old backpack half-full of clothes, and the dress Jane had lent me on a hanger. I set my load down by the front door and went to the kitchen to pack some food.

"Surprise!" my housemates yelled when I rounded the corner. All of them were awake—even Kelly, the relative newcomer, although I had said my good-byes the night before. Mimi stood at the stove flipping blueberry pancakes.

Arlene put an arm around my shoulders. "Just so you remember where you live," she said. "Families can take a person captive when she least expects it."

I said, "Oh, I'll be back. My rent's paid in advance." An unfortunately callous response, but to say more would have embarrassed me too much.

~ Ten ~

I didn't find my mother where I expected. I thought she'd be sitting where she often sat, where I had left her, her wheelchair pulled up alongside the windows in the front room. I thought she'd be gazing first inward, then outward—in to her soul, then out to the spruce trees that grew at the edge of the yard—waiting, passing the time until my father, or Consuela, or whoever else might be nearby would put Vera's needs, her well-being, on their agenda. She might have gone too long without a meal, depending on my father's mood, the day of the week, and whether Consuela was on duty or not. My mother's situation, I anticipated, would have improved. Now that Consuela lived in five nights each week, Vera would be less affected by Anthony's angry whims.

Clearly, I would have done all the changing; fifteen months away had made me an adult. I'd offer Vera my services, try out my powers of persuasion, and coax her toward taking control of her life. Because I had my own life in Chicago, I expected to reason with my mother, to talk sensibly and clear my conscience without yelling or accusations, more like an old friend in for tea than a panicked teenage daughter.

"Is that you, Anthony?" she called out when she heard my key in the lock.

"No, Ma. It's me." Inside and outside the house it was dusk; not a single light was turned on. The whole downstairs smelled faintly of piss.

"Frannie? I didn't know you were coming today. I was hoping your father would get home first." I followed her voice through the empty kitchen to her bedroom at the back of the house, the smell growing sharper as I went.

"Hello there," she said from her bed. "Let me look at you." Her hand fumbled for the chain on the lamp. I reached over and pulled it for her. She was still in her nightgown, lying on a pile of urine-soaked towels.

"I'm sorry," she said. "I didn't want to be in bed when you got here. Consuela's brother-in-law died. She needed a day off."

"Well where's Anthony?" I asked. I rarely called him by name in her presence; she had always found it disrespectful. But he wasn't Dad, or Daddy, not now. "How long did he leave you here?"

"Not long. An hour or two."

"If it was an hour or two, you'd be up and dressed and in your chair. Have you been alone since last night?"

"Don't be silly." A trace of annoyance colored her voice. "I had a bowel movement this morning. He brought me the bedpan." Things would have been much worse if he hadn't.

"Come on," I said, "I'll get you up"

"It's late," she told me. "I don't need to get up till tomorrow. Why don't you just lift me part way and change the towels underneath?"

"No," I said. "I'm giving you a bath."

It was the right thing to do. I tried to sound matter-of-fact, but I'm afraid I sounded petulant. I had never bathed my mother before, didn't particularly want to do it now. I conjured up Mary Nathan, and the nurses at the hospital, sturdy women who are kind whether you like it or not.

But I didn't have their skills. "You have to tell me how," I said. "How does Consuela do it?"

"Frannie, please," she told me. "Don't bother."

"Ma, I'm giving you a bath." My resolve grew to match her resistance. She deserved better, and maybe if I gave better she would adopt my belief as her own.

There was a plastic basin under the sink in the downstairs bathroom, a bar of Ivory soap in a plastic travel box, and a washcloth hung up to dry. I opened the hot faucet full-blast, then mixed in just the sweetest bit of cold.

"Take a clean towel from the upstairs hall closet," she instructed. "Don't take the ones from under the sink down here."

The towels under the sink were folded, stacked neatly, an odd assortment of colors. They were old enough to be cut up for rags, but had been put away carefully. My understanding of her situation warped, became liquid, and re-formed.

Although laundered, dried and folded, these towels still smelled like piss. They were the replacements for the wet ones underneath her. My mother left alone in bed for hours was not a single or occasional occurrence, but a regular one. A system had been worked out and at least three people shared it—my father, my mother, Consuela. And now me. My sense of purpose vanished; I lost momentum. One visit or one bath from me challenged nothing at all.

I soaked a washcloth in the basin of warm water, wrung it out and dabbed at the crevices of my mother's body. I used the Hoyer lift to help her sit upright, to move her onto the clean side of the bed. I pulled the nightgown up over her head, swiped across her back with the wet cloth. Her skin, soft and lightly freckled, was never exposed to the sun.

I looked for parts of myself in Vera's body, but a well-defined waistline was all we shared. Otherwise Anthony won the genetic lottery in me. I had his shoulders, his wrists, his eyes. On this side of birth, he was the one who picked me up, rocked me and sang to me when thunderstorms ripped the sky. He was the one who held me close with one hand—an infant, still blameless—even as he smacked my brother and sisters with the other. A bottle-fed baby, I knew my mother's breasts only from a distance. They filled out the top of her hourglass dresses, but I knew my father's chest, his heartbeat, up close.

I washed Vera's breasts, bathed the back of her neck and behind her ears. "This feels very nice," she said, "the water is a perfect temperature."

It wasn't half the bath I could have given. I sponged disappointedly at her toes. They were stiff, curled under. She hadn't stood on them for more than a year.

She chuckled to herself.

"Does it tickle?" I asked.

She said, "No one ever remembers my feet."

Probably no one remembered her crotch. Her leg muscles spasmed even more than the last time I saw her, her body had drawn itself into a tight question mark. I rolled her to one side to reach her butt, and the backs of her thighs, knees, and calves. I rolled her back and washed the front of both legs.

"Shall I?" I couldn't say "crotch," much less "cunt,"—not out loud, not in her presence. She used to call it "down there." She taught us to scrub it cursorily, quickly, and last of all—when the washcloth was already cold, denying any tendency to linger or explore.

"Shall I?"

She took a breath and let her knees fall open. I brought the washcloth to her still warm, trying to handle her more gently than she once would have handled me. I tried to be quick, because she wouldn't release her breath until I finished.

I blotted her dry with the clean towel, and we dickered about whether or not she should go right back to bed.

"We have to change the sheets," I told her. "And you should change your position. You'll get bedsores."

"No I won't," she said. "Bedsores don't happen that fast."

It was only eight o'clock, and neither of us had eaten supper. She finally agreed to stay up a while in her bathrobe.

"I feel so bad I have nothing ready for you," she told me. "We should have made a welcome home dinner." She hadn't cooked an actual meal in years, but still liked to think of herself as the lady of the house—the one who could plan menus, give instructions, organize to make special occasions spring to life—not on her behalf, but on mine. But she didn't even have groceries on hand.

"Don't worry, "I said. "I'll call the pizza parlor."

"How will we pay for it?"

"Where's your stash?" Anthony had always given her a weekly allowance, and a small lump sum before Christmas. Whether Donna and I bought or shoplifted the items Vera ordered from town, she'd squirrel away the meager change we brought her.

"He won't let me accumulate cash. He says someone will steal it. Besides, he comes in with the groceries now."

"You're married," I said. "His money is supposed to be yours. He ought to leave something around for an emergency."

"You think I like this life?"

"I don't know. You've always claimed it was good enough."

"Well, what was I supposed to do?"

"Do something. Want something."

She shook her head, indicating that this argument was over.

"I'll pay for dinner," I said.

Anthony called while we were waiting for the pizza delivery. Vera reached to answer the phone, but it took her a half minute of shaking to raise the receiver to her ear. "Frannie's here," she told him.

He still hadn't come home by the time we finished eating. I washed our dishes, then stripped and re-made Vera's bed with a clean plastic mattress cover and clean sheets.

"Don't you want to put down towels?" she asked as I prepared to swing her from the chair back into bed.

"How often will you need to go in the night?"

"I won't. Once now with the bedpan and I'm good till nine, ten in the morning. That's the miracle, it's the one thing that's working."

"Don't go to bed tonight planning to be alone tomorrow."

"Just to be on the safe side," she said, but I ignored her.

I asked, "So where is Donna?"

Donna was living with Billy in his parents' basement in town, working with him to rehab the old farmhouse they'd move into, while his parents worked to clean and rearrange the small plumbing sales office attached to their house, making room in their family business for my sister. Already Donna had taken over Audrey Paletta's job—answering phones, scheduling bids, keeping the books, plus putting the finishing touches on her wedding. Was Donna privy to the towel scheme? I wondered how my sister could live in town and keep her life so separate.

"What about Mrs. West, or the other neighbors?" I asked Vera. "Doesn't anyone come over anymore?" Even Mrs. Camden, the born-again neighbor lady with the Pat Nixon hair-do and sanctimonious smile, whose praying over my mother used to make me want to spit and slam doors—even she would have been better than utter isolation.

"No," Vera said. "Not really. I wouldn't want them to see me like this."

Like what? I wanted to yell. Like what? There's nothing wrong with you, except how you're living.

"Listen." I deliberated over my words, resisting the impulse to plead or scold. "I think it would be nice if you had some visitors once in a while."

"I'm going to sleep now," she told me. "We'll talk in the morning."

It was going to take a miracle to get her out of that morgue. It would require all the resources I could muster. Alone, I might have gotten a gun, might have carried off an act of destruction. But my mother needed an act of creation.

When Anthony took over Jimmy's room in 1966, he left Gloria's untouched, although she rarely came home from college. She spent every semester break with girls she met in the dorm, visiting their families as far away as southern California, as nearby as Long Island. Donna was granted permission to sleep in Gloria's room but not to move one of Gloria's things, not an inch. Our oldest sister's nearly-empty cologne bottles on a tray on top of her dresser, her too-small clothes hanging in the closet, her music box that played "The Isle of Capri" had all better be where she left them. She had pennants on her walls which said Princeton and Yale, one of which was supposed to produce her future husband.

Donna pushed the limits a bit, and then a bit more: first moving her own skirts and blouses out of our shared closet and into Gloria's. Then—not without a screaming fight—she succeeded in shaming Gloria into boxing up the too-small clothes and sending them with the cologne bottles and music box to the basement. The pennants stayed up until the day of Gloria's marriage to Michael, a U Conn man. The instant we came home from their reception, Donna plastered the walls with Lou Reed and Patti Smith.

I slept with Lou and Patti the night I returned to my parents' house. The room I started out sharing with Donna, which then became my own, was now Consuela's. I had thought to sleep in the truck—out in the driveway, or parked over at Pound Ridge Reservation—but it would have been wrong to leave my mother alone.

All the bedroom doors at the top of the stairs were shut tight, a ring of blank white slabs obscuring any view of clutter, reinforcing the impression that no life was lived in this house. Even in the darkness on the landing, I noticed Consuela's door—a different shade of white, a smoother texture than the rest. My shattered door had been replaced.

I let myself into Consuela's room, careful to keep the hinges from creaking, although clearly no one would catch me. Consuela had snapshots of her family stuck into the frame all around the mirror. Other than that, the room was spare and clean, all the books and mementos I left behind most likely moldering in the basement. The wall behind the door had been smoothed over and freshly painted. The whole room wore a cleaner coat of yellow. I wondered who had patched the sheetrock—my father reading out of a how-to book or maybe some anonymous handyman. Not Donna, who was still in Ecuador when Consuela moved in. And not Billy, who from the moment he started going out with Donna had avoided Anthony like the plague.

"Not so fast," I said out loud. "You don't get rid of me so fast."

I left, pulling the door behind me, took off my clothes and lay down in Gloria's old bed. I didn't sleep, and I didn't dream. I watched the numbers flip over on the digital clock and listened for my father to come home.

~ Eleven ~

Strategy #1: Kidnap my mother. Throw her wheelchair and Hoyer lift into the back of the truck. And take her where?

Strategy #2: Court my mother. Bring her to realize that life without Anthony was preferable to life with him. And take her where?

Fast or slow, any talk about changing Vera's life meant deciding where she would go. Everyone shuddered at the thought of a nursing home, but how could it be worse than what she had? Alone all day in a puddle of urine, this was grounds for an exposé by Geraldo Rivera—the old Geraldo, New York's folk hero journalist. Doctor's Wife Neglected in Mount Kisco Home, details at six and eleven.

He'd come storming in with his Eyewitness News cameras rolling, shirtsleeves pushed up, film crew trailing cords and cables. They'd grab what footage they could before my father showed up to threaten them with a lawsuit. Anthony's home, his castle, even if he was infrequently around to defend it.

Geraldo's light person would shine a lamp into every corner of the house. True, there wasn't a lot to see. A pile of mail, a stack of towels—neglect could be awfully subtle in the suburbs. Lying in a urine-soaked queen-size bed and lying in a dry, comfortable one looked pretty much the same on TV. But Geraldo would ask the hard questions, the probing, muck-raking questions: Mrs. D'Amato, how long have you been in that bed?

Not long, she'd tell him, because now her daughter Francesca was here. But before Francesca arrived how long were you alone? Would she open up or cover for her husband? Either way, Geraldo had a scoop.

We'd do a long shot of him and me on the back steps of my parents' two-story modern. I'd look unflinchingly into the camera as it closed on our faces. I'd reveal articulately, indignantly, what went on in the room behind the rhododendrons, and place the blame squarely where it belonged. Geraldo would deliver me to three or four million viewers.

Strategy #3: Involve my sisters in figuring out where my mother should live. How we should pay for it—that was the other big question. The three of us were all in New York for the first time in more than a decade—Donna settling down with Billy, and Gloria starting a residency at Columbia Presbyterian. I could be the outside agitator, the one to get things rolling. With some organizing on my part, my sisters and I would join together, rise above our differences, and sweep our mother into a better realm on the tide of our collective insistence. My timing was rotten, but when would it ever be perfect? Maybe Gloria—even with her ungodly schedule—could help research and line up some options. Maybe Donna would contribute quick assent.

Strategy #3A: Trick my sisters into coming to a meeting. Con my mother into setting it up.

Anthony came in well after 2:00 that morning. The front door shutting startled me awake. I listened as he climbed the stairs to his room, right across the landing from me. He didn't even look in on Vera.

~ Twelve ~

My father's initials were AD—Anthony D'Amato. When I was in second or third grade, the coincidence of this fact with the other AD, *anno domini*, amazed and amused me. And Anthony was lord over everything—the supper table, people he met on the street, our destinies and his own, even our bodies. Technically his initials were AD, MD, DS—the medical degree and diplomate of surgery, once earned, a permanent and essential part of his signature, the thing that made him a god even with respect to my uncles Bernie and Frank. Although older than him, his brother and brother-in-law were bricklayers. They were lesser lords, and only in their own homes, and only by virtue of being working men.

It isn't easy having power, he told me once. I was fourteen. We were alone in the car on a Saturday afternoon, on our way home from the A&P with a week's worth of groceries in the trunk. With Donna away at college and me too young for a driver's license, Anthony did all the food shopping. Usually, he went alone on his way home from the hospital, tacking the housewifely task onto the end of his surgeon's day. This time he'd postponed the trip until the weekend and I had agreed to ride along.

There had been a lull in our combat, in my constant barrage of accusations, his aggressive dismissals. We had, without planning it, both taken a break. "Do you want to come?" he asked. Not because he needed my help. He seemed to want my company.

Power, he told me that day—a sweltering early-summer day, the windows of the white Buick rolled down, the triangle vents pulled open—power arises out of dependency. Those of us in the world with money, good health, of middle age, bear the burden of those who are young and old, who are poor, and sick or crippled. Power arises out of that responsibility. What makes us human, what elevates us above the animal world, is that we don't leave the dependent ones behind. He, for example, accepted Medicaid patients, filling out forms in triplicate for the smallest of claims while other doctors catered only to the rich.

This was my coming-of-age lecture, planned by Anthony for God-knows-how-long, delivered the first chance he got in the quiet of an unnegotiated cease-fire. He did not distinguish between men and women in his scheme. I would be joining his camp soon.

But I didn't want to join his camp, didn't even believe such a thing existed. The tables could turn for him in a minute; one car accident and he'd slide right down the scale. And how could the inevitability of his own aging make no dent in the way he treated people? I'm not like you, I wanted to tell him. I owed Jimmy at least this much. But I just shifted away from my father on the front seat until my ribs were pressing into the armrest.

I hadn't yet learned to argue using ideas and logic, or artfully constructed rebuttals. As a teenager, I oscillated between sulking and rage. I wanted to tear like a hurricane through the house, knock down the walls, wash everything out into the street. Pick my mother up out of the rubble and carry her off to someplace better. What place, I never figured out. It didn't matter, because the walls always held.

I woke in Gloria's old room when the sun came in hot and white over the tops of the trees, pulled on my clothes, and went downstairs. Anthony sat at the kitchen table, his hands wrapped around a cup of coffee—a big cup, American style. A jar of Sanka and dirty spoon sat on the counter. Daylight ricocheted off the walls. My intestines knotted up at the sight of him. His shoulders were slumped, his face slack and grey.

"Here," he slid a five-dollar bill across the table. "For the pizza." He kept his fingernails perfectly trimmed and clean.

No, Hello, how are you? No, How are things in Chicago? One night, and it was as if I had never left. But I wasn't the Frannie he used to live with. I was teaching myself to store up challenges for the right time, instead of carelessly spending my breath.

It may have seemed cold-hearted of me as a child to refuse Anthony's love, to point out every day how he ought to be loving my mother. But fighting was engagement—it caused friction, kept things hot. This was true iciness, a disciplined scorn, to neither sulk nor scold, to value strategy above all else.

I picked up the five-dollar bill and put it in my pocket. "Thanks," I said as neutrally as I could muster, and headed into my mother's room.

"Good morning," I told her. Phony, but it was a start. She still lay in bed. I refrained from pointing out the problem. Although a criticism of Anthony, it would have twisted around to reflect on her, lending support to his contention that she was useless, a pain-in-everyone's-ass.

"Good morning," she answered, a little trill in her voice. The beginning pleasantries came naturally enough. She'd been a telephone operator before they married, with the looks and poise of a Hollywood starlet.

"You want to get up?" I made my voice light but foresaw no good answer. No would have her opting for self-deprivation. Yes might have me doing it forever.

"No, don't bother." I almost lunged after that one, but I jerked on my own leash. My self-control was immediately rewarded. "Because Connie called. She'll be here in just a few minutes."

"Okay," I said. "Then I'll go see Donna. Maybe you and I can have lunch together? I can get some Chinese take-out in town."

"I'd like that," she said. "I haven't had Chinese in years."

We were speaking the language of two people on a first date. "You know how you mentioned last night about making a dinner?" I asked. "I think it's a good idea. Could Gloria and Donna come too?"

"I can try," she said. "It would be great fun."

I heard the back door shutting, and Consuela came in. "Good morning, Doctor D'Amato," she called as she passed the kitchen.

She was a slight woman. Her wavy hair, the same medium-brown as her skin, was held back with a tight row of bobby pins. She wore a yellow t-shirt and blue cotton skirt—surprisingly girlish clothes for someone with such a serious face.

"I'm Fran," I told her.

"Yes," she said, "You look like your father." She flashed a smile and proceeded to ignore me. "Time for your bath, Mrs. D'Amato?" She opened my mother's curtains, a model of professional briskness and cheer.

"You won't believe it, Connie. Frannie gave me a bath last night. So I'm ahead of you, I don't need one today."

"You had a bath," Consuela said. "That's nice."

"No, it's not nice." As soon as I spoke, I regretted it. But too late.

86

Consuela's face swung shut. Vera hastened to explain, "Frannie didn't like my being alone so long yesterday."

"Not because of you, Consuela," I, too, scrambled to correct the insult I had caused. "Because of my father."

"Well, then, let's get you up," she told my mother. She walked around me like I was a chair, only worse. A chair she might have picked up and moved out of her path. I felt wooden, stupidly immobile. I had wanted to no longer be needed. I hadn't expected to feel so left out.

Well then, Connie could help Vera to maintain the status quo. I'd spend my efforts plotting a change. I'd get out of their way and go look up Donna, whom I hadn't laid eyes on in more than three years.

"I'm sorry, Consuela," I tried as I went out the door.

She said, "Nothing to be sorry about."

~ Thirteen ~

William Paletta & Son, Plumbing & Heating had had a face lift since I left town—new blacktop on the driveway painted with bright white lines to indicate parking for six cars, and a new green-and-yellow striped awning. I pulled the Datsun into a space.

Before I could slam the door, Donna was crossing the blacktop, saying, "Let me look at you." Then we were hugging and kissing and I wondered how we had waited so long.

"You've lost weight." She took a step back to make this appraisal.

"I finished growing," I told her.

I was twelve when she first left for Binghamton, fifteen when she took off for South America. People always called her my mother's daughter and me my father's, but looking at Donna felt like looking in a mirror. A fun-house mirror, maybe, or the kind they put in department store dressing rooms to trick women into thinking they're ten pounds lighter. I'd never be skinny and flat-chested like her, but we wore similar jeans, the same style of t-shirt. I had left my hair down, while hers was tamed into a French braid. But here was the important resemblance: I had reached adulthood in the time she'd been gone.

"Come on," she said, and I followed her inside. Only a half wall separated Bill Senior and Audrey's kitchen and family room from the small sales office where Donna worked. An accordion-pleated divider had been pushed open to let in the light. Billy's mother sat in an easy chair at the far end of the kitchen, knitting something blue, a cigarette burning in the ashtray next to her.

"Audrey," Donna said, "Frannie is here."

"Hello Mrs. Paletta," I called out, and for a split second I thought what a good thing I wasn't Donna. Odd enough to be getting married, but impossible to imagine spending my days working in the same space with my husband's mother trying to enjoy her retirement.

"Glass block," Donna whispered, pointing at the half wall, "that's the next project." We weren't so different after all.

She was figuring out a seating arrangement for the wedding reception, and showed me a paper chart with circles representing tables of eight. The paper was thin in spots from being erased too many times.

She said, "I'm sick of thinking about who can't get along with who. I want to say if you can't forget your stupid feuds for a few hours, then don't come to my fucking wedding." She talked tough, but I spotted a certain twitchiness around her eyes and mouth, as if she was suppressing the urge to cry.

"Too bad you can't have general admission seating," I said. But that would have been much worse, causing people to hover in doorways trying to figure out which half-empty table to approach, looking anxiously for someone to wave them over. It was the bride's responsibility to ensure that everyone had fun at her wedding.

"I give up," Donna said. "Let's go for a ride. Let's see how that truck of yours handles." She called goodbye to Audrey and hung a little clock sign in the window.

Donna wasn't throwing an elaborate wedding, not like Gloria with her eight bridesmaids in floor-length gowns. Donna had one, her girlfriend Carla, as a maid of honor. She insisted that Carla buy a calf-length dress in a color she liked, one she might use again on a fancy date, and planned a reception that wouldn't thoroughly embarrass her when she thought about how far money could go in Ecuador. She had needed to explain to Audrey that Anthony wasn't being cheap but that she wanted it simple.

I should have known my sister would be too busy fretting—about whether or not there'd be enough veggies and dip at the party, and would the band really show up—to join my crusade to rescue Vera from her life. A person only gets married for the first time once.

Before she left for Quito, I had overheard Billy and Donna fighting for probably the hundredth time about the same subject: why they couldn't commit, but couldn't quite give it up. "You can split whenever you want," he said. "You'll always have your father's money to float you." That pissed her off no end.

So here she was, finally, at the age of twenty-four, home from college and Ecuador, making a public ritual out of her decision to become the next Mrs. William Paletta. A low-budget ritual, which was just fine with Billy. He didn't want Anthony's money as a guest at their party.

When Donna left for South America, I was still too young to drive. Now I was taking my big sister for a ride, steering the little truck on a circuit of back roads, tracing the reservoirs, passing through towns and tiny unincorporated villages, and looping back around to Mount Kisco. The day was perfect, hot but not humid, the blues and greens shining brightly. We drove with the windows halfway down, a fresh wind scouring the inside of the truck's cab. Sometimes the road hugged the lake shore, sometimes it pulled away into woods and rolling meadows—once pasture land, now the front lawns of rich people's estates. I took every bridge, every turn to prolong the trip.

I had learned by tagging along with Donna and her friends. In bad weather we'd stay in the car, in good weather we'd swim, sit and gaze at the water, or walk out across the high stone-and-concrete dam that had created the reservoir. They'd pass a joint and a quart of beer, careful until I was in at least ninth grade to pass neither to me.

"Fucking A," Billy always said from the top of the dam. "This is New York City's drinking water supply."

On the stroke of their sixteenth birthdays, my classmates got their licenses and started borrowing their mothers' Volvos, but I held out. Driving meant grocery shopping and running errands, and by then I was already cooking dinner for my parents every night.

"Why don't you get your license?" Anthony would say. "Make yourself useful around here."

I did get my permit, which I kept secret from him, and enrolled in driver's ed by forging my mother's shaky signature. I learned to drive for future reference, for when I got out on my own.

I felt happy now behind the steering wheel with the windows down, the breeze messing up our hair, the lake coming in and out of view. As we rounded a tight bend, Donna asked, "Did you bring any pot?"

"No," I said, "I don't smoke much anymore."

Before I could decide how to explain my newfound political insights, my sister said, "Are you living in a cult or what?"

Already everything felt wrong. For years, I had imagined what a perfect reunion she and I would have, running to embrace each other. We had our moment in the Palettas' driveway, but Donna was not how I remembered her, not inspired and audacious, but suspicious, pinched. I wasn't how she remembered me either, no longer just an adoring kid.

"What's that supposed to mean—a cult?" I asked.

She said, "Everyone wants to know how you're doing. Why you moved so far away."

"Chicago's not far, Ecuador's far."

"I didn't go there forever."

"I've been in Chicago a little more than a year. Who says I'll stay forever?"

"It seems like it."

"Nobody cared how I was doing when I was stuck at home with two crazy parents."

"So that's the issue?"

"What do you mean 'the issue'? I'm just having a life." I tried to change the subject, to ask her about Ecuador. Nothing confrontational like, Were you really in the Peace Corps or what, Donna? Just, "Do you miss Quito?"

"I can't go into it right now," she told me, and I heard that same twitchiness in her voice.

I turned on the radio and spun the dial, looking for Marvin Gaye, Diana Ross, something we'd both know how to sing.

"Let's just turn it off," she said, her hand already twisting the knob.

So we didn't sing, and nobody talked, until I pulled the Datsun off the road, and we walked out across the dam. The sun on the water sliced the world into ribbons of light and shade.

"Why did you come back here?" she asked. We stood side by side, looking out at the lake.

"What do you mean? You're getting married."

"And you think it's a good idea?"

"You've been with Billy on and off for eight years." I couldn't see at first where she was leading.

"Would you get married?"

"I doubt it," I told her. Then I said, "Everyone I live with is a lesbian, including me." I wanted to sound calm and brave, but instead I sounded like a gangster.

"I know that already," Donna said. "I'm not dense."

"Then I don't follow you."

"Why come to celebrate something you don't believe in?"

I said, "I'm sure it's right for you."

She drew a deep breath, and then launched into her speech. "Don't define yourself too quickly, Frannie. Don't close any doors. Maybe you haven't met any boys as creative as you. Any men who are truly your equals. You're still young." Her jumpiness seemed to subside as this straightforward mother-to-daughter talk gathered steam.

"How old were you when you decided to be heterosexual?" I asked.

"I didn't decide—" she started, and then narrowed her eyes. "You ought to go to law school."

All of a sudden, I dreaded our lifetime ahead, full of opposition where I had expected harmony.

Donna bent down to pry a small rock loose from the top of the dam. She threw it into the open expanse of water, and softened for just a minute. "Do you like Billy?" she asked. I heard no challenge, no offense in her question.

"Sure I do. He's always been really nice to me." An insufficiently enthusiastic answer. But how was I supposed to provide enthusiasm when she didn't generate any of her own?

She said, "I've tried being with other men. None of them put Billy entirely out of my mind."

Sex is glue, in my opinion, even when you start out insisting it's not about love. It's only a matter of time before the adhesive sets and two people are bonded. Whether or not they make a good fit is irrelevant if they haven't managed to pull away soon enough.

But Billy must have appealed to Donna beyond being her first and most familiar. There must have been some reason she kept coming back, and a reason that without promising he made himself available when she did. Whatever the reason, she couldn't express it. She was doubting her decision to marry him, and I'd have been a fool to explore that doubt with her.

"I love Billy." I tried to put things right. "You know that."

She asked, "Would they let you keep living where you're living if you started dating a man?"

I said, "What do you mean 'they'? It's my house too," although in fact Jane and Arlene held the lease.

"I'm just saying hypothetically. Would you still be welcome?" She was the one who should have gone to law school.

"I would be welcome, but he probably wouldn't sleep over. So if I had a boyfriend, I'd probably choose to move. But don't hold your breath waiting for it to happen."

"So Billy and I can't come visit you."

I should have said, Of course you can. Are we talking lovers or family? Arlene's brother and Jane's brother-in-law visited all the time. But I was on the defensive, and didn't feel like making nice. I said nothing.

"What if Jimmy was alive?" Donna asked. "Wouldn't you want your brother to visit?"

To me, Jimmy was a shadow, the ghost of a boy my own age. Donna spoke of a Jimmy I could hardly imagine—a flesh-and-blood man, pushing thirty.

"I don't know what I'd want," I told her.

She drew her shoulders up, and turned away. It looked bad, I could tell, like I didn't care about my brother. But I didn't rush in to correct her impression. I didn't tell her I still lit candles for Jimmy at Saint Andrew's, right around the corner from my house.

"Donna," I finally did say, "if you and Billy want to come to Chicago, you can come. I'm here this week to have a good time." In that moment I had literally forgotten about my mother, about all my schemes for breaking her out of prison.

"Okay," Donna told me.

"Promise?"

"Promise." But her face had folded into a frown. She turned and headed back to the truck.

"What?" I asked, almost running to catch up. "What are you thinking about?"

She said, "Nothing. I don't want to go into it. I just have a lot on my mind."

Culture shock, I imagined. Leaving behind one life, reentering another. Planning a wedding. Joining the Paletta family business. Living so close to our parents again. I could see how these things would occupy my sister, and I wanted to give her a break. Still, I wondered why her forays into the world never brought lasting change, why nothing she experienced in college or Ecuador had knocked Mount Kisco out of the center of her life. I had found a new center, and Donna, I was afraid, couldn't forgive me.

~ **Fourteen** ~

On the second day of Jimmy's wake, Gloria, Donna, and Jimmy's girl-friend Gina all got in a huge screaming fight. None of us had heard of Gina and there she was, acting like people's lovers do. Like she knew Jimmy best. She knew he had a family, for instance—two families, counting Al and Marie. We didn't even know he had a girlfriend. The stakes were high, because this wasn't just some Christmas dinner; it was the end of our brother's time on earth.

"Look at that eye liner," Gloria said out loud to no one in particular. "Like a cat."

Gina looked like lots of other girls in the Bronx, like any other day—when she wasn't at her boyfriend's wake—she'd be hanging out in front of the candy store in black stretch pants. Gloria was already stodgy at twenty-three. She glared at Gina across the funeral parlor and Gina glared back.

Jimmy came home in a casket no one was allowed to open. We wouldn't recognize him anyway, the sergeant told Al and Marie. Although Anthony had seen plenty of gruesome sights, he didn't push the point on this one. Instead of a proper wake where people get to visit with the dead person, to verify that the body has grown waxy and cold, we got Jimmy in a locked box with a flag draped over it and the framed eight-by-ten glossy of him in his dress uniform propped up on top.

But Donna, who was sixteen, walked in carrying a huge green poster-board and a bag from the drugstore up the street. She reached into her pocketbook and pulled out a small stack of photos—some black-and-white, some in color—of Jimmy at all ages. She and Gina went off to a love seat in one of the little anterooms and spread the pictures out on a coffee table. I tiptoed over to watch. Gina had some snapshots too, of Jimmy as a teenager after we lost track of him. Donna, like the rest of us, had just met this girl the night before, and here she was, acting like her friend, working with her on a project.

Gloria strode over. "Donna, what in the world are you doing?"

"Making a photo collage."

Gina shot Gloria this double-edged look that girls from the Bronx were so good at, a look that said: on the one hand you are beneath consideration, and on the other I would gladly kick your ass.

Then Gloria went apeshit about how Donna was ruining the photographs, and Donna had to explain six times that rubber cement doesn't ruin anything, once it dries you can rub it right off. Well, it was inappropriate, this was Gloria's next angle, to have pictures of ourselves in a funeral home. Naturally, pictures of Jimmy included some images of us too.

"Fine," Donna said, and she slapped a photo of Jimmy and Gina all dressed up for a date right on top of four-year-old-Gloria playing in the sandbox with one-year-old Jimmy—that snapshot itself a relic from a time when Vera bothered to take the old Brownie out of its box. Gloria didn't appreciate that either. She was convinced that the rubber cement on the back of Gina and Jimmy had ruined her four-year-old self forever.

"Jesus, Gloria," Donna said.

"Watch your street language," Gloria told Donna, looking straight at Gina. But Gina sat quietly, a small smile playing at the corners of her mouth, and let my two sisters go at it.

"Jesus, Gloria," Donna said again. "You're twenty-three years old. Quit acting like you're fifty."

"What are you doing, associating with this stranger?" Gloria said. "You don't even know her."

She packed the two words, "stranger" and "her," with so much venom, they clearly referred to the most loathsome object in the universe. Gina—quite long-suffering, or perhaps just awaiting her cue—all of a sudden jumped up and started screaming at Gloria about calling her a slut.

I stood there watching—my feet, ankles, knees, thighs pressed against one other, my arms pressed against my sides. I didn't even know for sure what "slut" meant.

Gloria said at the top of her lungs, "If the shoe fits, wear it."

Donna and Gina both wanted to know what the hell that was supposed to mean and Gloria went into some off-the-wall tirade about Gina being loose and not caring about Jimmy.

Donna, for the third time, took the name of God in vain. "Jesus, Gloria," she yelled. "Quit being a hypocrite. Everyone knows you've been fucking Michael all year."

I did know what that meant. All of a sudden everything got very quiet—in our little alcove, and out in the main room where my mother and father, aunts, uncles, and cousins were sitting with Jimmy's coffin.

"How dare you say that?" Gloria whispered. Still seething, she had lost interest in making a spectacle.

"You deserved it," Gina commented just as quietly.

"Stay the hell out of our family's business." Now Donna jumped on Gina, but before things could re-escalate, Alida and Al were on the scene.

"Everything all right now, girls?" Aunt Alida asked.

"Fine." Gina picked up her stack of photos and put them back in her pocketbook. "These two," she said—pointing to Donna and Gloria— "these two deserve each other." Then she stalked off in her short black skirt and black platform sandals.

Gloria stood there fuming. Donna sat back down and stared at her hands. I stood nearby, watching. Al patted the back of my head. "Funerals are like that," he said. "It's a tense time for everyone."

He, Alida, and Gloria drifted away. Donna picked up the rubber cement and kept working.

"Can I help?" I asked.

She scooted over to make room for me on the love seat. We worked without talking. It was like fitting together the pieces of a puzzle—Jimmy in swimming trunks, Jimmy with a basketball under his arm—but it wasn't as much fun without Gina.

~ Fifteen ~

And now here came Gloria, the resident in reconstructive surgery at Columbia Presbyterian Hospital, with her husband, ascendant mystery writer Mike Ferris, startlingly handsome, although I'd never paid it much mind. Straight women fell in love with the photo on the dust jacket of his books. This was the joke he liked to tell on TV talk shows: "My wife is studying to be a plastic surgeon but honestly, folks, I looked like this before I met her."

Mike and Gloria had deposited their daughter Tina, now six-and-a-half, at the home of a private school classmate. In her entire life, Tina had probably spent a total of five hours in my parents' presence. Gloria and Mike arranged it that way. On this particular night they came to indulge my mother, who so rarely asked for anything. They parked their Mercedes in the driveway next to my truck, and came up the walk to the house, each carrying a bottle of wine.

"What a joy," my mother greeted them at the door in her wheelchair. "All my girls together again." The last time was at Jimmy's funeral; Gloria didn't fly home for my grandmother's.

"We'll be together Friday at the rehearsal dinner." Donna was crabby. She'd maintained from the outset that this gathering was a waste of her time. She could have been home rewriting her lists, or helping Billy set the tile in the shower he'd just built.

"This is different," my mother said. "That's about adding another branch to the family. This is just us."

I kept quiet, trying to exude indifference. All week, I had let my mother do the persuading. She was actually quite effective at fulfilling her occasional, minuscule desire. If only I could have inspired her to want more. A better life. Not the way the Christian ladies defined it, or the medical professionals. To them, a better life required a cure. Once the prayers and experiments failed, all that was left was to manage Vera's condition. But I was talking about a social life, about all the hours Vera spent alone in the house. A safer life. Safety, I had decided, was the tack I would take.

The preceding five days had been a lot like sailing, like the time Alexis took me out on Lake Michigan in a little Sunfish on a windy day, reducing the risk of capsizing by sneaking up first from one direction, then the other. Hard to believe we would ever get anywhere. All week, I'd let my mother make the calls, overcome the resistance, negotiate schedules, plan the menu, send me out for groceries, explain to Consuela how to stuff and roll and tie *braciole* with a string, how to let the little flank steak packages simmer all day in a red sauce on a low burner.

"Why doesn't Frannie cook?" Donna asked when my mother first proposed the dinner. "I hate how Dominicans reinterpret Italian food."

"I'm making the party," my mother had insisted. "For Frannie. For all my girls."

And I—out of guilt somewhat, but also to keep out from under Consuela's feet—donated my time and truck to Donna and Billy, ran whatever errands they tossed my way, picked up bags of Portland cement and cases of Jordan almonds, so they could keep working their day jobs. In the evening, I met them at the half-remodeled farmhouse and let Billy put me to work so Donna could be free to make yet more lists and phone calls.

"No one sees all the labor that goes into a wedding," she told Billy, and he—ever affable—admitted she was probably right.

He enlisted me to hold oddly shaped pieces of sheet rock at impossibly obtuse angles while he screwed them in to build a closet up under the eaves in the attic. Moving out of Audrey and Bill Senior's basement and into the farmhouse would serve as Billy and Donna's honeymoon for now—although Donna had sweet-talked Billy into accepting a trip to Puerto Rico, which they planned to take in January, from my father. For the time being, my sister hustled together a wedding, her boyfriend of eight years hustled together their new home, and I hung around feeling like a tagalong kid again.

I did manage to wangle one day to drive out to the beach by myself. It turned out to be the only cold cloudy day in an otherwise summery week. Even so, I took off my shoes, put on a pair of shorts, and waded in the shallow water until my calves grew numb. I sat on the sand with a blanket around my waist and my sketchbook in my lap, but the only things to come out of my pencil were weird abstract doodles of arrows, circles, and triangles—less like art and more like the strategic maps made by football coaches or generals.

For five nights, I took the truck to Pound Ridge Reservation—just a few miles from my parents' house—and camped there. Sleeping in their driveway seemed silly and sleeping inside with both Anthony and Consuela home made no sense, especially given my vow to hold my tongue.

"Frannie has always loved camping out-of-doors," Vera said to Consuela to explain why I preferred a pickup to the newly changed bed in Gloria's old room.

Alone or with my sister and brother-in-law-to-be, in the truck or in the house, at the lake or the ocean, I turned over the same questions: Once everyone had assembled on Sunday, how would I bring up the subject of rescuing my mother? What would I say and when?

When seemed straightforward: neither too close to the beginning nor end, somewhere in the middle when people were already committed to their digestive systems and not yet psychically preparing to leave. Not in between courses when there was so much traffic, the distraction of all the ups and downs from the table. Right after the ziti were served, after the bowl of extra sauce and *braciole* had been circulated. In the pause, that moment of quiet when all plates were full and everyone was set to dig in. I'd launch my discussion. But what would I say?

As long as we're all here, there's something we should talk about.

I know this is a party, but I think we need to talk.

Listen, everyone, we've got a problem here.

We have to talk about Vera's safety. About Mommy's safety. About Mom.

The fifteen minutes before dinner with everyone just standing around were the most strained, especially because Consuela had finished setting the table, down to the salt and pepper shakers and grated cheese. My sisters and I had nothing to do.

"Hello, Frannie." Gloria looked me over, then looked away, a dismissal which struck me as both familiar and new. She had never related well to other adults. I clearly was reaching an adulthood beyond rehabilitation—not worth her time unless I wanted to consult about a nose job.

My father's pride in Gloria stayed high through the early years of her medical studies, peaked when she selected surgery for a career, and then faltered as she narrowed down to plastic surgery. "Excessive specialization," I'd heard him say. Gloria could rationalize all she wanted about rebuilding faces after auto accidents and serious fires, but plastic surgeons were first and foremost hucksters. Elective procedures, face lifts and tummy tucks, would be her bread and butter.

My brother-in-law was charming as well as handsome. He chatted up the people Gloria preferred to ignore. This evening, Consuela and I made the top of his list. Did I ever get to Wrigley Field? he wanted to know. Who was that hot new ballplayer from Santo Domingo?

Gloria sidled up to Donna to ask how the wedding plans were shaping up, if the band had gotten their calendar clear. She wore a pained smile, like talking to Donna was the least of all available evils. She's so uptight: I tried to catch my middle sister's eye, to exchange some non-verbal commiseration, but Donna wouldn't play.

I took my wine glass off the table so Mike, who was pouring, couldn't fill it. I intended to keep a clear head for the sake of the revolution.

"Let's sit," Vera said. Mike went upstairs to get Anthony, who was resting in his room.

More than a decade had passed since so many people last sat at the table. My father, my mother, Donna, and I took our old places. Gloria now had Jimmy's and Consuela had what was once Gloria's, close to the kitchen. My mother pulled up to the table in her wheelchair. Her old dining room chair was squeezed in between my two sisters for Mike.

Vera's once-interesting china was now faded and chipped, having withstood fifteen years of daily use, but she didn't seem to notice that her dinner party looked a little shabby around the edges. "How nice," she said. She was positively beaming. "Let's say grace"—and we all mumbled our way through.

I felt like a skunk, a Judas. I toyed with the roasted red peppers on my plate. I considered abandoning my plan, but when would this crowd ever be assembled again?

If I hadn't fixed on a time to make my break, the whole evening might have slipped away, minute by excruciating minute. The antipasto plates were cleared, the bowls of macaroni passed around.

"Wonderful food, Consuela," Mike said.

I felt like the guy who kept his finger on the nuclear trigger. Boom! My stomach dropped out of me and onto the floor. "There's something we have to talk about."

"A toast?" Mike reached for his wine glass. My sisters and Consuela all set down their forks. Without looking I could feel Consuela stiffen right next to me. From across the table, Gloria and Donna eyed me with suspicion.

"Not a toast. Mommy's safety. The other night I found Mom alone in bed."

I glanced around the table and painted in long, broad brush strokes; there would be time to fill in the details later. I concentrated on sweeping each person into my story, careful not to lock in on Consuela. All week I had practiced not being derailed by what she thought.

"Mom was lying on a pile of urine-soaked towels," I said. "Consuela needs her days off, no one person can be here every minute. Someone should take responsibility for Mom's well-being. She shouldn't be alone in bed twelve, fifteen hours at a time."

I was talking, not screaming. My voice trembled and quaked. My heart pumped with the desire for someone to step into my belief that something could be changed here. Donna. Gloria. Michael. Step in.

"Frannie," my father interrupted, "You're embarrassing your mother."

"I'm sorry, Ma. This is important."

But the spell was broken, and in through the breach came the attack on my credibility. "What fifteen hours?" Anthony said. "You don't know what you're talking about."

Donna said, "Fifteen hours. I don't believe it."

I did know what I was talking about, and my resolve stayed strong. I was talking about sometime Monday morning until two o'clock the following morning.

"You were here," he told me, but he didn't know that until nine o'clock that night. So it was sometime between Monday morning and nine o'clock Monday night. Would they believe eleven hours? I wanted to talk about the undeniable problem of towels soaked in piss.

"Maybe a few hours," Anthony admitted. "I left in the afternoon. I had work to do."

"Till two in the morning?"

"Gloria," he appealed to my sister, "You know how it is, being a doctor."

"Frannie," Gloria said, "Daddy works hard."

"A tough situation," Mike addressed the whole lot of us. "Being a doctor is stressful enough and then Anthony has the added burden of arranging Vera's care. Consuela does a magnificent job. A funeral, Frannie," he concluded. "That's a special case."

But I didn't cave in. "This wasn't a one-time thing," I said, "there's a system set up for the towels."

I stole a look at Donna. Had she or hadn't she been hip to the towel scheme? She seemed blank, lost, innocent, most likely. Consuela seemed impervious to both Mike's compliments and my supposed insults. My mother just looked down at her plate.

"Listen," my father said. He took a drink of water, and it dawned on me he wasn't yelling either. I had planned on behaving reasonably and thought he, in contrast, would be shown up as a madman. He said, "I've been thinking, for these unavoidable instances, that temporary catheterization of the bladder would solve the problem we're talking about."

My heart joined my stomach on the floor.

"Daddy!" Donna said. And then, "You okay, Ma?"

"No," Vera said. "I don't like this discussion. So public." In place of the pride she wore earlier she now seemed miserable and deflated.

"I'm sorry," I told her again.

Gloria said, "You may have hit on a plan, Dad. We don't have to go into it at the dinner table, but it might prove a very practical solution."

"Great idea, Dad," Mike agreed.

It was a rotten idea, your classic technical fix, a bid to make neglect more palatable. I couldn't stand another minute of polite chat about catheters. I hated to hurt my mother, but couldn't stop now. "You wouldn't leave an infant alone in a crib all day," I said. "What if the house catches fire?"

"Frannie!" Donna exclaimed. "Mommy's not an infant."

"Ma, I'm sorry," I said yet another time, "but the only comparison is if you had to leave, you couldn't."

My mother looked like she had folded in half.

"There won't be a fire," Anthony said.

A ludicrous statement, but before anyone could grasp it my brother-in-law came after me. "What are you suggesting, Frannie? What do you think is the solution?"

I had launched the discussion before concocting a solution. I'd thought an exposé, a scathing indictment, would be enough to move my sisters to seek an answer.

"Better coverage when Consuela's not here." I needed to think fast, and talk fast. "We should hire a second person, because even when Anthony is here he's inconsistent in his care."

"Don't be ridiculous," my father said. "You don't understand the expense involved."

I told him, "You can afford it. You just have to decide my mother is worth it."

Mike said, "Your rhetoric is laudable, Frannie, but it won't pay the bills."

Then Gloria started in. "You haven't been here, Frannie. You're living eight hundred miles away. You don't understand the situation, you don't have the right to judge."

I could have said, I lived here and cooked dinner every night when you were six hundred miles away, and now that you live in the city how often do you visit? But my time was running out. "I bet there are nursing homes where Mom would be better cared for," I said.

"Frannie!" The best Donna could do was muster shock and surprise.

I said, "I'm sorry, Ma. I know you love living here. I just don't think it's safe anymore, not the way it's set up."

Gloria pushed her chair back from the table. "You're crazy to mention such a thing."

"Gloria, honey," Mike said.

"Are you satisfied?" She glared at me. "You've ruined a perfectly nice dinner."

"Frannie's just upset." Anthony said. "She's never gotten over the sad fact that there's no cure for her mother's disease."

"Not true," I told him. "I've never gotten over the way you mistreat her."

"Vera," he said, "would you like to take up residence in a nursing home?" He stretched the phrase "nursing home" into an extended sneer, like it meant snake pit, like it meant loneliness, dissolution, and decay. And who was I to argue otherwise? How could I be sure institutional neglect would be more benign?

"This is my home," my mother said. "If the house burns down, at least I'll have died at home."

"Frannie," Donna finally materialized to assert an opinion, "did you take Mommy out for a walk this week? Did you do anything to make her life better? You're like the goddamn Shining Path—don't ease her situation one bit, and maybe she'll buckle under. Mommy wants her marriage to last, Frannie. Even if you don't approve, you have to respect her choice."

The discussion had become a hall of mirrors. I needed to stick with what I knew: my mother alone in that bed.

"Ma," I asked, "What are you talking about dying? I'm talking about the quality of your life. You've got a good twenty, thirty years ahead. You want twenty, thirty more years of this?"

"Yes, I do," my mother told me, with five people there to witness. "Now please. No one leaves until we do justice to Consuela's dinner."

~ Sixteen ~

A different daughter would have fought harder. A different daughter would have taken charge, solicited outside help—at the state level, the county level—would have forged a plan. She'd have appointed herself boss, bullied people. She would have forced a change.

This daughter desisted, temporarily. Tried to abide by her mother's wishes, act like a family member, eat a few bites of food. But the food tasted like sawdust, like failure.

I pushed my plate away and stood up. "I'm out of here," I said. "I'll see you Saturday, Donna."

I was attempting a grand dramatic exit, but first I needed to squeeze between Consuela's chair and the wall, and then Anthony detained me on the way out. "It was you," he called after me, "who mailed that letter once, wasn't it? That letter pertaining to karma?"

"I don't know what you're talking about," I lied.

A different daughter would have stayed on for another round of persuasion, would have threatened to kill him then and there.

This daughter got into her truck and drove: across the Throgs Neck Bridge, east on the Long Island Expressway, south again and east, away from the red smear of evening sun, past potato fields and wealthy towns, out to the furthest little green triangle marked on her map—a spit of land with dark sky and ocean all around, Hither Hills State Park in Montauk. This daughter paid her camping fee and backed her pickup into an open site on a small rise above the beach. She lay down on her bed, listened to the pounding waves, felt the wind rock the truck, and dreamed this dream:

Donna and I were bicycling under water. We pedaled side by side on a nice smooth road, at the bottom of a large, quiet lake. We moved in slow motion like things do under water. The going was easy. I turned and said something to Donna, but my words just formed silvery bubbles that rose through the water and burst above its surface. My sister smiled at me, and we kept on pedaling.

I made myself scarce until Donna's wedding. I slept at the beach for six nights and by day wandered the towns of eastern Long Island. The night air was cool and hazy, wisps of cloud veiled and unveiled the moon. During the day, the sun blazed strong and hot. Even out over the ocean, the sky was sparkling and clear. I didn't swim, I didn't feel like playing. I carried my sketchbook around, sat in town squares and public parks, stared at the rough white paper, but the pencil in my hand was inert. Nothing came, not even those odd strategic doodles. The part of my brain that works at seeing had shut off. I was overwhelmed by hearing—not the ocean, gulls, or traffic, but a constant stream of words, a running argument with Donna: How could she be so wrong about me?

I ate granola for breakfast, bagels and cream cheese for lunch, tuna straight out of the can for supper. I ate the last peaches of summer and the first apples of autumn. I lived like a hermit, like a person with nowhere to be. The invitation to my sister's wedding was tucked up against the windshield of the Datsun. The things I should have said to Donna sped and rattled inside me like B-Bs in an empty tin can. They woke me up at four in the morning, clattered after me all day long. They drove me away from the beach and into the towns, out of the parks and into the stores.

It began with a leotard on a consignment shop rack—shimmering royal blue, the same blue as the sky, with spaghetti-thin straps, and the price tag still on. A photo of Rudolph Nureyev, mid-leap, graced the tag. On the same rack, a tropical print rayon skirt—royal blue and magenta and forest green. Just down the block, a Capezio store sold the exact same leotard. The saleswoman at New You sent me down there. She was thin, maybe sixty-five. She wore a brown wig and a deep purple pant suit with beige trim on the lapels. She wanted me to see for myself the deal I was getting on a brand new item. More importantly, the Capezio store sold opaque sapphire tights to match.

"You will look beautiful," she promised.

I still had the embroidered Mexican dress I borrowed from Jane, good enough for my favorite sister's wedding. But when the leotard winked at me, I realized I could do so much better. I carried all three pieces into the dressing room at New You.

The leotard and tights fit tight, like a thousand hands pressing against me, and I felt oddly free—encased from chest to ankle in throbbing blue light. I floated the skirt over my head. It settled on the curve of my hips, and swirled around my calves. I grinned at myself in the mirror. I'd found the perfect suit of clothes. I felt fetching and pretty. I looked smashing.

No coarse cotton dress for Donna's wedding. No begrudging if-I-have-to-go-I-might-as-well-look-good kind of attitude. Although my legs weren't shaved, they were wrapped in slippery blue light. They slid up

103

against one another, and threw sparks when I walked. I'd go to celebrate Donna, home from college and Ecuador at last, and Billy, the man she came home to—a sane, calm person, so self-contained, so untouched by D'Amato family bullshit. No disapproving dour lesbian, no frumpy hippie-dyke here. I'd go to their wedding dressed as the ballerina-flower girl-water sprite-naiad-little sister I'd always wanted to be.

I'd give everyone a synthetic eyeful. To rest their eyes, and in case the warm weather didn't hold, I'd top it all off with a white rayon blouse straight out of the forties—gussets and darts making ample allowance for breasts, and then narrowing like an hour glass, and short, just barely grazing the waistband of the skirt. I'd leave the blouse unbuttoned to keep the blue chest-to-toe unity.

I'd pay close attention in the ceremony, search for meaning in the priest's words, key in on Billy and Donna's loving faces. I'd look at the rings, the flowers, Carla's dress, and do my best to overlook the fact of Anthony giving Donna away. At the party afterwards, I'd dance with Aunt Alida and Uncle Robert. We'd count out the steps to the cha-cha and Alley Cat. I'd drink wine, but not to excess. I'd laugh and flirt with the old people and little kids. I'd show Donna, and the rest of our family, and Billy's family too. I'd prove, once and for all: it wasn't marriage we were quarreling about here.

~ Seventeen ~

In the foyer between the church sanctuary and banquet hall Gloria cornered me and said, "What in God's name are you wearing?" Before I could even begin to formulate an answer she was shrieking at me, a barrage of insults, a flood of accusations that made no sense, and all my cousins' kids—the little ones, the six- and seven-year-olds—had gathered around to listen: Selfish. Disrespectful. Immoral. Thumbing my nose at Donna's choice to marry. Deliberately embarrassing Donna in front of Billy's family.

"You're wrong," I answered. Only I didn't say it, I screamed it. "It's none of your fucking business. Leave me alone." Then there was nothing to do but stay or go.

I wouldn't let her run me out of Donna's party. My two sisters had never been close, had never found a single thing to laugh or gossip about, had both been living in New York for almost six months and hadn't even seen each other until this week.

"I'm not a child," I told her, "and you don't own me. Do you get on Aunt Julia's case if you don't like what she's wearing? You should turn your attention to more pressing family business."

I had already turned and started my long stalk across the banquet hall to my assigned place at the corner table when I saw Cousin Al, ever the peacemaker, approaching. We met in the middle, on the glossy parquet dance floor.

"Everything okay?" he asked, catching my arm to keep me from passing by.

"It will be."

"Maybe you'll save a dance for me?" He was doing his replacement big brother routine, which was sweet enough, but also staring at my breasts. Well, okay. The clothes were a mistake. "Huh, Frannie?" Al said again. "You gonna dance with me later?"

"Sure," I told him.

But when I got to my seat, I didn't want to move. I didn't want to laugh and flirt and joke around with my cousin Angela who could have been Nancy Sinatra, or with Billy's cousin Ralph the mortician who wore mutton chop sideburns and wide lapels to match. "I'll be there in a minute," I told Angela when she stood up to fill her plate at the buffet. I waited until the line had cleared, and by the time I got there the stuffed mushrooms were gone. I stared at the empty stainless steel warming pan with the puddle of oily brown juice in the bottom. Back at the table, I ate fast, my head down, like I was alone at a lunch counter, like I would never see another meal.

"Come on, Frannie, relax." Angela slipped a mushroom onto my plate. "Everyone knows that Gloria is too hard on people."

"She's nuts," I said.

"Fine. Right. She may be nuts. So have a good time."

Besides Angela and Ralph, two other wedding guests sat at our table. They pretended not to notice my ill humor. They were strangers, to me and each other—some woman Donna knew from the tub and tile showroom in Bedford Hills, and some guy who played softball in Billy's league. Although we were all unattached—Donna's theory behind the seating arrangement—I felt like an intruder on a double date. My invitation had read, "Francesca D'Amato and Guest," but who would I have brought with me? No one from Chicago. Not Nancy or Raymond, my high school friends, who'd both had the sense to go to college after all. No matter who I might have brought, there was no escaping my niche: the sullen kid sister with conspicuous clothes.

The musicians climbed up on the little stage and started tuning their instruments. Across the room, Donna and Billy made the rounds—spending just a few minutes at every table, toasting with just an inch of champagne in their glasses.

"Can I pour you some wine?" Ralph asked me.

"No thanks," I told him. "I'm on the wagon. It's a long drive home to Chicago."

But first it was an all-night waiting game between Gloria and me, to see which of us could righteously outlast the other.

The P.A. system came on with a pop and a crackle. "Tonight's first dance," the lead singer announced, "is dedicated to the bride and groom—and to high school sweethearts everywhere." It'd be a snowball, he told us. Corny, yes, but it was important to get everyone into the action. And a one, and a two, and the band launched into the Beatles' "I Saw Her Standing There." Billy and Donna danced alone together in the middle of the floor while everyone else watched.

"Change partners," the band leader called and they split. Billy came to get Angela, Donna went after Al. Change again, bring a new partner into the mix. And here came Angela with her eye fixed on me.

"You're leaving town tonight?" my cousin said. "Better have some fun before you go."

I let her lead me onto the dance floor, but all I could think about was my clothes. That and who I would pick next. Should I break down and put on Jane's dress, or let things slide?

Change again. Angela went back to our table for Ralph. I went to get Aunt Alida. Stick with the costume choice, I decided. Admit no mistakes. A costume—that's all it really was. I tossed aside my embarrassment. Fuck Gloria. Fuck her prudishness.

The band slipped from the Beatles to Steely Dan. The snowball ended with half the adults and all the kids out on the dance floor—all except my niece Tina who might as well have been chained to her parents' table. Over Uncle Bernie's shoulder I watched them: Gloria sitting back, her face carved in a permanent scowl, Mike leaning forward to chat with the other adults at the table, and Tina, the sum of two vectors—perfectly upright in her chair, perfectly alone in a white dress with a green sash, her skirt smoothed underneath her, her feet dangling inches from the floor. She wore a look I recognized, the blank look of a child under stress who must concentrate every second to keep her body, her family, the whole universe from flying apart.

My mother sat at a separate table, resplendent in a deep violet dress, beaming her movie star smile, flanked by Consuela and my father—both as impassive as pieces of scenery. Vera turned her head this way and that—to absorb all the activity in the room, to bestow her immense gratification and approval, to commune with the lovely guests at her middle daughter's wedding. Few of the guests approached her in person.

I was my mother's counterpart—younger, able-bodied, inappropriately dressed I now realized, but determined to whip up my own good time, to deny Gloria the pleasure of thinking she had put me in my place. I danced and danced. I burnished the room with blue light. I danced alone. I danced with Angela until Ralph cut in to whisk her away. I gathered the little kids into a circle. I partnered up with Aunt Alida. Already sixty-two, she'd gone out of her way to learn the jitterbug, the twist, the hustle—all the hottest dances of the previous three decades. I did my best at faking some steps to keep up with her.

Alida wore a beaded magenta dress—tight over her rear end, I noticed with some satisfaction—and one-inch open-toed heels. When the band gave us a cha-cha, my aunt pulled me in close. "When are you getting married?" she asked. Even in her heels she was shorter than me, and staring right at my chest.

"Never," I said. One, two, cha-cha-cha.

"You want to catch a man," she said, throwing a glance at my parents' table, "you give him the false impression he can tame you." Alida was no fan of Anthony, her younger brother, but for years she'd proclaimed, to anyone who would listen, that Vera brought her own predicament on herself.

I didn't answer, I just smiled and cha-cha-chad. When Uncle Robert—teetering a bit more than the last time I saw him—got the band going on the Alley Cat, I took my place right next to him, right at the front of the pack. I did it all without a drop of liquor, still keeping sober for the sake of the revolution.

Only my revolution had failed. My potential ally Gloria—admittedly never a promising one—was now inexplicably my sworn enemy, and the only plan left was to put sixteen hours of Interstate 80 between myself and the entire clan.

When the Alley Cat ended, I thanked Uncle Robert and headed back to my table. Time to start tanking up on coffee. If Gloria didn't leave soon, I'd have to let her win. Angela and Ralph had been tanking up on vodka tonics, and Ralph flirted in earnest. Angela, it seemed, was an oscillating system—returning his attention one minute, but dodging it the next. Poor Angela. Not a good sign, to be ambivalent after so much time and alcohol. The other two from our table were getting along famously on the dance floor. For them, Donna's matchmaking had paid off.

The crowd was starting to thin out and I'd come within inches of calling it a night when Gloria finally conceded the game, using the excuse of her daughter's bedtime. She sent little Tina over to make the concession speech.

"Goodnight, Aunt Francesca. Mommy and Daddy and I are going home now." Even in a white dress with a green bow, Tina looked more like a foot soldier than a little girl.

"Good night, sweetie. Travel safely." I didn't offer to kiss her; it would have wrecked her equilibrium. She turned and marched away.

Gloria and Mike circled the banquet hall to say their good-byes—to my parents and Consuela, Billy and Donna, our own relatives and the Palettas. All except Angela and Ralph, guilty by association with me. My sister didn't come near our table.

"We got Tina," I told Angela.

"Your sister's a piece of work," Angela said. "We definitely got the better deal."

As soon as Gloria and company had gone, I traced the same circuit, making false promises to my aunts and cousins: I wouldn't be a stranger. I'd visit more often, and not just for the big events. "Your wedding next," Aunt Julia said, "Or Angela's." My cousin had had her share of boyfriends, but never the marrying kind. Or maybe she was as skeptical about permanence as I was. Unless one of us succumbed to marriage, the next big event would be a funeral, but no one said this out loud.

I crossed the room to my parents' table, where Donna had taken a seat. She'd kicked off her shoes, hiked up her white silk skirt, and put her stockinged feet up on an empty chair.

"I'm getting on the road tonight." I addressed myself to my mother.

"Are you sure?" Vera said. "Please, drive safely. You look beautiful. I'm so glad you came."

"Thanks," I told her. "You too. You look beautiful too."

This leave-taking was more public than fifteen months before, more civil, and in an odd way more final. Then, I hadn't known where I was headed. Now, we all acted as if Chicago was my home. I had at least the outline of a life to run toward, not just the people and place I kept running from. In Chicago, everyone who knew me best generally acted like they liked me.

"Don't stay mad," Donna told me. "Come back and visit."

"Okay. You visit too," I answered. Although I couldn't imagine when or why.

My father and Consuela said nothing.

Billy embraced me more hesitantly than usual, perhaps because of my outfit. Just before releasing me, he tipped his head forward and muttered into my ear, "Get out and stay out, Frannie. You'll thank me in ten years."

"And you have a happy marriage," I told him.

I remembered to swing back by my table to retrieve my party favors—a commemorative matchbook engraved with Billy and Donna's names and a handful of Jordan almonds tied in a pale pink net with a pink satin ribbon. Ralph had scooted his chair around the curve of the table and pulled up close to Angela. She leaned away from him, but didn't tell him to move. She staggered when she stood up to hug me.

"Drive safe," she said. "Keep the faith."

Ralph gave me a little leer and a wink.

On my way out, I stopped by Gloria, Mike and Tina's now-empty table, littered with crumpled pink napkins, coffee cups and wine glasses. I reached around the glassware and helped myself to the bundles of almonds they'd left behind.

Emboldened by that move, I stopped again in the foyer, at the table piled with gifts for Billy and Donna. The fruit bowl I had bought—packed in a big square box, wrapped in blue and silver paper—rested at the top of the stack. I picked it up, tucked it under one arm, and carried it back out to the truck. I wasn't exactly stealing, just changing my mind about whether or not to give it.

PART THREE
When Love Returns • (1977-1983)

~ One ~

The night nurse first noticed the blood. It burst from my newly-made navel and spread in a bright crimson bloom through thick cotton diapers. The nurse called out over the intercom: Doctor Fields, Doctor D'Amato, Doctor Fields, Doctor D'Amato, come to the neonatal nursery. Doctor Fields, my mother's obstetrician, the man who tied a lousy knot. Doctor D'Amato, my father, a staff surgeon at the hospital. The emergency call echoed at five a.m. through empty, salmon-tiled corridors. My father answered it first.

He drew blood from his own veins and performed the transfusions himself, cutting with a scalpel into my tiny newborn ankles. For weeks after, my mother didn't know. How she escaped knowing has always mystified me.

At first she was groggy from the anesthesia; she would have had no awareness of the crisis in motion. But what about the days that followed, once the danger was past? Didn't every mother play with her baby's feet, suck its toes, kiss its strong fat kicking naked legs? Wouldn't any mother have discovered the raw scars on her newborn's ankles?

I take a closer look at the 1950s—at Vera sitting up, pretty as can be in her hospital bed. Clean white sheets and lightweight blanket, fresh bed jacket, yellow roses on the bureau, her thick auburn hair brushed away from her face. She's more rested than she has been since the days following Donna's birth. Now a nurse comes into the room carrying my little baby self and a bottle. I am fully dressed, right down to my diminutive yellow booties. My mother balances me on her arm, on top of the blanket. She smiles just a bit and guides the rubber tip of the bottle between my tiny sucking lips. There is no skin anywhere in this picture. Sometimes, if Vera is napping, the nurse will feed me herself. Better to let the mother rest; she'll have plenty to do after she leaves the hospital.

I can forgive her that first week, until she brought me home. But how could she remain so oblivious? Didn't she unwrap the swaddling clothes to change my diaper? Didn't she bathe me, or at least look me over? My grandmother would have noticed the scars, had she hung around to view me naked. But she most likely kissed my round face and bustled off to her own apartment, careful not to outstay her welcome.

Vera remained ignorant of my close call until she started to plan my baptism. "She's been baptized," Anthony told her. While he was suturing my veins, a priest had hurried to the nursery to christen baby Caroline D'Amato *in perilis mortem*. Anthony had pulled the name out of the air.

"Why didn't you tell me?" my mother asked, and she walked up the hill to the rectory to talk with the monsignor about christening me again. She had her heart set on naming me Francesca Anne, and Donna had been calling me Frannie all month. I was re-baptized in the church as Francesca Caroline, in a long white embroidered dress with Aunt Alida and Uncle Frank standing up as godparents.

My father's blood was flushed out of my system, processed by the liver and completely gone in a mere four months. Washed out of my dirty diapers, to be exact. But I didn't know this until after I could read. I learned from the *Golden Book Illustrated Encyclopedia*, one of the handful of books we had around the house, that new blood arises in the bone marrow and old blood cells are carried away in the feces. The body's entire volume of blood is renewed every one hundred twenty days. I spent much of my preliterate childhood convinced Anthony still ran in my veins, certain I owed him a pint. Learning to read broke this one bond, but it couldn't even shake the others.

The Sicilians believe if someone saves your life, you are bound to them forever. The psychologists believe an infant will attach to anyone who furnishes a nurturing touch. As much as I hated my father, railed against him, strived to rid myself of him, I also loved him. I loved Anthony without any choice in the matter, and sometimes I am him.

I am Anthony when I notice my own hands—cutting a silkscreen, or stirring a can of ink, or especially driving the pickup. It's that casual single-handed way of holding the steering wheel at the bottom, my wrist resting in my lap, my other hand free to gesture in conversation or fiddle with the radio dial. I see my hands dedicating only ten or twenty percent of their effort to steering, and they are Anthony's.

I am my father on the road with Ruby, the woman I love, crossing the Rocky Mountains in Montana. She's taking a turn at the wheel, but I can't relax because I've got my nose in a road atlas. There's the Sleeping Child Hot Springs, I tell her, a natural stone bridge, some ancient petroglyphs, only fifteen or twenty or forty miles out of our way. I get so excited about planning how to take in all these wonders I forget to notice the riot of purple and yellow flowers lining the highway, the red-winged blackbirds startled into flight, the slope of Ruby's forearm and wrist as she grips the steering wheel single-handedly at the top.

I am Anthony when inexplicably my love for Ruby becomes brittle, when I feel as cornered as I have by every lover before her. Only I do my best to ride it out. I know better than to say too much, particularly not "You're just like Arlene"—or Nicole, or my sister, or father—because no one takes to that well. I am the one, after all, just like I was with Arlene, like Anthony was with Vera—who possesses the fear and rage sometimes too big to tuck out of sight.

~ Two ~

The night I drove back to Chicago from Donna's wedding, I thought I was all alone. Only eighteen years old, and I had no family. One third was long dead, the rest had just squeezed me out. Only the second floor kitchen window was lit when I pulled up. The one light we always left on tossed a small splash of yellow out towards the alley. Disappointment washed over me; I had been hoping someone would be home.

As soon as I opened the door, the smell of coffee rushed at me—powerfully fresh, recently ground and brewed. My stomach clenched. I had downed too many cups of thin, acrid coffee, first at the disastrous wedding banquet, and then at roadside oases. I'd eaten nothing except almonds in twenty hours. My knees went weak as I climbed the stairs.

Jane sat at the kitchen table—her textbooks, the *Anatomy Coloring Book*, and an array of colored pencils spread out before her, her hair shining like copper under the incandescent light.

"You're back," she said, without looking up, like maybe I had gone to the grocery store. She held up two sharpened pencils to compare their shades of green. She didn't ask about my trip, or why I came back two weeks early.

"There's a ton of food in the fridge," she did offer. "Arlene made enchiladas."

I was being dismissed. Not that she could actually have kicked me out. House rules said first priority in the kitchen went to those who were cooking or eating. Had I insisted, Jane would have packed up. She might

112

even have liked me better for it, but I didn't insist. I went to the refrigerator and scooped some leftovers onto a plate, then interrupted her once more to ask, "So where is everyone else?"

Kelly was playing basketball at Truman College. Mimi and Arlene were at meetings. Jane put her head down to trace a nerve with the tip of an orange pencil. I took my food into the living room and switched on the lamp.

I finished eating in under a minute, but refrained from carrying my plate and fork to the kitchen sink. I didn't want to be another Willow, skulking in the corners of the common spaces, reeking of unmet needs. Still not ready to turn in for the night, I took up watch on the living room couch.

Keys in the lock, footsteps pounding up the stairs. Kelly. "Welcome back," she said without breaking her stride, and barreled straight up to her room in the attic.

I heard the door a second time, and Mimi's lighter step. "Frannie, you're back early. Your timing is great." She moved my plate to the floor and sat down on the hassock in front of me. "Have I got a job for you."

It was a production job at Hard Rain Posters, our local left-wing graphics and printing collective. Their politics were lacking, Mimi had to say, their analysis mushy, verging on liberal. Still, it might be perfect for me.

Mimi would've had higher hopes for me if I was a different kind of person. If I was a comrade, I would have organized the guys at the gas station. That accomplished, I'd move on to organize Hard Rain, to deliver the collective to the Party. But I was still getting used to the fact that "liberal" was a nasty epithet, and Mimi understood my limitations. She was in quite the generous mood that evening, advocating something purely for my personal gain.

"Think of the skills you could learn, Frannie. You're exactly what they're looking for. Dexterous. Energetic. A self-taught artist."

"I don't know," I told her. I didn't feel like much of an artist. I felt like a dull girl, a lost girl, someone bearing gifts that would be rejected at every turn. I heard the downstairs door again, and Arlene's measured tread on the stairs.

"There she is," she sang out when she came in from the hallway. "Our dexterous and energetic young traveler." I couldn't help but grin. They'd been talking about me.

Something about Arlene looked different. Same short light brown hair, same baggy clothes and square body. Same sweetness in her face, but it was less diffuse, more focused. I saw something in her I'd never noticed before—a certain cunning, an edge. She sat down right next to me on the couch.

"So," she said, "we missed you. How did it go? How was your favorite sister's wedding?"

I shook my head.

"You okay?" she asked, probably because I was staring at her, hard.

"A total drag," I finally managed to say. But I was busy discovering it was Arlene I had come home to.

"Well you're safe now." She put an arm around me. "Is Mimi giving you the scoop on the job? Mass-producing images for the revolution. Seems tailor made for you, Frannie. Talk about right livelihood."

"Oh, please," Mimi told her.

For a few months, Arlene had been reading Buddhist books, leaving them open face-down on the bathroom floor or kitchen counter. Sometimes she'd slip talk of "suffering" and "acceptance" into our suppertime socialist conversations. She had started going out a lot at night, to Alanon meetings and Buddhist study groups. Arlene was thinking small. While the others strived to make the world safe for workers, farmers, revolutionary doctors, women athletes, she concentrated on making an emotional home in the universe. Reproductive labor, Mimi might have called it.

Even before it became Arlene's project, it had been her tendency. The first day I met her, she was the one who argued in favor of taking me in. While Mimi was out learning to quote Trotsky to her co-workers in Spanish, Arlene had been busy practicing these simple English phrases: How are you doing? How is it going? We missed you.

"Frannie," Mimi said. "The cold weather's coming on. Wouldn't you jump at the chance to work indoors?"

I jumped at the chance to forget completely about the boy with the gun—the one who loitered in the back of my mind, who was bound to show up some day to test the theory that we cashiers didn't have access to the safe. But I didn't admit, even to myself, how much I worried about that boy until I was done at the gas station for good.

"I don't know," I told Mimi. "I guess I'd feel bad about leaving Eddie."

"What did Eddie ever do for you?" Mimi practically screamed, and then she was lecturing me, a tidal wave of words about the evil of identifying with one's bosses.

I wasn't listening; I was trying to clear away the brambles, to uncover the thing that kept me loyal to Eddie. He gave me a job, treated me decently, no more and no less than Mimi. I couldn't explain to Mimi that I was equally loyal to her, and she was equally undeserving. I couldn't tell her that some days, riding the bus, I fell in love with total strangers—young men, old women, just because they smiled at me nicely. That right before Mimi's eyes, I was falling in love with Arlene just because she'd laid a hand on my shoulder.

"I'll check out the job in the morning," I told my housemates. They weren't going to let up until I did. And I had to agree, it beat telling Eddie I was back.

~ Three ~

As a child, I thought of Vera as married to Anthony—but not vice versa. He didn't seem to need her. I hadn't clued in yet to all the emotional and ethical profit he reaped from his sacrifice, from counting himself among the ten percent, not the ninety—among the men who stayed with their wives, who didn't ditch and run when the diagnosis came back Multiple Sclerosis. But only once did I notice him talking to her like a peer, like she possessed something he needed:

It was evening in early April, the sky that color I love best—anxious blue-green at the horizon, deepening to inky blue-black overhead. I was in third grade. I slouched at the kitchen table, struggling to write a report about Argentina. I'd cut photos out of *National Geographic* to paste into my report—the traditional costume of the pampas, the modern-day dress of the urban Argentinean, and had already planned my layout—how I'd stagger the photos on the page, squeeze my sentences into narrow columns that snaked around and between the pictures. But the sentences were not coming; anything I could think of had already been said. I looked out the window, imagining the sky as a swimming pool. I felt my heart tip as I prepared to dive in.

The evening was quiet. My parents took naps at opposite ends of the house—my father upstairs in his bedroom, my mother downstairs in hers—sleeping with their clothes on, on top of the covers, because it was too early to call it a night. Jimmy was still overseas, Gloria away at college. Donna had gone off to a high school battle of the bands—which actually meant what she said. It would be another year or two before "choir concert" and "school play" became code for fucking in the Palettas' basement and drunken drag racing around the reservoirs.

115

My father was the first to stir. I heard the ceiling creak, the upstairs toilet flush, a radio coming on in his office. And then he was running. The ceiling thundered.

"Vera," he called out from the top of the stairs. And then he was running down, past me and into her room. "Vera," he shouted, "Put your radio on. King has been shot."

In a matter of minutes, his shock subsided. He went back upstairs to his paperwork, muttering. My mother and I turned on the TV. The wavering dot of blue light steadied itself, spread across the tube, and King's broad mustached face appeared. I recognized the face, and the man, from the pages of *Life*. I recalled the snippets we had learned about him in school. I saw the file footage of crowds, heard the newscasters' words: junior—memphis—doctor—strikers—martin—reverend—luther—assassination, and the gaps in my understanding knit closed.

But in that very first moment all that registered was this: King was the thing that made my father come running for my mother.

~ Four ~

Hard Rain Posters occupied the ground floor of an old candy factory eight blocks away from our house. The morning I set out to walk there, a fall wind was gusting hard. Empty boxes and bags turned into tumbleweeds, and the dirt on the street flew at my eyes. I caught the bus going south on Broadway.

A woman with long fine hair a shade lighter than my own handed me an application. Her face was broad—American Indian, I guessed. She pointed out a chair near the front window, red vinyl with a cracked seat and chrome arms, salvaged from a bus station waiting room. Framed posters hung on the brick walls, and unframed ones with cardboard backings were stacked upright in rough wooden bins.

What was my ethnic background and gender? the application form asked. What experience did I have in consensus decision-making? In silkscreen processes? In running an offset press? Except for high school art class, I had little to show. Under "How did you hear about this job?", I wrote, "My housemates," and then went back and squeezed in Mimi and Arlene's names. At least I had friends, and my friends told me I was dexterous and energetic.

"Italian-American," the woman read my application out loud. "I was thinking you might be Latina."

"You are?" I asked.

"Yes," she said. "I'm Rennie."

They had serious goals about who they'd hire at Hard Rain. Not a policy or quota, Rennie explained, just an ideal: they never wanted their collective of eleven workers to have a majority of white people, or straight people, or men.

"I can't fucking stand it," Mimi said that night at supper. "All this emphasis on sex and race." But they had every kind of person in their collective, and we were still all white women at our table. Although I merely thought this, I sat up a bit straighter to find myself disagreeing with Mimi.

Gregory called from the poster studio the same night to say they'd give me a try. They'd put me to work at unskilled tasks for a day. If that went well, we could schedule an interview. "I'll show you the ropes in the morning," he said.

Gregory was barrel-chested, muscular, and black. His lover Martin was skinny, equally muscular, and white. Serbo-Croatian, to be exact. They headed straight to the Y from Hard Rain every evening. From the first, Gregory seemed to delight in walking me through the work—even restocking paper or hosing down screens. He treated me like he genuinely liked me, and I soon found out all my assumptions about my application were backwards.

"Art students are slobs," Gregory said. "They might as well take a bath in the ink. No offense to my friend Martin."

Although Martin stood clear across the room, and some punk rock music was wailing in between, he flashed a sly, straight-toothed grin at his lover. He knew exactly what was being said.

Gregory told me, "We who are not of the elite learn to clean up as we go." Then he patted me on the back and left me to finish the screens.

If having no art school training made me look good, having friends was hardly the boon I had imagined. "You stay with those women on Greenview?" Marvette asked me. "They don't let black women in."

I had stacked the clean screens, hung the hose up on its hook, and was taking a break in the back room to eat my bread and provolone lunch. I sat on a green couch so sunken I may as well have been sitting on the floor. Marvette stood up—she'd come to look for something in the old refrigerator. She was a small woman—tiny, really, but right then she was towering above me, and I needed to think of something to say.

I couldn't say they would because they hadn't, and although no one black had asked since I'd moved in, I could see that was no excuse.

Marvette or some friend of hers must have asked once, must have failed some test I had passed. She'd been rejected and I'd been admitted. Saying I wasn't there at the time wouldn't cut it. Asking why she'd want to live there anyway would have been worse.

She stood with the refrigerator door open, letting the cold air and yellow light leak into the room. She wasn't taking anything out or putting anything back in.

"I didn't know that," I finally answered, "but I believe you."

With something like a "harumph" she shut the door and walked away.

It surprised me when Gregory called to set up the interview and when, without much more fuss, I was in. Soon I was learning greedily—about hand printing and machine printing, about papers, inks, and emulsions. I resisted the impulse to ingratiate myself with Marvette, and instead focused on what she could teach me: how to make a second and third ink line up perfectly with the first, how to get even distribution across the page.

"You request your days off before I make the schedule," she said. "Remember: asking doesn't necessarily get you what you want. I got eleven people's preferences to juggle."

No one could fault me on this last score. I lived in a collective, I worked in a collective. I spent my days and nights cooperating.

~ Five ~

My second winter in Chicago brought a second Christmas card from my mother, a Japanese-style print of snow on trees. And essentially the same message as the first one:

The tree looks great.
Stay well.
Love, Mom & Dad

This time, all of it in Donna's writing—the first scrap of communication since her wedding. By cheating my sister out of her gift, I had cheated myself out of a thank-you.

In those ten words I could read that Donna had gone down to the basement, dragged up the carton of decorations, and unwrapped Vera's beloved hand-blown ornaments from their cotton batting. The previous year, she'd been in Ecuador and Consuela had written the cards. I had been getting my bearings in a new city. This time, I could feel my own absence.

118

Once again, no question came in my card, no invitation to write back. I was still not welcome to make things harder on Vera. I was still unwanted, unless I could leave well enough alone.

Winter had passed by the time I could consent to her terms. Cold winds still gusted off the lake, but the daylight grew longer and stronger. One morning I woke up brimming with desire. I wanted to call Vera, to ask if the forsythias at the end of the driveway had started blooming, if spring had come on yet through her window, that shock of yellow against the blue spruces.

Dialing her number, I readied myself for her protests, her admonishments to call when Anthony was at home. Instead she asked, "Oh. Did you call about the surgery?"

I hadn't known about any surgery.

She was going in the next day, had been planning it for months. First Donna's wedding got in the way, then the holidays, then the neurologist went on a cruise. Now he was back and ready to sever the nerves in her legs, to interrupt the signals that caused her calf muscles to endlessly contract.

She said, "I must have told you."

I said, "You didn't. You knew about it before the wedding and you didn't tell me."

"You weren't here long. It must have slipped my mind."

I hated myself for arguing with her. "Tell me again what you're having done," I said.

It was a quick procedure, in and out of Columbia Presbyterian in one day. The neurosurgeon was a colleague of Gloria's. He'd clip the motor nerves in Vera's legs so the muscles would no longer spasm. He'd leave the sensory nerves intact so she'd still be able to feel. Her legs and feet hadn't borne any weight in months. Once cut, they would dangle instead of clenching up uselessly.

"Who said that?" I asked. "Uselessly?"

"No one. I did." But I could hear that it was my father or Gloria.

"You think this is best?"

She said, "I won't walk again, but I will be able to sit more naturally."

"Naturally," I echoed. "This is about appearances?"

"More comfortably. I meant to say more comfortably. Aren't you going to wish me luck?"

Cutting nerves like this was irreversible. A quick procedure, an act of destruction. The doctors had decided there would be no more remissions.

"Walking again," I told her, "that's not the goal. Having a good life, that should be the goal."

"Yes," she said, "I do. I have a good life." Meaning her husband hadn't abandoned her, like most women in her situation.

For years, my mother had been filling up on *Reader's Digest*. Through all her hours alone, the possibility of a cure ran like a silver thread, now to be snipped away, and she wasn't supposed to mourn it. No one, not Anthony or Gloria, not the neurosurgeon or the nurses on the hospital ward—would help her deal with the significance of this unraveling. And what did I contribute by telling her that walking was irrelevant, that it had been stupid all along to want a cure?

"I'm sorry," I tried. "It sounds like a tough decision."

She said, "It's nothing, in and out the same day. Please, Frannie, don't worry about me."

"Do you worry about me?"

"Of course I do. Alone in a big city."

"I have people," I told her. "I have structure; it's not what you imagine."

She said, "This isn't what you imagine either."

But I had witnessed her life. She'd never so much as glimpsed into mine.

I asked, "Is there anything I can do?"

"Wish me luck."

What was the point in always goading her to want things if I then rejected her requests? "Okay. Good luck," I said.

"Thank you, and take care now." She hung up.

I wanted to stop her. I wanted to get in the truck and drive cross country like a maniac, double park on Riverside Drive, run upstairs, throw myself across her legs, place my own body between hers and the scalpel.

Wait! I'd shout, and the knife would flash in mid-flight. The neurosurgeon and I would play tug-of-war with her body. She'd go limp like a rag doll.

Do something, I'd yell at her, I can't do it all for you.

We're here to help you, the surgeon, Anthony, and Gloria would say in chorus.

By the strength of my determination I would wrestle her out of their grasp and we'd tumble into a heap in the corner. Then what? Would I forbid her to have her nerves cut? It was her autonomy, not her nerves, I wanted to salvage. I'd glare at the doctors across the room and say, I don't like how this decision came about.

She'd say, I've made my choice. Help me up please. Wish me luck. It wasn't supposed to go like this, the rescued so damn ungrateful.

I got in the pick-up, but not on the freeway, and went to work. I stumbled through the day, responded when people talked to me, but had no idea what they or I said, had a tough time getting my screens to line up, a tougher time knowing what to do next.

I came home that night to an empty house. Everyone was out—changing the world, or changing herself. Not me. A note on the kitchen table said, "Lentil soup on the stove, cornbread in the oven." But I didn't feel like eating; I felt like smashing something. I sat and brooded.

Arlene came home first. "What is it?" she said, "tell me." She pulled up her chair so our knees were touching. I saw her glance around the kitchen, at the stovetop, the floor. This time I hadn't cleaned up; I'd gone right into collapse.

I couldn't speak, and I hid my face. I didn't even know where to start. But she leaned in, tipped her head to make me look at her, and soon I was telling her everything about cut nerves, my mother in captivity, my father's malevolence. About how I did my childhood best to free Vera and finally, like my brother and sisters, had to free myself. Although that should have been the end of the story, it never was. I was haunted, every cell in my brain a compass needle aligning itself to the woman I left behind. I rarely called, I didn't write or send Christmas presents, but every move I made was dedicated to my mother, every day an occasion to experience determination and pleasure enough for two.

I told Arlene about Anthony the surgeon, about Gloria the plastic surgeon. They viewed my mother as a failure, an affront to their faith in medicine, but I knew medicine was mere technology. I had faith in human beings. I told her about the forsythias and deciding to call just in time to learn about the operation. Not in time to do anything. I had flung myself away from Mount Kisco, but was always turning back. I kept the key to my mother's house on my ring. I hated my father and sister, despised all doctors, loathed the entire medical system. I was afraid I even detested Jane sometimes, but Arlene shouldn't worry, I didn't hate her, although she too worked at a hospital.

"What do you need?" she asked. What a crazy, crazy question. Need was more infantile than want, more primal, not allowed.

I wanted her to lie down with me, to touch my face, to talk so softly only I could hear her, but I couldn't imagine asking, not yet.

"I want to break something," I said. "Let's go outside."

She got her jacket. She didn't ask, Where? What are you going to break? What do you mean by that, Frannie? I wasn't sure what I meant, but it didn't matter. Arlene had faith in human beings too.

The sky was cloudy, the night warmer than it had been in months. We could see our breath when we stopped under the orange-grey light of a street lamp. We walked fast, our hands in coat pockets. Arlene turned when I turned; I set the pace. We traced a large circuit through back streets. She told me about her father, about his drinking and his decay. I listened because it was equitable, but I missed half the details because I was still thinking about cut nerves, still swallowing all the crying I'd almost let loose.

We stopped in front of an abandoned factory, slated for renovation like others in the neighborhood. Soon the inside would be gutted and subdivided, the old windows replaced, the brick front sandblasted clean. A new security door and buzzer system would be installed, and arty rich people would move in, but for now the building was empty, a somber hulk. Arlene and I walked all around it. At the back, hidden from the street, weeds pushed their way up between paving stones. We found an old gear, other rusty bits of machinery, a small pile of rubble, chipped and broken bricks.

My first throw was too feeble. It grazed the window and dropped back to the ground.

"Put your shoulder into it," Arlene coached.

On the second try, I heard the sharp crack of the window, the brick landing with a thud, the sprinkle of glass all around it. We snatched up one brick for my mother who was not permitted to want anything, one for Arlene's father and his whiskey. One for not wanting, one for needing too much. We danced back and forth at the foot of the building, sailing one brick, then another through the windows, laughing at the rainfall of glass inside.

Although we'd walked half the night, we were only a few blocks from home. "Let's go," she said and then we were racing each other back, jostling our way upstairs, tumbling gleefully into Arlene's bed.

We didn't call it fucking in those days, but that's what it was. It was exuberant and tender, rowdy, inventive. Somewhere out there in candle-lit rooms, women were actually writing and publishing that penetration was wrong for us lesbians, not sufficiently egalitarian. But that didn't stop us. We had fingers, tongues, and kisses, thousands of places to enter, and jokes about who might hear. Then the jokes stopped because now we were

122

flying, new realms opening before us. Just when I thought I would die of exhaustion, that I'd lived through the last orgasm I would ever have in my life, we were kissing again. I was riding her, and she was rolling and riding me and I came and she came and finally, just before the street lamps clicked off, we fell together into the richest slumber.

In the morning the room was awash with light—not my room; Arlene's. I was in Arlene's bed and there she was, sitting on the edge of the bed, half dressed for work already in a shirt but no pants, putting on her socks. When she heard me stirring, she turned to face me. Every muscle in my body expected she would lean down and kiss me. But she didn't.

"How soon do you have to leave?" I asked.

"Twenty minutes."

Something in her tone made me sit up, made me pull the blanket and sheet up with me, to cover my shoulders and heart.

"Frannie," Arlene said. "We probably shouldn't have done this. Let's not do it again."

She was wrong, of course. We were just getting started.

"It would be so complicated," she said.

"It already is," I told her, which I immediately regretted. "Don't worry, Arlene," I assured her. "We can stop if that's what we decide."

Sex does not equal love, I knew this. I had kept my eye on the difference, had proved the point with a dozen or more men, a half dozen women. But what about when love and sex line up, and not only that, but you already happen to live with the person, you've just treated her to your whole life story, even the most gruesome parts?

"We'll talk later, Arlene," I said.

"But not tonight," she told me. "I need time, a day or two of normal life. You think we can do that, Frannie, talk in a couple of days?"

"Sure," I said. "We can do that."

I was scheduled to work another late shift anyway. I'd cut out of Hard Rain at a quarter to eight, take myself to a movie, then come home when she slept, and sleep until she left for work. The following night was my turn to cook. I'd ask Kelly to swap with me, and invite myself over to Gregory and Martin's for dinner. I tried not to leap to any conclusions about moving out. I tried not to think about the taste of Arlene under my tongue.

But there was no avoiding her. She was awake when I came in from seeing *Three Women*. Waiting up, or so it seemed, at the kitchen table. I could have said hello and kept walking, but I sat down.

"I have the day off tomorrow. I can sleep in," she told me, and she reached over to tuck a strand of hair behind my ear.

We didn't talk, we went straight to my bed. After that, there was little to discuss.

There was only the question of telling the housemates—one-on-one, in a meeting, or not at all. Not at all, I said. Why make a big deal out of it? Recently Jane had broken up with Kim and started bringing home a black woman named Clarice, a second year medical student with a narrow, solemn face. Everybody made room for Clarice in the kitchen in the morning. Nobody asked what she and Jane had been up to all night.

"They're studying," Arlene said, and she kissed the small of my back. "But you and me, Frannie. This changes the whole dynamic of the house."

"Doesn't have to," I told her, although twenty-four hours earlier I'd been thinking about moving out.

"Okay," Arlene said, "you do what works for you."

In the morning she made coffee and carried it to my room. We sat with our backs propped on pillows against the wall. She told me about her twelve-step meetings and meditation group, about the endless reservoir of peace in her heart.

"So are you still a socialist?" I asked.

"Of course I am," she said, "but we're shaped by much less than history."

Arlene had never given up looking into the faces of downtown winos in hope or dread of finding her father. Her mother Vi still lived on the far south side of the city, and Arlene spent Sunday afternoons with her at least once a month. She brought flowering cacti and begonias on all the right holidays—Christmas, Valentine's Day, Mother's Day, Vi's birthday—and never complained about Hallmark having invented most of the occasions.

She moved my coffee cup off the bed to lean over and kiss the inside of my wrist. "Acceptance changes the quality of love," she said. "There's freedom in loving without an agenda."

Later that morning, on my walk to work, I stopped at a florist's with an FTD delivery sticker in the window. A bell chimed when I open the door. How much would they charge to wire a simple bouquet to Mt. Kisco? I asked. For my mother, who was recuperating from surgery. When pressed to choose an enclosure card, I picked out the one that said "Get Well." I had officially begun training as a lady who visits.

~ Six ~

I can point to the exact moment I decided to never have children: It was in May of sixth grade, the end of a long, hot, uneventful afternoon. In a few minutes, the bell would send us spilling out to the line of yellow buses waiting with their motors idling, their exhaust drifting in through open windows. Mrs. Dolan sat on the front edge of her desk, close to her students. Her green cotton skirt was hiked up a little and I could almost reach out from my first-row seat to touch her knee, covered in nylon. She was telling us about an article she had clipped from the *New York Times*. Too sleepy to listen well, I leaned back and watched the words form on her lips. "Sociological," she said, and it looked like she was blowing smoke rings. "... report on research results."

Then in a flash I became alert to what she was saying. "People who were abused or neglected as children grow up to do the same to their own kids." She didn't say "more likely," or "unless they work very hard to do it differently." She said unequivocally "they do," and "they" meant me.

Maybe Mrs. Dolan wasn't speaking directly to me. Maybe she didn't know about my life at home—my father's cruelty, my mother's slow fade, my brother first gone and now dead. Or maybe the researchers meant something different by "abuse" and "neglect." Even so, the knowledge rang through my body: I am never having children. I looked around to make sure I hadn't spoken this vow out loud.

It wasn't a new thought, only confirmation of the danger I'd always felt, the dread that tightened in my twelve-year-old chest at the sight of infants in strollers. I begrudged them their neediness. This, I feared, made me selfish.

I knew only one adult woman, Uncle Frank's sister Bea, who had no children—and it was not that she didn't; she couldn't. My other aunts tut-tutted over Bea's barrenness, much as they did over Vera's illness. Even so, my instinct was to refuse motherhood. Now, thanks to Mrs. Dolan, I could recast this impulse as a righteously selfless stance. I would use my own body as a roadblock.

Mrs. Dolan set the clipping on the desk beside her thigh. "Questions?" she asked. "Comments?" No one said anything. My classmates and I sat, suspended in awful silence until the bell rang.

"Have a good weekend," she called, as if nothing had changed.

~ Seven ~

Arlene drove with me back to New York exactly one year after Donna's wedding, stood behind me in doorways, watched like a stage mother while I stepped into rooms and played my parts—the lady, the daughter, the sister, the sister-in-law who visits.

Sister and sister-in-law to Donna and Billy only. Gloria I couldn't handle. "I can't draw a circle big enough to hold us both," I told Arlene. But Gloria, Tina, and Mike lived in a separate world. Only an hour away, they turned up on my mother's doorstep as infrequently as I did. I could act as if they didn't exist.

Arlene stood witness while I practiced detaching with love, resisting the urge to persuade anyone of anything. "Notice the urge," she coached, "honor it. Just don't act on it."

Vera was up and dressed when we arrived. She wheeled herself to greet us at the front door. She'd just had a bath; I could tell when I bent down to kiss her and came up with a noseful of talcum powder. And she did sit more easily in her chair, the result of having had her nerves cut. I was traveling, I had told her, with one of the women I lived with—a manageably ladylike half-truth.

"Pleased to meet you," she said to Arlene. "How good of you both to come."

I heard a footstep on the stairs above us, lighter than Anthony's, and I fished around for a smile with which to greet Consuela, but the woman who came down was darker than Consuela, and broader in every dimension.

"I don't think you've met Nadine," my mother said.

"Hello." Nadine nodded. "How nice of you to visit your mama."

I might have run and hid from embarrassment, but Arlene was blocking my exit, looking on, slow and steady as a metronome. I slowed down my breathing to match hers.

"Nadine stays with me on the weekends," Vera told us, "when Consuela goes to her own family."

"That's good," I said.

So Anthony had listened to me, more or less, but had excused himself from the attendant care rotation. Now he could come and go guilt-free at all hours. My mother no longer stayed alone for a day at a time. Instead of piss, the house smelled like some cloying chemical air freshener. I resisted the impulse to tell Vera, You see?

"You're doing great," Arlene told me in bed that night in Donna's guest room. "Things can change for the better. Let your mother claim it as her success."

But some things had changed for the worse. Vera, for instance, no longer lobbied me to visit when Anthony was around. Much as I had chafed at the requirement, it troubled me to see her abandon a strongly-felt principle. If I hadn't asked when he'd be home, not an easy question to broach, we would have spent a week in Mount Kisco without ever crossing his path.

"I'm unsure of his schedule." Vera's dignified bearing could not mask her embarrassment. "Why don't you leave a message with his answering service?"

I left the message, and he showed up at five-fifteen on the dot the night Arlene and I were there for dinner. "Nice to meet you." He shook her hand. "Is this your first time in New York?"

"No," she said, "I visited seven years ago, with a different friend." She'd been eighteen at the time, traveling with an older lover who was prone to jealous fits, but she spared him the details.

Anthony looked less weary, more buoyant, than he had the week of Donna's wedding. He carried fifty-nine years as if they weighed nothing. "This tastes excellent," he told Consuela, gesturing with his fork at the lamb chop on his plate. "Quite tender."

His mannerisms and polite chat reminded me of my brother-in-law Mike, but Anthony's routine was a little rough around the edges, his repertoire of pleasantries underdeveloped when it came to addressing his own wife and daughter. Near the end of the meal, while the rest of us concentrated on our roasted potatoes because we'd run out of things to say, he raised the indelicate subject of welfare cheaters.

"Did you see it in today's paper?" he asked. "One woman was cashing five checks every month, three of them issued to people in prison. That's how they are."

Were the people in prison actually women in prison? I wondered. Who was taking care of their kids? But while I mused about how to lodge a lady-like disagreement without ruining Vera's good time, Consuela took up Anthony's statement and ran with it.

"Americans look at me and think welfare just because I'm an immigrant. I worked hard since I got here, my sisters and children too. People who don't work, they should leave."

"Just as my father worked hard when he came," Anthony told her.

"Yes," she said, "the same."

I could tell we were watching a ritual drama, listening to speeches that had been made possibly a dozen times before. Far from bringing up a controversy, Anthony had introduced the one topic that joined him to someone at the table. I felt bad for my mother, left out as usual, but if she minded, it didn't show. Vera sat quietly, breathed deeply, and savored yet another success: her husband, attendant, daughter, and daughter's friend eating together, and no personal insults traded. Consuela and Anthony were still agreeing vociferously when Arlene and I stood up to clear the table.

The wedding present I had bought for Donna and stolen back sat on the floor of my closet in Chicago for months. The big square box wrapped in silver and blue paper made me flinch every time I walked past. Opening it and putting the bowl to use would have been worse. So I'd kept it around, a chronic reminder of unfinished business.

"Ship it to them," Arlene told me more than once. "Tell them you made a mistake."

I took her advice finally, a month or two before we drove east for our visit. I packed the gift in a carton in a nest of shredded paper and enclosed a note that read, "This is a wedding present I brought with me last year. In all the commotion that day I forgot to carry it in from the truck." An innocuous lie, and it worked.

When Arlene and I arrived at Billy and Donna's, I saw the bowl piled high with nectarines and plums, displayed at the center of the dining room table. There was no need to speak about the gift, the wedding, or the fight that preceded the wedding, and we didn't talk about Vera either. I'd resolved to leave my sister alone on that score. She had taken care of me as a kid—by letting me tag along, by climbing into my bed at night after the worst of the screaming matches with Anthony. She's the one who calmed me down, who kept me from spontaneously combusting. Who was I to fault her now for not looking after our mother?

Perhaps Vera didn't need looking after. No more shouting or violence erupted in her home. She could count on a bath and three meals every day. Neither Consuela nor Nadine seemed to bear any grudges. They responded efficiently to her infrequent requests. A fog had drifted in to fill the rooms of her house, a polite and perennial hush. I could still imagine better for her—true companionship, joyful noises, more inspired menus. But I could no longer imagine pressing my point.

Arlene rode along with Donna and me all over the county, followed us into the woods and out across the dam, let us drag her to all our old favorite haunts. We roused her at dawn on the morning we saved for the beach, so we could beat the traffic out to the Island, be first in line at the toll booth to Robert Moses State Park, find that perfect spot near the edge between dry sand and wet to spread our blanket. Arlene flattered Billy about the beauty of the house, complimented Donna on the delicacy of her cooking.

Donna had no such praise for Arlene, but neither did she ask why I brought her. She escorted us to the double bed in her guest room without batting an eye, and on several occasions handed the plumbing business back to her mother-in-law so she could pal around with us. I reaped the benefits Arlene predicted of loving with no hidden agenda, no need to harp on what had—or should have—transpired. My friendship with my sister was magically restored. Billy seemed notably distant, but he and Bill Senior were booked up at work. And he and Donna had already sailed into choppy waters.

Not content with the house she'd married into, Donna had pushed Billy that first year to expand and refine—a screened-in porch off the kitchen, a deck off the bedroom above, a half bath in a downstairs closet. Instead of ignoring his work as she had in the months before the wedding, now she stayed by his side, and persuaded him to teach her the skills. "I'm not confident of the roughing-in yet," she told Arlene and me, "but I can handle the finish work on anything he starts."

She had her eye on a second farmhouse down the road, abandoned longer and even more dilapidated than the first. "We'll make a fortune if we fix it up and sell it," she said.

"I don't need a big after-hours project," he said that night at supper.

"I need it," she told him. "What do I do all day but sit on my butt? It won't be hard. You can be my foreman. I'll do eighty percent of the work."

"It's true," Billy grinned across the table at Arlene and me. "Donna's really quick. Pretty soon she'll be able to build a house without me."

"Until we have kids," she said. "Then my hands will be full."

Right then, on a hot August night, the room grew chilly. My brother-in-law said nothing. He looked like a wild animal in a cage.

"Billy doesn't want kids," Donna told us.

Arlene and I glanced at each other. I was starting to feel trapped myself.

"I'm not ready yet." Billy spoke with great deliberation. "Having a child is not like buying a house. It's a commitment to another human being."

But Donna was relentless. "'Not yet,' he says. We've only been married a year, but we've known each other nine."

Billy pushed back his chair and stood up slowly. His gestures brought Jimmy to mind. I recognized the body language of passive resistance, of methodically sidestepping a persistent and unreasonable demand. Which left Donna in Anthony's old role—exasperated, panicky, but still believing that badgering Billy would get her what she wanted.

He turned and carried a stack of plates into the kitchen. Arlene helped herself to salad and looked on.

"You haven't talked much about wanting kids in the past nine years," I said belatedly in Billy's defense.

My brother-in-law wasn't listening. He set the dishes on the kitchen counter and walked straight out the side door. I heard the engine on his Ford pick-up turn over.

"I was in high school," Donna said, "and college. I didn't want to mess up my life. But this is my life now—Billy, the house, the business. Tons of room for a baby and he's as unwilling as ever."

"He said he isn't ready."

"What the fuck will it take him to get ready? Back then, I thought he was so considerate. Came to my doctor's appointments, bugged me about taking my pill, volunteered to wear a condom even with the pills, to guard against that one percent of failure. He was doing all that for himself."

"Maybe he'll come around," I told her. I didn't mention how deeply I sympathized with him, how assuredly and viscerally I knew I wouldn't be raising children. It wasn't the same.

Billy could have been the kind of dad who'd stop in to kiss his kids goodnight, or take them bowling once a month on Saturday. No one in his world, including Donna, would have faulted him for playing a minor role. His refusal was enigmatic. He loved Donna. He wasn't a bully. His upbringing had been genuinely better than ours. Yet he steadfastly declined to consider parenthood, or even to explain why not.

"Not ready," Donna mimicked him. "He's a fucking broken record. What am I supposed to do?"

I was still sitting with her and Arlene at the supper table, picking at my salad and casting about for quietly reassuring things to say, when Billy came home through the front door carrying a six-pack of Michelob and a quart of Carvel. He put the beer in the fridge and brought out four bowls and spoons for the ice cream.

"I drove by your new house," he told Donna. "It has potential."

"Yeah?" she asked.

"Only if we get someone else to do the roof."

"Okay," she said, giving him a wide-open smile. Better than beer or Carvel, Billy had brought home a sentence employing the word "we."

A few days later, they stood in their front yard, waving goodbye as I backed the Datsun out to the road.

"Don't forget your seat belts," Donna called after us. "Have fun in Chicago." As if Chicago was a vacation getaway, not our home.

We, in fact, were getting on the road towards Jones Beach, with our bathing suits under our clothes. If my sister knew, she would have said we were crazy. The noontime sun had already chewed up half the sky. The parking lots would be packed, especially on a Saturday, and we'd end up spreading our blanket too close to a garbage can, but none of that mattered. Arlene needed to replace a bad memory with a good one.

The bad time was with the scary girlfriend who screamed at Arlene about everything and nothing, held the keys to the car, prevented her from taking a turn at the wheel, refused to drive her home to Chicago in time to save her job. Arlene ditched the woman at Jones Beach and hitchhiked back to Illinois alone. Whenever she told the story I pictured her as so young, so vulnerable. Only nineteen myself, I didn't depend on anyone for a ride.

We stripped off our t-shirts and shorts, and raced across the burning sand into the water. We dove under the incoming breakers, swam out past them, came up laughing and sputtering. We yelled back at the seagulls wheeling above us, wrapped our legs around each other underwater, let the waves jostle us together and pull us apart. When our skin and throats grew parched from the salt, we swam back to shore and stretched out on a blanket to dry. I reached over and traced my thumb along the line of her shoulder.

"I won't be mean," I said, thinking it would be that simple.

~ Eight ~

I was running an errand in the Loop when I met up with the disability rights movement—not the whole movement, but enough to know the thing I had always wished for actually existed. I was walking down the street carrying a manila envelope of original artwork I'd just picked up from a

131

woman on the Reproductive Rights Committee who temped as a legal secretary by day. The tall buildings downtown turned the street into a wind tunnel, and the wind made my big envelope into a sail. I had to trim it this way and that to keep from being blown over.

I saw the white guy in the wheelchair first—a Vietnam vet, judging from his Army fatigues. He'd parked his chair away from the curb—backed up against the corner of a building so he could catch pedestrians coming from all directions—and he chased after people with his deep, loud voice echoing off the stone façades around us.

"One minute. One minute to read about an important public policy question." He urged passersby to take an orange flyer.

About every fifth person accepted the paper, only a fraction actually read it. The rest were stuffed into handbags and jacket pockets, or dropped casually to the ground.

I snatched one off the sidewalk where it fluttered to my feet, and reached out to stop the businessman who dropped it. "Excuse me," I said sweetly, tapping him on the shoulder. It was an old trick I learned in high school from Nancy Levy. "Excuse me, sir, you dropped something."

He turned around to see. "Stupid bitch," he said, taking a step toward me. I took a step back, and he laughed at my fear. Then he strode off and I was left reading the flyer.

"ACCESS FOR DISABLED PEOPLE," it said, all in caps. The small print was about getting curb-cuts and lift-equipped buses.

A young woman in a wheelchair—a sporty low model, without side panels or arms—pulled up alongside me. "Nice going," she said. "Is it litter or no curb cuts that gets your goat?" She wore fingerless gloves, like bikers do, and held a sheaf of orange papers on her lap. Her light brown hair in a braid was unruffled by the wind. I had never spoken to anyone disabled except my mother.

"Both," I answered, pushing my own hair away from my eyes. "It's arrogance." I waggled the flyer I still held. "This is great. I mean it's terrible. I mean it's great you're organizing. My mother is in a wheelchair."

It would have been better to say "uses a wheelchair," but I didn't know that yet. Her eyebrows shot up.

"Not here," I hurried to correct her impression, "in New York." I looked across the street to the guy with the booming voice.

"That's AJ. I'm Margaret. Over there are Clifford and Pam." She pointed diagonally across the intersection to a black guy and another white woman, both using chairs, handing out orange flyers. I felt like I was looking through the wrong end of binoculars. I had never seen four wheel-chairs in one place in my life, not occupied.

"AJ's the most aggressive," Margaret told me, "although you'd run a close second."

I winced at the thought of the guy in the suit, and at this woman Margaret having witnessed my fear. I turned from her to look more care-fully at the two people across the street. He was another veteran, with both legs amputated above the knee—my own brother, perhaps, if the guy in front of Jimmy had stepped on the land mine. Her upper body was twisted so her chin and ear rested against one shoulder.

"We're done for today," Margaret interrupted my staring. "We demon-strate every Thursday from noon to one. A different intersection every week, two if we get enough people. You're welcome to join us." She put her fingers up to her mouth and gave the kind of whistle only jocks know how to make.

"I usually work on Thursday," I told Margaret, gesturing with the big envelope I carried. "I'm supposed to be working right now."

"Oh, well," she said, "If you ever get the urge." Then she was heading off to rendezvous with her friends.

I watched them take off against the downtown traffic—four wheel-chairs in single file, growing smaller until they became points of motion swallowed by the city. I would have panicked, but I knew how to find them again.

Actually Margaret found me. She came driving up to Hard Rain a few months later when I was working a retail shift. I watched through the front window as a brown van pulled up, the side door opened, and the lift unfolded like a drawbridge. Even before I could see, I was certain it was her, and berating myself for my certainty—a version of "they all look alike"—but it really was Margaret coming through the door, and I stood there grinning.

"Hey," she said, "I know you. Remember me?"

"Of course," I answered. Remember her? I was in danger of idol-izing her.

She had a flyer to print, a thousand offset copies. When I finished writing up the order, she said, "I also want to see about t-shirts."

"We don't normally print t-shirts," I told her.

She wanted to know where else she might try.

"Hold on," I said. "Sometimes we can do a special project."

She wanted to know if a dozen was too few.

"Few is good," I said—all the while thinking how stupid of me, we don't stock t-shirts, I can cut the screen but she'll have to go buy Fruit of the Loom, I should refer her someplace else.

"Are you sure?" she asked.

"Positive. Although you'll have to supply the shirts."

She said, "That's cool. My ex-lover's uncle is in the business—uniforms, men's work clothes, Army-Navy surplus."

"It's a deal, then," I told her. "I'll see you next week."

I let out my breath as I watched her drive away.

Margaret's ex-lover was Ruby, whom for the longest time I heard about but didn't meet. I knew her byline; she covered local politics for the weekly *Chicago Reader*. Ruby's mother died when she was eleven, her father on the day before her twenty-third birthday. She inherited his share of the clothing business plus the home she grew up in—an oddly suburban rambler tucked in among the bigger and older houses in Evanston. Ruby ramped the place when Margaret moved in. When they split up, Margaret stayed on and paid half of Ruby's rent on a third-floor walk-up in Rogers Park. It impressed me that two ex-lovers could be so amicably entangled.

The t-shirts I printed for her read "Disabled Dykes and Friends."

"You can come to our meeting sometime," she said when she came to pick up her order.

"Maybe," I told her, although I couldn't imagine I'd belong. She was the only disabled dyke I knew, and "friends" most likely meant "lovers." All I had was the mother I'd left behind.

Instead of dropping in on the support group, I joined the downtown protests. Just as Margaret predicted when she first sized me up, I became the best leafleteer on the planet—the most persistent, most rowdy, most zealously dependable person on the picket line, in all kinds of weather.

I met all kinds of people. Some had been disabled their whole lives. Some had survived recent accidents. Wounded Vietnam vets and people newly diagnosed with MS. Some lived independently in subsidized buildings, others with their parents. They went to work and school, defended the right to make their own mistakes, to get drunk at inopportune times, spend money erratically, fall into bed with the wrong people for the wrong reasons. A few, with and without disabilities, worked in the system, as rehabilitation specialists. The others eyed them with suspicion. I witnessed all kinds of hierarchical squabbles, and listened to Margaret wail about the difficulty of getting such a motley crew united behind the same civil rights agenda. For me, it was enough that these people existed, and by existing denied whatever their doctors, parents, husbands, wives would've had them believe about themselves.

AJ had a friend Sam who lived in a nursing home and wanted to get sprung, but so far hadn't lined up the resources. In the meantime, Margaret and I picked him up once a month and drove him to where we were leafleting. His friends were taking him shopping, he told the nursing home staff.

"If—I—had—the m-m-oney—to shop, I wouldn't be living—in—that—torture chamber," Sam used to say. I had to struggle to understand his speech, but this was a stock line.

I refrained from pointing out that some people get tortured at home. How did I know for sure he hadn't been one of them? I stayed in the closet, more or less, about my mother having MS, about my father and sister being doctors. I never mentioned to the vets about Jimmy being killed in Vietnam. I just listened, and learned, and made my internal adjustments. I'd been as guilty as the next person of wanting Vera to try, to work harder, to overcome, not necessarily to walk but to engage with the world. My world. But Vera had never been as passive as I'd thought. She used every ounce of her power to stay married to my father, to hold on to the home she had chosen.

I kept my mouth shut about my family and made a niche for myself in the movement: chasing after temporarily able-bodied strangers and imploring them to think about how they too might some day need accessible mass transit. Wouldn't they appreciate it if the buses with lifts were already part of the fleet?

~ Nine ~

My mother's absentee ballot for the 1980 presidential election came in the mail the week I was visiting, a manila envelope tucked in among the department store catalogs. I felt a little surge of hope, a lift in my step, as I strode back up the driveway. At least she still bothered to vote.

For two years we'd been developing our partnership as ladies—the one who visits and the one who is visited—neither of us requiring nor offering much else. But no matter how diligently I worked at paring down my expectations, I still hadn't gotten the knack.

I'd bought a birthday present for Vera at the Field Museum gift shop—a bird feeder with suction cups that stuck to glass. An appropriate present, even Arlene (who'd begged out of this trip) had concurred. I would fill the lucite tube with seed and anchor it to the outside of my mother's favorite window. I would introduce color and movement into her view of the otherwise unchanging spruces.

But as soon as she tore open the wrapping paper, I could see my mistake. The birds would come and eat, the seed would disappear, the time would come to refill the feeder. Who was I to add this task to Nadine or Consuela's job description, to tip the balance Vera had achieved in her domestic affairs? "How nice of you to think of my birthday," she'd said, and I had smiled graciously to conceal my shame.

"Look what's here," I told her now when I brought in the mail. "Have you decided who you're voting for?"

I learned this delicate phrasing as a young child, to ask "have you decided" rather than flat-out "who." Caught between my grandmother, forever loyal to the Democrats, and my father, who picked up Republicanism like a hand prop moments before walking on-stage and into the bright lights of the middle class, my mother always defended the privacy, the sanctity, of the voting booth.

"Let me know if you want me to fill it out," I said, striving for a tone of casual respect.

"Oh. Your father will fill it out."

"Ma." I couldn't stop myself and Arlene wasn't around to stop me. "Do you trust him? How do you know he writes down what you tell him to?"

She said, "He puts down whatever he thinks is right."

"That means he gets two votes and you don't get any."

She made a face like I was giving her a headache. "I don't keep up so well with the news anymore."

She had a radio right next to her bed. Maybe she needed a different one, with bigger buttons, a more manageable dial, but she didn't want me to bother.

"You mean you don't want to be bothered."

"Yes," she said. "Perhaps that's right."

"Then let me have your vote. I want two votes, I want two." I shook the manila envelope at her, rattling it just out of her reach. I felt how easy it could be—how natural, like water running downhill—to become the tormentor.

"Let me fill it out," I said. "Why him? Why not me?"

"Frannie, stop!" she yelled.

I stopped. She was not a person who yelled.

"Put it on top of the piano," she said quietly. "Gloria will help me with it. I have a few weeks to decide."

Gloria! Just hearing my sister's name sent a shock through me, similar to the one I'd experienced when I spotted Mike's book one day on the paperback rack at the Sulzer library. I wasn't prepared for the impact of his photo on the back, a ripple from head to toe: I used to know him, not very well, but now I didn't know him or my sister at all. Gloria, I assumed, stayed as distant from Mount Kisco as she had when I was a kid. That was why I didn't see her.

She had brokered the nerve-cutting operation for my mother, but since then I'd heard no mention of her. Vera passed along bits of news about Tina—her confirmation, her summers at horse camp, but never anything about Gloria or Mike. If my path didn't cross Gloria's, it was not by my design. It hadn't occurred to me that she might visit Vera with any regularity, might stay away on purpose when she heard I was coming to town.

"Do you see Gloria much?" I asked, trying not to sound accusatory.

Vera looked caught, as if calculating her odds of escape. "Sometimes," she said, and for some reason this was a big admission.

Surely Gloria and I weren't still fighting about Donna's wedding, about my misbegotten too-tight clothes. For me, that memory had lost its sting.

"We were confused, Frannie," Billy had said to me one night when we'd all gone one beer beyond our limits—six for him, four for Donna, two for me. "How could a person who objects to the use of the word 'tits' go to such lengths to show us she has them?"

Donna had tried to shush him, but I didn't let myself take offense. "You've got a point there," I said, and, chortling sloppily, we'd closed out that chapter of family history. Was it perhaps still open for Gloria?

I rattled the absentee ballot one more time before putting it on top of the piano. "Donna is the best person to help you with this," I told Vera.

"We'll see," she said, very firmly.

Billy and Donna were working arduously the week I was in town to get farmhouse number two in shape for a walk-through by a potential buyer. Donna had worked too painstakingly on her own, had lagged far behind schedule. Summer had slipped into autumn and they needed to put the place on the market. Billy would be damned if he was going to heat an empty house through another winter.

I sat on an empty pail in the corner of the kitchen while the two of them brought a ceramic tile backsplash to life. The rasp of the tile saw underlined their words.

"All right, already," Donna told him. "I'm too slow. Next time I'll be faster. At least I rounded up a buyer."

"Don't count your purchase agreements before they're signed," he said. "For all you know she keeps calling you because she's lonely."

"This time, we'll break even," Donna said. "Next time, we'll turn a profit. That's a pretty good learning curve."

"If there is a next time," Billy told her.

I didn't have the nerve to ask what had become of their baby-making discussion.

Later that same week at their house, I was again reminded of Gloria's existence. Donna, Billy, and I were watching the eleven o'clock news. Or rather, they watched and I watched my step, careful not to criticize or judge, not to complain too much about the poor quality of information— all arsons and neglected children, interrupted by ads for Honda station wagons and laundry detergent. One ad would have slipped right by me, if not for Donna's peculiar reaction. It showed a series of earnestly beautiful people, three or four women and one man, shot through gauze or a greasy lens, talking dreamily about the changes plastic surgery had wrought in their lives. A woman in voice-over, authoritatively resonant yet nurturing said, "You have the right to feel good about how you look." Then a screen of text came on, with the name and phone number for a Manhattan plastic surgery clinic.

Donna, who had sacked out on the couch, now sat bolt upright and stared at me with an unmistakably guilty expression.

"What?" I asked her.

She looked caught, just as Vera had. "That was Gloria," she said.

She meant our sister's practice, not any of the actors in the ad. By her own industry's standards, Gloria is nothing to look at. "Weird," I said, for lack of anything better.

Billy snorted and rolled his eyes, his opinion of Gloria no better than that of Anthony.

"That's a nice car," I said about the next ad.

Donna sank back against the couch cushions, apparently satisfied there would be no confrontation. Poor Donna, caught in the middle between one sister who marketed nose jobs as an inalienable right and the other who didn't even shave her legs. Around me, she acted like our oldest sister had ceased to exist. Did she do the inverse with Gloria? Better not to ask, I decided. Better not to lose any sleep over what I might have been missing.

I found it easiest of all, once I quit trying to reform him, to carry on a casual conversation with Anthony. He had his work, his mobility, his travel. He had the hours he donated to a new mentoring program at the hospital, one that matched more established doctors with those who were just starting out.

"In my day," he told me, "we were left to sink or swim." He filled a demi tasse for me and one for himself. My mother and Nadine were both in their rooms—Vera sleeping, Nadine reading the Bible.

Anthony took a swipe across a fresh lemon with a peeler, and floated a ribbon of rind in each of our cups. His days of drinking Sanka had come and gone. If I moved my spoon, I could hide the chip in my saucer.

He was planning his semi-retirement and had found a new slant on international travel—his own Great Humanitarians tour of the world. No more Cook's vacation packages for him. It had started with an article in the Times about Albert Schweitzer. Next Father Damien caught his interest, and of course Mother Teresa. He drew a timeline with his fingertip along the edge of the kitchen table, and marked off his itinerary in reverse order for the next few years: Calcutta, by 1983, to witness the Missionaries of Charity's work up close. Schweitzer's hospital in Lambaréné, Gabon in '82. One needed to make an application there; at the moment he was looking into the requirements. For this year he'd already booked his ticket to Hawaii, where he planned to visit the former leper colony at Kalaupapa.

"People were stigmatized and horribly mistreated," he told me.

These days, they called it Hansen's disease, not leprosy. Medical breakthroughs had made it more manageable. The desolate point of land where in the past leper outcasts were dumped had recently been developed into a national park. A few survivors still lived there by choice. The only ways in were a day-long hike, by mule pack, or small plane.

"I'm deciding between the mules and the plane," Anthony said. "At my age, the walk sounds much too strenuous."

"Who are you going with?" I asked. It was just an intuition.

"No one. By myself," he said.

By the time of Ronald Reagan's so-called landslide election, I was safely back home in Chicago. Arlene and I sat in the kitchen, reading the front page of the *Tribune*, when Mimi came down for her coffee that morning.

139

"As if electoral politics change anything," she said.

"There are going to be a lot more poor people," Arlene corrected her. "We'll see more burglaries, and a lot more prisons."

If we didn't get all vaporized first in a nuclear war. Here we were, facing doomsday, and Gloria, the thief, had probably gotten two votes.

~ Ten ~

It was Donna who suggested and scheduled her visit to Chicago. "I'm working too hard; I need a change," she told me on the phone.

"Why not wait a couple of months for summer?" I said. "The lake will be beautiful, and there's a ton of free music."

But she was raring to book a ticket on a seven-day advance. She and Billy were having a rough time. Their after-hours business—by now farmhouse number three—could provide only so much distraction.

Arlene and I were getting along well enough to share her room for four nights and make mine into the guest room. I cleaned it from top to bottom, bought sorely-needed new sheets for the bed, left little chocolate mints on the pillow. I imagined scooping my sister up, letting her relax in our care, but she was about as easy to scoop up as a sea urchin.

From the moment she walked in, Donna ran an appraiser's eye around our house. She paid scant attention to the architectural details I loved so well—the radiators painted gold, the octagonal tiles in the bathroom, the way the maple in the kitchen glowed like a still-living tree in the afternoon light. Instead, she focused on every poster and refrigerator magnet, every emblem of lesbian pride. She stood in front of the bookcase to pore over the titles, sat on the edge of the sagging couch to flip through a crate of records.

"Why does everything have to be about women?" she asked.

I found myself defending the art I was fond of—my favorite Joan Armatrading album, a polarized photograph by Tee Corrine of two women, one in a wheelchair, getting it on—along with the things my housemates and I routinely made fun of, but nevertheless seemed to collect—songs about cats and unicorns, pen-and-ink drawings of vaginas as flowers, badly-rhymed poetry about finding love with a sister.

"It's like red-white-and-green flags," I told Donna. "Or t-shirts that say, 'Kiss Me, I'm Italian.'" Embarrassing, but essentially harmless.

She shivered as if frost was settling along her spine. "I feel like I don't belong."

I wanted to say something to melt her. You're my sister, of course you belong, but the words stuck to the roof of my mouth.

She liked my bedroom, at least—the spaciousness, the abundant light. She set her backpack down at the door, and wandered over to my painted table and chairs. "You did these?"

I nodded, held my breath, and waited for a compliment—a comparison to the paintings I did as a child, a chance to tell her how the landscapes poured out of me that first month in Chicago. But no compliment came. She sat down on the bed to pull off her Frye boots, and the chocolates on the pillow went sliding to the floor. I hurried to retrieve them and set them on the table.

"Why don't you leave your boots on? We'll go to the Art Institute," I said. Anything to get out of the house. I'd take her to see my new favorite paintings.

Somewhere along the way, I had lost interest in the Dutch Masters, and had become enamored instead with the Blue Riders. Gabrielle Münter in particular caught my interest, but I didn't tell Donna. You see, she would have said, it's women, women, women.

Diversion was the name of our game. For three days, I dragged her to all the tourist attractions in town—the Museum of Science and Industry, the aquarium, the planetarium. At night, I took her to restaurants for sushi or pan style pizza. Out in the world, in the midst of strangers, she seemed to remember that we were related. "Look at that wacky fish," she'd say. "Look at that guy's baggy pants." Even as I debated with myself about whether or not her jokes were funny—the old drunk she ridiculed, after all, might have been Arlene's father—I gave in and laughed along with her.

We walked everywhere, our collars turned up against the April wind. Donna hardly saw my housemates, not even Arlene, except in passing. By the time we'd get home at night, she'd be ready for a hot bath. I'd climb into bed with Arlene, who held me while I shivered, who smoothed the hair away from my face and kissed my brow.

"You're doing great, Frannie," she said. "You're doing exactly what you have to." Why I had to was a mystery, except that I'd started and the only way out was through.

Arlene said, "Donna is a very sad person."

I had always thought of people like Willow as sad, people who were watery and diffuse. Donna seemed pissed off to me.

"Try scratching the surface sometime if you can stand it," Arlene said.

"Saturday night, I'm signed up to cook," I told Donna. "We can make a big feast for the housemates."

141

Of all of them, Mimi fascinated her. She was skinny and pretty enough to be a fashion model, but often didn't even bother to comb her hair. "Is she Italian?" Donna asked.

"On her mother's side. On her father's, Greek."

"Doesn't she want to have a baby?"

So that's what was bugging Donna. "Not that I know of," I said.

Plenty of lesbians around town were choosing children, claiming motherhood as a revolutionary act, scheming to bring sperm into their lives—fresh and frozen, from known and unknown donors, delivered by doctors, midwives, friends who were go-betweens, or sometimes by the donor himself in a jar wrapped in a brown paper bag. Sometimes even by fucking. But that's not who we were, my housemates and I, nor what my sister wanted. She had a husband; she wanted him to want a family. They had made no progress in that direction.

Motherhood was stupid, both Mimi and Jane routinely said, an anti-revolutionary waste of time. My own reasons for wanting no children, although more personal, were compatible with theirs. No one said anything so damning in Donna's presence, but we could hardly have been her ideal refuge.

In my fantasy, my sister and I spent all day Saturday cooking up a storm, a five-course meal reminiscent of Sundays at Aunt Julia's. We carried plate upon plate to the dining room table, while my housemates marveled at the abundance and exquisite flavors, and we all basked in mutual appreciation.

In reality, Donna and I got home from the Museum of Contemporary Art with forty-five minutes to spare. Mimi and Monica, Kelly's successor, had both left notes saying they'd gone out for dinner. Donna and I peeled and cubed an eggplant, salted it for just a few minutes, and sautéed it with onions, mushrooms and a big can of plum tomatoes. We boiled a pot of water for rigatoni. The windows fogged up and I sliced some cucumbers for a salad.

"Eggplant with cucumbers?" Donna said. "It's like eating the same vegetable twice." That started a stream of criticism: the knives too dull, the carrots too wilted, the pot for the rigatoni too small. My sister seemed hell-bent on discrediting my life, as if one of us needed to be all wrong.

We carried our bickering from the kitchen to the table. Only it wasn't truly bickering, because I had made an unholy bargain, had given up defending myself and started counting the hours until she left. Only eighteen, and eight of them would be spent sleeping.

142

"The rigatoni is cold," she said.

"Oh, well."

"There's a hair in the salad."

"Oops!" I leaned over to pull it out and gave everyone a huge, fake smile.

It embarrassed me to have Jane witness all this, but she seemed to handle it fine. She and Arlene lavished praise on me and my cooking, but the two of them working at it full time couldn't begin to offset Donna's accumulating complaints. If they couldn't tell that the eggplant was bitter, the rigatoni starchy, what good was their approval?

"She hated cooking at home," Donna said.

What I hated was needing to act as my mother's surrogate. What I hated now was being spoken about in the third person.

"No," I answered, "I liked cooking. I didn't like watching our mother get tortured."

Donna stopped. Three different emotions played across her face in quick succession. Horror first. Then blame—a piercing look that said, How could you? Then, a kind of angry composure.

"You don't know what torture is," she said.

"Yes, I do," I told her. "You weren't home for three years. You didn't see what was happening."

She said, "I was in Latin America, where people really get tortured. Where they get their hands cut off."

"Did you see that?" I asked—not as a challenge, but because the possibility awed me. She still hadn't talked much about her time in Ecuador.

"No, I didn't see that. I'm just saying, that's what torture is."

"Donna's right, Fran," Jane spoke up. "Especially in Chile right now, there's some pretty serious stuff going on. I wouldn't use the word torture so readily."

Donna flashed me a look of sheer triumph.

"Okay," I said. "I misspoke."

No one asked what I'd meant to say, and I didn't try to explain. There was no discussing anything with Donna. Now Jane would think less of me for minimizing how bad things were in Chile.

When my housemates stood up to do the dishes, Arlene gave my shoulder a little squeeze. She was heading out for the evening, to help a friend paint her kitchen. Don't go, I wanted to beg. Be my girlfriend, share my misery, but for the most part, that's not how we operated.

Sitting around with Donna felt like sitting in a smoky room. I picked up the *Chicago Reader*, to scan the weekly calendar and film reviews for something we might both like—not too lesbian, not too left wing. The Art Institute was showing *Fort Apache*. Hitchcock I could have handled, but not a western. "What do you want to do?" I asked her.

"We don't always have to be doing," she said. "In Ecuador, we never did anything at night." Her mouth twisted, like a valve shutting.

I couldn't paint with her hanging around. I couldn't read. We paced our cage until I was about ready to scream. Then I invented an errand. "Walk with me to Hard Rain," I said. "I left my book under the counter."

"Okay," she said. "You haven't shown me where you work."

I hadn't shown her any of my world beyond the house, had entirely blown off a "We Will Ride" rally and Margaret, who got a kick out of meeting other people's families. Maybe I had held out unfairly. Maybe I should have escorted Donna through more parts of my life.

I didn't think we'd find anything happening at Hard Rain on a Saturday night, but through the darkened front windows we could see a light on in the back of the studio. When I unlocked and pushed the door open, a blast of sound hit us—Grace Jones growling, at the top of the volume control, "from the nip-ple to the bot-tle never sat-is-fied." That would be Martin.

I flipped on the hall light so we wouldn't sneak up on him. Even a light coming on would have startled the hell out of me. But Martin was unflappable. He turned down the music and grinned.

"Who's the beautiful babe?" he asked just to mess with her.

"What are you doing here on a Saturday night?" I answered.

"After-hours project." He handed us each a copy—an announcement about a surprise thirtieth birthday brunch for Gregory. Five dollar suggested donation, proceeds to Black and White Men Together. "Everyone's welcome," he told Donna, "even sisters."

"I'm leaving tomorrow," she said.

"Why tonight?" I asked him again.

"Gregory's on a date," Martin smirked. "He thinks I am too."

This was gay open marriage for you—passing up a chance at a friendly fuck so you could sneak around and plan your boyfriend's birthday.

"My date's still on," Martin glanced at the wall clock. "It'll have to be a fast one. If I cancel altogether, I won't have anything to report to Gregory when I get home."

So now Donna knew one of the men in my life. I expected this sort of talk to offend her, but she was relaxing. "We better let you get back to work," she told Martin. "Have fun."

144

Outside, the clouds had lifted. The sky was moonless and far away—full of stars, probably, but only a few reached past the light pollution of the city. Donna and I clutched at our jackets to fend off the cold and walked with our faces tipped up toward the stars. We didn't talk. For the first time all week this seemed fitting.

We wound our way home past the Standard station. "This is where I used to work," I told Donna.

It was a slow night at the station, sort of spooky, with not a single car pulled up to the pumps. As we got closer, I could hear the bass, and then the tinny guitar, and finally the words to "Walk This Way." That would be Eddie's nephew Danny, the one who replaced me, the one who played air guitar for Aerosmith. He was standing at the far end of the cement pad, his back turned to us and the street. There was something familiar about his posture—bent ever-so-slightly forward—and about the rhythmic motions of his upper body and right arm. Then I saw it: he held the nozzle from one of the pumps, he was writing in gasoline on the cement. Just like the time one winter I came across Jimmy and Carl Delassandro pissing in a snowbank behind our house. I was five, pretending to walk silently in the woods like Donna's school books claimed Indians walked, seeing if I could sneak up on the boys. When I did, they were standing side by side, hunched over just a little, with penises in their hands, writing their names in the snow. A common enough activity for teenage boys, but at the time I thought it was magic.

"He's crazy," Donna said.

I didn't see him strike or toss the match. I heard the woosh of the gasoline catching fire, and instinctively braced for an explosion, but none came. And there it was, D-a-n-n-y, written in flames—high erratic yellow ones that gave way to low blue dancing ones. They flickered, sputtered, complained, and died out. We, and the buildings around us, were all left standing.

"He's crazy," Donna said again. "He could set the whole neighborhood on fire."

Danny went inside and sat down. He was drumming with two pencils on the edge of the counter when we walked past the window. He recognized me, I'm sure, but acted like it meant nothing. Clearly, Donna and I posed no threat.

"What an asshole," Donna said.

"I'll call Eddie when we get home," I told her. But I couldn't keep the amusement out of my voice. Way to go Danny, your name in lights. And all those months I'd believed the whole place would explode if someone so much as dragged on a lit cigarette.

~ Eleven ~

Arlene and I, lying on the couch reading the Sunday *Tribune*, her head pointing north and mine south, our legs a tangle in the middle. Arlene and I, getting a jump on things at the laundromat, at six o'clock every Monday morning. The two of us, sitting in the Japanese garden, watching the falling snow draw an outline of each pine branch and stone lantern. Arlene smiling, watching over, approving, disapproving—for five years. Her faith in me persistent as the sunrise. Every move I made a confirmation, or a disappointment. I knew you could do it, Frannie. I know you still can. I felt so crowded sometimes, I wanted to hit her. The blanket I threw over that impulse muffled the more joyful ones as well.

Arlene, the butch big sister—always standing by, always doting. I admired the person she wanted me to become, but other women turned my head on the street. With Arlene, I didn't walk so tall. I had deftly avoided the pitfalls of mistaking sex for love, but what if I had mistaken love for sex? As much as I tired of it, she did too. Neither of us knew how to say, "That's all folks," how to put it into forward or reverse.

Arlene's biggest worry was that I'd leave her, mine that we'd commit to a lifetime of mutual deprivation. I'm the one who became hateful first, who tapped in to that daily dose of meanness—the curt words, the jealous reactions, just like a teenager. We hissed at each other in the kitchen and hallway, held full-blown whispered arguments in our bedrooms, slammed doors with only a fraction of our strength, always toning it down in our housemates' presence. At Foster Beach we yelled at the top of our lungs, not caring that strangers listened. We fought about everything and nothing. I'd order her out of my sight, then chase after her to say I didn't mean it. She's the one who walked off the set eventually, but it took idle threats, false starts, structural adjustments. It took me saying, "I've never lived on my own."

"Okay," Mimi and Jane both replied when I announced I had rented an apartment in the neighborhood. Their indifference I accepted as my penance for all the verbal swipes they'd seen me take at Arlene.

On moving day, Arlene lent a hand. She hauled my boxes up three flights of stairs, looked around the apartment, and said, "It's a nice space.

You'll be happy here. Good for you, Frannie." I wanted to kill her. I didn't even thank her for helping. I waited until she, Gregory, and Martin had gone. Then I locked the door, put the chain on, and smashed a box full of thrift-store plates and glasses—one at a time, hard, against the oak floor. I swept the pieces back into the box; they'd come in handy some day for an art project. Years later, I'd find an occasional shard with my bare feet.

Arlene slept over, but only when invited. I gave back the keys, stayed out of the fridge and house business when I went to see her. It was their house, not mine, not any more. I gave the exact same considerations I took for myself, never expecting her to invent her own. But Jane was applying for residencies in other states and Arlene had grown weary of adjusting to strangers. She took a job at the Belmont Community Hospital and rented an apartment on Milwaukee Avenue.

"It's such a pain in the ass to get there," I said. "The parking, the traffic, and the public transportation all suck." As if she should have made my life easier, should have invested in "we" with or without me, kept a fire burning in case I came home. I hated myself for thinking like this, and even more for letting it show.

We were sitting on the Belmont Rocks, eating pickled herring on crackers while the sun set behind us. "I'm finished, Frannie," she said. "This time I mean it. This time I'm making it stick." She threw a cracker to the gulls, stood up and walked away. I didn't run after her, or shout her name, or demand that she finish the conversation.

I should have called her on the phone to thank her. But I was too busy learning how to live between girlfriends without her—how to sail alone in my bed without saving her a space, to sleep in the middle so the bed wouldn't capsize.

~ Twelve ~

A month or so after Jimmy left for boot camp, my father asked my mother on a date. It was near the end of summer, a few days before her forty-fifth birthday, and the wind that whipped itself up before a rainstorm was just starting to stir through the trees. For the birthday itself, Donna and I planned to bake a cake for Vera from a Duncan Hines mix. We planned to give her the same writing paper and Esteé Lauder cologne we gave every year. On the birthday itself, Anthony would end up having a jealous fit about the card from Jimmy. But on this night, he tried something new.

He came home from the office, spread a newspaper on the dining room table, and told her, "Come on, I'll take you to a movie."

I was nine. I was playing on the staircase with plastic horses, making them climb the high narrow slope of the banister, then leap and bound down carpeted steps to the bottom. I spied on my parents through the open archway.

"What movie?" she asked, and it was as if she doused a single candle with a bucket of water.

He said, "Sit down with me and look." But whatever spark he carried home with him was gone. All he had left was his plodding determination.

They sat side by side to pore over the listings. My palomino pony drank at a mountain spring. No matter how many times Vera smoothed down the paper, the breeze from the open window came and rustled the pages. Anthony said "no" as often as she did. They took turns reading off titles and rejecting the other's suggestions. Irritability curdled the air between them.

And then, "Heh, heh," my father said, "We could always see *The Killing of Sister George*."

"Please, no!" My mother's shriek which meant they were talking about sex was an octave higher than usual. My palomino pony froze in mid-flight.

"Why not?" Anthony pressed Vera. "It says it right here: they were three consenting adults in the privacy of their own home."

An inexplicable insight sped through me. This movie my father named which I knew nothing about, this sex joke he told which provoked double the usual horror in my mother—this joke about a movie was not merely about sex. Somehow, it was particularly about me. A secret I didn't know I'd been keeping was now exposed. I understood this without logic, and without taking the time to calculate that three adults must have included either two men or two women. Just the word "three" resonated with possibility.

"Yes," Anthony carried on with the same villainous chuckle. "It's rated X. Don't you want to see it?"

"No, I don't," she said.

"Come on. People do these things. It's good for you to take a little look."

"Stop!" she nearly screamed, and you could tell she meant business.

~ Thirteen ~

The first time I met Ruby, she was reporting on a big "We Will Ride" demonstration where I was behaving badly. But not nearly as badly as the schmuck in the delivery van who tried to nose his way through our barricade by rolling into Margaret's wheelchair.

"Leave my friend alone," I yelled. Forgetting all the agreements we made in civil disobedience training, I scrambled up the front of the van. So now what? I hung onto the windshield, nose-to-nose with a guy not much older than me who was not laughing anymore, now that he had a lunatic in his face. I hadn't the slightest idea what to do.

I heard Pamela say, "Get his license plate."

"I've got it," Margaret said, and she meant it literally. She grabbed hold of the frame around the van's front plate and started tugging and rocking, which made it difficult for me to keep my perch. The driver threw the van into reverse. Margaret let go to save her hands. I jumped clear, landing in a heap at her feet.

Margaret laughed and rubbed at the scraped-up leather palm of her glove. I looked up from the ground to a woman standing above me with a steno notebook and bemused smile. "I guess you two showed him," she said. I stood up and brushed myself off, so Ruby and I could be properly introduced.

I thought Margaret would be mad at me for calling so much attention to myself, as if she needed me to protect her. But a couple of days later, when I went to her house for dinner, she only wanted to tease me about Ruby.

"You two sure had some sparks going."

"Really?" My face flushed a hot red.

Margaret was making vegetarian egg rolls, her latest obsession from the *Moosewood Cookbook*. They turned out spectacularly the first time, and for a few weeks were all she ever wanted to eat. She, of course, owned a Cuisinart. She had no patience with temporarily-able-bodied types like me who imagined that the labor-intensive way was the counterculturally righteous way.

"Hell, yeah," she said over the clamor of motor and blades. "Ruby admires the fight in you. Same thing she admired in me."

I might have thought Ruby and I eyeing each other would bother Margaret, but she was already eyeing David Kushner, Ruby's photographer.

149

"A man," she said with exaggerated brattiness. She piled the shredded ginger in a bowl and started in on the cabbage. "There's no accounting for sexual taste." Then she stopped. Head cocked, eyes wary, she looked braced for me to dump her right then and there, but I didn't care who she slept with. I was impressed all over again by how smoothly she and Ruby managed their transitions.

Times change. People change. No matter how often Arlene and I chanted these sentiments, we couldn't simply allow the changes to come. Somehow we'd been condemned—or had condemned each other—to the realm of all-or-nothing.

"Let me know how it goes with the photographer," I told Margaret.

"And you? You going to give that muckraking journalist a call?"

"Highly unlikely," I said, "I may look, but I won't touch." At the time I still lived unhappily with Arlene.

Several months passed before I saw Ruby again; this time we didn't have a chance to talk. She was covering a tax night protest sponsored by Women Against Militarism at the downtown post office, usually one of my favorite actions. The people lined up in their cars were a captive audience. We clearly knew something they didn't, because while they waited with motors idling to hand over their plump envelopes, we pranced and roller-skated around, dressed up like car-hop waitresses. We carried a tray to each driver's window: Here's your order, sir—or ma'am. The Israeli invasion of Lebanon. What? You didn't order it? But your tax dollars paid for it! Then we'd hand a menu through the window, a leaflet which detailed Pentagon spending. Most people accepted the flyer willingly; it beat reading the owner's manual for their car.

That year, one of the women in the street theater group showed up with props for our trays—clear Pyrex bowls of red Jello, with one or two tiny plastic soldiers floating face-down in each. Brilliant performance art, perfect imagery, everyone said. For a minute or two, I smiled in false assent. But all the while, the fact of my dead brother was hot lava, threatening to burst my seams. I said nothing. I walked away, untied my apron and set down my tray. You can take this demonstration and shove it.

I drove up to Foster Beach and sat for more than an hour. I didn't cry, or think much about Jimmy. I just looked into the blackest part of the lake, rocking myself back and forth to keep warm, and waiting for the explosion that never came, that would have sent the pieces of me flying. When the fire inside me eventually simmered down, I could feel the numbing coldness of the hard sand under my butt, and the prickle of danger when a car pulled up and some guy strode onto the beach. I stood up and took myself home.

A couple of weeks later, Ruby turned up at Gregory's second annual birthday brunch—organized by Martin like the first one, but obviously not a surprise. Ruby had come as a paying guest, not a reporter. It was a chilly blue-sky day, too cold to be outdoors in a cotton shirt, but I slipped out to the back porch to take a break from the body heat inside. Ruby may have followed me, or she may have wanted some fresh air herself. In either case, she pulled up the lawn chair opposite mine and set her mimosa down on the porch railing.

"So, tax day," she said without even a preliminary hello. "First you were there, and then you were gone. Did something happen?"

"The cherry Jello happened," I told her.

She waited.

"I had an only brother who died in Vietnam."

She still waited.

"It was like a game to everyone else, but I couldn't play."

Ruby nodded and said, "I felt a twinge about all the gore myself, and I was only writing about it. That soldier business must have been a direct hit."

Never once did she say, Good for you Frannie. I'm glad you took care of yourself. I'm glad you left when you needed to. When Ruby talked to me, the world became more spacious.

I said, "I couldn't help wondering if someone in their car felt like I did. Trapped on line, just wanting to drop their envelope in the bin and then suddenly being handed this load of grief."

Ruby listened.

I said, "Guerrilla theater, political art, is supposed to do that. Shake people up. But some of the things that get shook—some of the people doing the shaking haven't a clue."

She said, "In theory, the feelings that get stirred up will incite you to say, 'Never another war.' To act towards making that possible."

"No," I said. "I just wanted to kill the woman who brought the Jello."

Ruby smiled at me.

I felt all tuned up when she did—vibrant, resonant, like a pipe blown into, a plucked string. Like a plucked apple, chosen. I took a long look at her: green eyes, slightly crooked nose, straight hair as dark as mine lit red by the sun behind her. Green paisley shirt with the sleeves rolled up to the

151

elbow. Small hands, resting lightly on the arms of the aluminum chair. She emanated a liquid warmth, a glowing force field I could wade right into. Submerged, I could grow gills, learn to breathe underwater. But I didn't even make a move to kiss her, not yet.

~ Fourteen ~

Martin was the one at Hard Rain who insisted that no one worker become indispensable. Two or three of us should learn every task, he believed—ordering, scheduling, bookkeeping, machine maintenance. "No martyrs. We all need vacations," he used to say. This was simply good business sense, which put ours a cut above other movement jobs.

But in the few months before he split, Martin had relinquished each of his skilled tasks, had gradually and imperceptibly demoted himself. By the end he was performing an entry-level production job and none of us—especially not Gregory—understood why. Although Martin had the decency not to leave the business in the lurch, he crafted no such easy letdown for his boyfriend.

"We made love that very morning," Gregory would say—"making love" not a phrase I'd ever heard him use before. "Martin made me late for work. We made love. It was goodbye for one week, not forever."

Martin had booked a ticket to see his sister in New Orleans, had apparently planned all along to stay there. Gregory came home from the poster studio that night to discover dresser drawers and closets half-empty. Martin had packed every stitch of clothes—and the few books, art supplies, and trinkets he'd carried into the relationship eight years before. Everything they bought together, or made together, he left behind.

Gregory, of course, called the sister in Louisiana—a dozen times, a hundred times. Wouldn't quit until she finally put Martin on the line, so that Gregory could extract the most meager information: no, there was nothing to talk about. No, there wasn't anyone else. Gregory could not have done anything differently. Martin didn't plan on returning to Chicago. Yes, he would drop Gregory a line if he ever did. This last one freeing Gregory. He could limit his search to the empty mailbox, could quit hunting for Martin behind every lamppost.

Gregory staggered like a dead man through his day, carrying his suffering heart around in his hands. He wept openly, accomplished little, never could decide where he wanted to be. His work and home had both had the centers gouged out. New centers would grow, but not any time soon. One day, I'd find him circling want ads—determined to rent a place he could better afford, to walk out and shut the door on eight years, to salvage only his own books and clothes. The next day, he'd set fire to the same ads in the bathroom sink. His home, his work, his life. No one could take that away.

"You're in shock," Marvette told him. "Don't make any decisions right now."

The rest of us were not in shock, perhaps our biggest retroactive clue. The two men had never been known to bicker, had scrupulously kept their personal fights—by all accounts, few and far between—out of the workplace. But Martin had become a hazy, abstracted figure toward the end, someone who revealed a diminishing fraction of what he was thinking.

"I knew he was having a hard time. I just didn't know it would swing around and hit me." Gregory had taken to sitting on the old green couch in the back room, repeating the same sentences to anyone who would listen.

I listened, and Marvette. The rest of the collective skirted the back room, and ate their lunches in other parts of the studio. They insulated themselves from the lingering stages of Gregory's grief. Together, Marvette and I made a tag team, a pair of complimentary opposites. She listened standing up, on the fly, quick to dispense advice—most of it useful, I noted with admiration—which she expected Gregory to follow. "Did you box up that stuff like I told you? Did you get some new pictures for your walls? Did you try the wild lettuce drops for sleep?"

Having no advice to give and little to say, I'd sit next to Gregory on the couch and just listen. How they made love that very morning. How he couldn't have expected Martin to leave. The story barely changed, but Gregory did, his voice sometimes tremulous, and sometimes forceful, underlined by his old booming laugh. His body stiffened against the heartache, or sometimes was unexpectedly yielding to my shoulder, my thigh, or my hand against his.

The minute I started kissing Gregory, I thought: this reminds me of something. Some movie, or maybe some lesbian novels from the 1960s where the only way the heroine could make the first move was on the pretext of offering solace. In the 1980s, self-respecting lesbians had sex on purpose. We didn't need to sneak or fall by accident into bed. We had lifted ourselves out of the pulp stereotypes.

In those stories, the touching that starts out as comfort gives way to full-blown passion, but not with Gregory. I felt a thrill rise and expand

153

inside me, no doubt about it—but just when it should have surged and taken over, I felt it evaporate, as delicately as a soap bubble. Gregory and I, giggling a little, managed to back off enough to untangle our arms and legs. We sat on the couch like good friends again—my hand resting matter-of-factly on his knee.

Honey, I thought, some man's gonna scoop you up. I didn't say it. There's no point in rushing a person through his mourning.

~ Fifteen ~

The first time I kissed Ruby, and later when we had sex, she didn't taste right. Meaning, she didn't taste like Arlene. You'd think six months on my own would have reset my olfactory clock, but there I was, still biochemically bonded to someone who no longer spoke to me, recoiling ever-so-slightly from the woman I'd been flirting with for months. I hid my reaction, and who knows what else along with it. It took a couple of weeks—maybe seven or eight tries—to switch my allegiance, to give being with Ruby my all.

We were at my apartment on a February afternoon. Ruby, the expert gardener, had brought over supplies to re-pot my two little house plants—the only living creatures who depended on me for a meal. I was ignorant of their needs, I admitted it. As she finished her task, I came up behind her. Mixed in among the damp earth smells of the potting soil and the newspaper covering the table, there was the smell of Ruby's skin—suddenly familiar in a way that made me think: she's the one. Relief and delight overcame me, and I reached for her. Soon we were fucking like we never had before—with every cell, every molecule. All our edges blurred, but I came first, and when I did, I started crying. A huge sorrow rode in on the wake of the orgasm, and stayed. It brought back my edges, the reality of the bed, the hard winter sunlight coming through my window, our clothes lying in puddles on the floor.

I reached for the top sheet and wrapped it around me, but Ruby seemed undaunted. She drew me closer until my sobs died down. Then she pulled herself up to study me. "Ready?" she asked. And I was. And we were at it again.

I was climbing her back stairs a few months later when I encountered the possibility of forever—not advertising itself, not rushing at me, just sitting there among the pots of shocking blue lobelia that lined the edge of her porch. Ruby had been working at home—alternately banging out an article on her computer and wandering down to dig in her garden in the empty lot across the alley. I was coming from a noon-to-eight shift at Hard Rain directly to her house, as I had two or three nights a week for six months already.

The setting sun burnished the red bricks of her building, making them glow with a life of their own. Many hands had worn the wood of the banister down to satin. The wooden stair treads were scalloped from years of use. As I climbed them I thought, I will never tire of coming here. I could do this every night.

I had already established myself as a person who sticks it out through thick and thin, with people and at jobs. But this was different, more active, rooted in desire. Before I could entirely lose my head, I conjured up a picture of Gregory and Martin, smiling and looking like no end was in sight. I could say what did anyone ever know, but I wanted there to be no end for Ruby and me.

I pushed open the door to her kitchen. She stood there in near-darkness, a mountain of freshly cut oregano on the table in front of her. She was plucking the leaves from the stems. The last bit of sunlight cast a bright orange square on the wall.

"Here," she said. She sniffed her fingers, and then held them out as an offering for me.

When the time came to take a vacation with Ruby, we put the truck on I-90 pointing west. She'd have to meet my family another day. She had already seen the Grand Canyon, so we were heading to the Olympic Peninsula. I had never been any place, except back and forth between Chicago and New York.

I thought the Poconos, the Catskills, the Adirondacks were mountains. All the *National Geographic* photo spreads in the world didn't and couldn't have prepared me for how the West would rise out of the prairie, how the Bighorns and then the Rockies would rise and rise again out of the West. We turned onto side roads, winding our way up through alpine meadows where summer slipped backwards into spring. Cows and sheep wandered insouciantly in front of the car. I recalled paintings I had never appreciated before, ones by artists who lived in the West and whose color schemes always struck me as improbable—pastel oranges and pinks, and grey against beige. In the Badlands and the Columbia River Gorge, those paintings all of a sudden made sense. With Ruby, life on earth made sense.

The further we drove, the more I felt myself tugging and straining against a thousand invisible tethers, each strand as fine as a spider's web, but together they made a cable that would have yanked me back to New

York, would have had me spending my seventh summer vacation in seven years driving east to see my mother and sister. Every time we rounded a curve and an unimaginable view opened before us, I felt a few of the threads snap. Maybe a hundred broke free when I caught my first glimpse of the Pacific, shining in the midday sun. And another hundred when Ruby and I scrambled down to a beach to find that entire spruce trees had become pieces of driftwood, tumbled in the surf and bleached white as a giant's bones.

"Can you believe it?" I asked.

"Oh, yes, Fran." She kissed me. "Yes, I believe it."

"Will you swim with me?"

"You swim. I'll wait."

The Pacific tasted just as salty as the Atlantic, but the breakers seemed colder and more ready to knock me down. While I dodged in and out of the surf, Ruby walked the beach, gathering an armload of driftwood—a dozen or more pieces the size of human forearms and femurs. She'd build a fire, I assumed, but she laid the pieces in a row suspended between two long rails. I got out of the water to watch.

She took the bone she'd selected as a mallet and struck each of the others, tipping her head to listen to the tone the wood gave back. She rearranged the pieces, listened, rearranged again—until she got them perfectly ordered from low to high, and knelt down and played a little tune on her xylophone.

"You are the best," I said.

Later, when the sun disappeared into the water, I pried open the clams we'd bought on the side of the road, cooked them in olive oil and onion over her Coleman stove, and served them on top of linguini in tin bowls.

"Ruby," I said, "I could do this forever." I didn't mean the clams or the Pacific, I meant being with her.

She looked up at me and winked, and I felt the last of the threads giving way.

~ Sixteen ~

When Donna was in tenth grade Home Ec class, she made a dirndl skirt out of brown acrylic tweed with flecks of red, turquoise, and yellow. It turned out lopsided, with a seam that ran curved instead of straight up the hip, and some kind of torque between the skirt and the acetate lining. My mother put it in the orphanage box.

"Why would girls in the orphanage want to wear a lopsided skirt?" Donna asked.

"Well, you're not wearing it and you're not throwing it in the garbage," Vera said.

It was 1968. Vera had stopped going to her Ladies of Charity meetings, but the Ladies sent Mrs. O'Meara as their emissary. "I'll keep you up to date," Mrs. O'Meara told her. "We've adopted Saint Ann's orphanage as our project."

I was only nine, but certain words that came out of this woman's mouth made me cringe. Adopted. Shut-in. Just because Vera was a shut-in, didn't mean she couldn't participate. Mrs. O'Meara brought the orphanage box for our front hall closet—an empty cardboard carton covered in flowered gift paper. Every time we bought something for ourselves—nylon stockings, a lipstick, a sweater—we should buy one for the Saint Ann's girls too. Vera shouldn't worry; one of the Ladies would come and empty the box.

Sometime after Christmas, Mrs. O'Meara showed up with all the supplies for making yarn octopi. The yarn was wrapped around a styrofoam ball for a body and then braided into eight floppy legs. Black felt circles were pasted on for the eyes, and a pink felt crescent tipped up for a mouth. She had a finished sample to show us, a kelly green one, which spread out nicely on a made-up bed, the legs flopping in every direction. Just because Vera was a shut-in didn't mean we couldn't do our part. Every Ladies of Charity household had committed to making six octopi for the orphanage.

"I think we can manage six," my mother told her. But Vera's hands were too shaky, and the task fell to Donna and me.

Donna said, "Nobody wants a stupid octopus on their bed."

"Let them decide if they want it," Vera told her. Besides, she had promised. We had finished four when the bad news came about Jimmy. Once his funeral was over and the casseroles eaten, Mrs. O'Meara didn't stop by. The orphanage box sat for years on the floor of the front hall closet with four octopi, the skirt, and a few Avon soaps unclaimed.

~ Seventeen ~

Ruby and I had been home from our West Coast love-and-freedom-fest extravaganza just a few days when Donna called. Her voice was shaky, and plaintive. "Billy said, 'Not now, not ever.'"

On the first pass, I couldn't hear the distinction. My brother-in-law had insisted for years that he didn't want children. Only by switching from

"I'm not ready" to "No, not ever," did he withdraw the scrap of possibility that had been sustaining my sister.

"What should I do?" she asked.

I hadn't the foggiest. Deep down, I still couldn't imagine caring for a child—nor could I conceive of how or when motherhood had become Donna's strongest desire. Not that she expressed desire very often. The last time may have been fourteen years earlier, when she lit up a cigarette in the back yard and told me, "Billy Paletta is hot. Carla says he's going to ask me out." After that she mostly issued proclamations—I'm going to college, I'm dropping out, I'm going to Ecuador, I'm marrying Billy—statements as likely to obscure as to reveal what she wanted.

"Have you tried counseling?" I asked. Always a safe suggestion, although I'd hardly tried it myself. I must have sounded like Ann Landers. But Billy and Donna had skipped over counseling; they were headed straight for divorce.

"He moved back to his parents' yesterday," she said, sounding dazed, and stricken—like Gregory once had.

I said, "I can be there by the end of the week."

"My sister needs me," I told Marvette, begging forgiveness for messing up the Hard Rain schedule.

"I'm sorry, babe," I told Ruby.

She was retying tomato stakes in her garden, and having heard only a fraction of my family history, had no reason to question me yet. "I'll miss you," she said, and she tore a strip off an old cotton sheet.

"Me, too, Ruby. I'll miss you."

"Will you call me?"

"I'll try. But no promises, okay? Time gets away from me there, something else takes over."

"One call, Fran." She ripped another strip. "That's not asking too much."

"I love you for asking, but it makes me nervous. What if I forget?"

She stopped working and looked at me like I had two heads.

"All right, I won't forget."

I imagined Donna sitting catatonically at the kitchen table, unwashed and unloved, drinking gin all day out of the same cloudy glass. I envisioned walking into her house, prying the glass from her hands, picking her up out of her chair, reminding her that life was worth living.

But Donna had already picked herself up. She was talking on the phone with a lawyer when I arrived. The house looked a trifle neglected, nothing a vacuum cleaner and dust rag couldn't correct. Billy had taken only his clothes, tools, and tropical fish tank. On the surface, it was hard to see the disruption.

"I want to be fair," Donna was saying to the attorney. They were sorting out a proposed compensation for her contribution to the plumbing business. As long as she named a reasonable figure, Bill and Audrey would probably not contest it. Billy's stubbornness had already caused them enough embarrassment.

"Thanks for coming," she told me when she got off the phone.

"No problem." I felt foolish standing there with sweat running down the back of my neck, thinking she needed me. It was the hottest August in New York since 1962.

"Can you help me with some yard work?" she asked. "We were fighting so goddamn much it went to weeds."

"I don't know," I said. "It's pretty muggy out there. Maybe it'll rain soon and cool things off." Of all the domestic arts, gardening was my worst. If I'd wanted to do yard work, I would have stayed in Chicago and picked beans with Ruby.

"What can I help you with inside?" I asked. "Under the ceiling fans."

"How about dishes?" Donna was not as pulled together as she looked. One towering pile of dishes in the sink and a couple more on the counter were starting to smell funky.

She poured a gin and tonic for herself and one for me and sat down at the table. I had correctly predicted her choice of booze, but she didn't belt it down, she sipped it. I stood at the sink with my back to her, tackling the glasses first, then dishes and cups, then silverware.

For a while no one talked, and then Donna said, "I never told you about Ecuador."

"No." I kept my back to her and busied myself with rinsing a bowl. "Not the Peace Corps?" I tried to ask lightly, so I wouldn't frighten her off, but also to let her know I had guessed. She could skip the preliminaries and get to the heart of it.

"Mommy said the Peace Corps, not me. I said 'like' the Peace Corps."

"I don't remember," I admitted.

"I was dropping out of college," she said. "I needed something to do and Melanie Kurtz offered me a deal."

Melanie Kurtz was Donna's freshman year resident assistant in the dorm, a pale, earnest woman from Staten Island. At first Donna had mocked her, but at some point they'd become friends. Melanie had even eaten dinner once at our house.

159

"Missionary work?" I asked. I was pushing my luck, but who knew how long she was good for? I considered pouring her a second drink.

"An outpost of St. Helena's parish," she said. "All expenses paid."

"So why didn't you say missionary work?"

"It sounded too queer," she said, meaning nerdy, or dipshitty. "I thought I'd go along for the ride. Melanie's mother, a widow, was our group leader."

I filled the sink to soak the pots, then dried my hands on a dish towel and sat down across from her. The ice in my drink had melted entirely away. I asked, "Why do Catholics need missions in Ecuador? It's a Catholic country."

"Not any more," she told me. "They're losing ground. The place is crawling with all kinds of fundamentalist wackos. Daddy didn't even argue with me about dropping out."

I said, "He already had his doctor in the family." Irritation flashed across her face. He had gambled unproductively on her bringing home a college-educated man. Two years of tuition down the drain, and Donna still ran home on weekends to see Billy. At least it was only state tuition.

She said, "It was really pretty, in the mountains. The buildings were cinder block, but painted lemon yellow. Orchids grew up the side.

"It was embarrassing. We were supposed to teach Indian kids to read and write in Spanish, but my Spanish was for shit. Often the kids didn't show up. At least the workbooks weren't about Jesus. I skipped the folk masses at night."

Missionary work only benefits the mission, Jane and Mimi used to tell me. The same for international development—it paid off best for the Harvard MBAs in their Land Rovers. But Donna had needed to get out of town, to fit herself into any structure besides the one waiting for her in Mount Kisco: married to Billy, answering phones for the plumbing business, running over at lunchtime to fix Vera a dish of cottage cheese and peaches, to plump her pillow. She got on a plane to Ecuador.

Once there, she saw two kinds of Catholicism operating side-by-side—the love for Jesus that Melanie's mother wanted to bestow on the rest of the world, and a love for humanity that reeked of Marxism, that required involving oneself with the political struggles of the poor. Donna embraced neither; she felt no fervor. The young Americans and some Ecuadorian students would get together at night to swap folk songs and talk about Liberation Theology. The whole thing made Mrs. Kurtz pretty nervous, downright uptight, Melanie used to say. Donna skipped the rap sessions, and went for walks in the cool mountain air. Sometimes she ran into Hector, who worked for the mission. He kept things trimmed and well-oiled, indoors and out.

"I got pregnant," she told me while she fixed herself another gin and tonic.

"I get it." Liberation Theology might have kept her out of trouble.

She said, "At least he wasn't married. He might have offered to marry me if he'd known. I had to get out of there, fast. I had to come up with an excuse for Mrs. Kurtz about why I was abandoning the mission, and still get St. Helena's to buy me a ticket to New York."

She invented an inconsolable case of homesickness—hard to believe, given how people knew her around the mission. She was the one in the group most eager to take excursions down to the coast, to eat octopi and squid which made the German-Americans turn green. It hurt her pride to fake it, but fake it she did. All her worry and stress, her fear about having to walk back to the States, her guilt over suddenly dodging Hector—she took these feelings and used them, pushing them to accelerate and echo inside her body, until finally Donna went to Mrs. Kurtz in tears and begged the woman to let her go home.

"It's called method acting," she said. "I could have become a professional actress when I got back here. I never told Billy about the abortion. I asked him to marry me. I thought the rest would fall into place."

Even if she never told him, Look what I gave up to be with you, it would have been there all along, adding that tinge of desperation to their talks.

"Billy already knows enough about me," she said. "I don't know anything about him."

~ Eighteen ~

Every year in August, starting when I was five, my father filled out my medical form for school. He sat at the dining room table and put a stethoscope up to his ears. I stepped in close to his chair and turned first my back and then my front to him so he could listen to my lungs and heart. The membrane across the stethoscope looked like a circle of wax paper. The metal rim felt cold under my shirt. Anthony made a few marks in the boxes on the form and then it was Donna's turn. He listened, he made more marks. Then he signed the bottom of both pages and folded them up. I put

161

mine in my book bag, alongside the tiny manila envelope that held my first week's milk money.

My mother had her own doctors, and she drove herself to see them. Dr. Kendall first, a gynecologist—one of those words she said with a shudder. Later, Dr. Horn, a neurologist. Every once in a while, Anthony came home from the office carrying a toaster-sized green metal box with an electric cord and an attachment that looked like a wand. He plugged the box into the wall. Vera sat very still in a dining room chair; he stood next to her. When he flipped the switch, the box started humming. He touched the wand to her neck, moved it, touched it again. It was a beauty routine—cauterizing, he called it—to take off the skin blemishes that grew there. To make her neck lovely and smooth. The whole house smelled like burnt hair, like one time when Donna leaned in too close to her birthday cake.

By the time I was ten, driving became difficult for Vera. Donna got a permit first and then a license, and she drove my mother to her appointments. When Donna left for college, Vera stopped seeing doctors. Anthony took care of refilling her prescriptions. She stopped going out into the world, and he no longer brought home the green metal box. He never even listened to her heart through the stethoscope.

~ Nineteen ~

"I feel so bad about Billy and Donna," Vera told me. We were talking in her kitchen on a Monday morning, over glasses of instant iced tea. I would have preferred iced coffee—even Sanka—but as a visitor, I accepted what was offered. "I wish I could help them," she said.

She? Help them? I couldn't imagine how. "They got together as teenagers," I told her. "People grow away from each other. They move on."

When I first rented an apartment on my own, I sent my mother a card—a change-of-address announcement ostensibly, but I enclosed this note: "Arlene has been my lover—more than a housemate or friend—for five years, and now we're breaking up." Five years, at that point, a bit of an exaggeration but I liked its weight. I also enclosed a pamphlet from a parents' group, "We Love Our Gay and Lesbian Children." I knew all too well that Anthony might open the letter first. Either way, I would put myself on someone's map. I addressed it to Vera out of stubborn practicality. She's the one who maintained the Christmas card list.

If I wanted a response from her or Anthony, I didn't get it—at least not for a few months, and then my Christmas card arrived. This time "I hope

162

you are happy" instead of "I hope you are well"—perhaps a significant difference, or perhaps the mark of a writer who paid attention in high school English class when advised to vary her word choice. I knew for sure the address change had been entered.

Now here I was—sitting at Vera's table, making unwarranted comparisons, wondering if she could have mustered any sadness over Arlene and me, any joy over Ruby coming into my life. Here I was, talking tough, as if divorce should mean nothing, as if Donna's fourteen years with Billy had been nothing.

"I know what you're saying," I tried to make it up to her. "I'm going to miss Billy too. Maybe they'll change their minds." But before I could tell if I'd successfully repaired the conversation, the phone rang.

"You answer it," Vera said.

"Vera?" The voice was ebullient, somewhat scratchy, and very Italian-American, a woman with unpolished edges. One of Vera's long-lost cousins from Queens, I ventured to guess, but too happy to be calling with news of a death.

"Hold on, please," I said, and carried the receiver to my mother.

"Hello?" she asked in a cadence much like my own. "Oh, Helen!"

There was no mistaking the delight that crossed Vera's face, and the annoyance that followed on its heels. I had seen the annoyance before: Vera's first line of defense against anyone who ever proposed a visit: Mrs. Camden who prayed, Mrs. West who chatted, Mrs. O'Meara and her charity drives. And yes, probably me. She probably made that put-upon face when I told her I'd be dropping by, but no one in my lifetime had elicited such a moment of uncensored delight.

"Can I call you back, Helen?" she said. "My daughter's here. No, Francesca. The youngest, from Chicago. Well, yes, you can meet her. Yes. We'll be here. Goodbye." Helen, whoever she was, was incredibly pushy.

A few minutes later, I opened the door for a stout, square woman. "I'm Mrs. Gennaro— Helen Gennaro," she said. "You must be Francesca."

She wore crisp linen slacks and an open-necked shirt, no-nonsense clothes for what the radio forecast as the hottest day of the year. She walked with a cane, identical to the slim pearly-handled model that had been tucked at the back of Vera's closet for a decade. Fashion turned over slowly at the pharmacy in town.

"Vera," she sang out on her way into the kitchen, "have I got a deal for you."

Helen was an activist, a community organizer, the wife of a Republican member of the school board. She first met my mother while door-knocking for her husband's campaign. That was before a dragging leg and temporary bout of double vision brought her into the hospital for a diagnosis of MS. Mildly affected, she called herself, and she plowed all her civic spirit into building her networks.

The deal she had for Vera was a date really, a luncheon and comedy act sponsored by the local MS Society. Most exciting of all, a ride on the new county paratransit system. The paratransit had taken ages to wend its way through funding committee discussions. Helen, as a concerned citizen, had pushed it along.

"We'd better use it, now that it's up and running," she said. "Otherwise, they'll stick us with medi-cabs again. That's like sending a person to the grocery store in an ambulance."

As if my mother went anywhere, in medi-cabs or otherwise. She'd last left the house six years before for Donna's wedding. It had probably been four years before that. No way would she give in to this woman. Although her standard argument—Who would want me?—this time could hold no water. Clearly, Helen Gennaro wanted her.

"I don't know, Helen," she said. "It seems like too much."

"What's too much? I'll ride along with you." Helen still drove her own Lincoln with hand controls. She'd go public, just to accompany Vera.

This sort of over-the-top enthusiasm had never gotten me anywhere, but I watched in amazement as my mother started to budge.

"I don't have a dress," she said.

Helen said, "Fran can shop. Can't you? Go to B Altman's, pick out something nice for your mother?"

"Of course," I told her. In hindsight, I had never been so cheerfully optimistic. Helen didn't plead or apply pressure; she presumed.

Donna was the one who shopped for my mother's necessities, which of course my father still paid for. But this was different, an unplanned and unauthorized expense. Not the sort of worry Vera would share with Helen Gennaro, but the one capable of sinking the deal.

"I'll buy you a dress for your birthday, Ma," I offered. "It's not for a couple of weeks, but I'll be in Chicago by then."

Vera said, "Oh, no! Really?"

"Yes, really."

"You heard the girl," Helen told her.

"I don't know if I'm an eighteen or a twenty." Vera was a size four once, but time and Prednisone had taken care of that.

Helen said, "Come to think of it, you can take the paratransit to shop for a dress. That's what it's for."

164

"I'd rather have Frannie or Donna go. Save my first ride for something more fun."

An honest-to-God preference! How could it be? This woman Helen was dangerous—to me, my mother, to our boring but balanced interactions, and I liked her. In my younger days, I would have loved her.

"Well, then, Fran can buy both sizes. Bring a few things home for you to try on. Keep the ones that work, return the ones that don't. That's how Donna does it, right?"

Just like that, a plan took shape. I'd shop on Tuesday. Consuela would dye Vera's hair on Thursday—something she did every few months in the kitchen sink. On Saturday morning, Nadine would set Vera's hair with electric curlers, and give her just a touch of makeup. In the afternoon, Helen would drive over to the house and the van from the county would pick them both up.

"Jerry will be out of town," Helen said. "Anthony can come, if he likes, or we could make it just us women."

A cloud came over Vera, as if she had forgotten about Anthony. "I don't know, Helen," she said. "I'll have to wait and see. He's been so busy with his work."

"But you're not busy on Saturday afternoon?"

"No."

"Then we're on, don't you think? I'll book us two seats on the bus."

"I guess so." Vera took a breath, and took the plunge. "Okay, I'll be ready. Frannie will help me."

"It will be great," Helen said.

Here was hoping Vera wouldn't fuck it up by asking Anthony's permission.

~ Twenty ~

When my mother married my father, she left her village, Queens, and moved to his, the Bronx. She left her widowed mother, her older brother Robert, dashing in his Army uniform, her girl cousins, the two skinny ones and the fat one, Ida, Rose, and Marie; and her nineteen-year-old boy cousin Gene, who played guitar and banjo. Vera learned to trust Anthony's sisters and to cook like his mother—a customary Italian-American marriage. For a few years, she raised her first two children—Gloria and Jimmy—in the Bronx.

Soon after Donna was born, Anthony moved the family to Mount Kisco. A commuter train served the town but only my mother's mother, who lived on her own in a Greenwich Village apartment by then, bothered to make the trip. Vera and her neighbors drove past each other in cars, exchanged hellos in the back of church and the produce aisle at the A & P, got together once a year at the public school open house and once a month as the Ladies of Charity. An ordinary suburban life, with an average amount of isolation—until the MS crept up on Vera and driving became impossible.

This is how Vera's neighbor Helen Gennaro would probably have told it. Helen volunteered thirty or more hours each week—lobbying on behalf of paratransit users, leading discussion groups for the MS Society, strategizing to get her disabled housewife peers back into the mainstream. Suburban life had its flaws, but it was worth living. That's why the barriers needed to come down.

But Helen Gennaro had never seen Anthony standing over Vera, screaming about a phone bill, forbidding her to ever again make a long-distance call to Queens. She wasn't on hand the day Anthony banished Mary Nathan from our home. She didn't sit at the table with me and my grandmother, didn't listen in on our lessons about love. She never witnessed the seventy-year-old woman sneaking around to visit us, hurrying out before he came home, or the fighting that erupted when Grandma's timing was off. His home. He paid the bills. He decided who came in, and when.

That was the old Anthony. The new one, who spent barely any time at home, now had loosened his grip on Vera's affections. He had no fondness for strangers, but neither did he drive them away. He'd made room for Consuela and Nadine, had grown to like them at least as well as he liked his wife and daughters. When he met up with me, Helen, Consuela, and Vera, all hanging out in his kitchen on a Tuesday afternoon, he looked completely unfazed. This man, who once blew a fuse when I so much as wrote my mother and not him, now didn't even quiz me about how long I'd been in town without letting him know.

We'd been discussing what color Consuela should dye Vera's hair. "Go darker, Ma," I said. "Seriously. That red is starting to look kind of brassy."

I was risking an insult to Consuela, but she seemed cheered by the whole undertaking, and far less suspicious of me. For once, I was making a constructive contribution. "Your original color, Mrs. D'Amato," she said, backing me up. "It will look better with the dress."

It had taken only one round trip to White Plains to come up with the perfect dress—a print of indigo flowers against a muted olive-grey background, with tiny sprigs of bright yellow strewn here and there.

"Pretty jazzy," Vera had said. To hear her tell it, she'd stayed in for six years because there was no paratransit and no one had asked her out. Now that she had Helen and a ride, everything else was falling into place.

When Anthony darkened the kitchen doorway, I was the one who gave a little gasp. I fully expected him to bust up our party, but he just stood there, blinking sleepily like a bear waking up from hibernation.

"What's happening here?" he asked, without a trace of malice or envy.

"I'm taking Vera out on Saturday," Helen smiled at him candidly, "an MS Society fund-raiser. You're invited."

The old Anthony would have forbidden Vera to go. It's her choice, I would have argued, and she'd have gone ahead to make the wrong choice.

"Thank you," the new Anthony told Helen. "Unfortunately, I'll be working on Saturday."

"Are you staying for dinner tonight?" he asked me.

"Sure," I said. "I'll stay." For a few minutes, it was just that easy.

~ Twenty-one ~

Donna's house sat at the end of a squat valley, the last of six on a quiet little road, flanked by a stand of tall pines and a row of gnarled lilacs, and skirted by meadows that give way to wetlands—what we used to call fields and swamps. Her house, oldest of the six, getting onto a century, rested in the shadow of the interstate. If not for this, she and Billy couldn't have afforded the place.

If you listened, you could tell when a car was approaching. There was the percussive drone of the freeway in the background, the familiar riffs of cars on the exit ramp, the counterpoint of the secondary road. Finally, the squeal and clatter of a right-angle turn always taken too fast into Donna's front yard.

Donna and I were cleaning her cool cave of a basement that Wednesday afternoon, restacking boxes and too far underground to hear anything except Gloria's rackety landing, the arrival of a visitor who'd been shot out of a cannon. We ran upstairs to investigate. I reached the side door first. Gloria was standing on the stoop when I got there. A cloud of dust still hovered near the ground.

167

"You!" she said pushing past me. And then, "Plug your ears if you're feeling sensitive."

At first, I was fooled by her tough-girl act—too busy feeling the sting of her insult and reflecting on how long it had been since we'd glared at each other across the reception hall at Donna's wedding—to notice how stricken she really looked. But Donna pulled out a kitchen chair just a split second before Gloria collapsed into it. The parts of her face were disassembling, her normally arrogant demeanor dissolving under a peculiar mixture of terror and rage.

"What happened?" Donna asked. She took a glass from the clean dish rack and went to the refrigerator for ice cubes and water.

Gloria held the sweating glass of cold water against her forehead. "Your father is a pervert," she said. "I caught him. At the Ginger Man restaurant, with a younger man."

I suppressed the urge to laugh and instead asked, "Doing what?" My mind made a quick flip-book movie: a men's room, tile walls, urinals, two men. They had no faces, they were groping each other's crotches, one was down on his knees. Now Gloria was barging in. The men must have had cartoon faces because theirs and Gloria's registered shock and surprise. But no matter how hard I tried, I couldn't make one of the men look like Anthony.

"They didn't see me," Gloria said. "There was a divider."

I abandoned the men's room for a dining room, Gloria peering out from behind a potted fern. I pictured Anthony in a white shirt and tie, sitting at a table. I tried to sketch in another man.

"Like a boyfriend?" I asked Gloria.

"More like a gigolo."

Donna was conspicuously silent. I pressed on. "How young? Not like a teenage prostitute?"

"Forty-five, maybe," Gloria yelled, "a goddamn middle-aged faggot."

"A man," Donna whispered. She seemed stunned, but also oddly accepting. I was not convinced. All I had so far was my father eating lunch with some guy twenty years his junior.

"So what were they doing?" I asked again. "I mean, what makes you say it was— sexual?"

"Trust me," Gloria said. She had regained command of herself, acting all hard-bitten and savvy, but I could tell she didn't want to talk about this. Not with me.

I ran another movie in my head: my father out on a date with a dark, slender man. An Anthony Perkins type, maybe. They pressed knee against knee under the table, they smiled and tossed their heads in laughter, they leaned in to kiss—but then the sprocket holes ripped, the film jumped and sputtered. Their moment of contact was lost in erratic motion.

"What were you doing there?" I asked Gloria.

She was having lunch with a colleague.

And Anthony couldn't have been doing the same—lunching with a drug company rep or younger surgeon?

"No." Gloria stalled one more time, then finally delivered her trump card. "They were eating off of each other's plates."

Instantaneously, I was convinced. I looked at Donna, Donna looked at me.

"It's a guy." She shook her head, a tinge of nausea in her voice.

"Frannie," Gloria became suddenly sanctimonious. "Donna and I have suspected for a while now that Daddy was having an affair."

"Join the club," I said, which was not entirely honest. For years, I had noticed the indicators—the vacations "alone," the late nights out, but I'd never thought it all the way through. If I had, would I have been an equal opportunity daughter? Would I have allowed for the possibility of a man?

"So," I directed my question to Donna, "Until now you've been willing to forgive it?"

"Yes," Gloria said.

"No," Donna said simultaneously. "It seemed wrong, what Daddy was doing, but I didn't want to intrude. It's their marriage."

Gloria said, "Frankly, I thought it inevitable he would seek out other women, given Mommy's condition."

Not true, I started to say, but I spared them the disabled-people-are-sexual-beings-too lecture. We weren't talking disabled people. We were talking about our one very squeamish mother.

"We're all old enough now," I told them. "You think we could call them Vera and Anthony?"

"He's putting our mother at risk for AIDS," Gloria said.

At this I jumped out of my chair. "He is not! He is not putting her at risk for AIDS! You just implied they haven't had sex in years. What then? Have they been shooting up together? You're a goddamn doctor. How can you talk so irresponsibly about AIDS?"

"Cool down, Frannie," Donna said. "Can't a person make a mistake?"

"Thank you," Gloria told her. As if she needed protecting.

~ Twenty-two ~

"He's such a hypocrite," Donna told me when we were alone in her car on our way to the big show down. "Remember last year, that letter you wrote to Mommy about Arlene? You put some kind of brochure in."

So Donna had read it. I felt a little flush of embarrassment. "Parents of Lesbians and Gays," I said. "I thought she might like to know they existed, even if she wouldn't make the long distance call."

"Yeah, well, anyway, Daddy found the letter and the brochure under the radio by her bed, and threw them both out."

"He was jealous," I said. "He gets mad if I write to Vera and not him."

"No," Donna told me. "I was there. I heard him. He said, 'You don't want this junk lying around. You want Mrs. West to see it? Or the ladies who take care of you? You want them to know this about you when they're wiping your behind?'"

The parking lot at the Yangtze restaurant was nearly empty when we converged on it. Four cars for five D'Amatos: Donna and me in her rusty Toyota, Gloria in her BMW, Mike in his Mercedes, and my father's champagne Cutlass parked up against the building. He'd gone inside already. His suit jacket hung in the back seat.

"Not a word," Gloria hissed at me.

This was Michael and Gloria's strong-arm show. They'd rounded up Donna to pad their numbers, but hadn't been counting on me. Donna had demanded that I be invited, had goaded me to come with or without their permission. Gloria's ultimatum, that only she and Mike do the talking, was stupid, but I had agreed to it. I didn't even know what I wanted to say.

I hung back a bit as my sisters and brother-in-law strode across the asphalt to the restaurant. They looked like an all-white rendition of the Mod Squad, gritty and righteous and ready for action. In my unwelcome opinion, they were tracking the right criminal for the wrong crime—a pervert, that's what Gloria had said. Undoubtedly, she thought the same of me.

Mike opened the gigantic carved wooden door and held it until I caught up. A blast of air conditioning hit my face. Anthony sat on a red chair in the foyer. He stood up when we came in, and nodded with great formality to the four of us. Then he did a double take at the sight of me.

"Frannie," he said.

"It's a coincidence," I hurried to explain. "Gloria didn't know I was at Donna's."

My oldest sister raised a hand, to smack me or shush me, I didn't know which. But that's all I said, and she let the hand fall to her side.

The restaurant had four or five separate dining rooms opening one on to another. The maitre d' summoned a waiter who led us to a round table in the furthest corner of the back room. Someone could have pulled off a hit at the table, and no one would have been around to witness it.

"I hope no one minds," Mike said as the waiter poured our water. "I was starving. I went ahead and phoned in an order." A smooth move all right, designed to minimize the need for chit-chat, to shorten the time before they brought out the big guns. Did he invent this shtick for the occasion, or had he used it before in one of his novels? I'd have to start reading suspense fiction.

In the few minutes we did wait for the food, no one talked at all. I was seated to the right of my father, and stared obliquely at his hands. One was wrapped lightly around the stem of his water glass, then both held the bowl of the glass like a chalice, bouncing it gently. All my life I had regarded those hands, had considered their skills, their contradictory capacities: to write, to shave, to stir coffee with a spoon. To cut, to sew, to hit. And now, I'd been told, to wrap themselves around some man's cock. Another man's, not his own. To grab hold of some man's shoulder, the flat of his belly.

The food came, huge platters that let off their steam when the domed stainless steel covers were lifted. Beef and hot peppers, egg foo young, garlic chicken, seafood in black bean sauce. Suddenly there was a burst of talk, plates being passed, rice bowls refilled. Did everybody get at least one shrimp?

Then silence again when our plates were full. Gloria allowed us exactly three bites before starting in on Anthony. She raised her right hand and pointed a shaming finger. A surgeon's hand also. Clean. Trim nails. But much less familiar to me.

"We know how you're spending your time," she told him. "We know what you're up to with that man. We didn't come here to argue. What I have to say is very simple. Drop him now, or we'll tell Mommy. We'll hire a divorce lawyer on her behalf, and sue for every penny you've got." Gloria lowered the hand, but pinned him with her gaze.

Anthony's face revealed nothing—not the old belligerence, and not any fear. Had he imagined this day would come? Did he think his dyke daughter might join in the confrontation? Perhaps he had rehearsed not responding, staying calm. Perhaps he had taught himself, as they do in karate, to look in the vicinity of the attacker's mouth, careful never to lock on the eyes. He rested his hands on the tabletop, restraining their movement, it seemed, lest they bring about a betrayal. Perhaps he had coached himself to count to one hundred, to subdue his heartbeat, rein in his voice.

"Gloria," he said, very quietly. "I don't know what you're talking about."

She said, "Fine. Maybe I'm wrong. Let's keep it that way. But let's say I'm right. It's not the sort of thing you want to make public at a Catholic hospital. Not the news you want your patients to catch wind of."

This couldn't have been what Anthony wanted in life, not in a son or daughter, this person wielding power, threats, and anger. But bullies beget bullies. She could push him around now, could hurt him more than he could hurt her. It was his turn to yield.

"Michael. Donna. I thought this was supposed to be a nice dinner." Anthony made no appeal to me.

"What you're doing is unfair to Vera," Michael told him. "Quit now and we'll forget we ever knew. Keep it going and we'll have to force a change."

Donna said, "Somebody has to think about Mommy."

I said nothing, less of a struggle than I feared, since so far no one had mentioned perversion, or Gloria's specious argument about AIDS.

Anthony's hands still rested, palm down, on the red tablecloth. He leaned his weight into them to lift himself up. "I'm going home now. It's been a long day at the office." Even as he said this, it rang false.

"We'll be watching," Gloria told him. Somehow I expected more out of her, more accusations, a citing of evidence, a fire-and-brimstone sermon, but she let him go without another word. As soon as he turned his back, she started downing her food. His plate sat on the table, still full.

I watched Anthony leave, his white shirt weaving around the red furniture and toward the front door. He didn't look back. "Okay," I told them. "He's gone. I didn't talk. Now why all the posturing? Why not hire that lawyer and get Vera the hell out of there?"

An unholy alliance I was proposing, a true coalition government. We'd unite against a common enemy, avoid discussing our motives. Gloria had stumbled across the one thing that put Anthony one down, and here I was, advocating that we exploit it. That we drag his queer behavior into court, make it the central issue of a divorce. The real problem was not what Anthony did with his dick, not even how he spent the cash he should have been spending on Vera. It was how he had managed, over the years, to rob her of all value. But given this opportunity to kick him out of the house, to sue for a better than fifty-fifty split, I thrilled at the thought of what we might buy her: accessible housing, in White Plains maybe, where she could get out on her own to the shops and theaters. Physical therapy, for the first time in a decade; maybe even Mary Nathan was still in business. Higher wages for her attendants, an independent living plan that really worked. Only if she wanted it all, but money was half the reason she had renounced desire. It was too expensive to want, and except for a few years as a phone operator between high school and marriage, she'd never had her own nickel to spend.

Michael pulled me up short. "You must remember, Frannie, Anthony's a big man when you consider where he came from, but we're not looking at very much money. That's why we don't want him spending it on ... some stranger."

"How much?" I asked.

"I really couldn't tell you."

"Then let's find out." I was certain they had checked into it already. "Let's talk real numbers, and make a budget and an investment plan. What has he offered her for the next twenty years? We can come up with a better deal."

"It will go faster than you think," Mike said. "There won't be anything left."

"Left for what?" I started to ask, but Gloria's hand flew up in that same gesture: she would have hit Michael, or silenced him if it wasn't too late.

"I didn't suffer all those years of abuse for nothing." I felt the earth downshift when Gloria said this. Sometimes I could be so dense, so thick-skulled, so lacking in suspicion. My sister and brother-in-law didn't want to run Anthony out of the house. Better to keep him in it, if that would stanch the flow of cash. All their years of bargaining to stay in the man's will, but what good was a will with nothing left to distribute?

"That's all you care—" I began, but Michael had his answer ready.

"Frannie," he said. "We all have our reasons for the choices we make. We need to focus on our points of agreement, and it seems to me the main one is this: no one wants to interrupt Anthony's earning power. So no one wants to make a sudden move, wouldn't you agree?" Mike talked like it was his own money. He talked like Anthony would never disinherit Gloria; that's how much our father valued genealogy.

What can you do if I don't agree? I wanted to ask, but it seemed wiser to keep quiet.

Mike rose from the table, and pulled a VISA card from his wallet. "Time to go," he said. "We'll be in touch. The important thing is to keep an eye on Anthony. Don't worry, ladies, I'll take care of the check."

Donna and I remained sitting. We watched Gloria and Mike trace Anthony's path to the exit.

"And you?" I asked her.

She said, "It's humiliating her, Frannie. He hasn't slept at home on a Saturday night in months." She knew this but hadn't told me.

"You like their solution—to chase him back to her?"

"It's a starting point."

"It's regressive."

"It's what she wants."

"But what if she allowed herself to want better? Would you allow that too?"

"Yes."

"Even if it's costly? Even if it whittles away at your projected inheritance?"

"Yes," she said, "even if. But you need to stop living in the past. There's nothing wrong with Mommy's life at home. It's our job to preserve it."

I had to admit, I no longer considered a nursing home a solution. But if anyone longed for the past it was Donna, a past I hadn't been born into, one where her Mommy and Daddy loved each other, or at least she thought they did.

"What if talking sternly doesn't get him to stop?" I asked. "Now that his cover is blown, he could decide to leave her. He could come out. People do that in their sixties."

"I know. Let's hope for her sake it doesn't happen." Then Donna was flagging down the waiter, motioning for him to bring take-out cartons for all the leftovers.

* * * * *

The phone booth at the Yangtze was painted red and trimmed with a pagoda-shaped roof.

"Hang on," I told Donna on our way past it. I stepped inside and closed the door.

"I'm in a Chinese restaurant," I told Ruby when she accepted my collect call. "Things are happening pretty fast here. I'll save it up to tell you over a bottle of wine."

"Okay," she said. "I'll be waiting."

"I love you, Ruby."

Assignment completed. Promise fulfilled. I did love her, I was aching to get home to her, but I could hardly let myself feel it with Donna watching through the glass.

~ Twenty-three ~

I wasn't raised with books or music, not music that belonged to either of my parents. Neither the upright piano against the north wall of the living room nor the portable phonograph in a laminated fabric case ever got much use. Gloria, who left for college when I was five, had excelled at piano lessons, but Donna resisted every step of the way. Her time at the piano might as well have been time on a chain gang. Her complaining wore Vera down, and she was granted permission to quit. I was never even invited to start. The lid stayed shut over the keys.

In fifth grade, I learned to memorize E-G-B-D-F, and F-A-C-E, whole notes, half notes and quarter notes, sharps and flats, and I came home from school to try them out. I helped myself to the sheet music Gloria left inside the bench, uncovered the keys, and plunked out the melodies to a couple of Haydn minuets. I imagined Vera might notice, might come around the corner into the living room to see who was playing, steady herself on the doorframe and laugh—because who could it have been but me? Or maybe she'd mention it at supper. But she did nothing of the sort, and I soon lost interest.

I never knew for sure what Haydn was supposed to sound like. My parents owned no classical albums, no opera, jazz, folk, or blues, not even any Frank Sinatra. I don't know why they owned the record player. Donna was the one who brought music into the house, who switched the old AM radio over the kitchen sink from news to rock-and-roll, but only for fifteen minutes each night while she washed the supper dishes. Before and after supper, Anthony was always napping, always trying to catch up on sleep and yelling at the rest of us to keep it down. The slightest ripple of conversation or mirth had him bounding out of bed and down the stairs, yelling about how he needed his rest. His job exhausted him, taking all those people's lives and viscera into his hands, sometimes on short notice, sometimes in the middle of the night.

Eventually Donna smuggled an AM/FM radio into her room, bought with the money she saved from our grocery trips. Months passed before

Anthony caught on, and only then because he walked past her open door and saw the radio. He had no grounds to complain. She always waited to turn it on until she could hear him snoring, and even then stuffed a towel under her door. Soon she brought home a set of stereo components and albums by Traffic and the Velvet Underground. All of it went with her when she left for college.

Anthony didn't explain what moved him to start buying season tickets to the Met. Ethnic pride, I guessed. An excuse to get out of the house on a Saturday. One more addition to his highly routinized schedule. He allowed himself few amusements besides traveling, but could certainly afford any one that caught his fancy. If he loved the music, he didn't let it show. He never tuned in the classical station at home or in the car, never followed the singers' careers, or compared one year's performances to the next. His pleasure came, as far as I could tell, from simply joining the crowd at the opera house, from being the sort of man who held two season tickets and could bestow the experience on some of the women in his life—his sister Alida, his sister-in-law Julia, and me.

I was twelve, an only child. Donna still had a few months left in high school, but all of her time belonged to Billy. Anthony had already treated each of my aunts to a day at the opera, and in the middle of supper one night he said, "Frannie will come with me next weekend, to *Madama Butterfly*." It was a declaration, not a question, and in spite of my habit of resisting, I found myself going along with his plan. I waged most of my battles against him on my mother's behalf, but this new interest he was cultivating had nothing to do with her. The possibility of her accompanying him was never even discussed.

I felt guilty for leaving her behind, and watched her face for signs of hurt. None surfaced.

"You look beautiful," she told me on the appointed day.

I felt ugly and out of sorts. The one dress I owned was too lightweight for March; I'd bought it for my confirmation coming up in May. It was silver-blue, with sheer white sleeves and midnight blue piping around the collar and cuffs, which seemed sophisticated when I picked it out, compared to the pastel frills and ribbons which filled the department store racks. But putting a cardigan sweater on top ruined the entire effect.

Anthony and I went several days without a squabble after he announced our outing. I felt off balance. It seemed unwise to relax my warrior stance, yet silly to maintain it.

I smoothed my skirt over my knees in the car on the way to Lincoln Center. "I don't want to get confirmed," I said. "I don't even believe in it."

He was a non-believer too, although he avoided saying so. Get confirmed for your mother, I expected him to tell me.

I already did a lot for her. When Donna got her license, my mother got it in her head to send the two of us to Mass. If she couldn't save her own soul, she could take responsibility for shepherding ours. Every Sunday we dressed in corduroy pants and our nicest sweaters, and drove off at a quarter to nine. We parked down by the reservoir and sat on the hood of the car. Donna smoked cigarettes and I watched the mist rising off the water. After an hour had passed, we drove home and changed into regular clothes.

Donna would have to start dropping me off at church if I planned to go through with the ceremony. I'd have to attend at least a few classes, to learn what to say, when to sit, kneel, and stand, and when to get on line with the other seventh graders to get slapped across the face by the bishop.

"You might as well go through with it," Anthony told me, "in case you want to get married in a Catholic Church."

"I'm never getting married," I said.

He said, "Don't be silly. You'll want a career, but you'll want marriage and motherhood too." Just like the Czech doctor he knew, who on top of her medical practice was raising hyperactive twin boys. "She has her hands full," he told me, "but a woman's not a woman until she's given birth."

My face flushed but I didn't challenge him. We had reached the city and he was busy circling for on-street parking, resisting the allure of pay lots and ramps. His persistence was rewarded. He found a space—to my eye, barely as long as the car, but with a few turns of his wrist and a few glances in his mirrors he brought our white boat of a Buick safely into dock.

I had to double my pace to match his stride, and even so I followed two or three steps behind him. I watched the square of his shoulders in his wool top coat, a sharp black edge against the milky white sky and grimy downtown buildings, against the tall glass facade of the new opera house.

As soon as we crossed the threshold into the yellow-and-red warmth of the foyer, I knew I was an unworthy companion. My father stood up even straighter, and breathed deeply to take in the grandeur. Although I could see what impressed him, I couldn't feel it. A twinge, maybe, for the two huge paintings by Marc Chagall. Otherwise, my heart was as small and smooth as a chestnut. Everything slid off. Nothing got in.

We ascended the grand staircase under the chandeliers, went down a hallway, and stepped through a door into our box—a perch looking out across the great bowl of the hall. An elderly couple had already taken two of the seats. Anthony nodded hello. The woman, who wore a fur stole, smiled when I sat down next to her. She must have come to every performance, must have sat with my Aunts Alida and Julia.

No matter how I fidgeted and adjusted my chair, it was hard to get a proper view of the stage. I could taste the old woman's perfume on my tongue. She was sucking on a lemon drop, and I wished she would offer me one. Anthony read his program from cover to cover, sat perfectly straight in his seat, prepared himself to absorb the spectacle about to unfold. I looked at the ceiling of the new opera house, already beginning to tarnish and turn green. Finally, the orchestra started—an odd, jerky kind of music—the gold curtain rose, and a burden lowered onto me like a yoke.

I hated these people, this man in his uniform, this woman in her kimono. Even before they sang love, love, love, I was thinking stupid, stupid, stupid. I did like the paper screen with separate square panels, the blue light coming through from behind. But I hated these people the same way I hated Lucy and Desi, the Honeymooners, my own parents. Always the same unimaginative crap. No matter that this was opera, not TV, not real life. I was justified in my scorn. Soon enough the man in uniform left. Their glorious love gave way to her ridiculous waiting, her inane suicide. But not before he returned to claim his kid.

My father on one side of me and the woman in mink on the other both leaned forward in rapt attention. She lowered her opera glasses onto her lap. Her eyes and Anthony's eyes glistened with unshed tears. I folded my arms across my chest and tucked my hands into my armpits. This is bullshit, I told myself. I wouldn't be coming back.

~ Twenty-four ~

In 1983 the heat was on. The time had come for Anthony to prove something to the world. This newest Anthony of all, accused of sexual perversion, under duress, did not forbid, destroy, or even ignore the plans Helen Gennaro had made with Vera. He usurped them. He had the wife. She had the hair, the make-up, the dress. He didn't trifle with paratransit. He didn't spare any expense. He hired a medi-cab to drive my mother all the way to Yonkers. We'd have a dinner party at Dulano's for the whole family, he said, just the family, not Nadine, to celebrate Vera's upcoming birthday. More importantly, to celebrate his and Vera's thirty-seventh wedding anniversary, which had passed the month before without any fan-fare, which he now regretted. I had never witnessed fanfare on any of their anniversaries. But my job, as I understood it, was to watch and wait.

"I'm sorry, Helen," Vera said when she canceled the date with her friend. "I can't turn him down. I mean, I wouldn't want to. He rearranged his work schedule."

"Of course you shouldn't turn him down." Helen stirred her iced tea with a long spoon. "You'll have a ball. There will be plenty of MS Society events. Now that you've got the dress, and we've got the paratransit, we'll catch the next one."

"He's been so busy," Vera said. "I've been boring, I'm sure, and now look. You got me motivated, and that motivated him!"

The dinner party was a piece of theater, a one-act farce. It was *When Love Returns*, an opera in one afternoon, written, directed, and performed by Anthony D'Amato, featuring Vera D'Amato as the unsuspecting, long-suffering wife.

My mother and I arrived at the restaurant first. She would have arrived alone except that I, at the last minute, had hopped into the medi-cab. Why wasn't Anthony riding along with her? "I have a small errand to run," he had said, with notable coyness. "Travel safely," he called out as the driver put the van in reverse.

An aging restaurateur now greeted my mother and me as we came in. "Mrs. D'Amato!" He took her hands. "How lovely to see you. This must be your beautiful daughter."

"Yes," she said. "Francesca, my youngest."

"I knew your mother and father before they were married," he told me. I just nodded and smiled.

Dulano's was a typical southern Italian place with red checked table-cloths and candles in Chianti bottles still unlit. Daylight shining in high-lighted the streaks on the plate glass windows. Except for Vera and me, the dining room was deserted.

"Right this way," Mr. Dulano beckoned us over to a table set for six. "What can I get for you ladies while you're waiting? A glass of wine?"

"Oh! No thank you, not yet," my mother said. "We'll wait for my hus-band to decide."

But when Donna arrived, a young waiter came to the table carrying three stem glasses and a carafe of red wine. "Compliments of the house," he said.

"Just an inch for me," Vera told him as he poured. "I can't get tipsy yet! Please, give Mr. Dulano my thanks."

Gloria and Mike arrived next. "Hello, Ma," Gloria bent down to kiss my mother's cheek.

Mike took one look at the carafe on our table and sent the waiter away for a bottled wine. " —a *pinot noir*, but please, not 1981."

"So, it's your anniversary," Gloria said.

"Yes." Vera smiled. "Thirty-seven years. An odd number, but worth celebrating, don't you think?"

At the time, I was twenty-four. Gloria was thirteen when I was born. My parents, we'd always been told, married a year before she was born. "Ma," I said, "this must be number thirty-eight, not thirty-seven."

I hadn't intended to tease Vera, but after a fleeting look of consternation, Gloria caught my meaning and began to play with it. "So how about it, Mrs. D'Amato?" she asked. "Have you been married thirty-eight years, or have you been keeping something from me my whole life?"

"No, of course not!" Vera blushed. "What's thirty-eight from eighty-three? We were married in 1945. Who could forget a time like that?"

Gloria said, "It's all right, mother. I'm an adult now. I can handle the awful truth." I had never seen my oldest sister joke around like this.

Donna glared at Gloria, as if that would get her to stop, but my mother seemed no worse for the wear. She said, "I'm sorry, Gloria. I hate to disappoint you, but I did everything on the up-and-up then, as I do now."

The door to the restaurant swung open. "Finally," Vera said, "your father is here."

But this man was not my father. This was the tenor playing my father, playing the repentant husband, the magnanimous dad. "I apologize for taking so long. I had an errand," he said.

Anthony dismissed the young waiter who approached the table carrying six large menus. "Mr. Dulano," he called out to the older man, "we'll do it home-style, don't you think? Bring out the best you have. Nothing is too good for my family."

Soon the waiter and restaurateur were dancing around, filling our plates with mussels in wine sauce, anchovy crostini, sliced tomatoes with fresh mozzarella—and all the while paying special attention to my mother.

The tenor playing my father began. "I have a story to tell," he said. "I haven't been a good husband."

"Now, Dad," Michael tried to out-sing him. "You don't have to—"

"No, listen!" Anthony stood up and drew himself tall to make a speech. He gestured with his wine glass, pointing here and there to the various places in the restaurant, bringing to life the scene he described: "On a Saturday afternoon like this one, almost forty years ago, at this very restaurant, a young man proposed marriage to a young woman. This distinguished gentleman was just a young waiter then. The couple sat at that corner table. The young doctor, the hopeful husband, had grand ambitions, and promised to work hard to support the family they would raise, but he didn't realize how easily work could crowd out love. As time passed, he neglected to keep love close at hand."

The tenor playing the repentant philanderer cast his eyes down. "My own children had to remind me this week that love must be tended, and sometimes love must be invited to return."

Was that a tear I saw in my mother's eye? "Oh my," she said. "I never imagined."

Gloria smiled sweetly at Anthony, another first in my book. "We're glad you've come to your senses," she said with unbelievable gentleness.

But Anthony's performance was just beginning. "I'm sorry you've waited so long," he told Vera. He walked around the table to stand beside her, continuing his story as he went: "At that table over there they spoke of marriage, and this is the very diamond he gave her." He pulled a velvet box from his pocket. Inside was her engagement ring, too small now for her finger, remade by a jeweler into a pendant. He bent over to fasten it around her neck.

"Oh my," she sang. "I always hoped—"

"Of course I still love you." At first the tenor echoed the soprano's melody, but soon he was actually singing her part, his voice climbing up and up, defying gravity, defying death itself, reaching into the highest registers for the climax of his song.

The reunited pair smiled and gazed at one another while the chorus started up. "To love!" the restaurateur exclaimed. "Take heart, young lovers. An old chicken makes good broth."

Everyone joined him in holding up their wine glasses to toast the return of love. Except me.

It was times like this that made me yearn to call Jimmy back from the dead. How would he have turned out, I wondered, what would he have done as a grown man in the face of my father's performance? Would he have called out, "Bravo, Bravissimo!" or thrown tomatoes and eggs? Lent himself to the furor or denounced Anthony as a fraud? Perhaps Jimmy would have perfected the art of detachment, not even stooping to get involved in such D'Amato family theatrics.

The brother I remembered dribbled a basketball in the driveway. He pissed his name into the snow. He was an overgrown kid, charming and goofy, who kept moving along, sidestepping every burden, until the U.S. Army saddled him with one too heavy to shrug off.

The trick, besides turning the clock back for Jimmy, would have been to turn a different set of clocks ahead. What if he had skipped Vietnam altogether, had managed in spite of Anthony to assemble a good life, a landscaping business up in Yorktown? All his youthful indifference might have shone like sheer privilege. My brother could have been thirty-six, lounging at home, watching the Mets on TV, tuning out Gina who'd be yelling at him to help with the kids, the laundry, to at least get his own fucking beer. Tuning out me, too, because I'd be pestering him to demonstrate some shred of interest in his own mother's well-being.

But maybe Jimmy would have parlayed his lightheartedness into an admirable middle-aged wisdom, would have known better than I did how to talk back to Gloria, even if she was the oldest, and a doctor, and rich, and married to Michael. Jimmy and I would have stood by the truth and our mother, and Donna would have gotten lonely and joined us. In the midst of all the clamor, maybe Jimmy would have known better than I did whether to disregard or confront Anthony's lies.

"Donna," I whispered to my sister who sat next to me at Dulano's, "are you buying this?" She was the one, after all, who that very same week had been telling me about method acting.

"Don't start in, Frannie." She shot me a menacing look, then turned her attention back to her Biscuit Tortoni and the happy D'Amato family tableau.

Mike raised his glass for yet another toast. "Welcome back to the family, Dad," he said.

Vera brought one hand up to her neck to touch the diamond that hung there. "This is lovely," she said. "I hope we do it more often."

PART FOUR

Show Some Respect • (1983-1985)

~ One ~

I was in the back room at the poster studio running the offset press when the call came in from Donna. I was submerged, heeding only the rhythm of the work, the slap-clunk of the machine softened by my OSHA-regulation ear muffs, my heart picking up the downbeat. With every slap a new face of Nelson Mandela slid off the roller and into the perfect stack. One-Nelson, two-Nelson, three-Nelson. I was still entranced by the pure repetition, not yet irritated by the boredom of the job. The longer I watched, the emptier I became—a room cleared of its clutter, swept clean, windows and doors left open to the sunlight and the breeze skipping through.

I was counting Nelsons when I noticed the shift—some presence gathering mass, gaining insistence. I looked up to see Gregory standing in the doorway.

He pantomimed a telephone and mouthed some words that turned out to be "Your sister." Because she had never called me at work—not at Hard Rain, not at the gas station, not once in eight years—I didn't understand him.

He crossed over to me, and I lifted up my headset to hear him say, "Long distance. Your sister." My heart stopped, dropped, rolled.

Gregory tied an apron around his waist. "I'll take care of Nelson," he said, and he laid a hand flat against the middle of my back, prodding me ever so slightly, steering me out to the front of the shop, because otherwise I would have stood there forever, swaying stupidly, my feet bolted to the floor, wondering who had died.

No one had died. Donna had awakened from a deep sleep—not slowly, languorously, but all at once sitting upright. "I can't tolerate the way our mother is living," she said.

I, of course, wanted to know what happened. What had changed for the worse?

"Nothing. I just can't stand it is all."

183

For me, realizations come on like the dawn, certain knowledge inching up my spine like the sun crawling up the back of a mountain. Donna came to with the throw of a switch, a person whose paid-up time in the sensory-deprivation chamber had just run out. All those years of looking away from our mother's problems gave my sister a crick in her neck. And now—quick!—she wanted a chiropractic adjustment, from me.

"I have an idea we could try," she said.

Who was this woman who called me at work in the middle of the day, who dropped "we" so easily after withholding it for so many years?

"I gave up on changing things," I told her. "I've already accepted defeat."

"You can't," she said. "Help me out, Frannie." And every gate inside me swung to let her through.

Gregory's brow furrowed in question when I stepped back up to the press. "Nobody died," I shouted in his ear. "But I have to go see my mother."

First, I had to break the news to Ruby, and clear it at a collective meeting—two weeks of vacation and two of unpaid leave.

"You're kidding," said Marvette, who had just posted a new schedule.

"You're kidding," said Ruby, who had caught me on the rebound from my last trip east and had been foolish enough to believe me when I swore I wouldn't go back.

"That was different," I told Ruby. "We shouldn't have let Gloria run the show. Donna swears she's ready to do it right this time."

"Call me jealous," Ruby said. "I barely had a mother, much less siblings, but Donna doesn't speak to you for months, even years. Then one word from her and you drop everything. I always imagined I'd be standing here encouraging you to go, to hold on to whatever family you've got. But they only call you in a crisis. I'm not sure I can compete."

"What the hell do you mean 'compete'?"

"If you're always on call for them, can you really be with me?"

"I am with you, Ruby. This is real life, right here in Chicago, but I have to go. It's my first decent chance to take care of my mother."

"It sounds like a set-up."

"Are you forbidding me to go?"

"What a stupid thing to say!"

"It was a ridiculous thing to say. And I'm going. And I'm sorry."

I marveled at my own conviction. One phone call, and I was talking like Vera's situation had flipped from chronic to acute. Well, if hers hadn't,

Donna's had. I was glowing, humming. No complaint or caution from Ruby could stop me. I was ready to swallow that highway whole.

The sun was just rising when I turned into the gravel driveway at Donna's house. The smell of roses thickened the air. Get up, stand up, Bob Marley called out through the open windows. Don't give up the fight. Six a.m. and the farmhouse was rocking. Before I'd made it halfway up the front walk, the door swung open. No one stood in the doorway. Six a.m. and Donna was playing hide-and-seek.

"Surprise!" She jumped out when I got within range.

Surprise all right. She was as suntanned and muscular as ever, but tucked up under her sleeveless blue tunic was an extra part—a high, round, unmistakably pregnant belly.

"Jesus Christ," I said. "You didn't tell me." I hadn't heard from her in ten months, not since Anthony's unconvincing performance at Dulano's.

"Amazing, isn't it?" Donna asked. "It worked on the first try."

"First try with who?"

She shrugged.

"Like, you didn't ask his name?"

"Didn't have a name. Just a number."

I reflected for a moment on the image of my sister—recently separated from her husband, appearing more butch by far than me—striding into a sperm bank and plunking down her money. I didn't actually know what a sperm bank looked like, so I pictured a library—a reception desk and shelves stacked with glass vials.

"It's what you would have done," she said.

"You" in this case meant lesbians, women who generally excluded men from their beds. Not me. I was only beginning to adjust to the idea of someone needing me. The baby was due in three months, in September.

"What about work?" I asked. Such a cloddy, pre-feminist question, but my curiosity got the better of me.

She had taken a job doing bids for Rocco Gianetti, her friend Carla's younger brother. Rocco was halfway in age between Donna and me, someone we each would have overlapped with in high school, except he'd been sent up to reform school by the time I started ninth grade. He was the *Mount Kisco Courier's* biggest scoop of 1973: busted for breaking into suburban homes, stealing only the cars, and driving them until they ran out of gas. Rocco Gianetti, once an aimless young thief, now an up-and-coming housing developer. He had regained the straight and narrow, had dedicated himself to integrity, hard work, and AA. Now he'd given my pregnant sister a sales job, not out of charity, but because he understood marketing.

"Yuppies trust me." Donna beat out a reggae rhythm on her belly. "They start out all aggressive about their three written bids. Then, they end up hiring Rocco even when our bid comes in highest."

Here was the Donna I used to love—animated, irreverent, talking like I was her pal. Next thing I knew, she'd pulled out the phone book and a spiral-bound guide with the United Way logo, a hand out, palm up, holding a rainbow.

"We need to mobilize our resources," she said. "To call in outside help."

Seeing her pregnant dampened my fire. It wasn't the baby on the way, only that she hadn't bothered to tell me.

"I've been driving all night. You think we could ease into this?" I said.

"Tell you what. We'll go to the beach."

The seduction was on. Straight to my heart my sister flew. Since the day she turned sixteen, she had a bag packed for the beach. She tossed in the phone book and the United Way guide, an extra towel for me, a notebook and pen.

"Just remember I'm sleep-deprived," I told her.

"You're the boss," she said. "Whenever you're ready, we'll talk."

She called Rocco's business and left a message on the tape: "My little sister Frannie just appeared on my doorstep. I'm keeping tonight's appointments, but I won't be in till then."

We were on the road at seven-thirty, an hour past Donna's usual time. We'd go to Jones Beach—closer, more crowded, and all-around less hip than Robert Moses. There'd be a line of cars at the park entrance and slim pickings for space on the sand, but Donna was uncomplaining, unflappable, completely lacking in irritability. I'd have said it was the hormones, but why concede a point to biological determinism? Instead, I said Donna was finally doing exactly what she wanted.

Every other word out of my sister's mouth was Rocco. Rocco and the twelve steps as we unfurled the brown plaid blanket. Rocco who believed that yoga, meditation, and psychological counseling could relieve anyone's woes. Rocco, Rocco, Rocco—as we shlepped across the lukewarm sand, as she smeared Bain de Soleil on her thighs, as she followed me down to my ritual first tasting of the water.

"Donna," I asked, "are you falling in love with him?"

She said, "God, no. He's married to Kathy Moran. Plus, he's a fanatic about emotional responsibility. I'm okay alone. For now."

I stared at her belly. She wouldn't be alone for long. I was going to be Aunt Frannie, to someone who, unlike my niece Tina, I stood a chance of getting to know.

I said, "I hate to ask, but have you seen Gloria?"

"Not since Christmas. She doesn't believe in divorce."

"Like I don't believe in Santa Claus?"

"Like I should have tried harder. I should have quit taking the pill and let Billy deal with what happened."

By my unofficial estimates, ninety-five percent of women in her situation would have done just that, but I hesitated to say so. She was bound to hear it as an insult.

"He counted pills," she said. "'Did you take it, did you take it?' He questioned me every day. That's how much he didn't want to be a father." We waded into the bracing ocean. I resisted an urge to reach over and pat the drum of her belly.

Back at the blanket, Donna set up her canvas chair. Where she used to hold an aluminum foil reflector in front of her face, she now held *Your Baby and Child from Birth to Age Five*. I dreamed about Ruby while the sun warmed me, waking up occasionally just to roll over. Every time I drifted off again, I resisted the urge to scoot closer to Donna, to wrap an arm around her legs.

At one o'clock she roused me. "You're starting to burn. Come on, I'll buy you some clams."

We drove to a seafood restaurant along the strip, a free-standing building ringed by parking lots—to one side a used car dealership, to the other a Hostess bakery outlet. Clam-bo-ree, it said on the side of the building. The kind of place where you never have to wait for a table.

"You want a beer?" Donna asked. "I'll buy you one." I was already groggy, but what the hell. She ordered two fried clam baskets, and a Heineken's for me. This was the big sister I used to know, generous and supple.

The clams were perfect, whole ones, their bellies spurting hot and sweet when I bit into them. The beer was cold and bitter, just the right contrast. We hardly talked, except to exclaim about how good everything tasted. How hard it was to find decent clams, with everyone selling clam strips these days.

The waitress laid down our check and cleared away our plates. "Okay," I told Donna. "Down to business. Let's take a look at those books."

Our mother's problem, Donna had decided, was depression—undiagnosed and untreated because Anthony, the professional nominally in charge of Vera's care, had a lifelong stake in not noticing. The solution was to get someone else involved—a mental health worker, not a doctor, one who made house calls, if such a thing existed.

Once upon a time, I would have sold my soul to hear my sister talk like this. Now I wasn't so sure. I chafed against casting any professional as our hero, against defining the problem in strictly individual terms. But there was no point in debating philosophy with Donna.

"We'll see what's in here," she said, with a couple of thumps on her United Way bible.

I leafed through the state and county pages of the phone book. She copied down only two items, the county crisis unit and social work department. I wanted to copy down everything—the battered women's shelter, council on aging, vulnerable adult protection, the center for independent living, and an intriguing item called the impaired physicians' program, listed under the state board of medical practice.

"What's that one for?" Donna asked, her voice cracking the tiniest bit.

"Just a possibility," I said softly. No need to alarm her. The conjunction of 'impaired' with 'physician' intrigued me—a chink in the armor, perhaps the only spot on earth where doctors admitted publicly to the fallibility of their own kind.

Donna's goal was short-term, well-focused, and achievable: get Vera to consent and follow through on just one meeting with a counselor. See what developed from there.

My sister had plans for me, too. I was to make the phone calls. Get put on hold at the county. Explain the situation. Hang around the farmhouse for the promised return calls. Explain that regardless of what Anthony earned, our mother had no money. Line up the best possible help out there. Convince them to take us at the bottom of the sliding scale. We'd work on Vera together when the moment came. Donna had a job, and a baby on the way. Yes, I was spending my vacation time to be here, but I could solve that by living closer, couldn't I?

I said, "If I lived closer, I'd be working this month—not sitting around your house," but she wasn't listening.

188

~ Two ~

Her phone rang that Saturday while I was cooking French toast at her house—9:01 a.m. on the stovetop digital clock.

"You get it," she said. "She's your mother too."

But I moved too slowly, and the machine picked up.

"Donna? Donna?" Vera shouted as if her voice alone could span the distance. Then quietly, "I'll try you later."

"Saturdays are hard for her," my sister said.

"Why's that?" I asked.

"Because he sleeps away from home on Tuesday, Friday, and Saturday nights," she told me without flinching.

I said nothing. I took the warm jar of syrup from the pan of water, and dried off the bottom with a dish towel.

"So what do you want?" Donna asked. "Should I say you were right?"

I turned off the stove and slid our breakfast onto two plates.

"It's complicated, Frannie. He's gone a lot, but when he's there he's more there than ever. He even took her to a Valentine's Day luncheon at the MS Society."

I stirred half-and-half into my coffee, poured syrup on my French toast, and cut it into small square bites. Donna did the same. By now she was playing the same waiting game as me.

"So how does he explain his absence three nights a week?" I gave in and asked.

"He's said he's working in the emergency room, but it's not like when he used to sleep at home and take calls. He said he has to work the entire shift because he's mentoring the younger doctors."

She didn't seem to hear any sexual implication in this, and I turned away to hide my smirk. "Do you believe him?" I asked.

"Of course not."

"Does Vera?"

"I don't know. She tells Gloria everything's fine. She tells me she's miserable. I had to make a rule—no calls before nine on Saturday. She was driving me crazy."

The Vera I'd spent my youth with was far less demanding. Even if they'd slept for years at opposite ends of the house, it had balanced her to have a husband at home.

Donna did bids for Rocco on both Saturday and Sunday, to accommodate all religious and recreational preferences. Usually, once her appointments were booked, she'd squeeze in a visit to our mother. This time, she wanted to send me in her place. Actually, she wanted to escort me, to drop me off and pick me up on her way to and from her job sites. That way, she could make an appearance, could spend a few minutes with Vera and me, without losing a whole afternoon.

"Fine," I told her. It seemed only fair.

The rhododendron in front of my parents' house was laden with plush pink blooms, so thick they almost blocked the walkway. Nadine opened the front door when I rang. She carried a Bible, her finger stuck between the pages to keep her place. "Your Mama's in the kitchen," she said, and headed upstairs to her room.

I shut the door on the sunshine, on the confectionery pink and green. Inside, it was shady and dim.

My mother sat at the kitchen table, looking uncharacteristically ready for action. "Welcome back," she said. "Isn't Donna with you?"

"What do you need?" I asked. "Donna went to work."

Her eyes had been bothering her, and she wanted Donna to help sort her mail.

"I can help," I said.

"I don't want to put you straight to work," she said. "It's so rare that you visit."

"It's not work, it's nosiness," I told her. It was something to do while I worked up the nerve to invite her to therapy in her own home in just two days.

She giggled and sent me to the kitchen drawer where she'd hidden a heap of papers for sorting. I couldn't help noticing that the linoleum floor was cracked and flaking, the kitchen cabinet fronts dried out and buckling, the handle on the drawer wobbly. I grabbed a screwdriver and tightened the handle, a manageable problem.

Vera said, "The place is a mess."

"It's not bad," I told her. Although old, the kitchen was clean, everything within Nadine and Consuela's power well taken care of. It was the long-term things your average homeowner should attend to that had grown dingy. My parents' house looked like rental property.

We made stacks of catalogues Vera might want to order from, piles of magazines she might want to read if her eyes cleared up, a bundle of seven-month-old Christmas cards so she could savor the brief personal notes. We collected a handful of address changes, including one from Helen Gennaro who had moved to Phoenix with her husband, and a small bag of trash.

"Throw it," Vera said about almost every item. "Oh, wait, but what if I want to read it again?" My job, as I saw it, was to support any and every decision, to support the act of deciding itself.

After the mail, it was time for her lunch, a can of Progresso minestrone and a few Saltine crackers. "Nadine will do it," she said, but Nadine was still upstairs, reading the Bible. She retreated whenever a daughter arrived, unlike Consuela who stepped in closer to Vera's side, reminding us by her presence that this was no longer our home.

Most days after lunch, my mother transferred to bed for a nap. "Nadine will do it," she said, again.

"I'll do it," I told her.

I was untangling the chains of the Hoyer lift and getting ready to hoist Vera from the chair to the bed when I heard Donna coming in the back door. "Hi, Ma," she called out, but she stayed in the kitchen. I heard water running, cabinets opening and closing, the refrigerator opening and closing too.

By the time I'd gotten Vera settled on top of the covers, Donna had washed the few lunch dishes and put away the leftover soup. Now she was packing herself a bag of groceries—a half string of figs from the fruit bowl, half the salami from a white paper deli package, one silly stalk of broccoli from the vegetable crisper, a can of frozen orange juice, a carton of cottage cheese. She lifted the lid on the carton and sniffed before putting it in her bag. Now she was pouring herself a scotch on the rocks.

She looked at me sharply. "Only one," she said, laying a hand on her belly.

I wasn't worried about fetal alcohol exposure. I was thinking about this: Donna hadn't had a drink at her own house, or at the beach. Didn't order herself a beer to wash down the fried clams. Didn't soak half a watermelon in rum and smuggle it into the state park like she and Billy used to. Donna was drinking this whiskey because it was free, but first, she went in to kiss my mother's cheek before taking a sip.

~ Three ~

The sedan that pulled up in front of the house on Monday had the county seal stenciled on the doors. If it hadn't, I would have sworn a child stepped out from behind the wheel—a diminutive, birdlike figurine. It was going to be difficult, on first glance, to take this social worker seriously.

I had expected a strapping Mary Nathan type, a physical therapist of the mind, someone who would push and pull on Vera's thought processes, massage her attitudes, rub hope like almond oil into the thirsty folds of her brain. Someone who would press her to look at her options and finally, when the time was right, would rip away the blankets and sheets and roust her out of bed.

I studied the bird-woman as she came up the walk, but refrained from answering the door until she actually rang. I didn't want to come across as eager—or worse, spooky. She already knew half our secrets: that I had called for help, that Anthony held office hours on Monday morning, that it was imperative to meet when he was gone.

Up close, she radiated intelligence. Evidence of this flashed and reflected off the many small planes of her face.

"Carol Keenan," she said, as she stepped across the threshold. Her voice was squeaky and high, completely lacking in resonance. My prejudice flared back up.

"Francesca D'Amato. Thank you for coming."

We balanced there in the foyer, two people who had just agreed to dance. The music was starting up, but I felt unsure of the steps. I stalled for time by checking out her gray linen suit and cameo pin, the light touch she took with her make-up, but she knew this dance, and had no trouble taking the lead.

"Your mother is—where?"

"Sitting up in bed, where it's more private. That's what she said," I added, because this seemed like an occasion for exactness.

"We'll meet together the first time," Carol told me. "It's Mrs. D'Amato's call as to whether or not I come back." The same thing the intake worker had said. Clarity was the name of this game. I liked it. I ushered her through the kitchen where Consuela, head down, scrubbed the stove top.

"Good morning," Carol greeted Consuela, who said nothing. I ushered her into Vera's room.

My mother's bed was a throne, my mother a queen granting an audience. "Pleased to meet you." She held out a hand to Carol. By her demeanor alone she made it plain that she would entertain this social worker's desires, accommodate them if possible, but there was nothing she herself, Vera D'Amato, either lacked or needed. That's why she could afford to be so generous.

192

"May I sit down?" Carol asked, looking around.

I went to the kitchen to get two chairs, and a flood of shame engulfed me: all the times I had talked to Vera standing up, towering over her. All the times I had lectured her with one foot out the door. The ways I had used being upright as power, an antidote to her enormous dejection, but perhaps symbolically a way of putting her down. It wasn't entirely my fault. She didn't encourage people to get close. Before today, she'd never had a chair in her room, and I hadn't thought to carry one in.

Carol took her seat easily, gracefully. The therapist began the conversation with the facts: who she was, where she worked, that she had come at my request.

"Yes," Vera nodded. "I'm glad we're talking. I've been worried about Frannie. She's been unhappy for so long."

"Not true," I said. "I'm happy about most things. I just don't like it that you think so poorly of yourself."

"But I don't." She spoke so graciously, so magnanimously, I worried about who the social worker would believe.

"Can you give your mother an example?" Carol asked.

I could have given a thousand, but I started with this: "Anthony calls you stupid every day. Denigrates you and your needs. Never has a kind word. And you tolerate it."

My mother said, "I think you're imagining things. He has never— maybe once or twice—as a joke."

"Not once or twice. Day in and day out for my first seventeen years. I'm not so sure what's been happening lately," I admitted.

"You remember back to the day you were born?" Vera betrayed herself on that one, her question much too haughty for the occasion. Before I could pounce, Carol Keenan called a time out.

"Mrs. D'Amato," she said. "I'm going to suppose you know best. Your life and marriage have brought the rewards you wanted. But even the most contented of people have aspirations. Little dissatisfactions, perhaps. Adjustments they'd like to make. That's where setting goals comes in. Your life is good if you say it's good—" With a dip of an eyebrow she silenced my impending interruption. "But let's just say: pie in the sky. If you could have one thing different, what would it be?"

"Pie in the sky?" my mother echoed.

Carol nodded.

Vera was troubled, she had to admit, by the house falling into disrepair.

"Great." Carol Keenan dug in. What could they do about that, she wondered out loud. What improvements could Mrs. D'Amato imagine making?

"None," Vera said. She'd been talking pie in the sky. In real life, improvements cost money. Look at how much he already spent on her care.

I opened my mouth to protest, but Carol Keenan beat me to the finish. She managed to both speak first and telegraph another silencing look, a cross between a wink and a grimace. Trust me, I imagined it said. And what choice did I have?

"I understand," the therapist told my mother. "Let's back up." Any other wishes Vera might make? Any desires that didn't require money?

The woman was a genius. I had called for help, but I hadn't really expected to get any. All my righteous indignation, my convictions, all my lonely insights, time to set those burdens down. Time to sit back and watch this woman at work, an itinerant saleswoman, peddling the possibility of self-worth. Like the Fuller Brush men my mother used to warn me about, Carol Keenan had placed her tiny foot squarely in the door. Most amazing of all, this bird-woman conjurer had gotten Vera talking. Not only talking, but admitting to desires:

She wished her daughters would get along with each other, and with their father. She wanted Anthony to stay home sometimes. She hoped that Donna's marriage could be repaired, that the baby would have a father. She'd love it if I, Frannie, would change my mind and find a man. She dreamed of having a manicure. She'd like to see her own feet. She regretted not going to Mass on Sunday. She missed her mother and son, and longed to visit their graves.

"Good," Carol said. "We've got a lot to work with here."

Not the list I would have written, but an impressive one nevertheless. Three impulses shot through me: to prostrate myself in gratitude before this social worker and my mother, to shower Vera with solutions, to run and call Ruby and tell her about this miracle, that I had been right to come after all. I followed the second.

"We can go to the cemetery together, Ma. The paratransit will take you there, and to church." A manicure would be easy enough. Her feet? Nothing a hand mirror couldn't solve.

"No, don't bother," Vera said, "I'm too old to change my whole life."

In a flash, I hated her. I wanted to retaliate, to flatten her, but the therapist checked me before I could start in. "Mrs. D'Amato," she said, "There's no magic in this process. We take your list, I help you figure out what's in your power to control. If something's outside of that realm, I can't bring it in. But you may be surprised at how much we can achieve."

With that, she secured an invitation to come back.

194

"All right?" she asked me lightly as the hour came to a close, and although my blood was still simmering I nodded yes. Better than all right. Beyond any reasonable expectations.

"Thank you so much," my mother said. "May I call you Carol? This has been lovely. Francesca will see you out."

~ Four ~

I could have gone back to Donna's with happy news, news of a revolution in progress. Thanks to my sister and me, our mother had spoken out loud of wanting things, to a stranger, no less. Had invited that stranger to return next week. Might even let her become somewhat of a friend. I could have praised Donna about how smart she'd been to initiate this, to go looking for outside help. But before she could even ask, "How did it go?" I besieged her about the cottage cheese.

"What cottage cheese?" she asked, but her insolence gave her away.

"The one in your fridge." I opened the door for emphasis, and a cloud of mist formed around me. "The one Vera was hoping to eat today with her cling peaches." I slammed the refrigerator door.

"Listen," my sister said. "A thousand times he's bought cottage cheese and it's spoiled before they eat it. They throw away unopened cartons all the time. Why didn't you just go to town and get a new one?"

"I did. That's not the point."

She didn't ask me to clarify my point. She didn't say anything.

"You're gaslighting her, Donna."

This time she regarded me with genuine innocence. "I don't know what that means."

I skipped the synopsis of the Ingrid Bergman movie. "You're making her—" I began, and then started over. "You're creating occasions for her to doubt herself. 'Oh, stupid me! I was so sure there was cottage cheese. I must be going crazy.' At the same time you're sponsoring a mental health intervention."

"Jesus," Donna said. "Every day's an opportunity for her to think she's stupid and crazy."

"Why add to it?"

"Why didn't you tell her?"

"What?"

"Donna took the cottage cheese."

195

"Why didn't you tell her, 'I'm taking it'?"

"It wasn't important to me at the time. If it mattered so much to you, you should have said it." This last line delivered as she walked out of the kitchen.

In the week I'd been back in New York spring had rolled over into summer. Clear days and crisp nights had collapsed under climbing temperatures, intensifying humidity, and finally in the last twelve hours, a full-blown metro-wide heat inversion. It made perfect sense that Donna and I were fighting. It was hotter than hell, she was pregnant, I was camping out in her home. All through the county, the air smelled like a wet dog. We had come to the edge of our map.

We had accomplished what Donna proposed to do, and hadn't even charted a fantasy about what might follow. If Vera had refused to see Carol, had seen her once and refused any more, my sister and I could have commiserated. We could have said, Well, we tried, and then carried on separately. But our mother had said "yes" for the first time in decades. Potential hung with the water in the air—burdensome, stifling, but silly to waste it. We needed each other as allies while we waited to see what Vera would do, and I needed to get off my high horse about small things like cottage cheese.

I followed the sound of rhythmic creaking out to the screened-in back porch. Donna sat in a maple rocker, rocking with a vengeance, her attention riveted to *Your Baby and Child*. I will not fight, I will not fight, I will not fight, the rocker seemed to say.

Sometimes a person doesn't know how to stop fighting—with lovers, with family. I sat down in the wicker chair opposite, and watched my sister for the longest time. I caught her glancing at me. She began to turn the pages, to actually read. The book became a book, instead of a shield.

"Listen to this," she said, looking up.

I tipped my head to show her I was listening.

She read, "A baby will not fully understand an object unless he puts it in his mouth."

"You think we were allowed to do that?" I asked.

"You weren't," she told me. "I doubt I was either."

Donna had been readying a nest for the baby, clearing out the attic space opposite her bedroom. The sewing room, Billy used to call it, under the rafters to the left of the landing. He had dragged my mother's pedal-operated Singer up there and set it up under the high window.

"Here," he'd told Donna, "take a look at this." She could make curtains, and at the same time watch the deer that wandered into the back yard. But my sister never opened the machine, never loaded the bobbins or gave the wheel a spin. She intended all along to turn the room into a nursery. While she waited for Billy to embrace the notion of fatherhood, the junk piled up—cartons of Christmas decorations, bags of clothes, boxes of her old college term papers.

Now all that had been carried down to the basement or the trash, and the sewing machine down to the dining room to replace Billy's aquarium. Donna had emptied and swept the nursery clean, to make room for a crib Carla promised her. In the meantime, she'd painted the sloping ceiling and low walls—a rich periwinkle blue that made me feel like I was free-falling through space.

"Is it too blue?" she asked, rubbing her belly. "What if this creature is a girl?"

"It's not blue like a boy," I told her, "it's blue like a sky." Not our happy sky overhead, a melancholy violet sky stretching from one galaxy to the next.

"Let me put some landmarks in," I said, "to brighten it up."

"You think so?"

I needed a project to deliver me from idleness, some reason to hang around her house. I could have gone to the beach or the city, could have walked in the woods or at least parked down by the reservoir, but the weather was oppressive and I was bound to miss something unless Vera knew where to find me. What, I couldn't say. Some watershed event. My mother's life was due to change course.

"I'll cut out some stencils," I told Donna. I could see it all: stars, moons, comets, planets with rings scattered across the walls of outer space. No primary colors, no pastels either. Just good strong colors, warm counterparts to the periwinkle. Red-orange, orange-yellow. They'd pop off the page. A deep eggplant purple for contrast—almost black.

"You really think so?" she asked again.

"You bet," I told her. "It'll be like no nursery you've ever seen."

For her second meeting with Carol Keenan, my mother wanted to get up and dressed. She'd wear a rayon frock with red, yellow, and violet stripes—as long as I didn't think it too gaudy.

"It's beautiful," I said, pulling the dress from the closet.

She had called me at Donna's at eight that morning, after Anthony left for the station with Nadine.

"Check it out," I told my sister when I hung up the phone. "Vera gave Consuela the morning off. She's just finagled to be all alone with the social worker, except she needs help getting into her clothes."

In my headlong rush to reform her life, to rescue her from days and nights of neglect, I hadn't considered what it would feel like for Vera to never have an hour to herself, not even five minutes when no one on earth knew what she was doing.

Donna slammed down the lever on the toaster. "She leaves it to the last minute. It's fucking presumptuous."

"So let her presume."

I wanted to say yes to anything my mother wanted. Anything for the next two weeks, and whatever could be carried out long distance too. Visiting more often. Maybe living closer. Not Mount Kisco, but New York City—Ruby often said she'd like to live in Brooklyn. No way, I always told her, it's too risky. But I could imagine it working, if Vera gave us good reason. If she could get in the habit of taking charge.

"I had a bath last night from Nadine," she told me when I got to her house. "All I need today are the finishing touches."

She raised her arms and I floated the dress over her head, tucked in the label, smoothed the collar from the inside. The backs of my fingers brushed against her damp skin.

"It's going to be another scorcher," I said. "How about a little powder?" The perfumed talc clouded the room and settled on my tongue.

She wanted a strand of yellow beads, and yellow clip-on button earrings, her red, sling-backed, open-toed shoes, a spritz of water on her hair to coax some of the curl back out. Now she wanted me to go.

"I'll wait here," she said, wheeling herself to her favorite window. "Leave the front door ajar, just this much."

"Have fun," I said on my way out.

I was stirring a brand new quart of slick orange-red paint when Vera called at just a few minutes past eleven. "The lady is coming again next Monday," she told me. "She wants to know if both you and Donna can be here."

I always heard therapists liked to meet an entire family, but Vera made no mention of Gloria. And just as well. This was Donna's and my project; Gloria wouldn't have approved.

"No problem. We'll be there," I told Vera, doing my best not to sound over-eager.

~ Five ~

When I was twelve, my father took me to Boston. "I have business there," he announced one night at supper. "On Friday, just for the day. Frannie will accompany me." The business was at his old medical school, and I was still heir apparent to the throne. Gloria hadn't shown up yet to change that.

A couple of nights before we left, Mr. Klein and Mr. Radke, the accountant and lawyer, came over for coffee and a round of signatures. Anthony planned to give the medical school money when he died; he wanted to deliver a letter to that effect in person.

"Please, Doctor," Radke said. "Registered mail is good enough. Better to keep a low profile in these matters."

"Don't be silly," my father told him. "One doesn't purchase something sight unseen. It's been over twenty years since I've laid eyes on the establishment."

Klein made another attempt. "If I may say so, Doctor. You're making a bequest, not a purchase. A modest amount, as it currently stands." He chuckled, and swigged down the last of his coffee. "You should feel good about it, by all means, but don't look for your name on a building. Not yet."

"Of course not," Anthony said. "A day trip to visit my alma mater. To show it to Frannie."

Thursday night, Anthony called Donna at her dorm in Binghamton and told her to come straight home, because he and I were leaving and my mother needed company.

It was early April, not yet spring, but the winter's snow had been washed away by rain. "We'll take the train," my father said. "It's more relaxing than driving."

On the train, we chose two seats facing forward, and shared a *New York Times*. Long before it was time to swap sections, I saw drowsiness overtake him, the paper dropping into his lap, and he surrendered to the hypnosis of the rails. I scooted over to the empty window seat across the aisle.

The day was overcast and drizzly, the bare trees sodden and dark. Under the dull sky a few bits of color glowed, left over from fall—the twiggy red and purple shrubs, the golden tops of tall grasses. I spent hours peering past the grime on the window, and then the open spaces began to thicken, to fill in with factories and apartments. When the train pulled into Back Bay Station, Anthony woke up.

"Ready?" he said.

Out on the street, the rain had stopped. The sun struggled to break through the clouds.

He said, "As a student, I'd walk from the station to school, for health reasons, and also to conserve financially." Then he went ahead and flagged down a taxi.

The medical school was an old red brick building with a modern addition built of a lighter, tan-colored brick. "All new," he said. The two colors and styles of architecture looked wrong side-by-side, but he was acting proud enough to have built it.

When he opened the door to the old wing, I saw him and me, the cars, brownstones, and sky behind us, all reflected in the swinging oval of beveled glass. Inside the school, the front hallway was carpeted, dark, and hushed. A few paces down the hall, a second ornate door lead to the dean's office.

"May I help you?" Although it was 1971, the dean's secretary wore a bouffant hairdo. Beneath her desk she had kicked off her pumps.

"Doctor Anthony D'Amato," my father told her. "And my daughter Francesca. I have an appointment with Dean Allen."

She made a face like she didn't believe him. "Just a minute." She got up, crossed the room, her stockinged feet padding on the carpet, and opened an inner door. She came back quite promptly. "All right," she said, and I wondered why she bore us a grudge.

Dean Allen was younger than my father, and thinner. Unlike Anthony's clothes, his suit seemed to drape the way it was supposed to. He and my father shook hands.

"Anthony D'Amato. Class of forty-seven. This young lady is my daughter, Francesca. Class of eighty-four, if she's lucky." He smiled so the dean would know it was a joke. If *you're* lucky, I thought, but only half-heartedly. It felt more difficult than usual to hate him.

My father continued, "I believe my attorney phoned you this week?"

"Yes." Dean Allen's smile was dim. "Quite thoughtful of you, Dr. D'Amato. And how may I be of service today?"

"Well—" Anthony reached into his breast pocket for an envelope. The corners were dog-eared from the trip. "I wanted to deliver this in person and perhaps my daughter and I could take a look around?"

The dean accepted the envelope and placed it to one side of his desk blotter. "Please, feel free to wander. I'd show you the new wing myself, if I didn't have another appointment pending."

My father's posture shifted ever-so-slightly, his back straightened. Other than that, you wouldn't have known he'd been insulted. Dean Allen held out his hand. Anthony shook it, and we were dismissed.

He led me up two flights to the top floor of the new medical school addition. We zigzagged along the corridor, and peered through narrow windows inset in closed classroom doors. We looked into lecture halls— some empty, some full. When we finished the third floor, we took up the second. Anthony wasn't much of a tour guide. "A class in there," he'd say occasionally—as if I couldn't tell.

Sometimes he caught a glimpse of what was written on the blackboard, a snatch of what was being said. "Physiology," he reported. "Biochemistry." I felt sleepy and disengaged, weary of humoring him at this game that went on and on. We continued like this until the basement.

"Laboratories," he told me as he tried the knob on one of the doors. It swung open, and we stepped through. The lab was empty. A row of windows stretched from mid-wall to ceiling. The sun had finally pushed past the clouds outside. Golden light bathed the room; it washed over the work tables in the middle and the gallon jars lining the shelves around the perimeter.

There were body parts in those jars—internal organs, probably from human beings. Brains, it looked like, and hearts, submerged in clear liquid like so many jars of pickles. In one, a slab of something dense and purple that reminded me of liver. I stood back as Anthony strolled around this odd museum, and I thought about the lamb heads they sold in the meat case at the A&P, one eye staring up through tightly wrapped plastic.

"Look at this, Frannie," he said, and I ventured further into the room. He pointed to a big jar with a tiny brain—a baby's brain, most likely, bobbing loosely.

"It looks like a cauliflower," he said and giggled, a high-pitched chortle I'd never heard before. The jar was so heavy, he had to heft it with both arms. He held it aloft and pressed the glass to his forehead.

"Imagine having this," he said, "in here."

For a moment, I liked him more than I ever had. Still, I felt relieved that he set the jar down by the time a student walked in. Just standing there embarrassed me enough. The student looked at us quizzically.

"Anthony D'Amato," my father told him. "Class of forty-seven. And Francesca D'Amato, my youngest daughter. You're a student here?"

"Yes," the younger man said, and turned to rummage for something in a drawer.

My father brushed a lock of hair from my shoulder. "Ready for a bowl of soup?" he asked. "A little repast?"

We exited the lab and the building. Out on the street, he hailed a cab to the North End.

~ Six ~

I was sunbathing naked on Donna's upstairs deck when I heard the neighbor's car turn in at the end of the road. I was listening to the bees in the lilacs and the frogs in the swamp and recalling how, at the age of seven or eight, I used to walk over to Shaffer's Pond on my own in the summertime. I'd scoop tadpoles and murky pond water into a wide-mouthed peanut butter jar, carry them home, and dump them into a fishbowl on top of my dresser. Sometimes their back legs would sprout, but usually not even that, before they died. No one told me they needed something green, a piece of plant in the water, to keep them going. Food, too. I made the same mistake a half dozen times.

I was musing about the unintentional murder of tadpoles, pretending to read a book about the Mexican mural movement, and wondering with some earnestness whether Ruby and I could truly make a life in New York when it became viscerally clear that the car I heard wasn't a neighbor's. It was coming to the end of the road. On a deeper level, I realized only one person on earth could drive a half mile at that particular over-confident but still leisurely pace. I grabbed Donna's seersucker robe and peered over the railing as the champagne Cutlass turned in under the pines.

Two doors opened. A man stepped out from the passenger side, younger than my father, more fair than I had imagined, and surprisingly bulky through his neck and shoulders. He wore an olive green knit polo shirt. Anthony wore his usual, a short-sleeved white cotton shirt. They spent a few minutes standing in the driveway, looking at the border of violets Donna had planted, and at my truck—the wood topper still as pretty as ever. Just from the cant of their torsos, the way they stood idly, I could see these two were indeed lovers. Your run-of-the-mill gay couple, I'd have thought, if I came across them at the Art Institute, spanning the high and low ends of middle age. Unremarkable except that one was still married to my mother.

I threw on shorts and a t-shirt and came down the back stairs to the garden. "So it's true," I said, walking up behind them. "If I knew you were coming, I'd have baked a cake."

My father gave me a peculiar look, a cross between proud parent and cornered dog. "Frannie," he said.

My Ethel Merman imitation was losing air; in a minute I'd have to think of something real to say.

"Fran." Another pause and then Anthony finished the thought. "This is Larry."

"Charmed," Larry said.

We didn't shake hands. His nasal voice and the thickness of his upper body called to mind a fourteen-year-old, a JV football player—or better yet, the most talented boy in theater club, the one who always lost the male lead to the boy who looked like Anthony Perkins.

I said, "Donna's not here. She's at the office today."

"I know," Anthony told me. "I stopped there to see her."

"You saw her too?" I asked Larry.

"No," he said, "we thought we'd start with the easy one first."

I said, "You've got to be kidding. Ever since I could talk, Anthony's had me pegged as the trouble maker, or ever since my brother left home."

Both men glanced at the car as if considering escape.

"Cup of coffee?" I offered. I didn't know Larry. I had no reason to be so hard on him.

They followed me into the house. What would happen if Donna came home early, I wondered. How much were these two gambling, and why?

I put the water on to boil, and set up a coffee cone and filter on top of the Melita pot. They sat at the kitchen table and watched me.

Finally, the kettle sang, and I joined them at the table. "I heard you were in town," my father began.

"I've been meaning to call," I said. "I've been at the house a couple of times, but you—"

"Don't worry about it," he told me.

Pretty soon, I'd have to quit claiming that this was the new Anthony. This was the only Anthony around, a man who had apparently shed his jealous habits. Twice in one week, I had opened his door to a stranger— not just a neighbor, a county mental health professional, tantamount to plotting treason. To my mother's credit, she'd kept her meetings with Carol

Keenan secret. But now there was a lack of vigilance, and some new need in my father.

He said, "We've been thinking we should talk to you, because you're... you've... you've lived... a similar... lifestyle... in Chicago."

I smirked at his awkward phrasing, and they both pitched forward to scrutinize me.

"Haven't you?" Larry asked, his voice just a bit shrill. This was no slick fellow. A computer programmer, I guessed. Had he quit his job, I wondered, or was Anthony only paying for the luxuries?

"I am a lesbian," I told them. "Not just in Chicago, all the time. Even here." I didn't complicate the story by mentioning that ever since kissing Gregory I'd entertained the thought of fucking men—the ones I already liked, not the losing sort I picked up as a teenager.

"This is love," Anthony said. "One can't control when and where love arises. Sometimes it comes unbidden." He sounded like a schoolboy who has memorized a famous piece of oratory. "Larry takes good care of me. He admires me and I admire him."

This was embarrassing. It was like those ads in the gay paper: daddy seeks houseboy. Seeks son. But Anthony had a son once, and blew it. He should have admired Jimmy enough to keep him around.

Undoubtedly it was Larry whom Gloria had spied on in the restaurant. But was he my father's first? I couldn't bring myself to ask.

I kept waiting to find out what he wanted from me. But this was it: Solace. Someone to confide in. A daughter who would approve, hold up a mirror, chit-chat about our mythical shared history. But I didn't approve. In principle maybe, their right to pleasure as they understood it, but what about my mother's pleasure, her need to be someone's beloved?

"I'm not like you," I said.

He recoiled a bit and looked down at the floor. For a second I regretted my meanness, but then he looked up again, and the clichés kept coming. "We fell in love at the opera. At *La Bohème*. Larry and I started sharing the box when his aunt and uncle gave him their subscription. We conversed for a couple of years; maybe we both indicated some interest. But often he had friends along, and I didn't know if I could make the leap. Then one day, we were alone. During Rodolfo's first aria, he reached over and took my hand."

This was not some weird pick-up scene. This was a relationship, complete with a proper introduction and courting period. Larry's aunt was the woman in the mink, the one with the lemon drops I had met when I was twelve.

My father said, "Your sister Gloria is very hard on you. Given a chance, she'd be hard on me too. She's not openminded like you and Donna. You get along well with Donna, don't you?"

"Well enough," I said, and I could see what he was after. He wanted to reassemble his family on higher ground, to use my experience to gauge who he might and might not count on.

"Your sister Gloria," Larry said, "is greedy and prudish, a deadly combination, just like those TV evangelists. And that husband of hers. What did you call them, Tony? Pecuniary extractors?"

It surprised me that Anthony tolerated him talking like this. "Gloria learned well," I pointed out. "Anthony can thank himself for that."

My father looked baffled.

"Graduate from college or you're out of my will. Marry Michael or you're out of my will."

"That's enough," he said.

"Well, why don't you just say, 'Accept Larry as the love of my life or you're out of my will'?"

Larry squirmed in his chair and looked out the window toward the garden.

"It isn't that simple," Anthony told me.

Although he didn't explain, I could guess what he meant: maintaining two households was expensive enough; divorce would have been even more so. Staying married was his best bet, emotionally and financially. Separate the doctor from his money, and you might find Larry back at the Met, sidling up to a better, more distinguished white-haired gentleman. One with fewer complications in his life. One without vindictive daughters like Gloria—and maybe me.

"So," I said to Larry. "You've been to Kalaupapa? Calcutta? Lambaréné?" I made my voice cheerful and inquisitive, and poured him a second cup of coffee.

I watched him tip off-center momentarily, then spring back up with his composure intact. "Yes," he said, "Beautiful places. Rich in human tragedy and heroism."

So they'd been at this at least four years. I had to give the guy credit for sticking around. He might have had Tokyo or Venice if he'd caught Anthony a few years earlier.

My father said, "Some people get stranded on conventionality. This isn't an easy life, but if an organism doesn't grow it will die."

"What about Vera? What about her need to grow?"

205

"I'm not holding her back. She's holding herself back."

"Your mother," Larry told me, "is a very lucky woman. Your father, so loyal, never skimping on her comfort."

He needed a new scriptwriter. We all did. But the two of them seemed convinced by what they were saying.

Anthony looked a thousand percent better than when he arrived—relaxed, unburdened. He was like one of those people you meet on a bus who gain relief by telling you their life story. "There was always something wrong with your mother," he said. "Something detached, unsympathetic."

That certainly was my experience, but I'd be damned if I'd discuss it in front of Larry. Anthony was the one who held me as a young child, and I frankly never knew which was worse: the loss I experienced when I decided to reject him or the failure to thrive that would have ensued if I'd been left alone with my uninterested mother.

He said, "She wasn't warm. A man needs affection."

"I don't want to hear about your sex life," I told him. "Why don't you just leave, have your own life, let Vera figure out hers?"

"Impossible," Anthony said.

Larry stood up suddenly, gathered the cups and spoons from the table, and carried them to the sink. "This has been very nice," he said. "Tony, we should go."

My father pushed back his chair to join his boyfriend. I stood too, so I wouldn't be the only one sitting. We were planted at three points of an equilateral triangle, Donna's round kitchen table filling the space between.

Now trouble crossed Anthony's brow "Your sisters—" he said. "You won't mention..."

Here was my opportunity to squeeze, to extort. I hadn't gone looking for his secrets; he had sought out a place to unload them. I could charge rent, a keeper's fee. Put me in your will, I could demand, although a will was never a sure bet. Send me a hundred, five hundred per week, starting now. Take out your checkbook. Better yet, beg forgiveness.

I gained scant satisfaction from imagining all this; he'd already cast himself as the victim in his own story. I didn't want money, nor to see him grovel. I wanted accountability, for him to make his choices, apologize for the rotten ones, and move on if he wanted. I neither threatened to tell, nor promised not to. I said nothing at all and the three of us spontaneously broke out of formation. Anthony led us in single file out of the house, through the garden, over to the Cutlass. They got in and slammed their doors. Larry buckled his seat belt, but Anthony didn't. I leaned over his open window and placed one hand on the roof of the car. The two men inside seemed trapped, like I could hurt them. But my father didn't roll up his window. They both stared straight ahead.

Finally, he turned the key in the ignition and revved the engine a few times.

"Listen," I said, still holding on. "I want you to let my mother go." Go where, I didn't know. It was the best demand I could make at the time.

"We'll talk about it another day," he told me. He put the car in reverse, and I stepped out of his way.

~ Seven ~

For her third meeting with the lady from the county, Vera selected a sleeveless dress with harlequin diamonds in yellow and royal blue. The yellow earrings and beads matched the dress perfectly.

Donna asked, "Where is your diamond pendant?" and rummaged around in my mother's night stand until she pulled out the hinged velvet box. "You should be wearing it," she said. I bristled at this false symbol of marriage being dragged out of its hiding place, especially since Vera didn't seem to miss it.

"Oh, yes," she said, "let's put that on."

I stepped back to let Donna operate the Hoyer lift. She handled her passenger quickly, almost roughly, but Vera didn't complain. She relaxed back into the swing as Donna pumped it higher.

Consuela had asked for the morning off again, this time for the choir concert at her daughter's school.

"Watch out," Donna said. "She'll start taking her Monday mornings off for granted."

I knew Consuela had adult kids, but was surprised to hear she had one in grade school.

"Nita," my mother told me. "Eight years old. The most charming little girl. She was an infant when Consuela started here. The aunt and older kids looked after her."

I stood behind my mother to brush her hair away from her brow. Donna kneeled in front, struggling to slip Vera's feet into navy blue low-heeled pumps.

"Do you ever think Nita could come live here?" I asked.

Donna scowled at me.

"Don't be silly," Vera said. "There isn't room. Besides, they have their own apartment."

It was silly of me to imagine true companionship for Vera, silly to recruit Consuela, of all people, for my romantic fantasy, to imagine her job would ever be more than a job.

When the car turned up the driveway, we all stiffened.

"The lady already?" Vera asked, but she must have known it was him. As surely as I could identify his voice, I recognized the rhythm and pitch of tires on asphalt. He squealed to an uncharacteristic stop, thrown off, in all likelihood, by my truck and Donna's car in the driveway.

"I'll go," I told Donna. Her eyes were wide, and she was holding her breath.

He lumbered as he came up the walk, a person whose every move required extra effort. I watched from the window and opened the front door before he could reach for his key.

"Visiting?" he asked, but didn't wait for an answer. He passed right by me and went straight to my mother's room.

"It is I, Vera," I heard him announce. "I forgot something on my desk for a patient. I'll see you tonight, around seven."

A pleasant enough, if oddly formal speech, but coming from him, still unreal. He didn't ask why we were there, why she was dressed so nicely. He headed upstairs, and I stood guard in the entryway. Coming downstairs, he tucked a small white envelope into his breast pocket. I could have sworn I saw him wink at me. Impersonating a solicitous husband was not all that demanding.

I didn't wink back. When we met again in the entryway, I went up on my toes a little, primed for a bit of verbal sparring. Quit being a scuzz, I wanted to tell him, quietly, so my mother wouldn't hear.

But his cockiness had faded already; a weary hang-dog look settled in its place. He stood flat footed, shoulders slumped. He wasn't scuffling with me, not today.

"Have a good one," I said. "See you later."

He planted himself there, unmotivated, unmovable, no longer in a hurry. Not to be ushered out the door, but as if he wanted something from me.

"I'll walk you out," I tried. "I forgot my bag in the truck." But it was too late. The Westchester County car was turning up the driveway. I felt like three people at once: a naughty child caught in a bind, a teenager pumped to fight, and an adult, if being adult means you keep your cool.

Anthony and I blinked at the bright midmorning sunshine as the bird woman came up the walk. He regarded her blankly.

"Doctor D'Amato?"

He nodded.

"I'm Carol Keenan, from the Westchester County mental health unit. I'm here to speak with your wife."

This was his cue to bar her entry, to banish her from his kingdom, to yell, It's my house I pay the bills, now get out. That would have been her cue to stand her ground, to assert flatly and professionally that in fact Mrs. D'Amato had a choice, and mine to start shouting, my father's to keep yelling, my mother's to address the social worker directly, to make her choice known, to say coldly and with great poise, You'd better go.

But that wasn't quite how it happened.

"I'm here to speak with your wife," she said.

"I see," he answered. "Unfortunately, I have patients waiting. Francesca, you'll make the lady a cup of coffee?" He shook her hand and lumbered off again.

His new-found politeness may have been pleasant for Vera, but it made me nervous. I found myself missing the authentic Anthony, the tyrannical bellowing one, whose feelings were inseparable from his actions.

Carol Keenan and I stood side by side on the front stoop, watching as he executed a careful U-turn at the crowded top of the driveway. He looked left and right before pulling out onto the street. He didn't used to be like this, I wanted to tell her. He didn't used to have anything to hide. But if this whole therapy business was going to work, I'd have to trust her to assess the situation herself.

My mother and Donna were sitting at the kitchen table when we came in. Donna's still-wide eyes widened even further.

I mouthed the word "fine."

"Mrs. D'Amato." Carol Keenan walked right over and took my mother's hand.

"Hello there! Wait, don't tell me." Vera laughed gaily, and searched her memory. "Carol!"

"Very good. How are you today?"

"Very well. You haven't met my middle daughter, Donna."

The room was bubbling over with positive regard.

"I saw your husband on his way to work," Carol told Vera. "We met on the front walk." A neutral statement, as far as I could tell, a sounding

209

device, like one Jacques Cousteau might set off underwater, to map out the submerged terrain.

Without missing a beat, my mother hardened, becoming brittle on the spot. "I've been thinking," she said. "This isn't really working. I've been planning to tell you, you shouldn't come back."

I watched Carol Keenan try to recover. Was there a reason, she wanted to know. Some different arrangement she and Mrs. D'Amato could work out?

"No reason," Vera said. "I was just thinking, that's all."

Donna and I held our tongues and listened as Carol backpedaled. "Perhaps I shouldn't have mentioned your husband. We seem to do fine, Mrs. D'Amato, when we focus on your goals."

"No," my mother smiled grandly. "That's not it. I like my life the way it is. There's nothing to talk about. I'm happy with what I have."

"How about you, Francesca?" Carol asked.

"What?"

"How do you feel?"

I glanced at my sister. "Pissed off."

"Can you tell your mother directly about your anger?"

"Look," I said. "I've been telling her for years. It's not the point. If we're done, we're done." That very morning at breakfast, Donna had been quoting Rocco: you can't change a person unless they want to change.

"How about sad?" Carol pressed. "Do you feel sad too?"

"Sad, too," I echoed, although at the time I couldn't feel it one bit. If this social worker expected to make me the subject of this meeting, she could go to hell.

"What do you need, Francesca?"—the same question Arlene used to ask, and I felt no better equipped to answer.

"Nothing. To go home to Chicago. Get back to my girlfriend, my job." Good thing I hadn't called Ruby to report on any so-called miracles. I'd be calling her back to say it was a false alarm.

"And you, Donna?"

"Back to work," Donna agreed. "They're waiting for me at the office." She stood up like a pregnant woman, pressing her hand to the curve of her spine. "I'll see you later Ma, all right? I promised Rocco I'd be in as soon as I could."

"My girls have made good lives for themselves," my mother said.

"I can imagine," the social worker replied. It seemed like an opportunity to get Vera talking again, but instead Carol asked me to show her out.

I caught her meaning. She was offering me private talk, privileged information.

She began when we got outside. "There's a pattern that's been documented," she squinted into the sun, "in which a prisoner comes to identify with his or her captor and with captivity itself. The jailer can open the door and walk away. Time and again, the prisoner chooses the cell."

"Why tell me this?" I asked. "Why not tell my mother?"

"One would hope that honesty would solve every problem, but it doesn't. Your mother has closed the door on my help. Why push her to lock it? You'll be fine, won't you? You did well to get out."

That was the consensus among the professionals who had dropped in on my mother's life so far. Then why do I feel so rotten, I wanted to ask her, but didn't.

Carol Keenan laid a hand briefly on my arm. "Call me if you need something more," she said, and got into her car.

I studied my arm as if she'd left a hand print. I didn't care, I told myself; this was Donna's scheme anyway.

Having witnessed the failure of the slow-cook method of social service delivery, I flirted for exactly one hour with the desire to overturn my mother's self-determination. That's how long it took me to drive back to Donna's, dig through the beach bag for the crumpled list I had made at the restaurant, call my way down the list, make and remake my impassioned plea. Vulnerable Adult Protection. Impaired Physicians Program. Bring on the authorities.

But the system was set up to protect people like Vera from well-meaning relatives like me—from daughters who would prevent their sixty-year-old mothers or mothers who would prevent their nineteen-year-old daughters from committing themselves to good-for-nothing men. Impaired physicians are usually alcoholic, the receptionist told me when I called. Besides, Vera didn't have to choose her husband as her doctor. Vulnerable adults must be incapable, cognitively or physically, of dialing a phone and asking for help. Unwilling just didn't cut it. She had the right to make lousy decisions.

County employees were trained not to feel the loss personally when someone refused help. It was professional ethics for them, all in a day's work. If the rejections accumulated too rapidly, the Carol Keenans of the world had their colleagues and spouses to talk to, their racquetballs and golfballs to smack around.

All I had was the swift, sudden knowledge that it was time to get out of town, crank Bonnie Raitt on the tape deck to ten and put sixteen highway hours between myself and the futile desire to rescue my mother. I would have blasted the desire into outer space, if only I'd known how.

~ Eight ~

A different sister would have said a charming goodbye, would have packed her bags, cleaned the house, dashed to the supermarket and fish market, cooked an exquisite dinner of chilled cucumber soup, baked salmon, and cornbread. She would have set the table, lit the candles, sat down with her sister upon her return from the office. She would have said, We tried, didn't we? We did our best.

This sister came close. She packed and cleaned and shopped, but halfway through the cooking routine, she started to trip over household goods. These mixing bowls. Those flour and sugar canisters. The mirror hanging in the hallway. All of them artifacts from her childhood. Even the table cloth and candlesticks, relocated from her mother's home.

A different sister might have managed to ignore the pattern as she had for the past few weeks. She might have seen one thing, a second, a third. But this sister connected the dots— the clock next to the bed in the guestroom, the small end table for mail in the front entry. And this is the picture she came up with: her mother lying lonely in her room. Her older sister, sneaking around like a cat burglar, filling up a giant sack of loot.

A different sister might have said an insincere and pleasant goodbye. But this sister wanted to come back again; her sack of things unspoken had filled to bursting. So she finished cooking, settled into the rocker, and picked up a copy of *Your Baby and Child*. Passed the time by reading about how to get one's toddler to eat. Waited for her older sister to come home from the office. Wasted not a heartbeat when she walked through the door. Pounced right on her, confronting her with the inventory of stolen goods.

I started with the candlesticks, made in Israel of smoke-blue hand-blown glass. I'd found them in a boutique in the Village one day when I was skipping school.

"Donna," I said, "I bought these candlesticks. I gave them to our mother as a present."

She was standing between the stove and table, her hand pressed into the small of her back. "I only borrowed them," she said.

212

Was that so? Then what about the mirror, the ice bucket, the bowls, the bottle opener, the knives? I was stomping and whirling around her house, talking so fast I was spitting, and pointing to this and this and this.

"Mommy doesn't mind," she said.

"You mean you asked her?"

"Nobody uses the stuff. They don't miss it."

"It's disrespectful. She's lying there in bed and you're pillaging the house around her."

"You come all this way and live with me for three weeks to hassle me about some fucking kitchen utensils?"

"It's not the items; it's the pattern. You think taking things will settle some score, but it won't, Donna. It doesn't work that way."

Even as I said it, I hated how priggish I sounded—like something out of *Catholic Bedtime Stories for Children*, a ten-volume set of water-damaged books that lived in a carton in my parents' basement. Every story was the same: good boy (or girl) flirts with badness, disobeys his or her mother, gets into a scrape, prays to Jesus, is delivered from danger and vows eternal obedience. Any way you sliced it, Donna was the naughty girl. Even as a child, I felt annoyed by those books, their virtuous pen-and-ink illustrations splashed with turquoise and pale orange wash. I hated myself now for preaching, but I didn't know how to stop. Didn't know how to climb down from the mountain and say: Donna, I always liked those mixing bowls. How come you get to have them?

"I don't have time for this shit," she said. "I'm having a baby in two months. What do you want from me? You want the candlesticks? Take them."

I said, "I want to return them."

"You do that." She shook her head and walked out to the porch, leaving me alone to realize the flatness of my gesture, returning functional objects to their rightful place in an essentially abandoned house.

"Think of it as a proper mourning period." I followed her out to the porch. "Why divvy up the booty before you've abandoned all hope of that house ever being a home?"

But Donna wasn't listening, she was rocking and reading.

"Donna," I said. "Donna, Donna, Donna, Donna."

"Go away," she finally screamed. "I'm not talking to you; just leave me the fuck alone."

"Well, then, I'll see you sometime." I left the exquisite dinner on the stove and took the candlesticks with me.

I rang the doorbell at my parents' house, then went ahead and used my key. The living room was dusky, with all but one Venetian blind pulled down to block the sun. My mother had parked her wheelchair in front of the only unshaded window.

"I'm getting back on the road," I told her. "I came to say goodbye."

Then I looked again, because there in the shadows beyond her my father sat on the living room couch. I had seen his car in the driveway, had pictured him lying upstairs on his bed—as far away as one person can get from another and still use the same address. But here they were, behaving like an old married couple—she doing what she always did and he acting like something more than a stranger. This, then, was Vera's reward for chasing the bird woman away.

Anthony seemed truly relaxed. "What have you got there?" he asked me.

"I'm returning some candlesticks Donna borrowed." I walked around in front of Vera to show her. "Where do they go?" I asked.

"Oh, those," she said. "They only collect dust."

"I gave them to you. I thought you liked them."

"Something else to get broken."

Anthony said, "Let me see."

He took them and turned them upside down, inspecting the tiny gold stickers on the bottom. "Hand made in Israel," he read. "Maybe Frannie would like to have these in Chicago."

"A good idea," my mother said, but I made no move to take them.

He said, "Let's have a cup of coffee before you get on the road. There's a Pepperidge Farm chocolate layer cake in the freezer."

Vera lit right up. "Oh, I've been dreaming of that cake. We've been saving it for a special occasion."

"Frannie's departure," Anthony said, "that's an occasion." I decided not to take that as an insult.

He got up and went to the kitchen, and I took his place on the couch to join my mother in gazing at the bright rectangle of glass. The spruces stood flat against the hazy sky, a blank wall of dull green against grey. I remembered buying a bird feeder for Vera, how I had wanted to inject color and movement into her view. Since then, I'd learned a few things, among them that people often give the gift they'd like to have.

I heard Anthony filling the kettle, setting the table, opening and shutting cupboards and drawers. "Shall we?" I asked Vera when the whistle blew.

214

She turned in her chair and started towards the dining room.

He intercepted her in the hallway. "It's cooler in here." He gestured towards the kitchen where he'd already laid out three place settings, the cake, in its box, sitting to one side.

"You do the honors," Anthony said as he handed me a knife.

The flap of the box was open. I slid the cake out. The cellophane wrapper had been ripped open too, and a slice cut off the end. A layer of white frost had bloomed between the chocolate icing and cellophane.

"Gross!" I said. "Someone cut it and put it back in the freezer."

"Oh, no." My mother was crestfallen.

"It'll be fine," Anthony said.

But the cake smelled like freezer burn. When I got the first forkful near my nose, I knew I wouldn't be able to swallow. Vera managed only one bite. Anthony, on the other hand, ate his entire slice, as if trying to prove something.

"I'm so disappointed," Vera said. "I was so looking forward— Who would have done such a thing?"

"One of your ladies," Anthony told her, matter-of-factly.

I said, "Don't be so quick."

"Did you do it? Huh?" He became suddenly jocular, but I was too slow to think of a playful comeback. His attempt to tease me rolled to a halt.

"Other people do come through this house," I said too earnestly.

"So disappointed," my mother trilled. "So, so disappointed. I was looking forward."

"Vera, it's only a cake." Anthony said this without malice, without even a deprecating sneer. Just the same, I could see that his term as an old married person would be short. She was being herself. Bound to grow bored with the act, he would continue to get nourishment from the larger world. The unfairness of it burned in my gut.

"This is driving me crazy. I'm going to the A&P for another cake."

"No," Vera said. "Don't bother. There'll be other occasions, I'm sure. Besides, we shouldn't have been celebrating. Isn't that right, Anthony? Frannie is leaving."

Anthony was no longer paying attention. He stared absently at my mother and me.

"Is he asleep? Alive?" Now it was Vera's turn to tease ineffectively.

I couldn't watch another minute. "I've got to go," I said, "Chicago is calling me," and pushed my chair back from the table. As if he were connected—the other half of a mechanical toy—my father did the same.

215

"I'll walk you out," he said.

"Goodbye, Ma." I kissed the soft powdery slope of her cheek.

~ Nine ~

I was thirteen and had been complaining about headaches for two or three weeks when my father took me to see my mother's neurologist. The pain felt like the kind of clamp that keeps a car's radiator hose in place, only this one wrapped around my skull like a crown and every day someone gave the screw another twist. I felt excited to have an appointment scheduled with a doctor other than Anthony, to miss school on a Friday afternoon, to be the reason my father and I were driving together in the Buick. Maybe something would be truly wrong with my brain, and would require enough outside attention to break up the logjam of Anthony, Vera, and me.

Doctor Horn's outer office was lined with floor-to-ceiling bookcases. The doctor, tall and angular, his hair greying at the temples, folded himself up like an origami bird and settled into his red leather desk chair. Anthony and I took the chairs opposite him.

"Any unusual stresses at home?" Doctor Horn asked.

"Nothing to speak of," Anthony told him. "My wife's condition appears to be stable."

This was not what I had hoped for. I had imagined a honest chat in private with a kindly doctor and his no-nonsense nurse. The truth didn't stand a fighting chance in this room.

"Family problems? Out of the ordinary conflicts?"

"None at all," my father said.

I stared at the blood-red Oriental rug under all of our feet, and ran my hand along the little brass tacks on the arm of my chair. After a few more rounds of questions and denials, Doctor Horn invited me into his examining room.

I took off my Levis and sat on a high table in my underpants and shirt. The doctor thumped me on the knee with a reflex hammer. He told me to close my eyes and then poked me lightly, here and there, with pins. I indicated where I felt the pinpricks by pointing.

"I bet things aren't so good at home, are they?" he said.

"I don't know." I was half-naked, there was only one door in the room, and my father waited on the other side.

216

"It must be hard to get along with your mother," Doctor Horn said.

"Not really."

"Oh, come on. She must be a real bitch sometimes, no?"

"No," I told him, and the questioning stopped.

"Okay, you can put on your clothes."

By the time I did so and stepped back through the door, he had written a prescription for Valium. "To calm your nerves," he said, handing me a sample package. "Take one now." He poured me a glass of water. If the Valium worked, Anthony could arrange for the refills.

But there wouldn't be any refills. That same night, Donna let me hang out at the party she and Billy were throwing in Billy's basement. Audrey and Bill Senior relaxed upstairs away from the young people and loud music. The ice chests full of booze were hidden in the garage. I didn't like the taste of beer yet, but I accepted the gin and tonic in a plastic tumbler that Billy handed me, light on the gin and heavy on the lime.

Soon I was wondering how a few sips could have gotten me so drunk. I felt woozy and limp. A lined had formed outside the downstairs bathroom, so I went upstairs in the Palettas' house to use the one on the main floor. I splashed my face with cold water and looked in the mirror to try and get a grip.

On the way back to the basement, I missed the top step and bounced like a rag doll down the entire carpeted flight. At the bottom, I stood up and brushed myself off, relieved that no one had seen me. Donna and Billy found me still grasping the newel post to steady myself.

"You're getting my sister drunk," Donna said.

"I'm not drunk; it's these pills from the doctor." I pulled them out of my pocket to show her.

"Holy shit," she said. "Valium. You're not supposed to drink and take downs. I don't suppose Doctor Horn would have warned you."

So Valiums were downs. I had already smoked a little pot in my lifetime, but had always sworn I wouldn't do downs—ever since the day I witnessed Billy and his friend Jack stoned on Quaaludes. They were drunker than drunk, oblivious to danger, and Jack ended up slamming his hand in the car door.

Billy poured the rest of my drink down the drain and got me a piece of Italian bread from the kitchen. "You'll be fine," he said, and he was right.

A couple of hours later, Donna walked into the bathroom to find me scattering tiny blue Valium pills into the toilet, letting them slip from my fingers one at a time like seeds sown in a garden.

"We could have sold those," she said. "Someone else could have enjoyed them."

"These are shit." I let the last one fall from my hand, and flushed the toilet.

~ Ten ~

On the left side of the proposed mural, a conveyor belt carried grey people past white-coated doctors with dollar signs in their eyes and syringes in their hands. They stood ready to deliver injections as their patients passed by. No talking, no healing, no compassion—just drug 'em up and move 'em out. Also on the left was depicted a block of run-down brick apartment buildings with a burned-out car parked in front. Some of the figures were stepping off the belt and crossing to the right side of the picture, an idyllically colorful scene of community self-care—people planting gardens, talking together, and dancing. This was where the trouble started on the planning committee.

Almost every one of us had a story to tell about getting fucked over in the medical system—through lack of access, or lack of caring, or both. It was easy to agree about the left side of the picture, about what we all hated and how to represent it, but much harder to bring a group of neighborhood residents, health care advocates, young artists, New Age healers, and workers at the community clinic whose back wall we intended to transform toward any kind of consensus about what "health care for people, not profit" might look like, how it should be symbolized in a set of images on a public wall.

Hazel, the artist directing the project, was a model of patience. She carried her drawing home each week to work on the changes put forth by the planning group.

"It's too pastoral," Corinne said. "Too escapist, too elitist."

Corinne was a friend of Margaret's, a family practice doctor at the clinic, and the person who had called me about joining the project in the first place. Her criticism was easy enough to satisfy. Hazel would sketch in the same block of apartment buildings, but spruce them up—put curtains and flower boxes in the windows, bicycles out front, but not too gentrified.

The talk got on my nerves, but I stayed. I was most interested in the practical knowledge I could pick up from Hazel—how to prep an outside wall, how to transfer a scale drawing—and besides, Hazel's artistry as a mediator fascinated me. All my years of collective this-and-that, and I still felt as muddy as when I first moved in with Mimi and Jane. I still got lost in the thicket of opposing viewpoints.

The group spent two long sessions tussling over how to represent a positive view of medicine. We are all healers, the New Age people often said. Another man in particular, a licensed practical nurse who lived in the neighborhood, was not so easily swayed. If we meant to criticize medicine in its present state, we should also show what it might become.

Still thinking I had no opinion, I surprised myself by saying, "There are all sizes and ages and colors of people in this picture, but there are no sick or disabled people."

"My God, you're right." Hazel, said.

I was not prepared for the controversy that followed—a flood of New Age talk about holism and how nothing was an accident, how given enough time to meditate and forgive we would all heal ourselves and be made well again. These were the Mrs. Camdens of my own generation, the batik-clad counterparts of the Christian ladies who used to pray over my mother. Far from lacking an opinion, I now felt ready to blow. I wasn't the only one. The LPN, a man with AIDS, a woman whose sister had just died of breast cancer, all spoke vehemently: this was health chauvinism, victim-blaming, the kind of attitude which, left unchecked, could lead to eugenics.

Hazel's bones were big, her shoulders and hands broad. At first glance, people often judged her to be a man, but in every other way she reminded me of Carol Keenan, who had almost succeeded in getting through to my mother. Both women had been fired in the same kiln. Both made it their business to talk calmly, to come up with the compromises and explanations that would keep players from quitting the game. Hazel made a left-to-right sweeping gesture with one hand above her drawing. "These people are in transition," she said. "This is not dystopia and utopia; these are two aspects of how we live right now."

In the finished mural, a woman in a wheelchair works in a raised-bed section of the garden. A very thin young man, possibly with AIDS, rests with his back against a tree. An older man, kneeling, pours him a glass of water.

~ Eleven ~

When Anthony first called me about dropping in to Chicago for a visit, he said "I" every step of the way: "I'm traveling to Winnipeg, and I thought

I'd come through Chicago, maybe spend a couple of days looking around, if you'll be there."

"What's in Winnipeg?" I asked, imagining some hospital or orphanage on the prairie.

"Nothing. That's where Larry is from."

"So you mean you and Larry are coming to Chicago?"

"Yes, of course, if it's all right with you."

"It's all right," I told him, but I felt heavy with an unfamiliar dread. I didn't want to play the good daughter to his gay father.

"Have you told Vera you're coming to see me?" I asked.

"I can tell her. Is that what you want?"

"I want to go back in time, to when you wouldn't allow her to write me a letter."

"I never kept her from writing."

"You were jealous. It's a double standard."

"I may have been jealous, but I didn't prevent her from corresponding. She prevented herself." An all-purpose justification, and one I no longer knew how to dispute.

"Just give me the flight information," I told him.

When they walked off the plane at Midway Airport, they were wearing almost identical sport jackets, both grey-blue like Anthony's eyes. No one hugged or kissed, but Larry did step up to shake my hand. He seemed more composed than when we first met—less defensive, genuinely poised. Still too corn-fed and blond for me, but this time I could understand the attraction.

I watched them as they dealt with carry-on bags, luggage, luggage claim checks, the fluent way they handed things off and helped each other without ever speaking, like some quiet improvisational dance. Jealousy seized me—on behalf of Vera, Jimmy, myself. Why couldn't he have been easy to get along with the first forty years?

"New car?" Larry asked when we got outside to Ruby's Honda.

"Borrowed car," I said, "roomier than the cab of the pick-up." My father sat in the front seat, Larry directly behind him.

On the way to their hotel, Anthony produced a steady stream of commentary—about the buildings and landmarks, the billboards, other drivers. I stole glances at his lover in the rearview mirror. Larry looked out his own window, only occasionally attending to what Anthony pointed out, but frequently reaching forward to place what I imagined was a comforting and desirous hand on his arm.

"Are you seeing someone?" my father turned his attention to me. "Arlene, wasn't that her name?"

""It's not Arlene anymore," I told him. "It's been Ruby for the past couple of years."

"Well, maybe the four of us—"

"We'll see."

Ruby had offered to make dinner at her place for the four of us, had already planned the menu—salad Niçoise with fresh tuna from the market and potatoes and string beans from her garden. I was the one who resisted. She had no immediate family, had made it this far without exposure to mine. Maybe I wanted to keep it that way. Or maybe I didn't want to be on a double date.

"We're going to take a nap." When I pulled up to their hotel, Larry leaned forward and gave me a little pinch on the cheek. I blushed, but didn't protest. "We'll call you in a couple of hours about dinner," he said.

"I'll be home," I told them as the bellhop reached for their suitcases. "I'll see what Ruby is up to."

Ruby found a thousand things to talk about with Larry—perennial flowers, Chicago architecture, the Lyric Opera, even Winnipeg. One of her grandfather's brothers had started a branch of the family clothing business in Manitoba. Levinson's; Larry knew it well. His mother used to buy her nurse's uniforms and his scouting uniforms there. As a kid coming up through the Evanston public schools, Ruby had taken the exact same architecture walking tours that Larry now planned for himself and Anthony. She could not only rattle off Sullivan, Mies van der Rohe, Graham, Burnham—names I too had picked up over the years—she could match the name with the style, and even quote the addresses of important buildings.

Larry said, "We're done with the big international trips for now. Tony comes home so tired." He wagged a finger at my father. "We'll stick to North America for a while, take in the best of the opera companies. San Francisco next."

Neither Anthony nor I said much. He watched his lover and my lover, and I watched him—so remarkably relaxed, so contentedly out of the limelight. Toward the end of the evening, however, something was disrupting his good time.

Finally, he came out with it. "Should we have gotten four tickets for the Lyric?"

"No, it's fine," I told him. "You two should go and have fun."

We waited with them on the street until a cab came to take them back to their hotel. Later, Ruby and I walked down to the sea wall at the bend in Sheridan Road. The moon and clouds threw shadows onto the lake.

"You all right?" she asked. "You making it through okay?"

"Yeah," I said. "Better than I expected."

She said, "I like them. They're entirely gracious, not that I don't believe you."

"Nothing to believe," I told her. "Larry seems solidly good, and Anthony seems to be rising to the occasion."

I, in fact, felt horribly burdened. Drop me in the water and I would have sunk away. I didn't want to like Anthony, or to betray Jimmy and Vera by forgiving him. I didn't want any part of his happy gay family. I didn't want to become his secret pal. Easy for him, maybe, to step out of one life and into another, but I wasn't going, not without a fight. What fight, I didn't know. He and Larry were much better visitors than Donna had been. That, in itself, caused me grief.

It wasn't supposed to work out this way—my sister lost to me, my father all at once my best buddy. And all based on some stupid delineation about who was fucking who.

Donna and Billy were reunited, Anthony told me when we went walking the next day. My sister had sent me a birth announcement and photo when Carly was born, and I had mailed a tiny tie-dyed outfit. That was all the corresponding we'd done. According to Anthony, Billy showed up with roses at the hospital, and started calling on Donna through the winter. Before Carly was walking, Billy had moved back in.

My father, Larry, and I were standing on the Michigan Avenue bridge, looking down at the jade green river and up at the white Wrigley Building against the sky.

"A little girl needs her daddy," Anthony said, and for a moment I didn't know whether to throw him or myself over the railing.

I did neither, because I got sidetracked trying to figure out what exactly he meant by "daddy." Was he oblivious to the circumstances of Carly's conception, or trying to keep the secret from me? Or was he so hip, so worldly, had having a male lover so shaken his faith in genetic posterity, that he knew and didn't care?

Anthony pulled a Saltine cracker out of his pocket and tossed it to a sea gull. "You should see your niece," he said. "She's a year old already. A very smart child."

"Have you seen her?" I asked Larry.

He said, "I still haven't met Donna."

"Why not?"

"No reason." He looked to Anthony to explain, but Anthony kept his eye on the gulls. Larry said, "Timing, I guess. We're still working on the easy one." His smile came too readily, as did the next idea. "Say," he fairly shouted. "I thought the whole mural scene had come and gone, but Ruby told me you painted one just this year."

"I was part of a team," I said.

"Well, we want to see it."

"Somebody else designed it," I demurred.

My career as a muralist had been short lived. As much as I admired Hazel, art-by-committee was not the art for me. Given my free time, my unsalaried time with a paintbrush or pen in hand, I wanted to put marks on a page exactly to my liking. First, I'd have to discover what that liking was.

"Come on." Larry wouldn't quit. "We want to see your Chicago."

I gave in, hailed a cab, and gave the driver the clinic's address. He had a green, white, and red decal that said "Iran" on his dashboard. He sat with his meter running and Janet Jackson playing on the radio while the three of us stood before the mural.

"You painted this?" Anthony asked.

"I painted part of it." Any minute now he would take exception to the content. If the shoe fits, wear it, I'd have to tell him.

"I like this." My father pointed to the conveyor belt and the doctors. "It's a portrait of the greedy insurance companies. They get worse every year. I used to think I'd practice medicine as long as I was healthy, but with all the bureaucracy and paperwork, I've pretty much decided to retire."

Arlene was right: we each do have our own reality. Here was Anthony the hero, the one who hated welfare cheaters but took Medicaid patients because it was ethical. Retirement would change a lot, if it meant splitting not just his spare time, but all of it between his lover and wife.

"You go into medicine expecting to help people," he said, "but soon the greedy insurance industry makes you into a robot. Then you're not your own man at all."

I glanced at the taxi driver, but he was looking the other way—smoking a cigarette and drumming along to Janet Jackson on his steering wheel.

Larry performed an enticing little disco step in time to the music and turned to me.

"Me?" I asked.

"Of course."

Tina Turner was singing now, "We got to show some re-spect, we got a love to pro-tect." We danced separately at first, and then he reached for my hand and put his arm around my waist for a Jitterbug.

"Really?"

"Just follow."

He was a skilled leader, better than Ruby or Arlene, old enough to remember when dancing had structure. He moved me smoothly here and there in spite of the rough asphalt underfoot, and my rubber soled shoes.

We took a half dozen dips and turns. By the fourth or fifth, Anthony was smiling and clapping, and I was giggling helplessly.

"There!" The song ended. "Isn't that better?"

"The meter—" I said.

"It's only money," Anthony told me.

"Let's go!" Now I was fairly shouting. "I'll take you to Belden Avenue to look at the stained glass."

Larry held open the back door of the cab so I could scoot into the middle.

"Nice dancing," the driver said. "Where to?"

I leaned forward to tell him, then leaned back between the two men. Anthony looked at me and I gave him a little smile. I guessed I could permit myself to have a good time.

PART FIVE

Maybe Now • (1985-1988)

~ One ~

I have never been more than an adequate artist. I've got proficiency, technique, good eye-hand coordination, a visual hit on the world. But there is one trait I lack. I am too enamored with symmetry. I lack the ability to stop making sense.

I share this deficiency with my siblings, not that I'd ever consent to calling it genetic. We were all subjected to the same style of care and raised in a similar environment. Donna became a competent tile setter. Gloria made a mint peddling symmetry. Jimmy, I always thought, could have been a chorus line dancer. He was nimble; he would have learned the steps, but would have made an unlikely choreographer. We're all a thousand times better at execution than design.

Every couple of years in my own life, inspiration has hit. A sharp burst of wind springs the catch, slams open the door, and I experience a fleeting transcendental moment of perfect insight. I've made the most of these occasions by buckling down to produce a smidgen of work, but I've been too finicky about messes, too unfriendly toward confusion to leave that creative door ajar.

You would think that understanding orderliness so well, I could learn how to tweak it, torque it, move it a degree or two off center, use it as an entry into something new. So far, trying has only resulted in strain. Even when I work diligently, my compositions are predictable. In another time and place, I'd have made a superb icon painter. In my own, I became a t-shirt printer.

There was always room to do more at Hard Rain, if I wanted, at the monthly open design meetings where new work got criticized and images selected for production. Over the years, a dozen collective members charged that the process was rigged—that first Martin and then Gregory held court there. An accurate assessment, although Gregory balked at admitting it. And who was I to complain? I brought forward two designs in ten years, and both got produced. I excused myself from taking further risks by explaining that silkscreen was not my form. This was my alibi; that I was painting alone at home. Sometimes I was painting, and sometimes just moving paint around. Often, I did nothing at all.

There comes a time when a person must admit all this out loud. The truths you can dance around when you're twenty threaten to bar your way as you approach thirty. Not that it's ever too late, until you're dead. With any luck, my life as an artist is about to begin.

~ Two ~

I was alone in my apartment, cutting up tomatoes from Ruby's garden for a salad when Gloria called. The sun had just set and the sky had a yellow cast. Ruby was off covering the third or fourth in a string of heated community meetings about police brutality.

"May I please speak to Francesca D'Amato?" my sister asked, as if she had reached my secretary.

Right away, I recognized her voice. I could have pretended I didn't, could have matched her formality, but I've never possessed much self-control. "Gloria?" I asked.

"Yes," she said. "I'm ready to change our mother's situation."

I felt like a double exposure. On the one hand, justly suspicious: Why her? Why now? And what could she possibly want with me? Yet I was enthralled by the symmetry, a powerfully stable configuration. I had tried. Donna had tried. Surely the oldest daughter would be the charm. With my two sisters and me pulling in unison, something would have to budge. I was almost, but not quite, willing to forgive Gloria a decade of hostility.

"Okay, let's meet," I told her. "The downtown hotels here in Chicago are running great deals on the weekends"—a suggestion with no practical value; I made it only to annoy her.

Donna had two young children already, Carly, two, and Emma, only nine months. I still hadn't met either, but Gloria didn't mention our nieces. "Chicago won't work," she said, "we need to be based in New York." As if we were talking about a corporate merger, but she was right. We would need to research legal and financial realities particular to New York State.

She called on the Thursday before Labor Day to schedule a meeting with Donna and me at her office in Manhattan that coming Tuesday. "Book a plane ticket," she said. "Save yourself the drive."

"I have a job; I'll come in a couple of weeks," I told her, trying to preserve some semblance of choice. But I felt like a trained dog, like an addict—all physiologically perked up just because the thing I'd never stopped wanting was being waved in front of my face.

"We have to move fast," Gloria said. "I hope to see you on Tuesday. Goodbye, Frannie." Then she hung up.

I sat down and forced myself to eat my salad. Then I ran a peach-scented bath and climbed in with a sketch book and pen. I drew the tiles on the wall in front of me, my legs and feet underwater, the curved belly of the wall-mounted sink, the glass shelf and the cup that holds toothbrushes. I topped off the tub several times with water as hot as I could tolerate on a late summer night. The heat worked like a drug to induce drowsiness. I lay down in my bed, pressing my cheek and breasts, hipbones and thighs against the smooth sheet. This was my life. I refused to think about anything else until the morning.

Usually, I'm awake when Ruby comes over late after work. I'm sitting up drawing or reading, on the couch, in bed, or at the kitchen table. The sound of her key in the lock makes my breath catch, my heart skip a beat. I want to call out, to jump up and greet her, but I hold still. I listen as she walks around my small apartment, looking in this corner and that until she finds me. When she does, she kisses me, and most nights I've been alone long enough. I let the newspaper or sketchbook slide from my lap. I let Ruby take me to bed.

The night Gloria called, Ruby found me already naked and sound asleep in my bed. I didn't even stir until she climbed in behind me and laid the length of her body against my back.

"You took a bath," she said.

"Yes." I pressed the bottom of my foot against the top of hers. Then I dropped off again.

I dreamt that Gloria, Donna, and I were rowing a small boat on a big bay. We were transporting a microwave oven on the floor of the boat. It was night, and we headed for land, but Gloria followed one red beacon, and I another. At first it didn't matter, so far off shore; the difference between the two lights was negligible. But as we drew closer, I knew we'd have to force a decision. Donna kept reaching down, as if to pet the oven, to make sure it was still dry. I toyed with the oar in my hand, tested its weight, slipped it out of and back into its lock.

"It's a shame," I murmured to Donna.

She gave no answer.

Any minute now, I would hit Gloria over the head and throw her out of the boat. I had to do this before she did it to me.

In the morning, I rolled over into Ruby's outstretched arm.

"What wiped you out?" she asked.

I told her about Gloria's call, and the dream, and that I'd made up my mind to go.

"Oh God, Fran," she sat up in bed. "Not again."

"I'll take a leave without pay from Hard Rain," I promised. "I'll save my vacation time for you."

"It's not about time. It's about how you live your life."

We were out of bed by now, pulling on our clothes and following each other from bedroom to bathroom to kitchen.

"If you were going away to a workshop or class, I'd say great," Ruby told me. "Something for you, not everything for these people who don't deserve or appreciate you."

"Don't tell me how to live my own fucking life. Don't tell me I can't take care of my own fucking mother." I sat down hard in a kitchen chair and started sobbing. "You don't know anything," I yelled. "You don't know shit about me."

But even as I accused her, I knew Ruby was right. Of course I couldn't take care of my mother. I hadn't yet.

She stood by the stove and counted out scoops of ground coffee. "Are you sure this is taking care of her? Gloria seems like a terrible bet."

"I don't know," I said, still crying. "Gloria is not to be trusted, but Ruby, something big is happening and I want to be on the scene. We're all getting older. If it turns out to be the same old shit, I swear I'll retire."

Ruby left off making coffee and came to sit with me. "Man alive," she said, "You sure do hang on to your hope."

"It hangs on to me. I feel like a goddamn prisoner."

"Maybe I should come with you," she said. "Maybe it's time to meet the rest of this family."

"You have work," I told her.

"We could fly. I'll reschedule my interviews, take a few days off."

I had to agree, the offer was appealing. But we'd promised ourselves a trip to someplace warm that coming winter. "Let's skip it, Ruby. I'll drive," I said. "Maybe I'm a fool to jump when my sister says jump, but what's the point of being two fools and wasting our money too?"

She said, "You don't know Gloria very well. Don't be surprised by anything she cooks up."

"I promise I'll be careful."

"Just promise me you'll come home."

I thought I could do much better. On Friday, while Ruby wrote her police brutality article, I packed clothes and food for my trip, took out the garbage, rooted through my storage closet to find a sleeping bag, checked the oil and tires on the truck, and stocked her fridge with food from the Greek deli. I called Margaret to back out of her "Piss on Pity" open house—a gathering in opposition to all the suckers who had their TVs tuned to the Jerry Lewis Telethon all weekend.

"Let's unplug the phone," I said that night. "Let's spend a couple of days together, just you and me."

Ruby did her best to go along with the plan. But sex felt clumsy and lounging dull, as if we were both waiting for forty-eight hours to pass. She had slipped out of bed and gone downstairs to water the garden when I left her apartment on Monday morning. The sky had lightened from black to grey with only a band of fuchsia at the horizon.

~ Three ~

Around sunset in rural New Jersey the rain began to fall—a light misty one that softened the edges of the hills and barely wet the pavement. I kept one eye on the speedometer and the other on the lookout for cops. There was hardly anybody else on the highway.

One minute I was cruising on I-80, rounding the gentlest of curves, and then with no warning whatsoever I was facing a smear of red taillights, barreling into traffic that had ground to a halt. I used all of my wits to bring the truck to a stop without skidding into the rear end of a Volvo wagon. For here were all the New Yorkers who had spent their holiday weekend in the Poconos, waiting on line fifty miles outside the city to cross the George Washington Bridge.

Maybe it was an omen, a supernatural warning to turn back. I considered taking the next illegal U-turn but spotted an exit first, jockeyed across the tangled lanes, and set out to noodle my way north and east to the Tappan Zee Bridge. I had no road atlas, and neither sun nor stars to guide me, but eventually I made it. I pulled up in front of the darkened farmhouse after midnight.

No point in disturbing everyone; I had my home on wheels. I knew the routine—I had invented it—yet my body resisted. The foam pad felt too thin, the roof too confining. The cold metal floor grabbed at me, the walls squeezed in. The hammering of the rain was a headache, not a comfort. I tossed and turned, layered on extra clothes. For the first time in my life I thought: I'm getting too old for this. I longed for the comfort of Ruby next to me, in either one of our nice warm beds. I dozed and woke in what seemed like fifteen-minute cycles. At some point, the rain let up.

In the morning the world was a kaleidoscope. Bright beads of water scattered sunlight and color, and everything looked like a corny springtime scene from Walt Disney. Only this was late summer, the day after Labor Day, the day when, in my mother's time, a woman put away her white shoes, pocketbook, and gloves until next year. I pushed back the curtain to look at the oversaturated orange and pink zinnias in Donna's garden. The screen door slammed, and I heard Billy's footsteps on the gravel. I opened the back of the truck, but didn't get out of bed. I sat in my little cave, and Billy came over to sit on the tailgate. It had been four years since I'd seen him. He looked the same, give or take a few gray hairs. He wore a khaki work shirt and pants, and carried his lunch in an ecologically sound, reusable red sack.

"You could have come in," he said.

"I got stuck in holiday traffic. Besides it's different with the kids. I didn't want to be bumbling around in the dark." I didn't mention that Donna and I had left off two years before in the middle of a fight. I doubted whether I belonged in their house at all.

"I told Donna I'm staying out of this plan," he said.

"Of course you are." That's what made him Billy. But I couldn't keep from asking, "What plan?"

"The whole business about getting the house fixed up. Donna thinks we can bid it like a regular job, but I don't even like to work for friends. No way am I working for Gloria. There will be hidden costs up the ass."

"Fixed up? Like to sell?"

"Oh Jesus, Frannie," Billy said. "I'm sorry. I should learn to keep my fucking mouth shut."

"No," I told him, "it's fine." It was my fault. I should have known Gloria would've had a plan, would have held private sub-caucuses before Tuesday's official meeting. I had no grounds to claim I'd been intentionally excluded. I could have pressed Gloria to tell me more, could have spoken with Donna, could have given them Ruby's phone number over the weekend. But I had stored up my questions for asking in person.

"I'll go inside," I told Billy. "Donna will begin at the beginning. I'll act like I know nothing."

"I'll see you tonight, won't I?" he said and he patted the foot of my sleeping bag in parting.

Inside, I found a new kind of uproar. Raffi, singing about apples and bananas on the TV, competed with the morning news program on the radio. Emma, the baby, sat in a high chair, and Carly in a booster seat at the table. I stepped carefully, to avoid smashing Cheerios into the floor. I had a hard time knowing where to focus. I didn't want to stare too long at the kids, the video, my sister, or the objects in her house.

"You made it," Donna said. She wasn't pregnant any more, but her body had rounded out some, like mine. "Say hello to your Aunt Frannie," she told the girls.

I smiled and gave Carly a little wave. She was strapped into her chair, and I didn't make a move to kiss her. Not yet.

Donna stayed clear across the room. "Where are you sleeping while you're in town?" she asked. It was not an invitation.

Fine, then. We wouldn't be three, not even two and one. We'd be separate—one and one and one. Unless she and Gloria were a pair and I was on the outs. But then why would they have summoned me at all?

"I'll camp at Pound Ridge, unless the weather turns," I said.

It was only eight thirty. We were due at Gloria's at ten. Donna put a bottle of juice, some books, and a stuffed dog into a diaper bag. "I have to drop the girls at their grandma's," she said.

Something inside of me snagged on that statement. She meant Audrey, of course. Vera would never have qualified as a babysitter. But did Audrey really claim both girls as her own? If so, was it out of generosity or because she didn't know Billy and Donna's whole story? Either way, I should have been minding my own business. But I couldn't keep from wondering how much my sister passed in the world as a person with an uncomplicated life story.

"Separate cars?" Donna asked as she rubbed Carly's face with a wash cloth. She framed it as a question, but it didn't feel like one.

"Sure," I said. "Separate cars." Then she was hustling the kids out the door. She didn't even offer me a cup of coffee.

"You need help?" I asked. She had Emma balanced against her hip, the diaper pack and her own bag slung over one shoulder, and she shooed Carly along in front of her.

"I got it under control," she said. "I'll see you at Gloria's."

231

~ Four ~

I don't know what possessed me to stop at my mother's house. Smarting from Donna's dismissal, I had thought to go into town, buy a cup of coffee, scan the morning headlines, give my sister time to unload the kids at the Palettas'. I was dawdling so I wouldn't arrive at Gloria's office first.

But I found myself turning away from town and up the hill. I hadn't dropped in unannounced in years, had trained myself to always call ahead. But here I was, in the thick of it again, scheming to change my mother's life. A daughter, not a lady who visits. At least I could go say hello.

The driveway was empty when I pulled up. No sign of Anthony, but that was to be expected. I rang the bell and prepared a casually innocent face for greeting Consuela. But Consuela didn't come. No one came. Did I sense a change behind the door, pressing against it, leaking across the threshold? I was too distracted by digging in my pocket to find the key I still carried on my ring.

When I opened the door, it came at me like a wave front—a quiet beyond quiet, an emptiness that was complete.

"Ma?" I yelled into the hallway. "Ma?" I yelled louder in the kitchen. Nobody answered.

Vera's blankets were rumpled on the bed, the shades in her room still drawn. I brought my face close to the sheets to smell the familiar faint mixture of talcum powder, urine, and sweat. But any clue I hoped to find there still eluded me.

A second look at the kitchen revealed only this: the previous night's dishes clean in the dishwasher, and not a sign of a breakfast cooked that morning. My mother had been spirited away in the middle of the night. All the times I had described her house as lifeless had never felt like this.

I didn't bother with pleasantries when Audrey Paletta answered the phone. "It's Fran," I told her. "I need to talk to Donna." When my sister got on I said, "I'm at Mom's house, and she's not here. Nobody is here. Donna, she's gone."

Within minutes, she came over. She retraced my steps through the front hall and kitchen and into Vera's room where we stood and stared at the empty bed.

I said, "I'm calling the emergency room."

232

"No. Wait," Donna told me. "She's been gone longer than that." She led me back out to the kitchen. "I washed those dishes on Sunday afternoon. Billy and I brought the kids over for a barbecue."

Donna discovered Vera's toothbrush and hairbrush missing from the downstairs bathroom. A few dresses and other items had been skimmed from her closet and bureau drawers. Upstairs we found both Consuela and Anthony's beds neatly made, but the one in the spare room mussed up. A trace of perfume still hung in the air.

"Fucking Gloria," Donna said.

I followed her into Anthony's office, still set up and in use. The bills on top of his desk had current postmarks. Even if he didn't live or love at home, he did work there, and he still had Jimmy's Army photo on display.

Donna picked up the phone and dialed. "I need to speak to Doctor Ferelli," she said. "This is her sister, Donna Paletta."

She listened, then said, "Yes, I'm on my way to that same meeting, but I've stopped at my mother's house, and there seems to be an emergency here."

Although I couldn't make out the receptionist's words, I could hear the placating rise and fall of her voice through the receiver. One woman's emergency is another woman's briefing. No matter what my sister said, the receptionist stayed true to her message: Doctor Ferelli looked forward to seeing us in her office.

"Good work," I told Donna when she hung up. She had confirmed it: we had nothing to fear, we could go ahead and be pissed.

I said, "I'm calling Consuela. I want to hear what she's been instructed to tell us."

"Your sister," Consuela said immediately when I identified myself. "She promised two weeks paid vacation."

"Yes, Consuela, I know—"

"I take care of Mrs. D'Amato, not the house. Your sister understands. If Mrs. D'Amato is not home—"

"Consuela, it's fine. I just want to know what Gloria told you about after the two weeks."

"After?"

"Yes. How did she leave off with you?"

"She'll call me after the procedure is over."

"What procedure?" I asked. What was Gloria doing to our mother?

Consuela didn't know what procedure or what hospital. "I don't ask," she said. "I just pray for Mrs. D'Amato's return."

"What procedure?" Now Donna's voice was laced with fright.

"She didn't know. I don't think it's real. Gloria is up to some shit. If mom truly needed medical treatment, we would have heard."

"I guess so."

I wanted to ask Donna about the alleged plans for the house, but didn't want to get Billy in trouble. It would all come clear soon enough. "Looks like we've been set up," I said. "Like we have no choice but to go."

Donna and I closed the door on the empty house and stood in the sunshine.

"You want a ride?" I asked her.

"You can ride with me," she said. "It'll be easier to park my car in the city."

Ach, Ruby, I thought. I wish you had come. This is exactly as you predicted.

~ Five ~

At Gloria's office, the receptionist greeted Donna by name and ushered us both into a conference room to wait. She put a pitcher of water and three glass tumblers on the table. She had that sulky fashion magazine look, and her lips—very full, for a white woman—were painted an incredible shade of plum. "Doctor Ferelli should be in soon," she said, and closed the door.

Donna and I were jumping out of our skins. She sat at the table, but could have drilled a hole through the floor with all her foot tapping. I walked the perimeter of the room to read the framed print ads for Greene, Ferelli, and Associates that hung on the walls: you have the right to feel good about how you look. The finest surgeons and a caring staff can help you achieve the beauty you deserve.

I made my way around the room: chemical peel and dermabrasion, surgery of the nose and eyelid, surgery of the breast, cheek, lip, and chin augmentation. I bet lip augmentation made the receptionist who she was. The next photo showed two smiling parents and a little boy: age four is not too early to surgically correct a child's ears.

"I apologize. My phone consultation ran over." Gloria's voice was large, as if addressing ten or fifteen people. She carried an expandable paper file made of kelly green card stock. The bright color of the file clashed with the muted mauves and greys of the room, and with the pale celery green of her knit dress.

Gloria and I joined Donna at the round table. Right away, I was struck by Michael's absence. "Finally," Gloria said, "we're all here." Just us girls, we were supposed to believe, but of course she represented her husband's interests too.

"Gloria," Donna said, "Frannie and I were at Mommy's house. We called here. We called Consuela. We almost called the emergency room. What the fuck is going on?"

Gloria poured a glass of water and took a sip. "No need for that language. I've moved our mother temporarily to a nursing home on Long Island."

"Why did you do that?" Donna asked.

"A better question is why didn't I—why didn't any of us—do it sooner."

I said, "But you did it with no notice—to either of us or to Mom. Donna and Billy just saw her on Sunday."

"A bed came open," Gloria said. "We had to jump. It's only for the short term, just to shake Anthony up a little. I've encouraged Mommy to think of this time as a vacation in a luxury hotel." She pinned me with a stare. "Not unlike the luxury hotels your father and that man are so fond of. But none of this is a surprise to you, Frannie."

So here we were, at the very confrontation I feared when I grudgingly agreed to spend time with Anthony and Larry in Chicago, and had ended up helplessly enjoying myself.

Gloria slid a thick stack of photocopies out of the green file, six years' worth of Anthony's bank and credit card statements. She had already highlighted in orange ink against the glossy photostatic paper every expenditure that might conceivably have benefited Larry.

"You knew," she said.

Donna also knew. She hadn't bought into his pious charade for long. She's the one who, two years before, had recited Anthony's schedule to me, and initiated our failed attempt at therapy. But knowing and consorting were vastly different crimes. She never invited Larry over for dinner or introduced him to her kids. It wouldn't have gotten me out of trouble to drag Donna into it, nor to ask how Gloria managed to remain ignorant for so long.

"So what's next?" I said. "You called me here to talk about our mother."

"I should have known you would keep their dirty little secret."

"Stop it, Gloria" said Donna, which heartened but didn't satisfy me.

"You sound like he's cheating on *you*," I told Gloria.

"How dare you—"

"Stop!" Donna yelled, loud enough to rein us both in.

Our oldest sister glanced at the waiting room door. "All this money down the drain," she said. "Mommy's money. Things have been so hectic at home, and here at the practice. I could kick myself for not investigating this sooner."

She shot me another deadly look. I had kept their secret a whole year—two, counting the first time I met Larry. But who would I have told, and how would that have helped Vera? I had chosen silence, but Gloria chose naiveté. "We'll be watching," she told Anthony, and then she didn't watch. Wading around in our parents' marriage apparently was something she did only in spurts.

She said, "In the next few days, I'm filing a petition for a divorce in Vera's name. It's just a formality, a means of establishing with the court that a share of the marital assets should pay for her stay in the nursing home, and a signal to Anthony to get real."

For Vera the marriage was the asset. "Has Mom agreed to a divorce?" I asked.

"It isn't a divorce."

"Even a pretend divorce. Time and again she's chosen the life she has—or had."

Gloria said, "We're doing what we can to reconstruct that life for her, but only on honest terms, and only if your father cooperates. He can't have it both ways anymore. He'll have to get in or get out."

"Vera must have known Anthony was lying all along," I said. "Even so, she's chosen to stay put."

Gloria ruffled through the pages in front of her. "That may be, but Vera hasn't looked at their joint checking account lately. She needs to learn that simply staying married is no protection for her, financially."

That much I had to give my sister.

She said, "The divorce petition outlines the ways in which Anthony has mistreated Vera: emotional and verbal abuse. Neglect when the MS first came on. Failure to secure medical care for the past fifteen years. One or more ongoing extramarital affairs. For this initial round, we do not mention homosexuality."

But it was homosexuality that brought Gloria to take offense at all the rest. Until Larry, she was never troubled by the indignities Vera suffered.

She said, "Vera is under the impression that Anthony has been seeing another woman. We will not disabuse her of that notion."

"No," Donna said, "it would ruin the possibility of them getting back together."

"Back together?" I asked.

"Together under one roof," Gloria explained. "No more expenditures for the apartment on West 20th Street." But I suspected Donna meant literally back together—like in love.

Gloria said, "We'll get the best leverage with Anthony if we keep that particular ugly detail under our hats."

So this was her plan: Donna would put together a bid for the house repair. Nothing structural, just cosmetics. The place had degenerated enough that some amount of work would be needed whether it was sold or Vera moved back in. Gloria would finish evaluating the financial picture. She'd bring a realtor over to price the house, but only after the most glaring problems had been fixed. She'd also finish tallying up how much Anthony had already squandered.

"I'll field all calls from him," Gloria said. Neither Donna nor I argued with that one. We had both known, but not tattled. We couldn't be trusted to play Gloria's style of hardball.

Only I lacked a job. "As long as we're assembling a financial picture," I said, "we should figure out the best possible living situation for Vera. The most independence for her dollar." No way would Anthony recommit to the married man charade, not under Gloria's new brand of scrutiny. Her brazen move, as creepy as it was, reopened all sorts of possibilities.

"Fine," Gloria said. "You research the options. We'll get together on Saturday to compare notes and walk through the house." She stood up to show us the door.

In the hall, I stopped Donna. "Four days isn't much," I said. "I don't want to spend half of it driving. You think I could camp in your side yard, maybe make some phone calls from the house?" I could have camped in my parents' driveway, but that would have felt too forlorn.

"Oh, Christ, Frannie, I'll make up the guest room," she said.

~ Six ~

Beckman Manor, my mother's supposedly temporary nursing home, did look somewhat like a luxury hotel. Gloria had booked a private room for the time being, with a view of a small patio and open field beyond. There was no telling yet how much cash would become available to Vera.

There'd be no telling at all how long she might live, how many years of support she would need. Fourteen or fifteen years at least, if she made it to eighty like her own mother.

The most independence for Vera's dollar, I had said, but we needed to consider her dignity too. Even if forced to part with the illusion of marriage, maybe she'd want to stay in her own home. Or maybe she'd want to hang on to the illusion.

When Donna and I left Gloria's, we drove straight out to Beckman, signed in at the front desk, and walked past a day room where two old women watched a loud game show on TV. We found Vera sitting in her room, in her wheelchair.

"Ma," Donna said and rushed across the room to hug her.

I hugged her too, and sat down on the bed to be at her level. It was a hospital bed, covered with a purple and blue patterned spread.

"Are you okay?" Donna asked.

"I'm sorry I scared you girls," she said.

I told her, "You didn't do it, Gloria did."

Vera said, "I could have called Donna, once I got here, but my head is spinning. I just told Gloria, I'll sign the papers, but not the way they're written. It wasn't like that, all those things she says about your father."

I said, "It's entirely up to you, you know. You don't have to sign at all."

Donna looked at me sharply. There I went, messing up Gloria's plans. But Gloria was using Vera, bodily, to tell Anthony his time was up. The least I could do was suggest that my mother had a choice.

"No," Vera said, "Gloria's right. I haven't been looking out for myself financially."

"We're going to fix up the house," Donna said, "make it a nicer place to live. You'll pick the paint colors when the time comes."

Vera said, "Thank goodness for my daughters. I was so stupid. I never should have let things go on like this."

"You weren't stupid," I told her. "You were holding out for what you wanted."

She gestured to the walls of her room. "This is not what I want."

"Then we'll take you home. Right, Donna? Right now."

Donna just looked scared.

Vera said, "I can't. I promised Gloria."

"Forget Gloria," I said. "What do you want?"

"I want somebody to take care of me. So far, Gloria's the only one who's offered."

"We'll take care of you together," Donna told her, as if that were possible.

I'd spent twenty years coaching my mother to imagine life without my father, when all along I should have been coaching her to imagine life under her own control. Now, like the fisherman in the old story, my chances were gone, wasted, flipping head over tail into the sea, the sun glinting off of pink and golden scales. No amount of stamping my foot on the hard wet sand would let me call back that magic fish, would let me rephrase my wishes for Vera.

"We'll take care of you together, Ma," I echoed Donna half-heartedly. But I couldn't get over feeling like the bad daughter.

~ Seven ~

I didn't know what I'd find at Anthony and Larry's apartment on a Wednesday afternoon: the two men together, or maybe Anthony at work and Larry at home. Larry at home with a young trick, that possibility crossed my mind. Or maybe no one would be there and I'd just look up at the window, read the names on the bell, verify another piece of reality, and be on my way.

When I buzzed to get in, someone buzzed right back, no questions asked. On my way into the building, I passed a tall man coming out, carrying an armload of clothing on hangers. I climbed to the third floor. The door to the right of the landing stood wide open. I looked in and saw Larry. He sat on a white leather couch, weeping.

"Larry?" I said from the doorway. He looked up at me, then kept right on weeping.

"Hey, Larry, it's the drawers on the right, right?" a voice came from the bedroom. Then a short man carried in a stack of knit shirts.

"Spying?" he asked.

"Hardly," I snapped at him. "Larry," I said, "I came to see you and Anthony." But even as I spoke I knew there was no more Larry and Anthony. Those were his suits going out the downstairs door.

"I'm leaving," Larry told me. "I can't stand it anymore. Your father. Your sister. The whole drama about money. I've had it."

"From now on you'll stay away from the married ones," the short friend said. "The ones with vindictive daughters."

I didn't know this man, but I hated him. "It isn't that simple," I said, waving my hand to take in the living room and the rest of the apartment.

239

"I have no quarrel with all of this, but my father has treated my mother like shit." Even in the middle of an argument I noticed that the apartment was beautiful, not only because of the fancy leather furniture, but because it looked like a home.

"And now he's treating Larry like shit," the friend said.

"Well lucky for Larry he can walk out when he needs to."

By now the tall friend had come back upstairs. He didn't get involved; he went in the other room and kept packing. My father's lover just sat there. I sat down next to him on the couch. "I'm sorry," I told him. "I didn't come to fight. I came to see what's up."

The tall friend came out of the bedroom. "We have to keep moving, Larry," he said. "You don't want to be here when you-know-who gets home."

My father's lover looked at me. "I'm not taking anything except my clothes," he said, "...and this." He reached for something on the coffee table—a white plate, about six inches across, made of marble or alabaster with an intricate inlaid pattern of colored stones, and bits of turquoise and lapis. Larry turned it over in his hands. "We bought it at the Taj Mahal."

"Oh, Jesus," I told him, "take everything. Better you than Gloria."

At this, he gave a sputtering laugh. "Thanks, Fran."

I stood up to leave. His friends were right; I shouldn't slow him down. From the doorway I said, "I'm in the Chicago phonebook—Ruby, too, you remember she's a Levinson—if you ever want to look us up." It was silly, the sort of thing people tell each other at high school reunions, but I was going to miss him, this person my father had chosen. I'd imagined a whole lifetime for getting to know him.

~ Eight ~

All that week, Gloria and Michael were tightening the screws on Anthony. They had his wife. Did he want her back, or not?

He wasn't sure what he wanted. He was living alone in the apartment on West 20th Street. His lover had left him. He needed time to think.

Go ahead, they told him, Think all you like, but on one condition: he was not to contact Vera. The time had come to make a decision; there'd be no more jerking her around. My sister and brother-in-law took credit for having sent "that gigolo" packing. They counted Larry's disappearance as a personal success.

240

I imagined Anthony sitting on the white couch weighing the possibilities, trying to get a picture of his future. And every day Mike and Gloria upped the ante. They intended to wipe him out financially if he left Vera. They swore to monitor his every move if he stayed.

Even with his lover gone, I fully expected Anthony to leave. His freedom had to be worth something to him, more than the hundreds of thousands of dollars he'd accumulated. Freedom, and love. There'd be another man, another woman, someone. Maybe even Larry again, if Anthony could convincingly demonstrate that he'd quit taking orders from Gloria.

While he spent his days thinking, Donna and I cleared out the house. With Gloria looking on, Donna signed a contract with Anthony. She would paint the walls and kitchen cabinets, sand and refinish wood floors, replace linoleum floors, gut and rebuild the part of the master bathroom that had turned to rot because of a leaky pipe. Billy, true to his word, kept the hell out of it. His mother Audrey was looking after the plumbing business as well as the kids. Donna hired me on as her crew.

For fifteen bucks an hour, I worked by my sister's side, emptying our childhood home. We were laborers, not daughters. We stocked the fridge with beer and blasted Michelle Shocked on Donna's boom box. We packed fast, leaving the closets full and the mementos unsorted. Everything out in the open got shoved in a box, including the candlesticks I'd brought back and a few stolen items Donna must have returned too. Had she tired of them or felt guilty? At this juncture there was no use in asking. We lugged all the furniture except the upright piano out to the garage and stacked it as if the garage was a moving van.

At night, we picked up the kids and met Billy back at the farmhouse. We took turns cooking dinner. I helped out by wiping up when the applesauce went flying, and wondered what my own babyhood had been like.

Every night, Donna played this game with Carly: she lay on her back and sat her daughter on top of her bent knees. She bounced her there, eye-to-eye, the two of them holding hands and singing along with the Raffi tape. And then without any warning, Donna would say, "Oops!" and open her legs, and Carly would fall in a giggling heap to the carpet. She'd climb back up again and the game would start over. I didn't join in. I just watched and listened. By mid-week I knew all the Raffi songs by heart, and the dread that knotted up in me at the mere sight of children had started to come untied.

"So how is it?" Ruby asked when I called her from Donna's guest room one evening.

"A mess. Gloria is behaving abominably. I don't know where it will all settle, but the good news is I'm not getting over-involved."

"That can't be easy," she said.

"Easier than you think. You're my home, Ruby. I'm ready to come home."

"Okay," she said, "but don't hurry. Do what you need to. I'll see you when I see you."

"Hey—babe," she caught me before I said goodbye, "I miss you."

I grinned and wrapped the phone cord around my hand. "You're not mad?"

"I'm a little bit mad and I miss you a lot."

"Fair enough. I love you Ruby. I'll keep you posted."

When we hung up, I missed her more than ever, and the ease with which we always passed our days.

The minute I saw Michael, I knew something was up. Donna and Gloria had scheduled a meeting at my parents' house to talk with Anthony about change orders, but that didn't require my brother-in-law's presence. Yet there he was, in the middle of the empty living room, straddling an avocado green kitchen chair backwards, looking like a blue jeans ad for the over-forty weekend set. Donna knelt on the only other chair in the place, her back bent over a spread of papers on a rickety card table.

I stood in the archway between living room and hall. "What's going on, Michael?" I asked, too forcefully.

"I beg your pardon?" he answered.

"God, Frannie," Donna looked up from her paperwork. "What's all the hostility for?"

"Something's happening," I said. "Otherwise Michael wouldn't be here. He only gets brought in for the man-to-man talks with Anthony."

"Very perceptive." He tossed me a brilliant smile. "I'm having a man-to-man talk with Donna."

"Lay off, both of you," Donna said. "I'm trying to get these numbers to come out right. Jesus, what is it about this house? Everyone starts bickering the minute they walk in."

She and I had worked together for three days without a single squabble, but just the sight of my brother-in-law put me on the offensive. "The walls have been saturated with it," I said. "Woe to whoever buys this dump." In spite of all our talk about giving Vera choices, it certainly seemed that we were cruising toward selling.

I heard Gloria's footsteps overhead—click-click-clicking, then stopping, then clicking again. With the carpets ripped out and the furniture gone, the tiniest sounds ricocheted endlessly. Then Gloria came down the stairs behind me and brushed past me into the living room. She had to struggle to walk across the drop cloths in her high heels. Even so, she did a commendable job of ignoring me.

"I can see what you mean about the bathroom," she told Donna, "but I think we should stick to the original bid. Remember, any work is an improvement."

"Michael," this time I tried it more calmly, "please tell me what's going on."

"Anthony's reached a decision," he said.

"What decision?" Suddenly the restraint I had exercised all week seemed all wrong. I'd taken my cues from Donna and stuck to the practical. On my breaks, I made phonecalls to attendant care agencies and the local Center for Independent Living to follow up on housing leads. I hadn't fought with Gloria, demanding that she make me an equal player.

Now, on hearing that my father had made some decision, I forgot caution. I wanted to jump in, to drive a hard bargain for Vera. All the wrong people were designing her future. What exactly had Anthony been struggling about for days? Why had such an obvious choice taken so long?

"We don't know what he's decided," Michael told me. "He's coming here to announce it tonight."

I said, "You've got him over a barrel about money. That can't be in Vera's best interest."

"He's got himself over a barrel." Gloria finally looked right at me. "Look how much he spent on that fag."

"Surely not half of what he had," I told her. "Are you seeking equity or punishment?"

She said, "Cut the psychoanalytic crap. I should have known you would defend him."

I looked to Donna to contradict Gloria, but she was still punching in numbers. "What about you, Donna?" I asked. "You think it's a good idea to drive the man back into a failed marriage?"

"He might not go back," Donna said as she set down her calculator. "And who are we to judge that it's failed?"

"You tell me. You're the one who watched his comings and goings for ten years. And what about those divorce papers Gloria keeps threatening to file? What about the so-called abuses itemized in there? That was your word, Gloria."

"Things would have to be different if he went back," Gloria said.

"Things wouldn't be different."

"Maybe we can push for counseling," Donna suggested. "Six months of joint counseling before Mom can be moved out of Beckman. Dad can give up the apartment and live here, and they can look into working things out." I couldn't imagine what they would work out, but it was the least drastic idea I'd heard all week.

"That could be a plan, if Mom goes along with it," I said. I hated talking about Vera as if she had no say in the matter.

"It's a great plan, Donna," Mike said. "The important thing is to curtail your father's lying and spending."

I said, "The important thing is to give Vera as much control as possible."

"As much comfort as possible," Donna corrected me, "and as much control as she's comfortable taking."

"Exactly!" Gloria said. "That's why we can't go easy on Anthony about the money."

My oldest sister is a sculptor of flesh, a wizard at reshaping surfaces. She can completely detach your nipple, float it through space like a lovely pink petal, set it down anywhere and build a breast around it. Likewise with ideas. It wasn't money or revenge she was after, we were supposed to believe, but Vera's comfort.

I must have looked horrified, because Michael got out of his chair to come stand by me. "Listen, Francesca," he said, "if your parents were to divorce today, Anthony would not be obligated to give your mother the money he spent outside the marriage before dividing up the joint property. It isn't equitable, but it is the law. Now if New York State won't twist his arm, we have to. So we scare him a little, threaten a contested divorce, just to have things come out even. He stays or goes, but either way we help Vera keep closer tabs on her resources. You wouldn't mess that up, would you? You wouldn't tell Anthony that fairness doesn't matter."

"No," I agreed miserably, "I wouldn't tell him that."

"Good," Gloria said, "then we'll do the talking."

But I didn't want to talk to Anthony about money; I wanted to talk to him about love.

He rang the doorbell, then turned the knob and let himself in. No one moved. He stood in the foyer, blinking at the emptiness, the harsh overhead lights, and the four of us in the living room—all four of his offspring, you could almost imagine, with Mike standing in for Jimmy.

"It already looks good, Donna," he said. "A little cleaning goes a long way."

"It can," she answered.

"Have a seat." Michael thumped the chair he had vacated against the bare floor, and Anthony crossed the room to sit down.

I saw an incredible weariness in his demeanor, a network of fine webbed fissures, like the crackle glaze on a pottery bowl. In the glaze, the cracks are only on the surface, but my father seemed in actual danger of crumbling.

Michael, Gloria, and I stood in a little semi-circle around Anthony and Donna. My oldest sister and her husband were conspicuously reserved. They were playing it cool, waiting for Anthony to announce his allegiance. Then they would know how to handle him.

"I've been thinking," Anthony said. "I need to give it another try with your mother. As soon as the house is fixed up, we'll move back in. It will be like starting over."

"Good choice, Dad," Michael said.

"What?" I asked Anthony. "Why?"

He said, "Your mother and I have been married for forty-two years."

"That's right," Gloria told him. "It's time to honor that."

"Wait a minute," I said, "you've started over before. At Dulano's. Maybe you even meant it, but you didn't make it stick. Why would this be any different?"

"Vera was my first love," he said.

"We're talking about a marriage here," Mike told him, "an honest partnership. No more double lives." He gestured to include my sisters and me. "No more looking the other way."

"Yes," Anthony told us, "one home."

"I don't trust it," I said.

"Larry is gone." This was the first time I'd heard Anthony speak his lover's name in front of my sisters. "There won't be any more men."

This I believed. "You were in love with Larry," I told him.

For an instant, Anthony looked like he might drown, but then he pulled himself up, looked right at Gloria and said, "No. It wasn't love. I was under his influence."

"I've been afraid of that all along," Gloria told him.

"Hang on just a minute," I said. "The next person may very well be a woman. I bet you a thousand dollars there will be a next person. Why would you drag Vera through this again?"

"Donna," Anthony appealed to my sister, "you know what it's like to repair a marriage. This is my family. Vera was my first love."

Donna replied with a little scowl.

"How long will it last?" I asked him.

"Well, it *has* lasted forty years," Donna said.

"It's a shotgun wedding," I told Anthony. "You're making a decision under duress, under pressure about money."

"It's what Dad wants, Frannie," Michael said.

"It's what you're shoving down his throat."

Donna said, "It's what Mommy wants."

This much was true. Vera had spent the past six days in a holding pattern, waiting in her room and putting her faith in Gloria. She had in no way made the nursing home her own. She didn't wheel herself down to the dining room with the white linen cloths on the tables, or even attempt to converse with the other residents. She'd be going home to Mount Kisco any day now, she told the nurses, and took her meals alone in her room. Of course "home" was more than the house; it was that gorgeous illusion of marriage.

"It's exactly what Mom wants," I said, "which is why it shouldn't be offered insincerely."

"I'm sincere," Anthony told me. "Maybe time will convince you, Francesca."

"There's not a bone in your body that wants to work things out with Larry?" I asked.

"Not a bone."

"I don't believe you." Even as I argued, I could see I was pushing him out on a limb.

"I'm going to call your mother," he said.

"You can't," I told him. "You're fucking with her head."

Gloria said, "Of course he can call her."

"What about Donna's idea? What about six months of marriage counseling first?"

"Don't be silly," Anthony said. "I don't need a third party poking around in my marriage."

"What do you have here?" I asked. "A fourth, fifth, sixth and seventh party!"

"We're your family, Dad," Mike told him.

I said, "Michael, you approved of the counseling idea. This is happening much too fast."

"I'm going to call her." Anthony stood up from his chair.

"No," I told him, "I won't let you." And then I yelled, "Don't you people see what's happening here?"

"There's no need to yell," Michael said.

But there was need, there was crushing need, to stop him. Anthony walked slowly, as if sleepwalking, from the living room to the kitchen. I ran around the other way through the front hall and dining room and I beat him. The kitchen counters were bare, except for an open red and gray Craftsman toolbox, and a phone, the only one in the house. All the others had been buried in a heap of boxes.

Anthony and I circled one other, each looking for an opening. Gloria, Michael, and Donna crowded the doorways like kids gathered around a schoolyard fight. I had threatened him with a knife ten years before in this kitchen. Back then, I had imagined myself willing to use it. Now, I wanted to stop him, not hurt him. I wanted to prevent him from taking my mother for a ride.

The phone was an old desk model, tethered by a long cord to the wall jack. "Don't do it," I said, as he reached for it.

"I have to." Desperation lined his face, not sorrow or defiance, but bleak despair. He picked up the receiver, but didn't know my mother's number. Chances are he would not have bothered to call her all week, even if he hadn't been abiding by Gloria's rules.

"I'll do it," Gloria said, and she stepped into the kitchen to dial for him. I squared myself for a fight with her.

"Francesca," she yelled at me, "stay out of this. It isn't yours."

"It isn't yours either. But you're right, Gloria, I should stay out and so should you. You want to make a deal? You want to say we'll both get the hell out of our parents' business?"

She put her hand on top of the phone.

"Why are you letting her bully you?" I asked Anthony. He looked lost.

"Come on, Dad," Gloria said, and she picked up the receiver.

The phone was a live thing in the middle of the counter. I had to kill it. But to cut or to smash? Precision or passion? To cut, I decided—a quiet act, one that said I knew what I was doing. I reached into the toolbox and came up with tin snips.

I made the first cut near the wall before Gloria finished dialing. Just in case someone thought to splice the wires back together, I kept snipping, a half inch at a time, letting phone cord confetti fall to the floor. My family watched until I was done.

"You're out of your fucking mind." Gloria was waving her hands, and her whole body shook. Donna took a step into the kitchen, ready to break up a fight.

But I was done fighting. "Yes, I am," I told Gloria quietly, and put the tin snips back in the toolbox.

Anthony still looked lost. Mike came into the kitchen and put a hand on his arm. "Come on, Dad," he said, "we'll go to town and find a phone."

I was already heading toward the front door, and both Donna and Gloria hastened after me. "Frannie," Donna called out, "what are you doing?"

"Nothing." I walked out, and the four of them crowded on the front steps to watch me. They were probably afraid for their tires. But I couldn't stop Anthony. At best, I had slowed him down. I got into my truck and peeled out of the driveway.

A different daughter would have raced to town to call her mother and warn her about the impending seduction. She would have begged her to be other than who she was: a woman who sat alone in her private room, who dreamed of her marriage spontaneously reassembling, the shards of a broken bowl leaping back together—not with careful fitting, delicate gluing, pressure applied evenly while the cement hardened, but with the remarkable ease of a film run backward through the projector, the bowl reappearing on the table whole and unmended. How much further backwards would we have to run the film—thirty, thirty-five years?—to find the last kind word, the last electrified touch?

A different daughter would have hastened to the nursing home, would have lain in bed with her mother, held her body against her mother's back, caressed her mother's powdered cheek and whispered, "Mama, you're so beautiful, so kind. Give someone else a chance to love you." But who would there ever be?

This daughter drove, past the exit for her mother's new home, out onto Long Island, to the campground on the spit of land with dark sky and ocean all around. This daughter had a hard time falling asleep. She sat outside the truck on the rise above the beach and watched the black waves.

~ Nine ~

I woke to a chilly morning, before the sun had cleared the horizon, and clambered out of the truck to survey the world around me. Ocean and sky were matching bowls—one upright, one inverted, both beginning to fill with pale blue light. Both clear and quiet, except for the ruffle of waves at the ocean's nearest edge.

I thought about following the edge, about walking for a mile or two on the sand, but that would have made me too late for Vera. Soon my sisters would be calling her—or worse, my father. Worst of all, they would drive down. If I wanted to be alone with her, I'd have to get to Beckman before they did.

Once I got there, I wouldn't be going back to the beach. Underneath my concern for Vera, a stronger current was running, calling me home to Chicago and Ruby. It was time to start my round of good-byes: to the Atlantic first, then my mother, to my father if we crossed paths. To the tangle of suburban woods, roads, and traffic jams, to Billy, and my nieces Carly and Emma. I'd quit my job with Donna if she hadn't fired me already. It was time to admit I had failed. The attempt I'd made to see my mother through to a better place had flopped, not for lack of trying but for lack of audience appeal. I'd rip the page of independent living phone numbers out of my sketchbook and leave it with Vera. I'd go home, tell Ruby she was right again, start living my own life.

Vera was already up when I reached her. She sat with her back to the door, facing her window where the sky turned watery yellow with daybreak. She wore a rose-pink housecoat.

"Ma?"

"Have you heard the news, Frannie? It's a miracle!" She wheeled around to greet me. "Your father and I are going to live together again. He's coming down here this morning."

"Have you been sitting up all night?"

"No," she said, "Although I didn't sleep well. There's a very nice aide on the night shift; she got me up and bathed a couple hours ago. I told her my husband has found his heart. She said let's wait to put on my dress, so it will be as fresh as possible when he gets here."

This was the advantage of an expensive nursing home—a staff that could adjust its early morning routine to accommodate a woman with pressing personal business.

"Ma," I said again, coming to sit on the end of her bed, "I don't think you can trust him."

"Don't argue with my good news, Frannie. He told me I was his first love."

So I held my tongue. We sat in silence. Vera was still, wholly alert, an incandescent bulb humming and shining from within. This was the event she'd always dreamed of, the reawakening of romance in her life. She was his first love. First, and now last. Here was her payoff, her reward for enduring patience. She had thought about giving up, other women would have given up, but through the decades she'd held onto her faith. I had doubted and scrutinized that faith, had tried to poke holes in it, but she had known to give it time.

We were holding a vigil in her room, she for her husband to come back, and I for her illusions to crash. But when would that be—this day, in a week, in a month? Soon, judging from the panic I had seen on Anthony's face. He had been reacting, not scheming. He would bolt in a day or two, I guessed, before Gloria and Mike could force any steps toward an actual reunion.

"Thank God Gloria never filed those papers," my mother said, and then she went back to her shining and humming.

An hour passed; my stomach rumbled. I hadn't eaten dinner the night before. "I'll be right back," I told her.

Out in the hallway, I approached the charge nurse behind her desk. She was a tall woman, her narrow face partly veiled by fine, chin-length brown hair. "Margaret Sinclair, RN," her name tag read.

"Will breakfast be delivered to my mother's room?" I asked.

Nurse Sinclair paged through a three-ring notebook on the desk. "Your mother canceled both breakfast and lunch," she told me. "She'll be going out with your— um— her— husband." It was a good catch, not to assume my mother's husband was necessarily my father. One never knew, in the 1980s.

"She thinks my father's coming," I shook my head and grimaced and Margaret Sinclair smiled conspiratorially.

"Not true?" she asked.

"He did promise," I hurried to explain. "But the odds are a thousand to one he'll stand her up. She might as well have food on hand while she's waiting around to get fucked over."

The nurse didn't flinch. "Consider it done," she said, reaching to dial a number on her phone.

I needed to bother her for two more things. "Is there a candy machine," I asked, "and a pay phone?" She directed me to the vending alcove on the ground floor, just around the corner from the beauty salon.

"So soon?" Ruby asked after accepting my collect call. "Any news?"

"Nothing definite," I told her. "Gloria is pressing Anthony to choose between Larry and his fortune. Anthony's not taking it well."

"What's your plan?"

"One more day with my mother. Tomorrow I get on the road."

"Barring any hitches."

"No hitches, Ruby. Enough is enough. Whatever these people do next, it'll have to be their problem, not mine."

"Okay," she said, "I'll see you by the end of the week. Call me if something unexpected happens."

I didn't ask what could happen.

"Next time I'll come with you," she added.

"I don't want there to be a next time."

"Okay. But if there has to be, I'll come."

My mother's breakfast tray arrived at nine-thirty with two of everything on it—single-portion boxes of raisin bran, glasses of grapefruit juice, half-pints of skim milk.

"Here you go, Mrs. D'Amato. A little something for you and your daughter." The woman who delivered our breakfast was short like me, but more stout. Dominican, I guessed. Her name tag said, "Angie." Her uniform pants and shirt were the color of raspberry sherbet.

"Thank you," I told her. It was Nurse Sinclair who had done me this favor, but she'd already gone off her shift. My mother didn't speak to Angie; she barely registered the interruption.

"Come on, Ma, we'll have some raisin bran together."

"No thanks." She was saving herself for dinner with her first love.

Donna showed up at twelve-thirty just when I could have collapsed from boredom.

"What are you doing here?" That's how she greeted me.

"Keeping watch. I thought you would call."

"Donna," my mother began, "have you heard the good news? Your father and I—"

"I know, Ma," Donna interrupted. "Have you and Frannie been fighting?"

"What would we fight about? Look at this, all my girls are here."

What was Gloria? I wondered. Her warden? Her dominatrix? But I didn't start in.

Donna beckoned me to talk with her out in the hall. "He's blown it already," she said. "The asshole is backing out."

"That's presuming he was in."

"He was convincing at the restaurant," she said. "Gloria and Mike drove him to the Yangtze. We all stood outside that stupid pagoda phone booth while he called. It was like, Don't come out of your room until you've cleaned it! When he did come out, he ate like a pig and chatted up a storm, about all the real work 'we' could do on the house. All the little luxuries the poor man had never allowed himself: screened-in patio, second floor deck, jacuzzi, expanded second floor bath."

Nothing on this list of improvements indicated a desire to make a life with Vera, but I let Donna keep talking.

"He slept at Gloria's," she said. "They let him drive his own car down. When they woke up at six, he'd already split. They drove straight to Chelsea and sent me out looking in Mount Kisco. Nothing. At eleven, he calls me. 'I can't go through with it,' he says. He's in fucking Boston."

"Will you tell her?" she asked me.

"No way," I said. "I'm not delivering any third-hand messages. Besides, I'm the one who tried to stop him from calling."

"Here we go," she said. "You were right."

"Thank you very much, but I'm not telling her. And I'm not convinced you should either. Will you say he's definitely not coming? What if he runs this film loop a few more times?"

"I'll break his neck first," my sister told me.

I followed her back into the room.

"Ma," she sat on the bed and touched Vera's arm. "Dad isn't coming down today—"

"Donna—" My mother spoke up automatically to contradict any naysaying. But I could see the moment of impact when she realized this was Donna talking, not me, and my sister was delivering hard news. I saw the flash of Vera's filament burning out. "He what?"

"He isn't coming. I don't know what he was thinking last night when he called you, but today he's back to his same old shit. I shouldn't have let him call you," she mumbled as an afterthought.

"Don't worry, Donna, it's not your fault," my mother said. "I feel so foolish."

For the first time in my life, I wanted to be wrong. I wanted to see Vera lit up again, for her hopes to be well-founded.

"You're not foolish," I told her. "There's nothing wrong with wanting things. You just have to direct the wanting at someone who can deliver."

"But we love who we love, don't we?" she said. "Gloria tried to warn me that this would happen."

Gloria! I looked at Donna, but she just rolled her eyes.

"Gloria? Ma, last night she was the one who encouraged him to call. She talks out of both sides of her mouth."

"That could be." Vera blinked her eyes and seemed confused.

"Can we talk about where you're going to live?" Donna asked.

Vera said, "No, I need sleep. I can't tackle that question today. Will you press the light for me, Frannie?"

Near her bed, a call button bore a symbol of a nurse with starched cap and cinched waist. It lit up when I pressed it. A minute later, the loud-speaker mounted on the wall came on with a crackle.

"Can I help you?" someone asked.

"Is that Angie?" Vera said. "I'd like to lie down for a few hours."

Donna and I both stood up to clear out of Angie's way. "We'll call you tomorrow, Ma," Donna said.

But I intended to get on the highway first thing in the morning. "I'll catch up with you tonight," I told Donna out in the hallway. Then I went into the day room, closed my ears to the blaring TV, and waited for my mother to wake up.

~ Ten ~

"I'm taking you out to dinner," I told Vera. A good start—telling, not asking.

"Oh, no. Really?"

"Yes, really."

I was taking her out for lobster. Maybe it would take her mind off Anthony.

I flipped through her closet, then decided this would be more fun for both of us if it seemed like she was making some of the decisions.

"Is the periwinkle dress okay?"

"Yes it's my favorite. It's a flattering color, don't you think?"

"Stunning. Black beads or white?"

253

"What do you like?"

My old habit of begging her to have an opinion rattled its cage, but that was all.

"White beads," I told her. "They stand out against the blue." Her diamond pendant had been locked away, thank goodness, in the nursing home safe.

We were in the medi-cab, all strapped in and hurtling down the highway, before she asked where we were going.

"A seafood place. Nothing fancy."

It was the Clam-bo-ree, where Donna had taken me a few years back. The dining room was noisier and brighter than I remembered it. Waitresses in sneakers slammed back and forth through swinging kitchen doors—in with cracked discarded shells, out with steaming platters of clams. Underneath the clatter of dishes and conversation, I could hear a cheery canned rendition of "When Doves Cry," Prince's big hit from 1984, made into Muzak already.

"That's your dinner," I said when we passed the tank of live lobsters.

She grinned at the mottled green creatures in the murky water. "Wouldn't that be something!" Most likely she imagined that we'd order for my convenience, something easy to feed her, like filet of sole.

"Oh, no!" she exclaimed when we got to the table. "We forgot my bib." She had a whole drawerful at home and two or three at the nursing home—cotton dishtowels fastened with alligator clips and a ribbon around the neck.

"They'll bring plastic bibs with the lobsters," I told her. "Tonight I'll wear one too."

"You're joking!"

"I'm not." When the waitress came to the table, I ordered a one-and-a-half-pound lobster, two plates, and two bibs.

It's important, in eating a lobster, to save the most satisfying parts for last. I pulled off a tiny hind leg, and held it up to her mouth. "Suck hard," I said.

After the legs and fins, I started on the claws—one big and one gigantic. I used all the tools at my disposal—the nutcracker, the little fork, the thing that looks like a miniature ice pick—to slide the meat out of its shell. She feasted on the pieces that were big enough to chew.

"A person could starve to death on those little legs," she said.

"I won't let you starve." When the claws were gone, I called the waitress over to bring us two glasses of wine. "Can you drink wine?" I asked, but only after the order was placed.

"Of course," she giggled. "I'm not driving."

We took a break with half a baked potato each. I doused mine with butter and sour cream, then offered the same to her. "So fattening," she said.

"So you buy bigger clothes."

She smiled brightly, like it was the wittiest thing she'd ever heard.

"When was the last time you had a lobster?" I asked.

"Before I got married. I was on a date. That was a very fancy date in those days, but I felt so self-conscious. Imagine doing this when you're trying to impress someone!" She raised a napkin shakily and made a few unsuccessful passes at her chin before finally wiping away a streak of butter.

That couldn't have been her last time, because the first lobster I ever ate was on a family vacation in Maine, but I didn't spoil her memory. "A woman with an appetite," I said. "It sounds pretty appealing."

Her brow creased. "When was your last time?"

"With Ruby, in a Chinese restaurant. It was smothered in black bean sauce. Have you ever had black bean sauce?" When I was a kid, Chinese cooking was celery and water chestnuts from a can.

"No," she said, "never."

We'll go out for Chinese next time, I considered saying, but I wasn't making any promises.

"I haven't met Ruby, have I?" she asked.

"No." Again, no promises. "She's waiting for me at home."

Only the lobster's tail was left. I used my hands to turn back the bright red shell, and the red and white flesh came free all in one piece. I sliced it down the middle, and put half on her plate. Her breath caught. "Oh," she shook her head, "that's beautiful."

We both stopped talking while we devoured the tail. When she finished she said, "That was worth the wait." Did she mean forty-five years, or this particular lobster tail—a rush of abundance after a delightfully frustrating meal?

"Why didn't you marry him?" I asked.

"Who?"

"The guy who took you out for lobster."

"He didn't propose."

~ Eleven ~

Anthony's car wasn't parked on West 20th Street, and he didn't answer the bell. He was probably still in Boston. A woman coming out of his building let me in. Her nose was pierced with a ruby-red jewel that glinted under the hallway light.

I carried a scrap of paper, dangling from my finger by a single piece of scotch tape. "I'm heading back to Chicago. Call me," my note said.

On the third floor landing, I found another note taped to the apartment door—a small beige parchment envelope, with "Tony" written on the outside. I recognized Larry's carefully upright penmanship; I had seen him sign a VISA slip in Chicago. That was Anthony and Vera's money he had been signing away. According to Gloria, it was hers and her husband's and daughter's as well. But Larry had not seemed diminished by greed or dependency, not caught up in proving nor refuting the love-money equation.

I fought a momentary urge to open his note. Instead, I taped my own next to his and left the building. We were Anthony's fan club, the ones who could not let him fade away. I'd be hearing from both men soon enough, I figured. Chances were, they'd turn up together again in Chicago.

~ Twelve ~

The next morning I found water—sprightly rapids and rivulets that gathered and tumbled through my parents' house. A thin veil of a waterfall rippled down the front stairs and into the foyer, turned the bend into the kitchen, then ran again down more steps to the basement. And that wasn't all. Rain dripped from sodden ceilings and trickled down the walls of this one-time house, now a cave.

I stood rooted in the open doorway, my key still in the lock, trying to take in the doughy smell of plaster, the horror of so much damage, and transfixed at the same time by all the lively music and movement.

"Holy fuck!" Donna came up behind me. "Frannie, why the hell don't you do something?"

Do what? What was I supposed to do? Then it sank in. This was no act of God, no hole in the roof or a personally monogrammed rain cloud releasing its load onto the site of so many losses. This was about plumbing, a mechanical failure, about water escaping containment.

"The water main?" I offered.

But Donna had already analyzed the source of the sound, and hauled herself up by the banister. I heard her footsteps in the bathrooms above me. I heard the music subside, the instruments cutting out one at a time. Water rippled down the staircase for a few more seconds, then slipped away.

Donna climbed carefully down the slippery staircase to meet me in the front hall. "Who did this?"

We were standing in a puddle.

"Who did this?" she repeated.

"Did what?"

"Who turned on every fucking faucet in both upstairs bathrooms and let them run God-knows-how-long? Twenty-four hours, at least."

The horror sank in a little deeper: this was about deliberate destruction. Vandalism. Or insurance fraud.

"I'm calling Billy," she said.

She had a brand new modular phone cord in her purse, a replacement for the one I had snipped into bits. I wandered through the house again and claimed a dry seat on the front stoop, where I could think about how this discovery affected my plans.

The truck was all packed to go. Billy, Donna, the kids, and I had just done our awkward hugging in the farmhouse driveway.

"Don't stay mad," Donna had told me. But I wasn't mad, just anxious to keep my promise to myself and Ruby.

On my way through town, I'd found myself turning impulsively again, back up the hill to my parents' house. Discovering Vera's absence a week before was the biggest surprise I could have imagined. All I wanted now was a souvenir. I was going in to claim one.

What souvenir, I didn't know. I'd look in the closets we hadn't bothered to empty, maybe climb around in the garage, dig through some of the boxes out there. You're crazy, I expected Donna to tell me. She'd offer to ship something, but I didn't want whatever she picked out. I wanted to retrieve my own fragment of my childhood home, maybe snitch a piece of broken tile, in case the house belonged to someone else when I came back. I certainly didn't anticipate finding the place destroyed.

"Call me if something happens," Ruby had said. I had stopped myself from asking, like what? Either she was prescient or she understood my family better than I did. But Ruby didn't know me yet, once I hit a wall.

257

I had existed for years, decades already, appearing to have no limits—slamming the door, then yanking it back open to yell just one more thing. This time felt different. For the most part the fight had already gone out of me, and somehow the flood finished the job. The seamlessness with which my mother had moved from living under Anthony's control to Gloria's shocked me, and even in the middle of that shock I knew Vera would end up at Beckman. Flood or no, her home would be permanently dismantled. I would end up reciting for her, on the phone or when I visited, what I thought of as the truth, but I would not spend my life arguing with Gloria.

My heart wasn't completely hard like a walnut. It still beat for a person in trouble, even Donna who so often let me down. She was feeling this water damage more acutely, taking it personally, I could tell. On the practical level, the sopping wet house was her job site. But underneath that, she was just now glimpsing the ending I'd already viewed head-on.

I could give Donna a few hours, even a whole day. By midnight, I'd be back on I-80. In Ohio, I'd stop to call Ruby. By the time my lover heard from me, I'd be more than halfway to her side.

Donna came through the house and sat down next to me on the front stoop. She said, "Frannie, will you help me with this?"

And then she was crying, huge wracking sobs that started at her tailbone and exploded in her throat. I did my best to put an arm around her, but she held herself so stiffly it was like having my arm around one of those bucking bronco rides we used to put nickels into at the A&P. She sobbed and sobbed, and soon the sobs turned to laughter. The laughs were just as violent, and oddly private, so I didn't join in. Finally they ran themselves out. Donna and I sat quietly, and I took back my arm.

"Sorry," she said, "I'm just sick of this place."

"What do we have to do?" I asked. I still had a talent for saying "we" when it counted.

We had to take steps to minimize the damage. We had to strip enough wet plaster off the walls and ceilings to protect the framing, beams, and floor joists from soaking through and warping.

Donna hadn't called only Billy. She'd called the insurance agent, who had read her the policy, had tried Anthony at both the office and apartment again to no avail, and had insisted that Gloria's receptionist pull Gloria out of a consultation.

To do the urgent demolition work, she and Billy would need to hire a crew. "You're the crew," she said, "if you're willing."

"We're definitely getting paid?" I asked. Vera had signed some papers giving Gloria power of attorney, but I was leery of any deal Donna made with Gloria.

"Of course we'll get paid. Somebody's going to end up with a new house, courtesy of State Farm. Entirely gutted, none of this touch-up shit. Too bad it won't be Mommy."

"It could be," I said, for the sake of the argument. "She made it this long without much of a husband on the scene."

But Donna had no interest in philosophical questions. "Billy's coming soon," she said. "In the meantime, we can't do anything."

What did she mean we couldn't do anything?

He was bringing rakes and shovels. Garbage bags. Cardboard boxes. Wheelbarrows. Electric fans to help dry the place out. A wet-dry shop vac. Until he got there, we wouldn't have any tools.

"We have sticks," I said.

I jumped up from the front stoop and ventured into the woods, where I pulled out a dead branch about the length and thickness of a broom handle. Donna followed me into the house. I darted into the living room, poked at the bulging ceiling, and jumped back as milky water and soaking wet plaster tumbled down with a splat. Jab and splat, jab and splat. I ran and leaped through all the downstairs rooms of the house.

Soon Donna was beside me, with her own stick in hand. Poke and splat. We were knocking plaster off of walls, off of ceilings. Lancing room-sized boils. Careening through the wrecked empty house, wrecking it more to save it from structural damage. And then Donna and I were laughing together—not the harsh, wrenching, really-crying laughs she'd had earlier all by herself, but rich pealing ones, like sisters having an excellent time.

~ Thirteen ~

On a Sunday morning in March, eighteen months to the day after my parents' house was destroyed by water, Anthony noticed his piss was pink. It bothered him enough to report it to Larry, who'd been living with him again for about a year, but not enough to go to a doctor. "I will," he kept saying, "I will, I will," and by the time he did he had pissed away half his blood—which certainly cast a new light for me on all the years I screamed at him about neglecting Vera, and the years since I myself had visited a dentist.

259

Larry called me that Tuesday afternoon from the cardiac intensive care unit. "A minor prostate repair," he told me. "At least it should have been, but the strain on his heart. They keep saying he'll pull through, but I can't shake this worry."

"I'll come," I said. "Ruby and I will book a flight, but even so it'll take us a day. Do you want me to call Donna?"

"Alida is calling Donna."

"You know Alida?"

"We've met. She seemed like the right person for the job."

She was the perfect person for the job. Anthony's heart had indeed called it quits before our plane skidded to a stop at LaGuardia the next morning, and by the time Ruby and I picked up a rental car and drove into the city, my aunt had single-handedly planned my father's wake and funeral. She settled with amazing dispatch the sorts of questions Larry, Donna, and I might have haggled about for hours. No, you don't mention the ex-wife in the obituary. Yes, you do mention all the children, even the estranged ones. Three surviving daughters, one son who preceded Anthony in death—there's no divorcing one's biological offspring. If Alida struggled at all dealing with Larry, who sat stunned and weeping at her kitchen table, she didn't let it show. She made him cups of hot tea, pushed the box of Kleenex in his direction, gave him billing as Anthony's companion in the obituary.

"What can we do, Mrs. Suvino?" Ruby had the sense to ask.

Alida sent us girls, Donna, Ruby, and me, to the florist in Yonkers. "Pick out five arrangements," she said. "Three tall, two short, and a string of rosebud rosary beads for the open casket."

"Skip all the banners; they're tacky," she called after us as we went out her front door.

"My aunt said no banners," Donna asserted when the florist flipped to that page in his glossy catalog. He gave her a wan smile and closed the book, and so we were spared the impossibility of pondering phrases like "beloved brother," "beloved husband," "beloved father," of trying to get all we knew about Anthony summed up in a few words in gold flock on white satin.

Ruby and I found Vera sitting up, fully dressed, when we showed up unannounced at the nursing home.

"Ma," I called out from her doorway. "It's Frannie. I've brought someone to meet you."

"Oh!" she turned in her wheelchair, pulling her attention away from the window which in March looked out on a field rutted with frozen mud. "Wait! Don't tell me. You must be Ruby. I can't believe you girls came all the way down. You must have so much to do."

"Hello, Mrs. D'Amato." Ruby walked right in and took Vera's hand.

"Please," Vera motioned for us to sit on her bed.

"The wake doesn't start until two," I told her. "The funeral's tomorrow. The flowers are ordered. There's nothing at all to do except sit around Alida's and drink too much coffee."

Vera laughed.

"Are you sure you don't want to come, Ma? There's still time to hire a medi-cab."

"Would it be appropriate? After all, I'm divorced." She pronounced "divorced" with great deliberateness, a word that still required practice.

"I didn't think about appropriate," I admitted. "I just wanted to make sure you'd been offered a choice."

Vera said, "That's nice of you, Frannie, but it's cold out, and far. And I think I'd be too self-conscious. Too embarrassed to see people."

"Anthony's relatives never drive out to visit you?"

"They haven't. You know, I always imagined I'd be a widow."

"Of course you did. I did too. After forty years of marriage, you can think of yourself as a widow, if you want."

"I have!" Vera said. "I do! But it didn't start with a death. It started with moving in here."

"Ma," I said, not even attempting to stop myself. "Do you ever think about living independently, maybe getting a condominium in White Plains, someone like Nadine to live with you?"

"Not really. I'm getting used to this."

An aide came to the door. "Oh, Mrs. D'Amato, you have company. Would you like to eat lunch in your room today?"

"No thank you, Bettina," my mother said. "I think my guests will accompany me to the dining room."

Ruby and I followed as she pushed Vera out of the room and down the hall.

"Do you ever wheel yourself to lunch?" I asked my mother.

Bettina glanced at me over her shoulder with what might have been marked suspicion, but she slowed her walk.

"I probably should, shouldn't I?" Vera said.

"It's up to you," Bettina told her.

"Then I will."

The aide stayed behind Vera, and I took a few quick steps to be by her side. "Remember Mary Nathan?" I asked. "Your old physical therapist. She always said you should protect what you have."

"She was a smart woman," Vera said.

"I thought so."

"Too bad she quit her practice and left me."

I didn't bother to correct her. We had reached the dining room.

"You'll help your mother with her meal?" Bettina asked.

"Sure," I said, "that's fine."

"All right, Mrs. D'Amato? I'm going to leave you with your daughters."

"Yes," my mother said. "Thank you, Bettina." She reached for her bib on the table. "Ruby," she said, "will you help me fasten this?"

I thought a thousand things at once when I looked at Anthony at rest in his coffin. Among them: Come back here, we're not done with you yet. Among them: I would gladly return that pint of blood I took at birth, if only it would help. Among them: Why the hell did he have to do himself in? Not in any quick way, any violent way—a gun to the head, a swift surgeon's cut under the chin—and not with any prolonged and gritty decline. Why did he piss away in two days his remaining and supposedly happiest years?

He'd been living a modest life, he claimed, the sweet life of a man who had mellowed with age. He had learned to treasure love more than money. Larry stuck with him even when the divorce cleaned him out. Vera's and most of Anthony's savings were under Gloria's control now. Anthony, in his retirement, had started writing his memoirs—his father's rocky farm in Campania, his own happy boyhood in the Bronx.

"A person doesn't need much," he had taken to saying. "Just a roof over his head, a little something to eat, someone to love."

"Oh, spare me," I'd tell him, and for a fleeting moment all over again, I'd wish him dead. Of course, I hadn't been asking for this—Anthony cold in his best suit, ready to be lowered into the ground. I'd been looking for change, a break, so we might be released from our interminable struggle.

Billy, Donna, Ruby, and I sat in the very front row at the funeral parlor, just a few feet from Anthony's body, and watched a handful of other people file by to take a look—Alida and Frank, Uncle Bernie and Aunt Julia, and a couple of nurses from the hospital, the sort who read the obituaries every day. A few friends of Larry's, one of whom I recognized from moving day, sat near the back of the room. At some point Larry came and took the empty chair next to me.

"How you doing?" he asked.

"Okay. You?"

"Okay."

For the moment, no one was crying. Everyone looked pale in their dark clothes, drained, like maybe we were all down a pint or two of blood.

Larry reached over to take my hand, and I let him. "I'm sorry we never made it back to Chicago," he said.

"Me too."

Anthony and I had gotten only as far as talking on the phone; we were still dancing around each other about tolerance and trust. Gloria, we agreed, had come to embody evil. But how often could I stomach my father's description of himself as harmless, and how close did he want to step into my jabs?

The last time we were together in person, I'd been snipping a phone cord into half-inch bits. He had been under terrible pressure that night, he wanted me to know. And this is what one did under pressure, fucked with the mind of a vulnerable person?

After eight or nine months of hammering at him like this, he apologized. "Apologize to my mother," I told him, and he said, "I will." But if he was so hard pressed to admit any mistakes to me, I doubt he ever admitted them to her.

Much as I wanted to, I never completely learned to keep the hell out of their marriage. I tried going cold turkey. I shook, I sweated. I became brittle. I almost drove Ruby away. I gave my statement to the insurance company about finding the house flooded, and otherwise let their investigation proceed without me. A teenaged vandal, they'd concluded, and nothing to confirm my hypothesis that Gloria had put him up to it. I let the divorce proceed without me. But how could history proceed if I was always correcting Anthony's version?

Sitting there at his wake, my thigh pressed against Ruby's, my hand still clasped in Larry's, I looked at Anthony, at the lavish display of flowers behind him, at the pale blue carpet under my feet, and I thought a thousand things. Among them: You were just starting to have fun. Among them: I wanted to give that sweet old man routine of yours a chance. Among them: Say hello to my brother if you see him. Maybe now I can quit being your conscience.